Dangerous
Paradise

Happy reading!
Debra Andrews

Debra Andrews

ELUSIVE STAR PRESS

This is a work of fiction. Names, characters, places and incidents are either the product of the author's imagination or are used fictitiously, and any resemblance to actual persons, living or dead, business establishments, events or locals is entirely coincidental.

Editor, Patricia Thomas

Photos for cover from bigstockphoto.com

Printed in the U.S.A.

DEDICATION

To my wonderful husband, John, and my children, Hayley and Eric,
and my mom, Rose. You are my inspiration.

ACKNOWLEDGMENTS

I have to thank so many who helped me with this story,
which began as a dream, first, my incredibly patient sisters, Brenda,
Teresa and Sharon. I also want to thank my critique partners over the
years, Sheila Viehl, Marilyn Jordan, Kathleen Pickering, the M&M
group, Mona Risk, Rose Lawson and Joan Hammond.

And a final thanks to my fabulous editor Patricia Thomas.

CHAPTER ONE

"What the . . .?" Kelly Cochran flicked on the light and stood rooted in the doorway of her bedroom in her Los Angeles apartment. The French doors to the balcony swung in the evening breeze, and the linen draperies billowed like sails. Her heart slammed against her ribs in a painful, warning rhythm. *She had locked those doors in the morning.*

Her gaze lowered to the shattered glass on the carpet. Panic raced through her. Why had the newly installed alarm failed to go off?

She fumbled in her purse and hit redial on her cell phone. *Please, Robert, answer.* He was the last person she'd spoken to and had dropped her off at her apartment only a few moments ago.

A thump from the closet sent cold, dark fright spiraling through her. She turned to run, but strong arms grabbed her from behind, knocked her bag and phone from her hands, and sent her flying onto the bed. The man pounced on top of her and crushed the breath out of her.

"Help!" she cried, kicking wildly. She tried for a knee-kick to his groin, but hit his thigh instead. "Somebody help me!"

He fisted his hand in her hair and jerked her head painfully against the headboard, then clamped his other grimy hand over her mouth. "That'll cost you, bitch. I heard about you redheads. I bet you like it rough," he said, in an almost casual tone.

Kelly shook her head frantically. He laughed and released his hold on her hair, then grabbed the front of her shirt. She pummeled her fist against his arm.

He chuckled, his rotten breath assaulting her. "I've been paid to off you, but it's a shame to take out a hot chick like you before we've had a little fun."

A nasty grin lit his face and frightened her more than his threats. She knew in that moment her death would mean nothing to him. Sheer terror sent adrenaline flying through her.

She jerked her mouth free and bit down hard on his hand.

He yelped. "Damn you, bitch."

Kelly managed one loud shriek before he clenched his hands around her neck, strangling her screams and cutting off her air supply.

With spots dancing before her eyes, she clawed at his hands, but couldn't pry loose his crushing death-grip. She had to do something to save herself. Wriggling frantically beneath him, she extended her arm and touched the edge of the nightstand. Her fingers curled around the base of her crystal lamp.

Thunk. He grunted and his hands fell away but his body weight slumped on top of her.

She shoved him off her and air rushed into her lungs. Raising fingers to her throbbing throat, she rolled from the bed. The man groaned.

A crash in the living room—as if the door had been broken down—startled her.

"Kelly!" Robert yelled.

Her breath rushed out in a tide of relief. *Thank God, he was here.*

She snapped her head toward her attacker who'd already staggered to his feet. Her previous adrenaline rush that had allowed her to fight so violently for her life had vanished. Now, she gasped for breath, and trembling consumed her body.

Instead of coming toward her, the intruder fled onto the second-floor balcony. He gave her one last menacing glare that promised he'd be back, then grasped a rope and was gone.

* * *

One Week Later - April Fools' Day

"I'm perfectly safe, Aunt Kaye," Kelly said into her cell phone. "I'm a thousand miles away from L.A. and that thug. What could possibly happen?"

Kelly opened the blinds overlooking her balcony on the luxurious *Royal Queen III.* Outside, a steady, wind-driven rain rapped the glass—a clear testament to the unpredictability of typhoon season in the South Pacific.

Despite her reassurances to her aunt, Kelly's throat tightened. Before the attack, she had taken the simple act of breathing for granted. *No more.*

"Sorry I left so suddenly." She hoped she sounded normal enough to soothe Aunt Kaye's fears. "If word gets out someone tried to kill me, it could hurt the company."

"*The company?* I'm worried sick about *you*," her aunt said in her raspy voice.

"Don't be. That's why Robert insisted I go on this trip. We need to consider our options and decide what I'm going to do. Now, please, don't worry. Perhaps, by the time I return, Detective Spagnola will have someone in custody."

"You seem to be spending a lot of time with Robert?"

"I enjoy being with him. Why?"

"But he was your father's lifelong friend," Aunt Kaye said. "I thought you always considered him as an uncle. With his mother working for your grandparents and living on the estate, he was almost like your dad's little brother."

"Yes, but we're not related by blood, Aunt Kaye. And you should have seen Robert. He was impressive. He busted down the door to my apartment and ran in like a hero. He risked his life to save mine—that killer could have shot him. That he did what he did, means a lot to me."

That night she'd flung herself into Robert's arms so thankful for his help.

"I'll allow you that he's compelling, and I'm grateful to him, too, for coming to your rescue," Aunt Kaye muttered, "but didn't the thug flee before Robert even walked into the bedroom? It sounds to me like you saved yourself."

"But, Aunt Kaye, I don't know how long I could have held the man off." Though she was surprised at how violent she'd been when put to the test.

"You're under a lot of stress with this maniac after you. Don't do anything—"

"Impulsive?" Kelly frowned. She had worked hard to curb her impetuous nature. And after graduating with her MBA, she had returned to work for the family company. Still, Kelly sensed her aunt needed reassurance. "This cruise is nothing more than a chance for me to regroup. And it's a business trip for Robert. He'll be busy with his clients. I'm just grateful for this chance to get away."

"All right, sweetie. I'll try to lose my auntie jitters. However, you're young and beautiful. Robert's no fool—"

When the ship's horn blasted, Kelly exhaled a sigh of relief. She didn't want to discuss her feelings for Robert. She wasn't even sure what she felt for him. He'd been her friend and mentor for so long . . . "Aunt Kaye, the ship's leaving port. I'll call you in a few days. I love you."

The ship moved out of the Port of Lautoaka and along the Fiji shoreline, blurred by the deluge. Kelly hadn't seen the sunshine since they'd arrived yesterday.

Bracing her hand on the door, she felt the change as the ship entered the open water where waves crested into peaks before plummeting into a green-gray ocean. Dampness mingled with the air-conditioning and the smell of saltwater. She shivered and rubbed her arms for warmth. A headache hammered her temples and she glanced around, nervously.

You're safe on this trip. As if to taunt her, lightning seared the darkening sky, followed by the loudest crash of thunder she'd heard all afternoon.

"Oh . . ." She whirled from the stormy view and paced the floor of the large, blue and gold cabin, agitated and second guessing her decision to take this luxurious trip.

Get a grip, girl. She stepped to the dresser and examined her reflection in the mirror. She brushed her long hair away from her neck and carefully traced her fingertips along the tender bruises. Although still a faint yellow, the bruises were barely noticeable with the makeup she'd applied that morning.

Oh, Dad, why did you leave me in this mess?

Thankfully, she had Robert in her life. When they'd arrived that morning, he surprised her by having two dozen white roses delivered to her cabin.

Kelly leaned over and inhaled the sweet fragrance, then reread his bold script on his card.

'Love always, Robert.'

She smiled. Did he mean the kind of love one had for a lover? She suspected his feelings for her had changed when he kissed her unexpectedly the day after the attack. And then, 'to ensure her safety,' he'd asked her to accompany him on this business trip.

She had almost been killed . . .

Had he been so shaken up that he realized he loved her?

With a sigh, Kelly walked to the closet and removed her blue evening gown from a hanger. The silk caressed her fingertips as she draped the dress over a chair. Tonight she'd explore this new romantic side of Robert. A girl could get used to this.

Deciding she needed a rejuvenating shower, she stripped down to her underwear. Then her gaze fell on a familiar gray envelope on the nightstand.

The terror had begun a month ago with the arrival of the first in a series of similar threatening letters. This was the first one since the attack.

Her pulse beat erratically as she reached for the envelope and sank onto a chair. The usual cut-and-pasted letters from magazines creepily spelled out her name and company address.

Despite her shaking hands, she opened the envelope and managed to read the letter's different-sized words.

You take expensive trips and don't repay your father's debts. Next time, you die.

Kelly leapt to her feet. Robert had paid for this trip and this elegant suite. Even though many clients had lost their life savings in the company's debacle after her father's death, she and Robert were going to make sure all were gradually repaid. Resisting the urge to crumple the letter, she stuffed it back into the envelope.

With it in hand, she slipped on her robe, hoping Robert was next door in his cabin. The clatter of something falling in the bathroom . . . made her pause. A chill edged her spine. She froze.

Her heart pounded in her ears as she strained to hear sounds from the bathroom. Only the familiar groans of the ship, and the titter of a woman's laughter from the hallway, broke the silence. Rain beat a rat-a-tat on the glass. The seconds dragged. Slowly, the bathroom door squeaked open.

Someone *was* in there.

The envelope slipped from her icy fingers and she ran. The lock clicked into place behind her as she hurried from the cabin. Exhaling a pent-up breath, she turned to run, but the hem of her robe snagged in the closed door. She tugged, but couldn't free herself and didn't have her keycard. She glanced down the hallway. It was empty so she tore off the robe and left it behind.

Appearances were the furthest thing from her mind as she made her escape.

Cool air hit her bare skin as she ran the few steps to Robert's suite.

She pounded on the door. "Robert. Open the door. Please."

When he didn't answer, she wrenched the knob. *Locked.* She shot a glance toward her cabin. The door remained closed. She choked out a sob, relieved that she'd not been followed.

She couldn't run through the halls of the ship dressed in her underwear so she needed to get into a cabin and call security.

She tried the door across from Robert's cabin. It opened, and she lurched inside. Crouching down, she leaned against the door, her breathing rapid. The room spun.

Calm down. As she scanned the room, she forced herself to breathe evenly. A man's white dress shirt lay on the satin comforter and a suitcase stood nearby on the floor. The bathroom door was closed.

She rose on shaky legs. "Hello?"

When no one answered, she exhaled and crossed to the desk where she found the ship's directory card and security's telephone number. She reached for the phone.

"Oh, this one is really good," said a man with a deep polished English accent, from behind her. "Much better than a fruit basket."

The receiver slipped from her hand and clattered onto the desk. She whirled to find the most handsome man she'd ever seen standing at the bathroom entrance. Every worry she had, left her on the exhale as she stared at him.

At least six feet tall, the Adonis raised muscled arms and casually towel-dried his dark blond hair. He looked to be in his late twenties, and he wore only a white towel draped around his sleek waist and hips.

He leveled his aqua-blue gaze on her. "Should I give my compliments to the captain? Or is this what thieves are wearing these days?"

Disoriented, she stared. Then remembering she wore only her new Victoria's Secret bra and panties, she clamped her arms across her chest. "I . . . "

With a flick of his wrist, he tossed the towel he'd used to dry his hair onto a chair and leaned a broad shoulder against the doorjamb of the bathroom. With one brow raised, he gave her a thorough going-over.

Her face warmed at his rudeness, but then she cringed. *She* was the one in *his* room. "I am not a thief."

"Of course you're not," he said, in a patronizing voice. "That would be unusual attire for a burglar." He shoved away from the doorjamb and stalked toward her, contempt obvious on his face. "Similar schemes to invade my privacy happen all the time, but this has got to be the best. So, what's your story? Why are you here . . . dressed like that?"

"Schemes? Story?" She retreated until the back of her bare thighs hit the desk. "Someone is hiding in my cabin. I heard an intruder and needed a place to hide. I need your help."

He stepped closer.

Intimidated by his nearness, she dropped her gaze—only to have it land on the rippling curves and planes of his muscular chest, still damp from his shower. She drew in a sharp breath and along with it the clean, soapy scent of male.

"Is that what they're calling *it* these days—*help*?" he asked, his voice husky.

At the flicker of heat in his eyes, everything inside Kelly stilled.

* * *

Alex Drake didn't believe for one moment that the stunning redhead was in his cabin for anything but seduction. With his career on the fast track, he'd grown accustomed to aggressive females. In fact, since he'd arrived on the ship this morning, three women had brazenly approached him.

He didn't like extremely forward women. He'd be the one to do the asking, thank you very much.

Just last week, in his hotel room, he'd found a stark-naked woman lounging in his bed. At least she'd been truthful about what she wanted. Nevertheless, he had sent her packing. He'd have no problem doing the same with this one. He didn't need a scandal.

His gaze swept over the woman again, and his anger faded. Although a beauty, with her large, sapphire-blue eyes and creamy fair skin, she wasn't the usual type to do this. And regardless, he preferred older women who understood he wouldn't get involved.

She seemed primed for her game of seduction though. Her long hair tumbled in thick, dark auburn curls down her back. She filled out a sexy, blue satin bra and panties, trimmed with black lace. Desire surged through him.

Bloody, bloody hell. It went against his better judgment, but he wouldn't mind kissing those full, red lips and sampling whatever else she had to offer.

And why not? For five years, English law had ensnared him. Perhaps it was time he enjoyed himself . . .

Then he gazed into those widened eyes and frowned. For a woman bent on seduction, she almost looked frightened and a bit too innocent for this sort of thing.

Dismissing that as just another approach, he hardened his heart. He'd been fooled by the most conniving of her sex. She must have bribed a maid to let her in—something he would take up with the ship's steward.

Still . . . Despite everything, he found himself intrigued.

Alex lifted her chin with his finger. "Well done. You've succeeded in attracting my attention."

"Your attention? But I need help."

He chuckled. "Oh, yes . . . my *help.*"

She blew out a deep breath. "You believe me. Thank you."

Next, he guessed she'd find an excuse to throw herself into his arms. As he expected, she swayed toward him. His mouth quirked as, he caught her curvy body against the length of him. *Damn it.* She was good. Perhaps his initial guess was wrong and she wasn't a lady looking for his favors—but was an actress. She played the damsel in distress to perfection with that phony swoon.

No doubt, she thought he could help her career as well. If he hadn't had to catch her, he would have applauded her acting talent.

Why not play along and see how far she would take it? "Are you all right, love? Should I call the ship's doctor?"

"Oh, no." Her warm breath on his bare chest sent a shiver through him. "I'll be okay in a minute. I'm just a little 'shook up.'"

"I'm a little shaken myself," he said dryly. His hands encircled her small waist, while her hair tickled his nose and reminded him of lavender flowers in an English garden.

An unwanted tremor ran through him. She was good, really good. And with her full breasts pressing against him, his body responded on command. He'd have a *hard* time refusing her. That was probably her intention when she practically threw herself into his arms.

Not wanting to reveal just how attracted he was to her, he held her a little away.

Bloody, bloody hell. For the past six months, he'd successfully avoided women and their accursed lies and manipulations, but now, he couldn't think clearly with this angel in his arms.

Why not taste those inviting lips before he sent her on her way? "I don't usually care for this approach, but you've been very persuasive."

Her eyebrows arched. "What . . . ?"

"You know what I'm talking about, little one. You've won. I'll *help* you."

He ground his mouth down on hers. For a brief moment, it seemed like she resisted him and her nails dug into his biceps. He assumed this was part of her act, because, dear God, she already trembled with desire.

As he expected, her grip relaxed and her lips softened under his. His desire ran rampant. He wanted more. Why not take what she so freely offered? He cupped his hand on the back of her head, his fingers tangling into the thickness of her hair.

He groaned inwardly and the ironic thought crossed his mind that clothing wouldn't be an obstacle, since they were both nearly naked. "You *are* incredibly sweet," he murmured against her lush lips.

A part of him couldn't believe he did this. He didn't even know her name.

Another part believed entirely.

Hugely.

* * *

To Kelly, time seemed in slow motion. His jaw scraped her chin, and his lips met hers. He deepened the kiss, widening her mouth, his tongue exploring. Heat shot through her and her knees wobbled. His English accent had been seductive, while the unexpected kiss stole her breath away and sent her senses reeling.

Did he just say, 'sweet'?

Finally snapped out of her hypnotic state, she jerked her lips from his. "This is not what you think."

"What?" the stranger whispered, his breath warming her cheek. "You ran in here, begging for my help," he said against her throat. "I'm only offering my assistance."

She struck her fist against his arm, meeting hard muscle. "What kind of assistance did you think I needed? Let go of me. I came in here to use the phone."

He loosened his hold, the passion vanishing from his eyes. "What game are you playing?"

Whirling out of his arms, she caught her reflection in the mirror and gaped in mortification. No wonder he had the wrong impression. Her hair looked wild, and without the rest of her clothing, her penchant for frilly, pretty underwear made her appear provocative and sexy.

She grabbed the white dress shirt from the bed and clutched it over her breasts. "I'm telling you the truth."

He ran his fingers through his damp hair. "You're a tease."

"No. Please, let me explain."

Crossing his arms over his chest, he nodded toward the shirt. "Put it on."

With her cheeks burning, she turned her back to him and quickly buttoned the shirt. Then she took a deep breath and faced him. "Someone was hiding in my bathroom. I ran in here to call security."

"Let me see if I've got this right. You ran into my cabin—practically naked and in that getup—because you feared someone hid in yours. How did you get in? Did you bribe a maid?"

"No," she said in exasperation. "Your door was unlocked."

He raised a skeptical eyebrow. "It locks automatically."

"I'm telling you, your door was unlocked."

He shrugged. "Perhaps it wasn't shut properly or the lock is faulty. I'll have maintenance check it out."

"And when I came in here, trying to get away from an intruder in my cabin, you . . . *you attacked me.*"

His eyes narrowed as he leaned his beautiful face toward her. "Hardly. I thought you were here for another reason altogether, love."

Her mouth dropped open and then snapped shut. Although he was devastatingly handsome with his classic features and high cheekbones—and had a body and face of pure masculine beauty—surely he didn't think a strange woman, wearing only her underwear, would come into his room and throw herself at him?

"You are the most arrogant man I've ever met."

He had the gall to glare at her.

"You entered my cabin, barely clothed, and kissed me," he scoffed.

"You kissed me first."

He shrugged. "You responded. Why you practically threw yourself at me."

"I was in shock."

"What was I to think? You're almost naked."

"I was undressing to take a shower. Sorry, I didn't take the time to be properly fashionable when I ran from someone hiding in my bathroom—*someone wanting to kill me*."

"Sounds like a farfetched excuse to me."

The towel around his waist unfurled. She caught a glimpse of a tan line, and as he turned to grab the ends of the towel, a bare white hip and muscular butt cheek. He tightened the towel and faced her, shooting her a cool look.

Her cheeks burning, she blurted, "Now, may I use your phone?"

"Be my guest," he said with a curt nod.

She picked up the telephone, checked the list of ship lines, punched in security's number and made the report. After hanging up, she turned to find his gaze on her legs.

Frowning, she tugged the shirttail downward and covered one bare foot with the other.

"A security officer is on his way," she said, using the most impersonal voice she could muster, treating him like the stranger he was—in spite of that crazy kiss they just shared. "He'll meet me at my cabin. Thank you for the use of your phone. I'll return the shirt later—"

"I'll help. I'll go with you."

"No thanks," she muttered. "I don't need the kind of *help* you offer."

"With a killer on the loose," he said, with a sardonic lift of an eyebrow, "I insist. It's the least I can do to make sure you get back to your cabin safely."

He removed a shirt and shorts from his dresser and stepped into the bathroom to dress.

* * *

A few minutes later they stood in Kelly's cabin while the security officer checked her bathroom. She stood frozen by the door, beside the handsome stranger.

"I was telling you the truth," she said, giving him a sideways glance. "I didn't run into your cabin for some kind of hook up."

The officer exited the bathroom and handed her a plastic cup. "This was on the floor." He swung the door back and forth. "Your door does have a squeak. Salt air can do that. I'll send maintenance to oil the hinges. Isn't it possible that, because of the storm, the excessive rocking of the ship caused the cup to fall from the counter and the door to swing open and that's what you heard?"

Blood pounded at her temples and Kelly collapsed in the nearest chair. "I don't know." The cabin seemed undisturbed. Only gusting rain hit against the doors to the balcony. Had she been mistaken?

The officer's eyes revealed he thought she'd imagined it all. He strode to the door. "I'll write a report, just in case, and have the lock across the hall checked, too. Call me if you have any more problems." The officer gave the man who had kissed her a wink before exiting the cabin and closing the door.

Of all the nerve. Neither one of these men believed her. She wrapped her arms around herself. Well, okay . . . It didn't matter what they thought. She'd be fine now.

No killer here. Then she remembered the date and winced. Today was the first of April—she felt like the biggest fool.

The man whose cabin she'd run to, bent down and retrieved the gray envelope from beneath the dresser. "What's this?" he asked.

She must have dropped it in her rush to escape. Here was the proof that she'd had a reason to be afraid. However, now she had no intention of telling this man anything. If word got out someone wanted to kill her, the old scandal would be dredged up and her father's name would be blasted in the news again, hurting Cochran Investments' chances for recovery.

She watched as he frowned at the pasted letters on the front, which spelled out her name and address. Then he handed her the envelope.

Grimacing, Kelly took it. "It's nothing important. Thank you. Now can we please forget everything that happened today?"

He didn't answer, but his gaze searched hers as if trying to read what she had every intention of concealing. "I didn't get your name. Or should I read the envelope?"

"I'd rather you didn't."

He crossed his arms over his chest and waited.

She let out a deep sigh. "Okay. Kelly Cochran."

She waited for the accusations, but he said nothing. Being British, perhaps he'd not heard about her father's U.S. embezzling scandal.

"I'm Alex Drake." He held out his hand to shake hers, but she ignored it.

She rose from the chair. "Let me give you your shirt. I'll be back in a minute." She returned from the bathroom dressed in her robe, with Alex's shirt in her hand.

Alex turned from the windows. "I want to apologize for not believing you. Let me make it up to you. Have dinner with me tonight."

Aside from kissing her unexpectedly, he *had* looked after her safety and was gorgeous enough to be any woman's dream date. However, she was Robert's guest on this trip.

"I can't." She held out her hand. "Thanks for letting me borrow the shirt. Should I have it laundered?"

"No, I'll take care of it."

When he reached out, her gaze dropped to the wedding band encircling his finger.

"You're married?" she blurted. "And you kissed me." Was there no end to the audacity of the jerks she met? She should've known. By the way he'd kissed her, he'd given her every indication he had loose morals.

He twisted the ring on his finger. "My divorce will be final— in a matter of days. I haven't taken off my wedding ring because I'm not ready for a public announcement."

"Sure," she scoffed. "What kind of idiot do you take me for?" She blushed, recalling how they'd already been in each other's arms, practically naked.

"You don't believe me?" he asked with surprising bitterness.

Robert's face loomed in her mind. She had to get this man out of her cabin. "It doesn't matter what I think. I'm with a friend . . . a boyfriend. He might be here at any moment. You'll have to leave."

Crossing his arms over his chest, Alex regarded her with disdain glinting in his eyes. "Do you usually return passionate kisses from strangers while on trips with other men?"

He had her there. The only excuse she had for that brief moment of insanity when she had melted into his arms was she had been in shock.

She pointed toward the door. "Please, leave. Forget we ever met."

He shrugged and strolled to the door. After opening it, he swung around to face her. "I did think your being in my cabin was an excuse to meet me."

Folding her arms over her chest, she said, "How conceited."

"It wouldn't be the first time I've seen a woman do something strange to get a man's attention."

She couldn't believe her ears. "You can be certain I wasn't trying to attract your attention, *Mr. Drake.*"

"Really? Well, I'd love to be a fly on the wall when you tell your boyfriend the entire tale. Don't leave anything out." His blue eyes glinted mischievously as he dipped his head in mocking farewell. "If you change your mind, or find yourself in need of *help* again, I'm across the hallway."

CHAPTER TWO

Still jittery from the afternoon's events, Kelly took a deep breath as she stepped into the ship's most elegant restaurant for dinner. Soft piano music, and the aroma of seafood and grilled steaks, permeated the air. In spite of her previous scare, she wanted to enjoy tonight's black-tie affair.

The security officer was probably right. No one had been hiding in her bathroom, ready to kill her. But then, how had the envelope gotten there? Fear *was* driving her crazy. Hadn't she just allowed a perfect stranger to kiss her? *Now that was crazy.*

His head bent, Robert wore a tuxedo and sat at a private table by the windows, studying a menu. Even from this distance, her tall and handsome friend radiated rugged sophistication. His black hair held just a hint of gray and she knew he kept in shape by boxing and playing tennis.

Kelly smoothed the skirt of her evening gown. With her hair worn down, did she appear mature enough to date a man sixteen years older than herself?

He lifted his head, met her gaze, and rose from his chair. As if an invisible current pulled her toward her destiny, she moved past the linen-covered tables topped with tropical flowers and lighted candles and approached him. His lips twisted into an appreciative grin.

Her nerves tensed at his visible interest in her. He had been a long-time bachelor and sought after by women for years, but he'd never married. Wealthy in his own right, he owned Hillyard Pictures, a movie-production company.

Tomorrow, at the next port, actress Vanessa Caine and her husband would board the ship. Kelly was thrilled at the prospect of meeting the world-famous movie star, especially since Vanessa and Robert were such good friends.

He captured her hand in a firm grasp. "You look gorgeous, but you seem nervous."

She nodded. "I am a little distressed. I've had quite the afternoon, and I couldn't find you."

"I was at the gym. I should've checked in with you." He pulled out a chair for her across from his at the intimate table. "So, what's got you so uptight? I wanted you to enjoy our one night alone before Vanessa arrives."

Kelly opened her beaded evening bag and pulled out the letter. "This was on my dresser this afternoon."

He took the envelope. *"What the hell?"* Then he tapped the postmark, his initial reaction softening. "I arranged for our office mail to be forwarded to the various ports. Your cabin steward must have delivered this letter to your room."

"I realized that later, after . . . never mind." How could she explain *that* fiasco?

He raised an eyebrow, but didn't question her further. He tucked the envelope into his inside jacket pocket. "I'm sorry if you were frightened again by this thug. Don't worry. We'll take the letter to Detective Spagnola as soon as we return to L.A."

She sighed. "There's still the possibility we've been followed. It would be easy to get rid of a person on a cruise ship. I've heard of people falling overboard, never to be found."

She stared out the expansive windows wrapping the restaurant on three sides. Under a twilight sky, the sea swirled black and turbulent. At the thought of someone flinging her into the vast Pacific Ocean, a cold chill swept up her spine.

She turned toward Robert. "Will I always be looking over my shoulder, waiting for another attack?"

"This letter is only a threat to scare you."

"It's working," she said, swallowing a lump in her throat. "I was spooked enough to think someone was in my cabin. I even called security." She offered him a grim smile. "I just might lose my sanity before we find out who is behind this."

Although she disliked omitting her encounter with Alex Drake, she wouldn't bring up the incident to Robert. She'd like to think Alex had forced himself upon her, but she had been lost in the feel of his lips on hers for that one brief moment. Frowning, she raised her fingers to her lips.

"Kelly, don't worry. I'll keep you safe."

Obviously he had misread her thoughts . . .

She grimaced and nodded weakly.

"I'm sure these latest threats were incited by the *Wall Street Journal* article about your inheriting partial control of the company on your birthday."

"You're probably right. The press always brings out the vermin." She had experienced that fact after her parents had died. "I can't endure all the bad press again. I just can't do it."

He reached across the table and took her hand. "I'm not going to let anything happen to you. Your father left me trustee of your interests. I don't take the responsibility lightly."

He didn't. Other than Aunt Kaye, Robert had been the one constant in her life—an uncle figure to her. He had been there eight years ago when her parents' plane had been discovered, crashed off the coast of France.

She had become hysterical at the news. Robert had held her and soothed her until her sobbing had subsided.

He had been there supporting her when the double caskets had been lowered into the ground.

"It's best if you don't see them," he'd said, while wrapping an arm around her shoulders.

The coroner told them her parents' injuries had been more than traumatic. Robert had identified them for her, to protect her from that memory.

Pushing away her sadness, she squeezed his hand. "You've been there for me since the day they died. Thank you."

Robert smiled warmly. "You're welcome. Wouldn't have wanted it any other way, Kelly."

"I wish we could reason with this monster," she said wistfully. "Once we get out of the red, we can reimburse him and everyone else."

"Him?"

"I know it's silly, but I think of him as 'Mister X.'"

"Whoever it is, I'd like to shoot the bastard. I don't like to see you frightened."

Kelly sighed. "Do you think David Lewis killed my parents?"

At one time, Lewis had been her father's associate and a client. He'd been one of the many whose investments with the firm had disappeared. While there were other clients who were angry because they'd lost money with her father, David Lewis was the one the police suspected, because of his violent criminal record, might actually have killed her dad.

Exhaling a deep breath, Robert leaned back in his chair. "When the police tried to make an arrest to question him about your father's death, he ran from them. It *made* Lewis look guilty, Kelly. However, it could be anyone threatening you now. Your dad left so many—"

"*Enemies*," she said, finishing his sentence with the truth.

"I was going to say disgruntled clients."

A nervous chuckle bubbled in her throat. "That's a nice way to put it. Thank you for believing in Dad. Not many people do. And now, so many people hate me because of what they believe Dad did."

"Don't ever stop believing in your father. And none of this is your fault."

The wine steward stopped by their table. "Mr. Hillyard, our best bottle of champagne, as you requested."

After he departed, Robert lifted his glass for a toast. "To a new beginning."

She clinked her glass to his. "I certainly need one." She sipped the expensive champagne. The bubbles exploded with a dry, fruity flavor in her mouth, while the warmth settled her stomach and nerves.

"When I used to tease you about your braces and knobby knees, your father would joke that one day you'd be as beautiful as your mother." Sighing, Robert twined his fingers with hers. "Do you remember?"

She smiled. "And I, all of eleven, with this gigantic crush on you, told you that one day I was going to marry you."

He grinned. "And I said I'd wait for you to grow up."

"But you were only teasing me at the time. You don't know how devastated I was when I left for college—which wouldn't even have happened if you hadn't helped pay for it. I owe you everything."

She chuckled and sipped her champagne, remembering how hard the crush on Robert had been to get over.

Robert shrugged. "I had no idea things would change once you grew up. You're a beautiful woman now."

He leaned across the table and brought her hand to his lips. "You are very dear to me. This might come as a surprise, but, Kelly, I want you to marry me."

She gasped softly, her glass pausing in midair. "You're proposing to me?" How perceptive Aunt Kaye had been about his interest.

His dark eyes held an intensity she had never seen before. "I don't care what has happened in our tangled past with your family or the fact that until now we've just been friends. You must know I'm in love with you. All I want is for us to have a happy, long life together. Will you marry me, my dearest Kelly?"

The man who had looked after her over the years patiently awaited her response, but it was the blazing passion she'd seen in Alex Drake's smoldering blue eyes that came to mind. She blinked to clear her thoughts. How could she think of an obnoxious stranger like that at a time like this?

"But, Robert, we've only had a few dates." While he had brushed goodnight kisses across her lips afterwards, they'd not shared anything passionate, nor had they been intimate. However, she couldn't forget those overwhelming teenage emotions she'd focused on him years ago. It was unbelievable that Robert saw her as anything more than a friend now.

He squeezed her hand. "I know it's sudden, but I've never felt more right about anything. You know your father would've approved. I'll cherish and protect you. I'm not like that young Ben, that jackass you almost married."

Kelly's chin shot up. Two years ago, 'jackass' Ben had broken their engagement the night before their wedding when he had discovered Cochran Investments was near bankruptcy. Her romantic dreams had lain like ashes on a dead fire. Ben's exact words before he walked out had been, 'Now you're not only as cold as a fish, you're as poor as one, too.'

The next day, with tears burning her eyes, Kelly had told Robert every humiliating detail. He had enfolded her in his arms, reassuring her that the right someone was out there for her. Later, she realized how lucky she'd been to learn the truth about Ben and his motivations before they married.

"Didn't the louse marry someone else?" Robert asked.

She cleared her throat. "Yes, an heiress to a chain of department stores."

After Ben, all her dates were disastrous. This afternoon, Alex Drake had been a bitter reminder that for some reason she brought out the worst in men. They either wanted the money they erroneously believed she had, or thought her body held an open invitation for sex.

A year ago, she had slapped the last man she'd gone out with, a man who had groped her breasts on the way to dinner—on their *first date.* That was when she had given up dating, though she never quite understood why she attracted such creeps. Just that she *did.*

However, Robert was nothing like those men. Every other man had betrayed her in one way or another—even her father. He had broken her mother's heart by having several affairs with actresses . . . Had he stolen money, though?

No. She wouldn't believe it. He may have cheated on her mother, but she knew he was innocent of stealing. She and Robert would find a way to prove her dad hadn't embezzled Cochran Investments' funds.

She clenched her hand on the champagne glass. These past few years had been filled with loneliness and despair. Why shouldn't she take this chance at happiness? She could easily fall for Robert. Heck . . . she was halfway in love with him already. He just told her he loved her, and she trusted him more than she trusted anyone.

She would never find a man who'd risk his life for her, as he had when he crashed into her apartment to save her. Her attacker could have had a gun, but Robert had loved her enough to dismiss the danger to himself. Not only that, but for years she had wanted him to see her as a woman, and now it was obvious he did. She was so weary of the jerks she always met and tired of the loneliness. After enduring so much pain in her life, she desperately wanted some happiness—and to be loved.

Despite the knot squeezing her stomach, she blurted out, "I'll marry you."

Relief lit his face. "You've made me the happiest man in the world."

He retrieved a black velvet box from his suit pocket and flipped open the lid to display a ring with the largest diamond she had ever seen.

"Oh, my! I can't accept it, Robert. This ring would pay off a few of Cochran Investments' debts."

He pushed the enormous rock onto her finger. "My wife-to-be deserves the best."

A little loose, the ring nearly slipped off. Sliding the ring back in place, she held out her hand and studied it. The huge diamond sparkled like fire and ice in the candlelight.

"It's beautiful, but I can't."

"Yes, you can." His smile widened with approval. "And to show you how much I love you, I'm forgiving the loan your dad borrowed from me. It will be tight, but when we return I'll do the paperwork."

She rested her palm on her pounding heart. "You'd do that for me?"

"I'd do anything for you."

"But that's nine million dollars. With that off the books, we can save the company and start a repayment plan for a number of our ex-clients." She sighed and leaned back in her chair, thinking of all the possibilities. She'd also been so worried about several of the employees who had invested with the company.

"All I've ever wanted was for you to be happy."

"Thank you, Robert, for being so generous. But," she said, shaking her finger at him, "I intend to somehow repay you every cent of that money."

"We'll be husband and wife," he said with a shrug. "Now, I don't want you worried about anything. Let me do the worrying. In the morning, I'll arrange for the captain to marry us on Saturday."

She choked on the champagne. "You want to get married on the ship?" She had expected a longer engagement so she could get used to the idea of them being a romantic couple. "This is so sudden. What about Aunt Kaye? She'd want to be at my wedding."

"She'll understand. Your life is at risk. Announcing our marriage will warn that bastard who is trying to kill you that you are under my protection. Besides, I want to start our new life together now." He caught her gaze. "But only if that's what you want."

The waiter interrupted them with two steaming plates of lobster.

She chewed a few bites. What should have been delicious, tasted rubbery tonight. Then the enormity of her decision hit her like a bucket of ice water. She would be Robert's wife, with all the intimacy of marriage. She gulped her champagne. Would she have to get drunk for their wedding night? Rip-roaring drunk? A vision of lying in bed with Robert's hands grasping at her breasts like lobster claws caused every muscle in her body to tense. She should have continued to see her psychologist. *Would she ever be normal?*

Before they married, she needed to tell Robert one important detail about herself, but he spoke first. "Kelly, I have another surprise for you. I bought your family's ranch when it was on the market. It will be our new home."

Tears welled in her eyes. The ranch had been sold years ago to repay some of her father's debts. To be able to live there again would mean everything to her. In his usual thoughtful manner, Robert had known how much she missed her parents and the house where she grew up. And he'd secured it.

"Oh, Robert, you are the most generous and thoughtful person I've ever met. Saturday will be just fine with me."

He kissed her hand. "Honey, our life together is going to be perfect." He was romantic, kind, and the most wonderful man in the world.

"I promise to make you happy and be a good wife."

* * *

Later that evening, Kelly danced with Robert to a rock song thumping the walls in the Tropical Harbor Nightclub. The lights in the club swirled in an array of colors.

When the band took a break, Robert ushered her to a small table, near potted palm trees decorated with tiny lights. "I didn't think they'd ever stop."

"I was enjoying myself," she said wistfully as she settled into the chair beside him. She didn't know if Robert even liked to dance?

He slipped on his reading glasses and tapped his watch. "It's one o'clock. Let's call it a night. I need to make calls to another time zone. You do understand I have business to handle on this trip?"

She nodded. "Of course."

A movement at the door caught her attention. Robert's assistant, Tammy Smith, maneuvered through the crowd. Around forty, and recently divorced, she looked attractive with her short, blond hair and wearing a slinky, black dress.

"Robert," she said when she approached the table. "I thought you planned to work tonight? And, *Kelly* . . . you're here, too?"

Kelly wasn't surprised Tammy's voice soured on her name. Her father's ex-secretary, Tammy, had been aloof since Kelly had returned to work at the company. When Tammy's gaze softened on

Robert she radiated her feelings. Now, Kelly understood why she'd been so sour.

"Yes, I had planned to work," Robert said, waving his hand toward a chair. "Why don't you join us?" Smiling, he placed his arm around Kelly's shoulders. "You can be the first to congratulate us. We're going to be married."

Her lips thinned as Tammy rose from her chair. "Don't let me interrupt your celebration. We can work tomorrow." She hurried across the floor and out of the nightclub.

Kelly frowned. "That was strange."

Robert squeezed her bare shoulders. "Am I sensing a little jealousy?"

To her surprise, she wasn't. "Not from me, but I think she likes you more than just as her boss. She wasn't too pleased."

"Whatever is behind her strange behavior, we don't want to lose her. She knows our businesses inside and out. I'll find out what's bothering her." He leaned toward her. "You trust me, don't you?"

She chuckled and kissed his tanned cheek. "If I can't trust you, who can I trust? Go make your calls."

"Honey, no one is going to come between us. *No one.* And I won't lie and tell you I haven't had plenty of women in my life, but Tammy wasn't one of them. I've never been interested in her."

Kelly could understand how any woman could be in love with him.

"You don't need to explain."

He stood and offered his hand to her. "I'll walk you to your cabin."

"I think I'll stay." She rose beside him. "I want to enjoy the music and every moment of the cruise."

"All right, but if any of these studs come around, tell them you belong to me."

When he brushed his lips briefly across hers, she compared his chaste kiss with the fire of Alex Drake's and silently cursed herself.

"Don't stay up too late," he said, flicking her chin. "We're going to do a lot of shopping over the next couple of days. I can't wait to spoil you."

"Don't forget I have the dive trip on Friday."

"That was before you found another threatening letter. You shouldn't go out alone, Kelly. Cancel it."

She frowned at what sounded more like an order than a request.

A plump, young woman with freckles and short, red hair approached the table. "Hello, if you're leaving, may I have your table?" she asked, in a soft, British accent.

Kelly gave her a welcoming smile. "I'm staying, but you're welcome to join me."

Robert kissed the top of Kelly's head. "Enjoy yourself. We'll talk later. Goodnight."

After he departed, the young woman grinned and shook Kelly's hand in an enthusiastic handshake. "I'm Susan Wright."

Kelly introduced herself and waved her hand toward a chair. "Now, at least I won't look like I'm sitting here waiting for a man to pick me up."

"Your father wouldn't like that?"

Kelly twirled her engagement ring on her finger. With their age difference, she'd better get used to this. "Robert is my *fiancé*. We were engaged tonight."

"Oh, best wishes for your happiness." Susan beamed a toothy grin and seemed completely at ease with her error.

The returning band members leaped on stage and soon a rock song filled the air.

Susan raised her voice over the blaring music. "With a looker like you off the market, I'll have a chance tonight. You must have had your pick of men."

"*Me?*" Kelly asked with a laugh. "Thanks, but except for my fiancé, I'm a magnet for lechers, losers, and liars."

Susan giggled. "Well, at least you attract them." She chattered on about how she had arrived with a business group from London. "I'm the secretary, or I couldn't have afforded this expensive trip."

Kelly glanced toward the nightclub's entrance and saw Alex Drake enter. She sucked in her breath, unprepared for how breathtakingly handsome he was in a black tux. Women's heads turned when he ambled with casual, masculine grace through the crowd.

Susan waved across the crowded room. "My cousin is here."

When Alex waved back, Kelly sank in the chair. "That man is your cousin?" How fast could she escape to the nearest exit? She had hoped never to see him again, which was probably ridiculous since he stayed in the cabin across the hall.

Susan beamed with pride. "Yes. His name is Alex Drake. He's an actor. Have you heard of him?"

"No."

"Isn't he handsome?"

Ridiculous to deny the obvious, Kelly nodded reluctantly. She refrained from adding he was obnoxious and conceited, too, and despite her reaction to his kiss, she'd like to think he'd taken advantage of a frightened woman when he'd kissed her.

"Maybe he'll stop by our table, if he can get through the crush of women. They're always coming on to him. He's becoming famous in England. His first American film, a suspense thriller, will be released in a couple of days. If *The Spy* is a success, he'll only have more problems. He's perfect in the role as a humorous, James Bond type."

Kelly silently agreed as she watched him proceed through the crowd, practically accosted by women. A few reached for his arm. Others bent their heads and whispered excitedly to their friends. Grudgingly, she had to admit he had some justification for his earlier assumption about why she'd entered his cabin. He lingered at a few tables and spoke to the occupants before heading in their direction.

Kelly frowned. "Susan. I have to go."

Before she could get to her feet, Alex strode up to their table. Like expensive champagne, he intoxicated with his dark blond hair, which contrasted with the crisp whiteness of his shirt and black tie. With shoulders broad in the tuxedo, he looked the epitome of the handsome movie star.

"Hello, Susan," he said, but his gaze rested on Kelly. Her heart lurched, and she berated herself. She shouldn't have this reaction, not when she'd just become engaged to another man. Was she more like her Casanova father than she realized? She winced.

"Kelly, this is my cousin Alex," Susan said by way of an introduction.

He grinned. "We met briefly today."

"I'm surprised you remembered," Kelly said through tight lips.

His grin sent shivers rippling through her. "Now how could I forget the way we met?"

Kelly glared at him, infuriated by his smiling eyes and the smirk on his face.

"Can you blame me for wanting to know you better?" he asked, obviously finding it amusing to annoy her.

Susan's glance flitted back and forth between them in confusion. "Alex, we were just discussing you."

"Oh, you were?" he drawled. He dragged a chair beside Kelly and sat at the table—uninvited. "*And?*"

Kelly thrust up her chin. "Let me assure you, it was only for a moment."

"I was telling Kelly about your latest film," Susan interjected. "She's from Los Angeles."

"I should have guessed you were an actor," Kelly muttered under her breath.

Alex leaned toward her, so close she breathed in his cologne. She found it hard to concentrate.

He smiled. "You must be in the industry as well. You're obviously a good *actress*."

"I'm not an actress," she admonished him. "I just received my MBA."

His blue eyes gleamed mischievously as he reclined in his chair. "So you're the serious, business type living in the film capital of the world. A strange combination."

She narrowed her eyes. To conceal her exasperation, she said, "Name one of your movies. Perhaps I've seen one."

He ran through a small list of British and American films. She recognized some titles, but she had not had the time to enjoy the luxury of movies these past months.

She shrugged. "No. I guess I've been too busy."

His gaze dropped to one of her bare shoulders, causing an unexpected tingling at that spot. Finally, he lifted his eyes. "I've had some parts, villains and such in the States, but this is my first leading role. I'm keeping my fingers crossed this is my lucky break."

With his English accent, he was different from the usual American movie star hunk—but devastatingly beautiful he was, with golden good looks and sophistication all in one package. Based on appearance alone, he seemed destined for stardom.

The waiter stopped at the table. Alex ordered a round of drinks.

Kelly shook her head. "I can't stay too long."

"Alex is the best actor in England," Susan said with unabashed pride and a toothy grin.

He smiled indulgently at his cousin. "Thanks for the compliment, but enough about me. Any more problems, Kelly?"

"No."

His eyebrows drew together. "After considering what had happened today, I've come to the conclusion after seeing the strange lettering on that envelope, something in that letter frightened you."

Susan's eyes widened quizzically.

Now knowing the threat had arrived by mail, Kelly had to keep the matter quiet because she didn't want anything leaked to the press—anything that might hurt Cochran Investments' chance of recovery.

"No, it was nothing."

Alex opened his mouth to respond when an overblown blonde in a white dress and swiveling Marilyn Monroe hips, ambled up to the table. She slid a napkin and ink pen before him.

"May I have your autograph?" Her ample bosom threatened to spill out of her 'V' cut dress if she leaned any lower. When she whispered something into his ear, he returned a smile, which appeared to dazzle the woman.

Kelly rolled her eyes, recognizing his type—a womanizer . . . and a lying, cheating, and married, womanizer at that. The blonde didn't seem to mind that he wore a wedding band.

His lips curved into a smile and that grated on Kelly's nerves as he scratched his pen across the napkin. He had the typical attention span of all the other vain actors she'd met while living in L.A. They were like butterflies, sampling one flower after another.

And why she cared, she hadn't a clue. She was going to marry the most wonderful man in the world. On Saturday. Her stomach tightened in a knot.

"Mr. Drake, why don't you join us?" The blond woman pointed toward a table where three more attractive women sat. They waved and lifted wine glasses. "We'd all love to hear about your latest movie."

Kelly thrust from her mind an unwelcome image of Alex lounging in bed with all four women. If he were truly separated, his wife probably filed for divorce because of his infidelity.

Kelly leaned toward him and asked in a low voice, "Yes, why don't you join them?"

"Pardon me," he said. "The music is loud. What did you say?"

"Nothing." She rose from the chair, having had enough of the Alex Drake Fan Club. "Goodnight, Susan. Nice to meet you."

"Night, Kelly," Susan said. "I'm off to bed as well."

Kelly gave Alex a curt nod as he rose beside her. "Mr. Drake, do enjoy your . . . your evening," she added dryly, tipping her head toward the four women who watched with interest.

He stopped her with a warm hand on her elbow, sending a tingle up her arm. "Must you leave so soon?" A hopeful glint lit his blue eyes. "Stay. We could dance."

She frowned. There were plenty of interested women to dance with. Was he interested in her because she was the only woman not fainting at his feet? He seemed sincere now and all cynicism gone.

Her heart fluttered. She loved to dance, while Robert hadn't seemed to care too much for it. What would it be like to forget about killers and bankruptcies, if only for an hour?

Then her jaw tightened. Maybe Alex wanted her to stay because he thought she would be easy to get back into his cabin and undressed . . .

As if he read her thoughts, he said, "I'm only asking for a dance."

Not believing him, she flashed her left hand. "No, thanks. I'm engaged."

He lifted her hand and examined the ring on her finger. To her chagrin, a warm sensation shot up her arm at his touch. She flushed miserably.

"You weren't wearing that rock this afternoon," he said. "I thought your claim of a boyfriend was a ruse to put me off."

"Kelly became engaged this evening," Susan interjected.

Alex cocked his head. "My, my, you've had a busy day. Where is the lucky guy?"

She tugged her hand from his grip, but the pressure of his fingers held hers fast. "My fiancé had to leave." Scowling, she jerked her hand from his grasp.

He lifted an eyebrow. "The disappearing fiancé. He's never around when you need him."

"I suppose that's somewhat similar to what must be a very *inconvenient* wife."

He ignored her comment. "Your fiancé left you alone, love? He's not worried someone might come along and try to snatch you away?"

She lifted her chin. "As if anyone could—and I'm not your 'love.' Now, excuse me." She turned to Susan. "Have a nice evening." When Kelly reached for her handbag on the table, she stared at her ring-less left hand in horror. "*My ring!* I must have just dropped it."

How would she explain the loss to Robert? She raised her long dress over her knees and lowered herself to the floor.

When Susan knelt to help, Alex shook his head and touched his cousin's shoulder. "Go ahead. I'll help Kelly find it." To the women who hovered nearby, he said, "Ladies, I'll try to stop by your table later."

Kelly peered up at the women from the floor. The sour expression on the blonde's face suggested she thought Kelly had been more clever in capturing Alex's attention. She was so wrong.

"No. Please, don't waste your time here," Kelly said to him. "I'll find my ring." She waved him off. The ladies leaned forward, interested.

He bent down near her ear. "I didn't invite them over. Let me help you."

She considered the serious expression on his face. Did he really find those attractive women a nuisance? Cautiously, she nodded, remembering the last time he offered *help*. He knelt beside her.

Trailing her fingers over the carpet, she said, "It has to be here. You must think I'm always getting myself into trouble."

"You do seem to have a few mishaps."

Tears pricked her eyes. "Well, this one tops them all. That ring has to be worth a fortune."

He raised an eyebrow. "Is the diamond real?"

"Of course."

He cleared his throat. "Of course." He turned back toward the floor.

Kelly searched beneath the table. She wrinkled her nose when all she found were a few crumpled napkins.

Several minutes later, Alex had stopped looking at the floor and his line of site was leveled on her cleavage.

Straightening, she gave him a stern look. He was so annoying. "I thought you were helping me find the ring?" She stared back at the floor and bit her lip. "What will I tell Robert?"

"Perhaps that the engagement is off?" Alex asked, with a lopsided grin.

She glared at him. "Will you ever stop?"

"No doubt, he'll be disappointed if his beautiful fiancée doesn't bear his mark." He moved to the next table and continued the search.

She followed him. "If you're trying to flatter me, you're wasting your time. Actors don't interest me. I've lived in L.A. long enough to know what you're all like."

He grinned. "All of us, love? Is that a challenge? I find you quite lovely even with your wild, red hair."

She raised her hand to smooth her hair. Having been teased about its color and unruliness all her life, she considered his statement an insult. "What's wrong with my hair?"

"It's untamed, like the captivating face that goes with it." An easy smile played at the corner of his mouth. "Like I imagine you are. Would be . . ."

How dare he? "Please, go away. I'll find my ring myself." She turned her attention to the floor.

He said to her back, "If your fiancé wants to break the engagement because you've lost the ring, I'll be happy to console you. But next time, knock on my door first."

She faced him. "If he did," she said, giving him her iciest voice, "and excuse this cliché, I wouldn't go out with you if you were the last man on the planet. Besides, *you're married.* I don't buy that about-to-be divorced bit you told me. Next time you hit on someone, remember to remove your wedding ring."

His eyes glittered.

She reveled in his reaction. He probably didn't receive many rejections. Too bad. He might benefit from a few more.

He looked down his straight nose. "Who said anything about going out? I thought we might pick up where we left off this afternoon." When she gaped at him, speechless, he added, "I almost didn't recognize you in clothing."

Narrowing her eyes at him, she said with sarcasm, "I could say the same about you."

"Yes, but you should be familiar with the shirt. It's the same one you wore against your sweet, nearly naked skin," he said, in a low seductive voice.

She turned to crawl away, determined to find her ring and get the hell out of there. Down on the floor, not two feet from her face, were a pair of men's black dress shoes.

She tilted her head upward and winced in surprise. "Robert. I thought you were working?"

"I wanted to check on you. You weren't in your cabin." A frown creased his deeply tanned forehead. "What's going on here?"

Despite the nightclub's cool air conditioning, heat stole over her. "I-I lost my ring. We were searching the floor."

Her fiancé threw a hostile glance toward Alex. "*We?*"

"Yes. He was helping me." She sprang to her feet and adjusted the long dress. "It's insured, isn't it?" she asked hopefully. Alex rose beside her.

Robert didn't answer, but glowered at Alex. "I'll help *my fiancée.*"

Caught off guard by the blatant jealousy on Robert's face and in his stance, Kelly gaped at him. She'd never seen him like this before.

Alex opened his palm. "I believe I've found it."

"Thank goodness." Then she caught the mischievous gleam in Alex's eyes. *He'd had the ring the entire time.* He pressed it into her palm, allowing his fingers to linger longer than necessary. She yanked her hand from his grasp.

"Thank you, Mr. Drake, for all your *help*," she said, through tight lips.

Robert narrowed his eyes. "Did you say Drake? *Alex Drake?* I should've recognized you. I'm Robert Hillyard."

She blinked at Robert, her heart thumping. "You know him?"

"Yes. We've never met, but he's Vanessa's husband and our guest on this trip."

CHAPTER THREE

Alex Drake was Robert's associate.

Could her luck get any worse? Thank goodness the nightclub's air conditioning cooled her heated face because Kelly thought she might faint.

Robert crossed his arms over his chest. "Drake, I expected you to arrive tomorrow with Vanessa."

Alex extended his hand. "I arrived this morning and left a message for you at the main desk."

Robert didn't shake Alex's hand. Clearly, he didn't like the man. *Why?*

"I didn't get it." Robert nodded his head toward the nearest vacant table, still littered with glasses from the last customers. "Take a seat." After he pulled out Kelly's chair, he whispered in her ear, "Feeling well, honey?"

Kelly drew a weary hand across her forehead. "It's late. I'm just tired."

He sat in the chair beside her. "We'll get out of here soon."

A waiter approached and cleared the empty glasses, but Robert waved him away.

"Nothing for us," he said in an autocratic manner. He glanced back and forth between her and Alex, then raised a dark eyebrow. "So you two just met?"

She didn't want to lie. "I think I need something to drink." She motioned to the waiter. "Water, please."

Alex leaned casually in his chair. "Actually, we met by accident earlier in the day. Didn't we, Kelly?" He turned amused eyes on her.

So much for him being a gentleman. After the waiter served her water, she drank to relieve her dry throat.

"Why didn't you tell me you'd met Vanessa's_husband?" Robert asked.

She met his gaze. "You never mentioned his name. I had no idea who he was." She shot Alex a disgusted glance. "So you're married to Vanessa Caine?"

"Yes," Alex said, with a shuttered look.

Robert shot her a quizzical glance. "Vanessa is due to arrive tomorrow."

Alex jerked his head toward Robert. "I thought you wanted to discuss an offer with *me*. I wouldn't have come if I'd known she was involved."

"Vanessa wanted this project to be a surprise."

Alex blew out a deep breath and sat back, his expression darkening. "I can work with her if I must, but our divorce will be final in four weeks. Nothing will stop that from happening."

Kelly's heart skipped a beat. So Alex had told the truth.

"Drake, my concern is signing Vanessa for another project. I'm only hiring you because this is what *she* wants. Frankly, I don't care if you do, or don't take the part. I preferred Timothy Michaels for the lead. You don't have the box office draw in the U.S."

Alex inclined his head.

Robert rose from his chair and offered his hand to Kelly. When she stood, he lightly stroked his palm against the small of her back as if she were his property. "Kelly and I will be married in a few days. If you don't want to stay with Vanessa, you can move into Kelly's cabin then. We'll discuss the details for the movie tomorrow at breakfast on the deck at ten."

Robert guided Kelly by the arm across the floor. "Hell. I leave you alone for a moment, and return to find the bastard trying to pick you up is Vanessa's husband."

"You don't need to worry about me. I can take care of myself."

His hand tightened on her elbow. "You're not experienced with men of his caliber. Drake had a reputation with women, which didn't stop with his marriage."

When they reached the doorway of the nightclub, she stole a glance toward Alex. At least now, he'd remain silent and drop the seduction bit. After all, her fiancé was the man hiring him.

The blonde and one brunette hovered around him, but his gaze locked on Kelly's. For an instant, she was entranced, until one of the women tugged on his arm and said something into his ear, and he turned away.

With a sinking feeling in her stomach, one she didn't understand, Kelly let Robert lead her out of the nightclub.

* * *

The next morning, Kelly stepped from her room and nearly stumbled over the mountain of luggage stacked in the narrow hallway. A porter wheeled a large suitcase into Alex's cabin.

Although his back was to her, she recognized Alex. He faced yet another female. Kelly shook her head in disgust and planned to walk right past him. Then she glanced at the woman, with long brown hair. Vanessa Caine. A small gasp escaped Kelly's lips. The actress's legendary talent had entranced millions of fans around the globe.

She was dressed in a beige suit that displayed her tall, toned figure while her skin glowed and her features appeared nearly perfect—except for lips that seemed puffier than Kelly remembered.

On the flight, Robert had boasted that when Vanessa's name was on a marquee, a movie was sure to be a box office success. Kelly knew he wanted Vanessa for this project, and he'd do anything to get her signature on the contract.

Afraid she'd been gawking, Kelly stepped forward to introduce herself, then paused.

With a gleam in her green eyes, Vanessa trailed a red manicured nail down Alex's arm.

"Not happy to see me, darling? You should be eager to make amends, since this part could make you a star in the U.S."

"Bloody hell, Vanessa. I don't want to be anywhere near you. You've set me up on this trip."

Vanessa peered past Alex's shoulder and pointed in Kelly's direction. "Where in the hell did you pick up this cheap slut? Get rid of the bitch."

Kelly stiffened in shock. The famous star's crude language was nothing like she had expected.

Alex whirled around, his eyes flashing in recognition when he saw Kelly.

"Vanessa," he drawled with a thread of warning, "allow me to introduce you to Robert Hillyard's fiancée, Kelly Cochran. Shortly, we'll be meeting them for breakfast to discuss this bloody contract you've arranged at my expense. Would you care to comment further?"

If embarrassed, Vanessa concealed it well. She languidly extended her hand toward Kelly and slipped back into the regal voice of her movies. "Forgive me. Groupies are constantly throwing themselves at Alex."

Still stunned, Kelly stood speechless.

Vanessa scrutinized Kelly's face. "My goodness, what is Robert thinking? Why you're practically a child compared to him."

The porter strode out of the cabin. "Anything else I can assist you with, Ms. Caine?"

"One moment." Vanessa turned to Kelly. "You could do something for me, dear. I need to speak to my husband, and I don't have change. Be so kind as to give the porter a tip, and I'll reimburse you later."

The actress peered down her nose as if she were a queen used to having her every command obeyed by the peasants. Kelly wondered dryly if she should curtsy now or later.

Alex retrieved his wallet from his pocket. "That won't be necessary, Kelly." He handed some bills to the porter. "And there is nothing between us to discuss, Vanessa." He stalked past Kelly and down the hallway.

With a huff, Vanessa flounced into his cabin and slammed the door behind her.

Kelly expelled an exasperated breath. This trip wasn't going well at all. She was supposed to be relaxing and recovering from a brutal attack, and now she had to deal with these people.

* * *

Twenty minutes later, Kelly reluctantly made her way to the sunny top tier café to meet everyone for breakfast. Alex sat at an outside table, staring, with a brooding frown, toward the green mountains of Suva's harbor—the capital of the Fiji Islands. There was no sign of Robert.

When Alex spotted her across the restaurant, she drew in a deep breath. Too late to do a hasty retreat, she greeted him with a half-hearted wave. He mockingly dipped his head in return. Perhaps they could make an agreement to put that little episode in his cabin behind them. She strode toward him.

Unsmiling, he rose from the chair, a bitter look firmly in place in his expression. Gone was his carefree attitude of yesterday.

"May I join you?" she asked warily.

"Of course. We *are* meeting for breakfast."

His sarcasm stung. She pulled out the chair farthest away from his at the round table.

After they sat, she attempted to be civil. "We've had a bad beginning. Why don't we clear the air?"

He stared at her, his lip curled in a cynical expression.

She gritted her teeth. Damn him. "I'm so glad the weather has cleared," she said, changing the subject. "It should be perfect for the dive tomorrow."

He shrugged and seemed uninterested. "Vanessa was rude to you."

"I guess I can overlook it. I admire her talent."

He shot her a hard glance. "Making excuses for everyone's darling? That always happens. And I'm painted as the rat."

She didn't know what to say. The silence grew between them, accentuating the voices of the other diners.

The waiter brought two steaming cups of coffee to the table.

While she sipped the hot beverage, she studied Alex. *Had Vanessa married him for his looks?* They seemed an odd couple. The actress had to be at least ten years older than her gorgeous husband. And it was an outrageous coincidence he would be working for Robert.

As if he read her mind, Alex pinned her with his gaze. "Relax. Your secret is safe with me. As you can see, I wasn't lying about my impending divorce. This won't create the best atmosphere for a-soon-to-be wedded couple, but since you'll be on your honeymoon, you won't be spending much time with us."

She bit her lip. He was right. She'd be alone with Robert. *In his cabin.*

With her napkin, she blotted the beading of perspiration along her top lip, then sank back in her chair, closing her eyes. What was wrong with her? She wanted to marry Robert and grasp some happiness? *Didn't she?*

Alex interrupted her thoughts. "You're pale. Are you seasick?"

Her lids flew open. She straightened. "No, I-I'm fine."

"Really? Not nervous about the upcoming nuptials?"

She narrowed her gaze on him and wouldn't dignify his question with an answer.

"I'd be anxious, too. I've had my fill of marriage. You saw what Vanessa's like."

"I'm surprised. In her movies, she plays such a likeable person. Everyone in America loves her."

His brows drew together. "That's her public image. Don't let her aristocratic manner fool you. Vanessa grew up in a rough neighborhood in London. She's as hard as nails."

"But Robert has known her for years and likes her."

Alex studied his fingertips. "He benefits financially from her, and he's not married to her." He shot her a glance. "Soon, I'll be free."

She crossed her arms over her chest. "To go out flirting with as many women as you please?"

A sardonic smile played across his lips. "Who told you that? Hillyard? But, yes, I can guarantee you there won't be just one woman for me in my future."

"Don't you even care who you hurt?"

"I'm not going to lie to anyone. Plenty of women are all right . . . without a permanent relationship."

"No wonder Vanessa thought I was a groupie. Besides, from what you've shown me, you're not exactly easy to get along with."

He stared at her for a moment, then turned to scan the port as if he preferred to be far away from this ship.

"Why don't you and I start over and try to be friends, or at least be amicable?" she asked softly. "We'll be traveling together for a while."

When he turned back to her, his eyes gleamed with mockery. "It won't work. I find I want you in a way that's none too friendly, and you know it."

A wave of warmth swept over her. It was worse when he leaned toward her and her pulse accelerated.

"Now, tell me, you didn't feel anything when I held you in my arms?" he asked.

Her face heated. He *would* bring up that moment of insanity in his cabin.

"You did return my kiss. Doesn't sound like a woman who should be marrying—"

"I told you I was afraid. And you took me by surprise."

"Surprise?" He chuckled. "And I don't believe I've gotten the whole story." He lowered his voice. "What was in that strange letter that terrified you?"

"It's none of your business."

As if dismissing her distress, he propped one elbow on the table and rested his chin on his fist. "Then I have to think you really wanted to get into my cabin to meet me."

She wanted to shake him. "Robert wouldn't hire you if he knew what you've said to me."

His eyes gleamed naughtily. "Frankly, I don't care about the part. As much as I wanted the work, I'm not thrilled to have to work with Vanessa." He lowered his gaze to her lips. "It's you I prefer to please, Kelly."

In spite of herself, her name on his lips sent a thrill through her. "I told you, I'm engaged," she said in a shaky voice. "Can't you understand?"

"But you weren't yesterday when we kissed. He's almost old enough to be your father. Did you agree to it for the money?"

The remark stung. She gripped the hot coffee cup. Would everyone think the same?

"You've no right to judge me. You don't even know me."

His lips twisted cynically. "True, but I can see right through you. You're marrying an older man for his money, and he gets a sexy young lady in the deal—"

She stood abruptly, practically knocking over her chair. "Robert doesn't need me for this meeting. Tell him he can find me in the gym—I'm going to check to see if there are any available punching bags."

Standing, Alex held up a stopping hand. "Don't get yourself in an uproar. I'm teasing you. Please, sit."

"Are you?" She eyed the passing waiter. "Because I'd love to dump that hot pot of coffee right into your lap."

With a glance around the café, she realized people stared at them. She dropped into her chair.

He must have noticed they'd garnered attention, too, for he settled back in his chair and said in a lowered voice, "Accept my apologies. I shouldn't take my black mood out on you. These past twenty-four hours haven't gone as I'd planned, and honestly, ever since I met you, you've piqued my curiosity. Let's dismiss that curiously passionate kiss we shared. Why don't you tell me what frightened you enough to drive you half-naked into my cabin?"

She narrowed her eyes. "You can't really be concerned about me. We're strangers."

He shrugged. "Don't you at least owe me the truth? I wore only a towel when you burst in on my privacy, and I nearly lost the thing completely."

Remembering how little he had on, her cheeks burned. "All right, but if I told—"

"There you are," Robert called out from behind her.

She turned to find him walking toward the table. An unsmiling Tammy followed him, clutching a briefcase.

Robert's mouth took on an unpleasant twist. "Where's Vanessa?"

She could tell he was angry to find her with Alex again.

"I'm here." Dressed in a flamboyant, sarong skirt, Vanessa strode toward them in high-heeled sandals that clicked on the deck. A wide-brimmed hat and large sunglasses shaded her eyes. Her long brown hair was held back in a ponytail.

Alex's cousin, Susan, demurely followed behind Vanessa with a downcast expression. She seemed as unhappy as Tammy.

Vanessa fanned herself with a paper. "Is it dreadfully hot out here, or what?"

Alex gawked at her. "You're in the tropics. What did you expect?"

"Darling," Vanessa said in a sweet voice. "I don't find it unpleasant. I'm only making an observation." She greeted Robert with air kisses before giving him her hand to kiss. "I've already met your little fiancée. How charming."

Robert grinned. "Isn't she beautiful? If she were an actress, you'd have something to worry about, Ness."

Vanessa laughed, but was anything but in agreement with him.

He winked at Kelly. "Everything's all set. The captain will marry us on Saturday."

Kelly's stomach clenched. *Was she really ready to get married so quickly?*

Vanessa stood and waited at the table. When Alex didn't make a move to assist her, Robert pulled out her chair.

Nothing like the bubbly English girl from yesterday, Susan seated herself on the other side of her employer and opened a notebook.

Vanessa seemed to have a searing effect on everyone, except Robert. He sat beside Kelly and leaned toward her for a kiss.

Pretending not to be aware of his intention, she dropped her gaze to study the menu with a grave fascination.

After the waiter took the food order, Vanessa peered over the brim of her coffee cup. A satisfied smile curved her lips. "You're a fortunate girl to be getting Robert for a husband."

"No." Robert picked up Kelly's hand and intertwined his fingers with hers. "I'm the lucky one."

Kelly met Alex's skeptical gaze, then managed to ignore him throughout what remained of breakfast.

After the waiter cleared the table, Tammy produced the preliminary contracts. Robert enumerated contract matters. Filming was scheduled to begin in June, a scant two months away. Barely known in the U.S., Alex would receive a mere pittance compared to Vanessa's large salary and her percentage of the movie profits.

With a glum expression, Alex sat back in his chair while Robert read aloud the numerous perks Hillyard Pictures would provide for Vanessa. After several minutes, Alex seemed bored and occasionally glanced Kelly's way, giving her subtle, yet knowing, looks.

Surprised by the warmth coiling in her body after each look, she fidgeted uncomfortably in her seat. Why did she have this reaction to him? Last night, after she and Robert left the nightclub, when he had kissed her goodnight at her cabin door, she'd felt no sizzling desire, nothing except wanting it to end. Was she making a horrible mistake with her life—and Robert's?

For some strange reason, she had this bizarre chemistry with Alex. And the way he looked at her couldn't go on. Robert would notice. After all he'd done for her, she couldn't hurt him. She owed him everything.

Keeping her eyes averted, she smoothed the tropical tablecloth beneath her fingertips. Her refusal of Alex's advances had only stoked his ego. She'd have been foolish to tell him about the death threats and the attack. Perhaps she'd just become some kind of game to him? Determined to be the most loyal fiancée that had ever existed, she focused on the mountain scenery and the seagulls scouring the surf—anything, except looking Alex's way.

"That should wrap up everything," Robert said, packing the papers into his briefcase. "Tammy will draw up the final contracts and get them to you this evening to sign. Now, let's enjoy the cruise."

Kelly sighed with relief that business was over. Everyone rose from the table.

Robert linked his arm through hers, and they made their way toward the restaurant exit. He smiled at her as if she were a cherished treasure, making her feel even guiltier. "Kelly and I are going to the island to shop. Would anyone like to accompany us?"

Tammy, who had been subdued throughout the meeting, shook her head.

Vanessa clutched Alex's arm and offered him a hopeful smile. "I hear the shopping in Suva is interesting. Would you care to go?"

"Not a chance." He extricated his arm from her grip. "I think the love birds need time to themselves, so I'm off to explore the city alone." His gaze rested on Kelly, and he added, "Mr. Hillyard, she'll make a beautiful bride. You *are* fortunate."

At the gleam in his eyes, Kelly seethed underneath what she hoped appeared a calm facade. The comment made in front of everyone sounded innocent enough, but she knew better.

She'd do well not to find herself alone again with Mr. Alex Drake.

CHAPTER FOUR

After returning to the ship from their shopping on the island, Kelly had pleaded a headache and left Robert to entertain his guests on his own that evening.

In the morning, she woke up from a restful night's sleep. Excitement bubbled in her when she thought about about the dive she'd signed up for. After showering and slipping on her robe, she tapped on Robert's door, bracing herself for his disapproval. She ran her fingers through her wet hair. He had to hear her out as she was going on the dive.

Robert swung open the door. Wearing pajamas, he urged her into his cabin. "What brings you by so early?" He sat on the bed, while she perched herself on a nearby chair.

"I'm not letting the letter ruin this chance for me. I'm going on the dive."

He scratched his neck. Heavy, gray-black hair protruded from his unbuttoned pajama top. She wrinkled her nose, unaccustomed to seeing him partially undressed.

"Kelly, we're getting married tomorrow. There'll be other dives on this cruise."

"But not this one. The same dive my mother took. She raved about it."

"Seriously, Kelly, we need to entertain Vanessa and Drake for a day or two. I don't plan to see much of them after the wedding as I want to focus all of my attention on you."

She mustered up the smile he expected, but her stomach rolled.

He sighed. "Although I don't know how pleasant she'll be with this divorce he's trying to force on her."

"How long have they been married?"

She could have bitten her tongue at her question, but she wanted to know more.

"Let's see. After Vanessa did *The Flaming Rose* . . . about six years ago. Drake, I believe, was a drama student at the time."

She frowned. "He must have been very young, compared to Vanessa, who was already a major star."

He looked thoughtful. "Yes, he would've been."

"Alex seems so bitter."

"Probably because he knows he's not going to get the fat, juicy divorce settlement he thought to get when he married her."

Was Alex the *gold-digger* and if so, why he had pegged her as one, too? "How terrible for Vanessa," she muttered.

He chuckled. "Don't worry about Vanessa. No doubt, he expected her to help his career, but that didn't happen, and he's paying dearly. What he doesn't know is Vanessa has him right where she wants him—under her thumb."

"He doesn't appear to be anyone's boy-toy."

"He married her, didn't he? She's older and wealthy. If he divorces her, he won't be able to land a job in Hollywood, even as a waiter."

She shoved a strand of wet hair behind her ear. "Now you're making me feel sorry for him." Ugh. How could she pity Alex after the way he'd harassed her?

"Your kindheartedness and loyalty are two of the things I admire most about you, but stay away from Drake."

She planned to. "Don't worry about me, but it's obvious you don't like him. Why?"

Robert shrugged. "Soon after they were married, Vanessa called me crying and told me he was cold and emotionally unavailable to her. I've always thought he used her." He stood and took her hand. "Enough about the *Caines*. Drake belongs to Vanessa, like you do to me, and clearly, Vanessa wants him back."

He lifted his hand to Kelly's hair and twirled one of her wet locks around his finger. "I can hardly wait to make you mine completely." Desire flickered in his eyes. "*But* I'll wait because I respect you, Kelly, and our wedding night will be something special. I'll take you slowly, making sure you enjoy every moment of our first time together . . ." He brought the lock of hair to his lips. "Beautiful."

A queasy sensation gripped her stomach. She frowned, not sure she liked the idea of being his, as if she were a possession. "Robert, do you like my hair?"

"I love everything about you. Why?"

"Oh . . . someone made an unflattering comment."

"Imbecile or jealous witch." When he pulled her to him, she tensed. "No need to be anxious with me, honey. We'll be married tomorrow. I'm still tired, but never too tired for you. I promise I won't take it too far today. Why don't you stay?" He ran his hand down her cheek and then pushed her robe away, baring her shoulder. "You have beautiful skin."

"*Uncle Robert*," she blurted, without thinking, and backed out of his embrace.

"*Kelly*," he muttered. "I hope you don't think of me that way anymore. We're going to be *married*."

At his frown, she babbled nervously, "I-I mean *Robert*, of course. I don't know why I said that. Anyway, I planned to grab something to eat." She hurried to the door and said over her shoulder, "Why don't you sleep? We'll talk later."

He said to her back, "I know how much this dive means to you, but we're not positive we weren't followed. You're not to go, Kelly. I mean it."

She stepped out of his cabin and couldn't believe she'd nearly freaked out when he touched her. He would be her husband, and of course, he would touch her.

This would take some getting used to.

And on top of that, should I really be worried about the dive?

A flicker of apprehension shot through her, but not enough to stop her from going. Later, she would explain to Robert that she couldn't pass up the chance. Besides, he didn't need to tell her what to do as she made her own decisions.

She had to hurry to get her things because the dive boat disembarked in an hour.

She was lost in these thoughts and nearly bumped into Alex in the hallway. Her heart thumped wildly at the sight of him. He was only inches away and she tilted her head to see his face.

She clutched her robe closed at her throat. "You're up early."

"Has the honeymoon already begun?" he asked in a cool voice.

No smile flashed for her on his handsome face today.

Her shoulders stiffened. Let him think whatever he wanted. She'd be married tomorrow.

"I'm so glad that what I do is none of your business," she said through tight lips. However, the imp in her couldn't resist adding, "And how was your night?"

He raised a cynical eyebrow. "Why, does Hillyard need some tips?"

"No," she choked out. Alex didn't move out of her way so she sidestepped around him to get to her cabin. *Infuriating man.* She slammed the door behind her.

* * *

Glad to get away from the stifling confines of the cruise ship, Kelly stepped down the gangplank onto the dock. She wore a black t-shirt and a short, green skirt over her bikini and had pulled her hair back in a French braid. Besides globs of sunscreen, she had donned a baseball cap to protect her face from the strong, tropical sun.

She was determined not to let anyone spoil her dive today. Inhaling the fresh sea air, she scanned the area. Already the docks bustled with suntanned tourists strolling in either direction down the street. The locals grilled and sold exotic, mouth-watering foods. South Pacific music floated on the breeze and mixed with a variety of languages.

Nearing the long dock that led to the vessels for the excursions, she halted. Ahead of her were Alex and his cousin, Susan.

"Don't ignore me, Alex," Vanessa called from behind her.

Not wanting to run into them, Kelly slipped behind a group of large metal storage lockers. She explored around the back and couldn't find a way out. *Damn it.*

"Alex, don't go," Vanessa said in a shrill voice as the three of them met up beside the lockers. "And, Susan, where are you going?"

"You usually sleep late," Susan said meekly. "I didn't think you would care if I went on the dive."

"Should I remind you that you're not here for a family holiday," Vanessa said. "Now do not make me get frown lines. If you value your job, you'll head back to the ship."

"I'll meet you back at your cabin," Susan said sadly. "Enjoy the trip, Alex."

Kelly peered around the corner of the lockers, hoping they had all departed . . . only to find Vanessa and Alex glaring at each other as if they were going to brawl. Kelly ducked back into her hiding place.

"You could've studied your lines by yourself for one day," Alex snapped.

"I pay her salary. She'll do as I tell her."

"Why do you have to control everyone and make them miserable?"

"I don't want to make you miserable." The actress's voice turned into a caress. "I haven't seen you in a while. I find it incredible that you're even sexier than the day we met. Why don't we spend the day together? *Alone.*"

"You're out of your mind if you think that's going to happen."

"Please, give me another chance to make our marriage work."

"Damn it, Vanessa. I never loved you, and you know why we married. Let's not pretend there was any other reason."

Kelly's eyes widened at his confession. Was he so unscrupulous that he married the actress for her money and his career?

"I'll arrange for dinner and champagne to be sent to the cabin tonight," Vanessa said in a lowered voice. "I expect you to be there." Kelly grimaced at hearing their intimate conversation. She'd die if they found her now.

"Don't," he ground out. "My part in the film, and your joining this cruise, changes nothing."

"I'd rather see you dead than to let you marry someone else."

"Remarrying is the last bloody thing I'd ever do after being shackled to you. Our legal separation time is up. There's nothing you can do to stop me."

"Oh? Think really hard about what you want, Alex. If the media gets word of a nasty divorce, negative publicity might hurt *The Spy*'s success. Hollywood won't give you another chance. I'll play the betrayed wife to the hilt for the press."

"Save the ultimatums."

"You bastard," she hissed. "You are mine. *This* is mine, and don't you forget it."

"Skip the crude groping. Nothing you could do would ever seduce me."

Kelly slapped her hand over her mouth to keep from gasping. She had a good idea where Vanessa's hands had roamed on his body.

He stepped backward and into her line of vision. Kelly held her breath and flattened herself against the locker. Her heel tapped the metal, making a clunking sound.

He turned his head. He saw her, and his eyes flared. Then he glanced toward Vanessa. "Vanessa, go back to the ship."

"Just remember, Alex, I can make or break you. It's all up to you. I'll be waiting for you in our cabin to rekindle our love. I'll need refreshing company after spending the day with Robert and his fiancée—now there's a real opportunist. Until later, darling. Don't disappoint me."

Outrage spread through Kelly. She stepped after Vanessa's retreating form. Alex gripped Kelly at the waist and pulled her behind the lockers.

She struggled against his tight hold. "I'm going to tell her I think she is the most obnoxious person I've ever met, even more obnoxious than you—"

"Don't say a bloody word to her. It's not worth it."

She stared down at his fingers, still clasped around her waist. A jolt of heated awareness shot through her. Disgusted with herself, she said, "You've no right to put your hands on me."

"Don't I?" His eyes flashed angrily. "What do you think you were doing hiding behind these lockers? Spying on me?" He released her and glared. "Well?"

"I wasn't spying on you."

"You heard every bloody word."

Vanessa called out again. "Alex, have you decided not to go? Why not spend the day with me?"

"Damn. I'll get rid of her." Alex gave Kelly a scathing glance, warning her to be quiet, and then he stepped from behind the storage bin out to the open dock. "Bloody hell, Vanessa, go back to the ship." His footsteps sounded on the boards as he walked away.

Wiping the perspiration from her brow, Kelly blew out a deep breath. No wonder Alex was bitter. He paid a heavy price for being married to the shrew. In addition, he had some nerve and was awfully pushy where *she* was concerned. She'd have words with him about that later.

She hurried to join the line behind the other divers waiting to board the *Blue Dolphin.*

A few minutes later, over her shoulder, Alex said, "Now I'm convinced you're following me."

"Me?" She whirled to face him. "I was here first, and this is my dive trip."

"Why didn't you make your presence known back there, Kelly? It's not polite to listen to other people's conversations."

"I didn't intentionally eavesdrop, if you must know. I didn't want to run into any of you. I thought I'd walk around past those lockers, but there wasn't another way out. Believe me, I didn't want to hear your . . . your *heated* discussion with her."

He sighed and gave her a long look. "It was more than hot, wasn't it? And I suppose you have every reason to avoid me."

"You've got that right," she muttered.

He shrugged. "So where's your *significant other?* I'm surprised Hillyard doesn't still have you in his cabin rehearsing for the honeymoon."

Bristling at his rudeness, she narrowed her eyes. "Were you always this rude, or did you pick it up from your wife?"

"Ah ha," he said with a chuckle. "Perhaps you're right, and I think you've finally realized Vanessa's true personality."

"I don't know why she dislikes me so. I've done nothing to offend her. And I admit she's not the person I expected her to be."

"Of course not. She's a . . ." Although he didn't elaborate, Kelly guessed what word he wanted to say. He pushed his sunglasses back on his head. "Seriously, where's Hillyard? You're not scuba diving alone?"

He was goading her again and she should be angry with him, but she was angrier at herself . . . at the way her breath caught at the sight of his glorious blue eyes that studied her. The sunlight made his hair gleam like antique gold. A man shouldn't be so good-looking.

Angry with herself for the attraction she felt for him, she finally said, "So you're a male chauvinist as well. How many other charming traits do you have? I've seen a few."

"Before you get on your feminist high horse, love, you know as a diver, it's not a good idea for anyone to dive alone. It's not safe. However, in your case, I only thought you'd be trailing after your rich fiancé. Aren't you afraid another woman might try to take him away while you're gone?"

Refusing to let him goad her again, she lifted her chin. "Robert loves me. We also have *trust*, something I doubt you know anything about."

Alex laughed, causing dimples to appear in his cheeks. "Trust? Really? What about what happened in my cabin?"

Her shoulders stiffened. "Will you ever drop that topic?"

"All right," he said, but she heard amusement in his voice. "I do agree with you on one thing. Trust is something I have yet to experience where women are concerned."

At an uneasy feeling someone stared, Kelly turned toward the docks. In the distance, Vanessa stood with her hands on her hips, watching them.

"She's jealous of you," he commented.

"Whatever for?"

At that moment, his eyes held a hint of bleakness. When he didn't answer, she frowned and murmured, "Is she jealous just because I'm speaking to you?"

He nodded. "It doesn't take much to provoke her." He seemed to say it more to himself than to her, but then he recovered and his gaze swept over Kelly. "With your provocative looks, it's hard to blame her."

She blushed. Did he really think she was pretty? She shot a guilty glance toward the docks. Vanessa whirled and headed, with a defiant stride, in the direction of the cruise ship.

The line to board the dive boat moved forward.

"Allow me to assist you." Before she could object, he picked up her bag, and then she had to follow him aboard the vessel.

A man with a freckled, sun-baked face, and the most startling, bright blue eyes Kelly had ever seen, shook their hands. "Welcome aboard. I'm Captain Brian. You're in for a spectacular sight today."

When they reached the cushioned benches, Alex set her bag on the deck and sat down. She reluctantly dropped on the seat beside him. He casually stretched out his legs.

His wedding band, with three diamonds, glittered in the sunlight. Vanessa had alluded that it was important for him to have a quiet divorce, but if so, why would he even wear the ring? Was it an attempt to keep the hordes of women away?

Feeling uncomfortable with his nearness, Kelly turned her attention to the diving vessel. Cushioned seating ran around the outer edge of the deck. She counted fifteen additional divers, plus the captain with a crew of two. In the center of the boat stood an air-compressor used for refilling the scuba tanks. Lunch and refreshments were stored in large coolers up front.

"As jealous as Hillyard is," Alex commented, "I'm surprised he allowed you to take this trip by yourself. All I have to do is look at you, and I see the hatred cloud his eyes."

So, she wasn't the only one who had noted Robert's jealousy. "My fiancé knows he doesn't have to worry. You're not my type."

He cocked an eyebrow. "Too young for you?"

She ignored the putdown about Robert's age. "No. Because you're an actor."

"Ah, we actors do get a bad rap."

The engines rumbled to life. A moment later, the crew untied the boat. Slowly, the *Blue Dolphin* slid away from the dock.

The captain's voice bellowed over the speakers. "We will be at the reef in forty-five minutes."

Alex nudged Kelly's arm with his elbow, then pointed toward the docks in the distance.

"Seems like your fiancé is concerned after all."

She shielded her eyes and gasped. Robert ran down the long dock, waving his arms.

"Oh, dear," she said, putting her hands to her face. "Vanessa must have told him."

Robert shouted something. Could he see Alex sitting beside her? She flinched, knowing she'd have some explaining to do later. Plastering a smile on her face, she waved at Robert.

"Doesn't look like he wanted you to go," Alex said blandly.

With a sigh, she slumped in the seat. "He didn't."

How would she explain this? Not only would Robert be upset she'd gone on the dive, he would be angry she was with Alex again.

"You're not even married, and you're not listening to your future spouse," Alex said, nodding his head knowingly. "Sounds as if the honeymoon is already over."

She grimaced at him. Was he still teasing?

"Getting married to Robert doesn't mean he can run my life."

"Don't be surprised if he tries." Alex must be referring to his own marriage.

The boat entered the open, rougher waters. Kelly lost her balance and hastily groped for a steadying hold on the cushion to keep from falling against Alex.

For safety reasons, the first mate came by and assigned each diver a partner. He pointed at them. "You two together." Before she could protest, Alex confirmed the pairing, and the man moved on to the next passengers.

She shook her head at Alex. "No way am I diving with you."

"Look," he reasoned with a shrug, "the man assumed we were together. Why don't we call a truce for today?"

She narrowed her eyes. "*I* never started the war."

He raised his hand. "I acknowledge that. Having to tolerate Vanessa hasn't put me in the best of moods. I'm sorry if I've taken it out on you."

"Do you mean it?" She would love not to deal with this stress anymore and not to have to worry about Robert finding out how she'd met Alex. And it was safer having Alex along on the dive trip—whether Robert approved or not.

Alex nodded. "Listen, I know you're marrying Hillyard tomorrow, and since I can't stand being near Vanessa any longer, I'm leaving the ship in the morning."

She gave him a sharp glance, surprised to recognize a small part of her didn't want him to leave.

"So, what harm would there be if we enjoy the dive together?" he asked, smiling at her innocently enough. "We probably won't see each other again after today."

He was right. After filming, she'd view the finished product, but Alex would be at a safe distance on the screen. Then she could smile and remember the day she had kissed a dangerously handsome actor—one who had made her senses reel.

She offered him a smile. "I suppose it can't hurt. At least you can't make any nasty comments under water."

He grinned, his dark blond hair ruffling in the breeze. "Dear girl, I promise while we're diving I won't insult you."

She laughed. "Is that the best I can hope for?"

* * *

The boat motored over the deep blue sea to the reef. Captain Brian gave a signal that the divers could prepare to enter the water. Kelly placed her sunglasses and engagement ring in her bag.

With Alex next to her, and self-conscious, she turned her back toward him to undress and suit up. She quickly stripped down to her pink and yellow, tropical-print bikini and slipped on her wetsuit.

When finished, she turned to face him. Looking muscular and fit, Alex zipped up his suit and watched her. She waited for him to make a sarcastic comment about them dressing together again, but he didn't.

He nodded toward the dive platform. "Let's go."

They donned their tanks.

During the diving safety procedures and the buddy-checks of each other's equipment, Kelly had misgivings about agreeing to be his partner. She was crazy to place herself in such close proximity to this man. His job was to make women swoon, and he did that merely by breathing.

No wonder Robert was jealous. He must have seen the smoldering looks Alex had sent her way over breakfast yesterday.

Had he noticed her heated reaction to Alex as well? She clenched her teeth. She wasn't going to think about Robert this morning. She was going to enjoy the dive, and Alex's company for what it was— nothing more than a fun excursion, and the last time they'd be together. Robert would have to understand.

Alex checked her tank and equipment. When he tucked a stray curl of her hair beneath her mask, his fingertips grazed her cheek. She knew the pulse in her neck beat faster. *Did he notice her reaction to him? Could she trust him to honor their truce? And keep his distance?*

She followed Alex to the dive platform. He jumped in first.

When she entered, the water refreshed her hot skin. In awe, she swam with him to a depth of about forty feet where the gentle rhythm of her breathing through the regulator the only sound. With crystal-clear water, the reef appeared close enough to touch and filled her with awe and a kind of regret. *Mom, I wish you were here with me.*

Alex motioned to Kelly. She swam with him, past multicolored corals and aquatic life. When he pointed toward two mating sea turtles, she narrowed her eyes and was glad he couldn't comment underwater.

After the first dive, they returned to the boat for air refills and lunch. Hungry from the morning's exertion, they ate sandwiches and drank coffee. True to his word, Alex behaved like the perfect gentleman.

The afternoon passed quickly. She checked her watch, disappointed that it was already three o'clock and time to board. She signaled to Alex. He motioned he would follow and waved her on.

While she swam upwards, she realized how much she had enjoyed the day diving with him. A stab of regret that he would miss the next dive hit her, but it probably wasn't a good idea to enjoy his company too much. He would leave the ship, and she would most likely never see him again. She didn't have time to examine these feelings because above her another boat, with its twin propellers spinning dangerously, pulled alongside the *Blue Dolphin*.

At the surface, she gripped the ladder and slipped off her mask. She had to tell the captain about this new boat. They had to shut off the engines because Alex was still below.

"Don't anybody move, and no one will get hurt," said a man with a deep voice, in an American accent.

In spite of the waves tossing her ribs painfully against the rungs, she clung to the ladder. She ducked low and peered over the edge of the boat. A large, dark-haired man of about forty stood on the bow of a sleek racing vessel. A thin, white scar zigzagged across his cheek, giving him the appearance of a pirate. However, instead of brandishing a sword, he waved a gun toward the divers.

Two men were with him. The younger one had a scruffy beard and wore a camouflage hunter's cap. He sat at the helm and grinned as if he enjoyed the moment. The other man, probably in his fifties, with salt-and-pepper hair, leveled an automatic rifle in the direction of the passengers.

Kelly hunched lower on the ladder, her heart pounding painfully in her chest. Were they being robbed . . . or hijacked? She searched the surface for Alex, wanting to warn him to stay low.

"We don't want any trouble," Captain Brian said.

"There won't be any as long as I get who I came for," said the dark-haired American who had spoken first.

She sucked in her breath. *Who were they looking for?*

A moment later, he said, "She's not here. Let them go."

She choked back a sob, thankful they were leaving.

"Wait," yelled one of the men. "Someone's on the ladder."

Her heart punched like a fist hitting her chest. The dark-haired man leaned over the back of his boat, his dark eyes piercing her. "Kelly Cochran?" he demanded with a motion of his gun, "Up. We won't harm you."

Inexplicable hatred blazed in his eyes. Despite his words, she *knew* he would hurt her. She dropped into the water and swam hard. Where she could go, she didn't know. She paused and fumbled to release air from her buoyancy compensator, so she could put her mask on and dive under water. Shots rang out, and bullets whizzed near her head, spraying the surface. Her heart nearly burst with fear. She was going to die.

"Mick, you crazy fool, you've hit their gas line. Get us out of here!" the man roared.

The racing craft rocketed past her, leaving a foaming wake in its path. Screams and shouts rang out from the dive boat. She whirled to see the *Blue Dolphin*, in an earsplitting explosion, burst into a volcano of flames. Debris rained everywhere.

A violent blow to her head caused a wave of pain. Then darkness.

CHAPTER FIVE

The *Blue Dolphin* was silhouetted above as Alex swam upward through the clear depths of the Pacific Ocean. A muffled explosion rang in his ears and a concussion of water tossed him back. His chest ached from the force.

Bloody hell! Kelly had gone up to the boat only a few minutes before him.

Once at the surface, he ripped off his mask and regulator. Smoke ravaged his eyes and seared his nose. "Kelly!" he shouted, his voice cracking.

Shielding his face from scorching heat, he whipped around, horrified. Everything was surreal. Fiberglass crackled and hissed as a ferocious fire consumed what remained of the diving vessel's hull. Cushions, coolers and debris littered the water. He made out a boat in the distance, speeding away.

Terror gripped him. Where were Kelly and the other divers? His heart raced as he swam, searching among the destruction. He passed a mangled body and drew in a deep breath.

How could anyone survive the horrific explosion?

He pushed through remnants of the dive vessel until he saw red hair. "Kelly," he said, his breath rushing out.

She floated face down in the water. Fear twisted around his heart as he gently lifted her head. Blood oozed from a shallow cut near her temple.

After unstrapping her tank, he fully inflated her buoyancy compensator. He then pressed his hands to both sides of her face. Sealing his lips over hers, he forced air into her lungs.

"Come on, Kelly, breathe," he begged between breaths. He repeated the action, again and again, until saltwater bubbled from her throat. She choked and gasped.

"You're alive." Relief rocked his body. He held her close, but her head lolled in unconsciousness.

Then his mind reeled. He had to find other survivors. He treaded through the floating wreckage, hauling Kelly's limp body with him past an empty soda can, a scuba mask—a severed arm with the fingers curved in a relaxed pose.

His stomach rolled. He drew in a deep breath and turned away from the nightmare to swim in another direction. A body popped to the surface in front of them. The half-blown away face of Captain Brian stared back. One bright blue eye remained in a fixed stare.

Gritting his teeth, Alex shoved the corpse away. Where were the cameras for this horror film? Except this wasn't fantasy. The smell of fuel and burned flesh tied the scene firmly to reality.

Was everyone else dead? The water had turned red around him.

Then it dawned on his shock-slowed brain. Sharks would be attracted to the bloodied site.

With a firm grip on Kelly, Alex moved through the water, looking for anything that housed a raft. He spotted a trunk marked: Emergency Supplies. When he neared the box, a large dorsal fin circled dangerously close.

He stayed still until the shark headed in a different direction, and then gently treaded water toward the floating trunk.

Grabbing the handle, he let the swell of the waves push them away from the blood-steeped area. The damaged trunk easily opened. To his relief, he found an inflatable raft inside. He pulled the tab. A steady hiss of gas filled the rubber raft. He pushed Kelly inside, having to boost her by her firm bottom to do it. He shoved the trunk in, then climbed aboard.

Relief and exhaustion overcoming his body at that point, he sagged against the side. Waves slapped the sides and though every muscle, nerve and bone he possessed ached, he considered what had just happened.

What had caused the explosion? An air tank or the compressor?

Alex studied Kelly's face. She should've come around by now. Blood trickled down her cheek. He reached into the trunk and found a first aid kit.

When he rolled her to her back, she remained motionless. Alarm gnawed at his insides. He leaned over her and pressed his ear to her chest . . . and heard a strong heartbeat. *Thank God.*

He gently shook her. "Kelly?"

Her eyes flickered open. "Robert?"

"No," he snapped. "It's *Alex*, not your beloved Hillyard. There was an explosion on the dive boat. *I* pulled you out of the water." His voice sounded gruffer than he intended.

She raised her palm to her temple. When she drew back her bloodied fingers, she gasped.

"You're going to be all right." He retrieved gauze from the first aid kit and wiped the blood from her hand. Her gaze locked on his as he gently bound her head.

"You're lucky." He gave her a brief reassuring smile as he tied the bandage. "You've only a bump and a small cut."

When she tried to sit up, he placed a hand on her shoulder and held her down. "Lie still. I don't want you passing out on me again. Can I get you water?"

"No," she whispered. "Just my bag, please." Then she closed her eyes and fainted anyway. Women. Even in the face of danger, they were concerned about their purses.

He lifted her wrist, reassured by her strong pulse. Kelly, no doubt, would live.

He took from the trunk two extendable oars and paddled back to where the accident had occurred. He hauled into the raft three slightly charred coolers and several bags that floated on the water.

When he spotted Kelly's green gear bag, he reached out. A shark surfaced five feet away. He yanked the bag into the raft. Bloody hell, he could have lost a hand in the deal.

He rowed away from the blood-saturated area and then rummaged through the emergency trunk. Among other miscellaneous items, he found a canvas tarp, a rope, a survival manual and a thermos with water, but no sign of the flares he'd hoped to find.

Shielding his eyes, he frowned and surveyed the horizon. *Where were the rescuers?* He checked his watch. Four p.m. The boat that sped away should have reported the accident by now. He could do nothing but sit and wait, taunted by regret that he had been unable to do anything for the other divers.

The tropical sun burned hot so he stripped off his wetsuit. Kelly hadn't moved at all.

He hauled her to a sitting position and gently shook her arms. "Wake up, love."

She sagged against him. "Too tired." Her warm, perspiring face pressed into his bare chest.

A tremor ran through him.

He clasped her chin. "Come on, Kelly, wake up, or I'll have to get you out of this wetsuit. Do you hear me? It's too bloody damn hot for you to wear."

When she didn't respond, he laid her on her back. He unzipped her wetsuit, down over her breasts, her trim flat stomach, and down further where the zipper stopped on her bikini bottoms. Good thing she was out cold or she'd be angry as hell about this.

Undressing an unconscious woman was a first for him. He peeled the wetsuit off her shoulders and traced with his fingers the yellow bruises on her neck. How had she gotten them? *From Hillyard?*

He tugged the wetsuit over her full breasts, managing to keep the small fabric of her bikini top in place, then dragged the suit down farther, past her slim flat stomach, over her rounded hips, off her thighs and knees to her slim ankles. Her legs fell open in an inviting position. He put his hands on her knees and closed them together, then pulled the suit off her feet.

His task finished, he let out a deep breath and checked his watch again. Five p.m. *Where in the bloody hell were the police and the emergency crews who should be out searching for survivors?*

Leaning against the edge of the raft, he scoured the horizon for a rescue ship or plane, but only the endless blue ocean lay before him. Wave, after rolling wave, rocked the raft.

* * *

Pain tugged Kelly from the darkness. She opened her eyes to a setting sun shot with crimson and gold. Where was she? She licked her dry, salty lips and tried to sit. A throbbing headache sabotaged her efforts. She fell back in agony and moaned. When the pain in her head subsided, she lifted her hand to the thick bandage. How badly was she hurt?

Alex . . . He had been with her. She jerked her head, searching for him. In spite of excruciating pain, she was comforted to see he was safe and sleeping beside her. His tank and diving suit discarded beside him, he wore nothing more than swimming trunks.

Why were they in a rubber raft? Memories of the attack and the fiery explosion flooded her mind. She shuddered. Those men . . . They had tried to kill her.

Trembling, Kelly sat up, fighting the blackness and nausea which threatened to lay her flat again. Where were the other divers?

She placed her hand on one of Alex's perfect, bare shoulders. Touching his smooth, warm skin only confused her, so she shook him hard.

"Wake up, Alex."

He bolted up and rubbed his eyes. "Damn. I didn't mean to sleep. How are you?"

"I'm okay, but my head hurts."

"I was underwater when the explosion occurred. Did you see what happened?"

Her mouth went dry. "Three men with guns attacked the boat. They were . . . looking for someone."

"Did they say who?"

Guilt burning her cheeks, she shrugged. She couldn't tell him those men had wanted to kill her because of her father. She couldn't risk this getting into the media. She had to tell the police privately.

"I don't have any enemies, unless this is Vanessa's way of getting rid of an ex-husband," he said dryly. He leaned back against the raft. "Did you get a good look at them?"

She shuddered. "I'll never forget their faces."

His expression grew somber. "We're the only survivors."

"No," she cried, horror engulfing her. "Oh, my God. No, please, don't tell me this."

"Kelly, everyone is dead."

Guilt assaulted her. Her worst fears realized. More people were hurt because of her father. Another tragedy that would be laid on him.

"How long ago did it happen?" she asked in a whisper.

"About six hours."

Hot tears slid down her cheeks. "If only I could've done something to help."

He shook his head. "They were dead instantly. How did you survive?"

She choked out, "I wasn't on the dive boat yet." She should have been the one dead.

"Don't worry. We'll be rescued soon."

Kelly hugged her knees. He didn't understand. This was her fault. If she had stayed in L.A., or had just gone with those men, this would never have happened. She stared over the moving ocean water through blurry eyes. They sat in silence floating on an endless sea.

Finally, Alex gestured to the containers at her feet. "Would you like something to drink or eat?"

"Yes, water, please."

He handed her a water bottle. "We have several more." Then he reached behind and retrieved her bag. "You were so concerned about this after the accident."

"I was? Thank you." She rummaged inside her bag. Her fingers grazed the diamond ring Robert had given her. He would be frantic with worry. She slid the ring on, fairly sure the piece of tape she'd wrapped around the back made the ring snug enough on her finger.

"Bloody hell," Alex snapped, causing her to jump. "Did you know I risked a shark bite for that trinket?"

"I'm sorry. Thank you for saving my life." She plucked the strings of her bikini top and realized he'd stripped off her wet suit. Her cheeks went hot. "You were kind to think of my comfort."

He shrugged a bare shoulder, which reminded her they were alone and nearly naked again. "The pleasure was mine."

When he turned back toward the water, she sighed in relief. He seemed appeased by her apology. She hadn't really thought much about the ring, except that she didn't want to lose it.

Kelly pulled a compact mirror from her bag and lifted the edge of the bandage to look at her temple. "Not too bad. The bleeding has stopped."

"Don't lose that mirror overboard. If we don't get picked up tonight, we might be able to signal an airplane or boat in the morning."

"Right." After she put everything away, she settled against the side of the raft.

Her head still ached, but not quite so fiercely. She shielded her eyes and searched for any sign of the rescuers. Nothing but blue water spread in all directions. To the east, the horizon darkened, while the setting sun to the west made the ocean turn into silvery ripples.

She wanted to confide in Alex that someone was out to kill her, but the thought that it would be blasted all over the news brought dread to her insides. "Why haven't we been rescued?"

"We've drifted from the reef. And there were no flares." He must have seen her despondence because he added in a positive voice, "They'll find us. It'll take a little longer, that's all. Don't worry. Hillyard will have an entire fleet out looking for you."

She sighed, supposing his remark was a compliment, even though coming from Alex it seemed more like a dig. However, he was right. Robert wouldn't give up.

Alex's words of hope rang hollow as stars gradually dotted the sky. She became increasingly uneasy when the wind picked up and pushed the raft on the vast black sea.

During a brief downpour in the night, Kelly followed Alex's lead and allowed the cool rain to wash off the salt and refresh her skin. The bleeding stopped, she unwound the water-soaked bandage from her head.

Though refreshed, she huddled beneath the canvas tarp and shivered while Alex bailed out the rainwater. When he joined her, their knees or legs constantly bumped.

Eventually, he stretched out in the raft. His even breathing indicated he'd fallen asleep. She wanted to lie down, too, but the only space was beside him so she huddled into a ball, rested her head on the edge of the raft, and let exhaustion overtake her.

* * *

Thunder crackled and boomed. Alex awoke and poked his head out from under the tarp. Cool raindrops sprinkled his face. Thankfully, the storm appeared to be moving away from them. With a new day, the rescue teams should find them.

He bailed out the rainwater which had accumulated in the raft during the night. Kelly yawned and stretched, causing her full breasts to strain against the string bikini top.

Disconcerted by the morning lust she had aroused in him, he asked blandly, "Thirsty?"

She rubbed her eyes. "Yes."

They had consumed the last of the water from the bottles yesterday evening. Alex scooped up rainwater he had collected in the cooler overnight. He handed the cup to Kelly. When she had finished sipping, he slaked his own thirst and watched as she busied herself by arranging the coolers and the trunk in a more orderly fashion. He sighed. He'd never involuntarily spent so much time cooped up in such close quarters with anyone, not even Vanessa. *Had Kelly?*

Although grateful they had food and drink for the moment, he feared the sandwiches would soon spoil. How long could two people survive without food on the Pacific Ocean?

Alex drummed his fingers on the side of the raft, deciding to voice his concerns to Kelly. "If this weather continues, we'll be pushed even farther from where the accident occurred. We must be miles away by now."

"Robert won't give up trying to find me."

At the mention of Hillyard's name, the hair on the back of Alex's neck prickled. He gritted his teeth and dropped his gaze to her engagement ring. Hell the sheer size of the diamond irritated him, too. *Was that her price? Would any rich husband do?*

"You'll find out marriage isn't all it's cracked up to be," he said coolly.

Her face paled. "Just because you married your wife for your career and money . . ." She ducked her head. "I didn't mean to say that."

"Oh, yes you did. That's what everyone thinks. You can believe what you bloody well want about me, but you'll learn. Marriage is a trap. Since you seem so naive, I'm filling you in on that fact."

"And I suppose you're so old and worldly?"

He deflected her sarcasm. "I'm twenty-eight. How old are you?" The conversation was ridiculous and more suitable to one they'd have a bar, not in a raft drifting aimlessly in the Pacific Ocean. Their lives were in serious jeopardy, but blast it, sparring with her passed the time.

Her chin shot up. "I'm twenty-four. Not so young."

He reclined against the edge of the raft and studied her. He'd assumed she was a couple of years younger. "Hillyard lusts for you, and I can't blame him, but there's something more. What is it about you that brought down this Hollywood icon?"

"Don't look at me like that. I've known Robert for years. He's loyal and he loves me, but I don't know why I'm trying to justify our relationship to you. My marriage to Robert will be perfect."

Alex contradicted her words with a smile.

Her eyes flashed with anger. "You don't believe in love, because actors can't care about anybody, except themselves."

He frowned. Had there been a time when he'd believed in romantic love? "So you think you're in love with Hillyard?"

"Y-yes. He's the kindest and most wonderful man in the world." She turned her back to him and hugged her knees. "So keep your opinions to yourself."

He crossed his arms over his chest. "Fine with me." He didn't know why he liked to torment her either, or why he cared if she married Hillyard. He didn't want a relationship with her. A one-night stand would be more in his sights . . . a week tops.

However, he couldn't deny his strong, mystifying attraction to her. Perhaps it was better to keep her angry while they were alone. Just how much longer would that be?

His jaw tightened. *Where in the bloody hell was the search team?*

They remained silent in the drifting raft until a stray bolt of lightning, far from the receding storm, streaked the sky and boomed like a bomb going off.

"Oh," Kelly cried out. She whirled toward him and laid her palms on his bare chest. The jolt of electricity from her touch startled him more than the thunder.

"Are you afraid of the lightning?" Without thinking, he wound his arm protectively around her.

"To be honest? A little." She squeezed her eyes shut. "When I was a kid, my family took a tropical vacation. We were stranded during a hurricane in a house on the beach. I never forgot the storm."

With a protectiveness he didn't know he possessed, he pulled her closer. He cupped her head and pulled it to rest against his shoulder and held her tightly. His heartbeat quickened and when she tilted a puzzled face up to him, he wanted to clamp his mouth down on her full red lips in an almost violent response.

Good God, he had a mind to test her loyalty to Hillyard and kiss her again, right now. That would certainly be far more enjoyable than arguing. When his body eagerly responded to that idea, he groaned. *Why did she affect him so?*

To hide his embarrassment, he teased her. He wanted to make her angry because if she remained in his arms, he would kiss her—possibly do more if she'd allow it. "If you don't want to talk, Kelly, what would you like to do?"

His strategy worked. She reeled away from him as far as possible in the small raft—about a foot. So much for putting distance between them, but that would have to do until he could leave her behind on the *Royal Queen III*—with her fiancé.

"How can you speak to me like this? Here? We're lost in the Pacific Ocean. We might die."

"I'm trying to make a bad situation more pleasant. You can *lean* on me any time, sweetheart."

"And that's all?" she said with a sarcastic lift of an eyebrow.

He shrugged. "Well if you want to do more, I'm not opposed to the idea."

Glaring at him, she folded her arms over her chest and turned away. That turned him on even more.

He knew she didn't return his desire. By her own words, she loved another—a rich man who had had his choice of women.

Alex's mouth twisted grimly. She just didn't mind returning hot kisses to other men . . . if the occasion arose.

He sighed. To be fair, it wasn't her fault his body went into overdrive when she was around. He should apologize to her—but he didn't.

They *needed* to be rescued soon.

The day slipped into afternoon before she spoke to him again.

"Where are they?" A worried frown creased her forehead.

"I don't know what's taking so long." He grew more concerned by the hour, especially with the horizon darkening and the wind whipping the waves.

He reached into the cooler, brought out two sandwiches and handed one to her. "Eat as much as you can."

"No. I'm not hungry."

His patience snapped. "Listen to me, the ice is nearly gone. We don't know how much longer we'll be out here, and this food won't be good tomorrow."

"All right, but with this rocking, if I get sick, it'll be your fault." She took a few bites of a sandwich. All the while, anger simmered in her eyes.

He shrugged and mentally disregarded her temper. If he wasn't mistaken, they were in for a huge storm.

* * *

Kelly's attraction to Alex flustered her to no end. He made her feel as if she didn't have a right to marry Robert at all. However, none of that mattered when the nighttime sky opened for a torrential downpour.

Wave after wave splashed cool water over the sides. Chill bumps edged her arm. She grasped the flapping tarp and tried to cover herself from the beating raindrops.

The waves tossed the raft like a toy. Shivering, she clung for dear life to the side to keep from being thrown out. At any moment, she'd lose the precious sandwich Alex had forced down her.

At the next wave, one of the coolers bounced out and was swept away on the waves.

Alex hurried and lashed a rope to the raft, then performed the nearly impossible task of securing the remaining two coolers.

He slid back under the tarp as another drenching wave of salt water sloshed over the sides. The next wave flung her into him and her breasts smashed into his face. He steadied her until she recovered her balance. Another time, she knew he would have remarked on the incident, but tonight they fought for their lives.

Mortified, she scrambled off him and groped for a tight hold.

As the storm intensified and raged, all she wanted to do was survive. Deafening thunder crackled and lightning brightened the sky. In near darkness, the raft rode a relentless onslaught of waves. Her heart pounded in her ears. The breeze slapped the tarp painfully against her skin, while the thin rubber floor rippled and bulged against her backside. Her arms ached from clinging to the raft.

A huge wave caused the raft to lurch. Her hand slipped from the hold she had on the side. She screamed, "*Ahhhh!*" then managed to clutch the side again.

"Hang on to me," Alex yelled over the roar of the storm. "I have a good grip on this handle."

"I can't," she choked out as a spray of cool seawater doused her. "You'll think—"

"I'll think what? Don't be an idiot."

Barely making out his outline in the darkness, she stared at him, frozen with fear and irrational thoughts. He held out his hand.

She shook her head. "But I can't."

The next huge wave dumped gallons of salt water into the raft. Her grasp slipped. She shrieked when she bounced onto the edge of the raft.

Then her braid yanked painfully at her scalp. A sob of relief burst from her throat. He had caught her by her hair. If she'd fallen out, he couldn't have saved her. She hugged the sides of the raft again.

He dropped his hold on her braid and grabbed her elbow. "Sorry for that. Come."

Her legs quivered as she crawled to him.

"Sorry I hurt you. Now, put your arms around me and hang on tight."

Kelly did more. Trembling, she nestled her face against his chest, slick and cold from the rain. "We're going to die," she hiccupped through sobs.

His heart next to her cheek hammered as rapidly as her own.

"No, I won't let us. We only have to make it through this storm. They'll find us in the morning."

He fought the weather for both of them, while she clung to him. She prayed for their survival as they rose on the crest of each wave. Each time they plummeted, an icy knot formed in her stomach. *Would the raft capsize?*

Alex counteracted the momentum by leaning into and riding each wave. The motion and the seawater she'd swallowed made her nauseous, but still she hugged him like a lifeline.

The wind and waves gradually subsided. The rain slowed to a drizzle.

He tapped her head. "We need to bail out the water."

Embarrassed, she nodded, and released the stranglehold she had on him. "Sorry," she said through chattering teeth.

As they bailed out the bottom of the raft, he threw a cooler lid full of water into the ocean. "It's a pity we can't save this rainwater, but it's contaminated with salt."

When they finished, he rejoined her under the tarp. This time when he pulled her into his arms, she was too shaken and exhausted to care. Their wet bodies were chilled to the bone and the breeze made it even worse. They needed any body heat they could generate so she clung to him once more.

* * *

Alex opened his eyes. Kelly's slender arm lay across his chest. Clad in only the tiny bikini she'd worn, she slept soundly. With each breath she took, her full breasts rose and fell intimately against his chest. The juncture between her legs pressed his hip as one of her thighs straddled him and pressed close to his morning erection. A familiar tremor passed through him.

Frowning, he scanned her face. Auburn tendrils escaped her braid and framed her face, while her long, dark eyelashes lay against her cheeks. With her mouth only inches from his . . . He resisted the temptation to place a kiss on her lips to wake her—she belonged to someone else.

And if she didn't—belong to someone else—would it matter? Kelly was one woman among millions, nothing special. He sighed. Not true. She had spunk. And something else he couldn't name. And unlike most women he knew, she had taken this disaster in stride.

He blew out a deep breath. He wouldn't wake her yet. They weren't going anywhere until the rescue crews found them. She felt too good in his arms, and he enjoyed looking at her.

The sun's rays broke through the morning clouds and a rainbow shimmered across the sky. A glimmer of confidence enveloped him. Today the rescuers would find them. For now, he was content to lie as they were and endure this bittersweet torture . . . and to resist a potent desire to caress her.

* * *

Realizing she lay prostrate, and comfortably snuggled against a warm body, Kelly's eyelids flew open.

Alex's smoldering blue eyes gazed back at her, and a cocky grin spread on his face. *What must he think of her?* It didn't take long to find out.

"Sleep well? I did." His lazy English drawl caused heat to spiral through her.

"Sorry." Her heart beat faster as she untangled herself from him, but she refused to let him provoke her this morning. He had been all tenderness last night. She owed him a debt of gratitude for saving her life *twice*.

Her gaze slid across his swimming trunks and the arousal he couldn't hide. She grew even warmer and had to get away. She jumped over the side of the raft into the ocean water to relieve herself, in more ways than one.

When she climbed back into the raft, dripping wet, and resettled herself, she couldn't stop staring at Alex. He stretched, limbering up what had to be stiff muscles from last night.

Overpoweringly male, he had the sculpted body of a Nordic god, combined with movie-star good looks. A strange longing washed over her. *For what?* A quick roll in the hay?

What was wrong with her? Even if she weren't engaged to Robert, getting involved with a self-admitted, fly-by-night lover was sheer lunacy.

Alex's eyes mocked her. He *knew* she was attracted to him, as he probably knew most women would be. She couldn't let him remain too sure.

She lifted her chin. "While I thank you for saving my life, Alex, I'm not interested in what else you have to offer."

With a shrug, he slipped over the side of the raft and swam a few yards in the ocean.

When he climbed back into the raft, the salt water dripped from his hair and beaded on his muscular body. If it were possible, he looked more incredibly sexy wet.

"Not interested, Kelly? Your eyes tell me differently."

"Do you think every woman has to be interested in you?"

"No," he said with a grin, "but you're not one of them." He could tease her all he wanted, but she'd never admit to the feelings he inspired in her, and they weren't all from his sex appeal. He'd been amazingly kind to her last night. There was more niceness to Alex Drake than he would have a woman know. However, *she* was engaged.

She turned her back to him. "I can't be the first person to tell you that you're conceited."

He laughed, but the sound died in his throat.

"Land," he shouted over her shoulder, startling her. A small mass was on the horizon in the distance. He reached for the oars. "Move back. I'll row. We might be in luck as the current is with us."

Hope welled inside her. Tonight, if things went well, she'd be back on the ship and safely away from the tempting allure of Alex Drake.

CHAPTER SIX

Robert Hillyard stepped off the search helicopter and shoved past the nosey press. The crew he'd privately hired had been over the vicinity ten times in the last six hours. They'd found mangled body parts and circling sharks . . . no sign of survivors. If the Fijian resources had been the equivalent of the U.S., and organized enough to start a full-blown rescue immediately, Kelly might have been found alive.

After entering the large dining room, Robert made his way to one of the tables where Vanessa and Susan sat, surrounded by other somber passengers waiting for information. He dropped into a chair beside Vanessa.

The *Royal Queen III's* captain strode in with two other men. The room fell silent. "We've arranged this meeting to answer all of your questions to the best of our knowledge."

After the captain stepped aside, a middle-aged Fijian man took over the podium. "The dive boat exploded. I'm sorry to say no survivors were found. While we think the cause was accidental, we will start a criminal investigation."

Robert's stomach clenched. The more time that elapsed, the less chance they'd find someone alive, or find out what had caused the explosion. "My fiancée was on the boat. You're not quitting?"

The investigator sighed. "Sir, we've called off the search. With the severity of the storms hampering our earliest efforts, it's unlikely we'll find any of the nineteen missing."

Robert leapt to his feet. "But we can't leave them out there."

The captain walked over and took Robert aside. "Mr. Hillyard," he said in a low voice, "I don't want to upset the other passengers, but we've done all we can. In the past three days, we've thoroughly combed the area. Your crew has been out as well. I don't want to alarm you, but we have accounted for enough bodies to know sharks attacked the victims." He raised an eyebrow. "Do you understand?"

Robert flushed. "The remains?"

"We will attempt to identify the passengers. Our sincerest sympathies are with you, Mr. Hillyard."

Robert returned to the table and sat beside Vanessa.

Her eyes red-rimmed, Vanessa grabbed Robert's hand and dug her nails into his palm. "I can't believe it either."

He squeezed her hand. "If only Kelly had listened to me and not gone."

Susan pressed a crumpled tissue to her eyes. "I just can't believe Alex is dead."

The investigator signaled the end of the meeting and opened the door to the press. Robert led Vanessa out to the lobby, keeping one arm around her. She might grieve, but he knew she'd get over Drake soon enough.

Why in the hell did Kelly disobey his order, and why was she with Drake that day? Had she been about to betray him? He didn't want to think so, but none of that mattered now.

When Tammy walked up, he stated flatly, "Kelly's dead."

"I'm sorry." She held out her hand, but he refused to grasp it. He had the distinct feeling she wasn't a damned bit sorry Kelly was dead. In spite of what he had told Kelly, Tammy was a jealous bitch over their relationship.

Vanessa wrung her hands together and seemed only half-aware of her surroundings. Had she popped some of her collection of pills to get her through this tragedy? "I know Alex would have dropped the divorce. He loved me."

Robert didn't refute her delusions. What did it matter now?

And he would have to forget what he could have had with Kelly.

* * *

The wind worked in their favor. Kelly shielded her eyes and watched the island grow steadily larger on the horizon. Hope welled inside her. "Would you like me to row for a while?"

He shook his head. "We have to reach the island before the current changes, or we might be pulled back out to sea." As he continued to row, the muscles flexed in his arms and chest. She was reminded of how he'd used those arms to keep her safe and warm the night before.

The sun sat low on the horizon when they approached the beach. They dragged the raft to a point above the high tide mark.

Alex, filled with exuberance and relief, picked her up and swung her around. When he set her down, her feet sank into the soft sand and her heart beat faster. To steady herself, she put her hand on his forearm and the other on his bare chest. She wasn't surprised her knees were wobbly, from being in the raft for so long and from being in his arms.

"Kelly, we've made it." He gave her a wide grin as if he didn't care whether she appreciated his hug or not.

She beamed a smile of her own. "We did. Land beneath my feet has never felt so good."

He ran his fingers through his ruffled hair and heaved a sigh. "I can't go one step farther tonight."

"Yeah, let's find help in the morning."

From one of the bags, he spread a towel in the dry sand. She placed another one about fifteen feet away from his, and then lay down and let exhaustion and the happiness of being on land overtake her.

* * *

Waves crashed onto the beach and then roared out to sea. The loud repetition invaded Kelly's sleep. She opened her eyes, disoriented by four seagulls hovering above her. They squawked and flapped their wings against the blue sky then flew out of sight.

Rising on her elbows, she spotted the birds farther down the beach. As far as she could see, turquoise water rolled onto white sand, but on this beach there were no tourists.

Uneasiness settled in the pit of her stomach. Today, they just had to find help. She stood and dusted off the fine-sugar sand clinging to her legs, and then walked to where Alex still slept.

The four-day-old stubble on his face gave him a sexy and dangerous appearance, and she realized her attraction for him was even more reason for them to be rescued quickly. She sighed. Let him rest for now. He had to be exhausted after rowing such a long distance.

She'd be forever grateful to him for saving their lives.

Perhaps, she should just go and check out the general area on her own. She shielded her eyes and surveyed the landward surroundings. Palm trees, with their fronds fluttering in the breeze, met hills with dense foliage. An unspoiled, deserted, tropical paradise lay before her—without a building in sight. She strolled down the beach for a while. Not finding any sign of humans, she returned to where Alex slept.

Determined to prove she could do her part and provide breakfast, she walked to a young palm tree and pulled off two coconuts that were easy to reach. She broke almost every fingernail tearing off the brown husks. Then she jabbed her dive knife into the hard flesh to make a hole. With the two coconuts cut this way, she strode to where Alex slept.

The epitome of masculine beauty dozed at her feet. She drew in a shaky breath. No wonder he was in the movie business. She lifted her hand to her own snarled hair, saturated with dried saltwater and still in a braid. How unfair that he still looked so good. She must look a fright, with her rumpled t-shirt and skirt that she'd prudently donned after sleeping the one night in his arms.

He opened his eyes. "Like what you see?" he asked with a lazy smile.

She let out an exasperated breath. "I'd say your conceit matches your looks."

"Thank you very much. Have you checked around? Seen a hotel or condo on the beach? Anything?"

She shook her head. "There's nothing in the general area. Beautiful island, but right now I'd be much happier if we'd landed at a gaudy tourist trap. At least we'd find help at one of those." She thrust the coconut she'd prepared for him, in his direction. "Here's your breakfast. I put a hole in it so you can drink the milk."

His brows rose in surprise. "Thank you. That was kind of you."

She kept busy by going through the rest of the bags Alex had salvaged, if only to remove herself from his intoxicating and unsettling physical presence.

Walking up to her, he said over her shoulder, "Found anything useful?"

"Matches and a lighter. Also, plastic utensils were packed in with the lunches but they won't do us much good . . . the food is spoiled." She dangled a plastic bag before him. "Except for one squashed peanut butter and jelly sandwich, which I think should be safe to eat."

He grimaced. "Bring the sandwich along. We can arm wrestle to see who gets it if we don't find help."

"Do you think we're still in the Fiji Islands?"

"Probably."

She turned toward the soaring, jungle-like hills. "The Cannibal Isles," she murmured, turning to him.

His gaze locked on hers. "What did you say?"

"The Fijians were notorious for eating people."

"That was hundreds of years ago."

"You're right," Kelly said, shoving those horrific thoughts from her mind. She loaded the bag with supplies they might need when they searched the island, while Alex checked the security of the raft and drained the remaining rainwater from the cooler into a thermos. He rummaged through the bags and found a t-shirt, shorts, sunglasses and a pair of shoes that fit well enough.

Once dressed, he set a wide-brimmed hat low on his forehead. "Let's go. Since no one has found us, we'll find them."

They strolled along the deserted beach. Kelly noticed no manmade items had washed upon the island's pristine shores.

In the afternoon, he pointed to a hill. "We'll use it as a lookout to see the other side of the island."

In the stifling heat, Kelly hiked upward through the overgrown foliage, behind Alex. At least the trees offered some relief from the hot afternoon sun. She paused to admire a colorful bush and stuck one of its peach-colored flowers behind her ear. Then she spotted a bush with clusters of purple fruit and ran toward it. The thought of eating one of them made her mouth water. She sank her teeth into the juicy fruit.

Alex came up behind her. "Do you know what you're eating?"

"Yeah. I'm pretty sure I recognize this from a tour I took at a marketplace in Suva." She handed one to Alex. "Here. They're delicious."

Grimacing, he tore the fruit from her hand and lobbed it in an arc down the hill. "Blast it, Kelly. You're not positive what you're eating. It could be poisonous. And even if it were all right, after the saltwater you've swallowed and the lack of food, you shouldn't eat so quickly." He stalked up the hill.

She stuffed a couple pieces of the fruit in her skirt pocket and ran after him. "I don't think I need you to tell me what *not* to do."

"Suit yourself, but I don't want you sick and holding us up."

After walking for another half hour, her stomach began to cramp. She swiped away the sweat beading on her forehead. She didn't want Alex to know he might be right about the fruit.

"Go on ahead. I'll catch up with you at the top of the hill."

He raised an inquisitive brow.

"I need a moment of privacy," she mumbled. "Okay?"

He gave her a reluctant nod and walked on.

Sighing, and glad to be out of his know-it-all presence, she sank to her knees in the grass. Her stomach lurched again. She hunched over and vomited, then slumped back against a tree.

Several minutes later she heard Alex shouting, "Kelly! I'm coming down for you—now."

She squeezed her eyes shut. "No," but her protest was barely a whisper. She didn't want him to see her like this.

Twigs and branches snapped. She raised her gaze and met his arrogant stare, glaring down at her.

He stood over her. "Damn it, Kelly. Perhaps you'll listen to me the next time?"

Her stomach lurching, she dropped her face into her hands. "There won't be a next time. I'm dying. Go away."

However, he didn't leave, but stood over her, frowning. Crouching on her hands and knees, she vomited again. Closing her eyes, she collapsed against the tree a second time.

After a few minutes, when he spoke, his voice was softer. "Better now?"

"I thought I told you to leave," she said through gritted teeth. How many times would she humiliate herself in front of this man? She heard him uncap the thermos and pour water.

"Kelly?"

She raised a pensive gaze to his and took the cup of water he offered. "Thanks," she said, taking the cup. The water refreshed her, washed the sourness in her mouth. She handed the cup back to him.

He shook the thermos. "We're almost out of water." His eyes reflected worry.

"Maybe that's why we haven't found anyone on the island. There isn't any water."

"No. We'll find it." He held out his hand. "Now, do you think you can make it?"

She nodded, grasped his hand and scrambled to her feet.

He circled his arm around her shoulder. "You can lean on me."

Taking him up on his offer, she draped her arm around his waist and they continued to climb the hill.

After a while, she said, "I should have listened to you. Do you know that through this ordeal you've been really good to me. If I haven't said it before, I am now. Thank you."

He shot her a wary glance, then gave her a faint smile. Her heart nearly jumped out of her throat when she saw the warmth in his eyes.

Her pulse quickening, she pulled away from him. "I think I'd better walk on my own now."

They continued to plod upward.

Please, let there be help over the next hill.

* * *

By the time they reached a clearing at the top of the hill, the sun sank in the west and the day had cooled. A large white bird soared over a sea of green treetops. In the distance, waves rolled onto the beach. Kelly sensed the thick and lush terrain was a dangerous paradise. In so many ways.

Alex gazed across the expanse. "We'll rest here. From this vantage point, we'll see from the lights tonight where the island is inhabited."

"I can't believe we've found no signs of anyone yet." She plopped down on a fallen tree trunk and massaged her aching calves. They had to find help, or she'd be with him for another night.

He sat beside her on the log.

She dangled the flattened sandwich before him. "I brought the last of the food."

They shared the sandwich gratefully. Peanut butter and jelly never tasted so good, but the small amount of food left her stomach growling for more. She knew that after the energy Alex had expended rowing, he must be even hungrier.

They each took one sip from the thermos. Alex swished the container. "Only a cup or so left." He lifted the survival manual from the bag.

"Is there anything I can do to help?"

He flipped open the book. "You can gather some palm fronds and brush."

Happy to have something to occupy her, she collected a large mound of plant material. When lit, they would have a huge bonfire.

Alex was still reading.

"Is this enough?" she asked him.

He glanced at the pile and nodded, then returned to reading. She resettled herself beside him and read along, waiting for evening. When a fly landed on her leg, she shooed the insect away.

Dusk settled over the island. Squawking parrots heralded the evening as they returned to nest in the trees that swayed in the breeze. The chirping and buzzing of birds and insects intensified. She didn't welcome the sounds. Soon night would envelope them. *When would Alex light the fire?*

"It's too dark to read." Returning the book to the bag, he stood and stretched and gazed again toward the horizon. "I'd hoped we'd see lights, or fires—something—but I don't see a thing."

"But we can't be on this island alone," she blurted out, rising to stand beside him. "There must be someone else out there." She scanned the horizon. Only the glow of the quarter moon and the brilliant stars provided any light. Her stomach clenched with fear. "On one of the tours a guide said there were about 20,000 to 30,000 islands in the South Pacific and not all of them are inhabited. This one *can't* be deserted, can it?"

"It could be."

A loud shriek filled the air. She stepped closer to Alex. "Do you think there are dangerous animals or snakes out here?"

He shook his head. "I don't know."

She pointed to the pile of palm fronds. "Are we going to light the fire to signal for help, or is it to keep the animals away?"

"Neither." Alex stooped to flatten the mound with his hands, then spread out their towels on top. Her face heated when she realized his intention.

He lay down, the brush crackling beneath his weight. "This is our bed." He patted the place beside him.

"I can't sleep beside you again."

"Suit yourself." He closed his eyes.

"Hey, I collected the brush and fronds myself," she grumbled.

He sighed and sat up. "We don't have enough for two beds. Look, it's just to sleep. It's safer. I won't try anything."

"You'd better not. Don't forget I have my dive knife."

He chuckled and reclined again. "Believe me, I'm too tired to ravish you, Kelly. Besides, you'd have to be a willing partner."

"Don't ever count on that."

"I don't. I know you're Hillyard's woman. You've made that clear. And because you miss his arms, I don't expect you'll want to make up the time in mine."

His assumption made her feel empty somehow, and that surprised her.

"Come to bed, love." He turned on his side, away from her. "Look at it this way, if there are any wild animals, we can look out for each other."

He didn't have to say it twice. Who knew what creatures were on the island? Over his shoulder, he said, "Think of me like a brother."

For some strange reason that bothered her, too. "I don't have any brothers," she said stiffly to his back.

She couldn't collect more brush tonight to make another bed, and the idea of sleeping on the dirt wasn't appealing either. With a sigh, she settled on her back beside him.

"It must be your curvy body and not your congenial personality that Hillyard is after," Alex murmured over his shoulder.

"What did you say?" she snapped.

"Why nothing, love."

She exhaled a deep breath. So what if he thought she were a shrew? Who wouldn't be after what they'd endured these past few days?

She struggled to get comfortable on the lumpy pile. "It's not exactly the Ritz."

A couple of minutes later, his breathing evened out. She was surprised by how quickly he fell asleep—almost insultingly quick. It must have been her throwing up that had turned him off, or her salt-dried, matted braid. Or perhaps he'd never found her attractive at all. She'd only been a game to him. She remembered in the nightclub, he'd said, "I find you quite lovely even with your wild, red hair." Which, to her, meant he didn't like it.

She groaned softly. Was she losing her mind to even care what he thought . . . considering what they were going through?

She stared upward, through the clearing in the trees. Stars sprinkled the dark sky. He was right. They'd been through too much together and their lives were in serious danger. It would be plain stupid to worry if she slept beside him or not, in these circumstances.

Robert would understand. That was if she ever told him the truth about all of this. He loved her, and she wanted to be loved. She tried to remember Robert's face, but she couldn't hold onto his image for long and then she dozed off.

Something thumped in the trees. Her eyes flew open. What kind of creatures lurked above them in the darkened night?

Alex rolled over onto his back. His warm arm and hip settled against her. To her dismay, her body tingled where they touched. If she moved even an inch away she'd roll into the dirt. She sighed. Great. Now, she couldn't sleep . . . for any number of reasons.

Even if she shook him, she didn't think he'd wake up because he seemed to be sleeping soundly. He probably wouldn't wake up if a bear came up and bit him on the butt. She chuckled with exhausted humor at the thought. Thank God, there were no bears out here. Then she sobered. She was losing her mind. Their situation was far from a laughing matter.

She scratched a mosquito bite on her elbow. She was being ridiculous to think that Alex might try to take advantage of her in her condition. Scratches streaked her legs from the walk through the brush, and she'd broken the rest of her fingernails, and what she really needed was a good bath. No one could be attracted to her in this state. Then her lips curved into a smile. He didn't realize how well she'd clean up. With that thought, she closed her eyelids and drifted to sleep.

Something long and rope-like slithered across her. She screamed and flung herself on top of Alex, her heart pounding.

He bolted up, their arms and legs entwining as he did so. "What's wrong?"

"A snake. It slithered across me."

"It's too dark to see anything. Are you sure?"

"Yes." She grasped his t-shirt in her hands. When she heard something swish though the palm fronds at her feet, she buried her face against his chest. "I hate snakes." She pointed in the direction of the sound. "There it is."

He chuckled and gently lifted her chin and turned her face. "Look, Kelly. It's only an iguana. I'm sure he's more frightened of us."

In the moonlight, she barely made out the three-foot long lizard—certainly not the gigantic boa constrictor she'd imagined.

She exhaled in relief and sagged against his chest.

Alex put his arm around her. "Are you all right now?"

She gave him a shaky nod, not ready to leave the safety and comfort of his arms. "Well, I'm relieved it's not a snake, but a giant lizard is not that much better."

Her secure feeling changed after a few moments as she became aware that her buttocks brushed against a hard ridge of male flesh.

He didn't think of her like a sister for one minute.

"Let me go." She shoved against him, but he tightened his hold. Her nipples budded at the brushing of his arms against the underside of her breasts. She gaped in amazement. Why did his touch do this to her? It was as if her body were telling her she should she just lie down and say, "Take me. I'm yours."

Despite the heat of the night, she shivered, frightened by her lack of control and her strong physical responses to him.

When Alex spoke, his breath feathered against her ear. "I'm not the one who jumped on you, Kelly. You'd be wise not to push me too far."

"Nothing you could do would ever make me say yes, Alex."

His stubble-roughened face brushed her smooth cheek. He lifted his hand to her face and stroked her jaw with his thumb. "I do believe this time you are challenging me. Shall I kiss you again, Kelly?"

"No. Please, don't. You know I'm engaged." As if that explained anything, but partly she didn't want him to because she hadn't brushed her teeth.

"Then have a care for my restraint, love. It's too much to have you all over me and not expect anything to happen."

He had to restrain himself from touching her. Oh, no, this wasn't good at all.

He loosened his hold, and she scooted off his lap. "Sorry, Alex. You're right. My fault." She lay down and faced away from him.

After a restless hour or two, exhaustion took over again and she slept.

She didn't argue when his hands clasped her shoulders and his lips brushed hers. She groaned and wondered why he kissed her now, when they were both dead tired.

She sighed. She'd known sleeping by him had been a bad idea, for both of them.

His mouth coaxed hers open, and he swept her up in his passion. She welcomed it and didn't have the strength or desire to resist him anymore. No. Instead she burned for him to touch her.

Tomorrow, she'd worry about the consequences, but now, she couldn't get close enough to him. She wanted him with an aching desire she hadn't known she possessed.

Somewhere in the recesses of her mind, she tried to recall promises to someone else, but she couldn't even remember his name.

Alex slid his hands under her shirt and untied her bathing suit top. She sucked in her breath and waited. When his warm hands cupped and caressed her breasts, she shivered in delight. All the while, he continued to kiss her and drive her wild.

She should make him stop, but she wanted some relief from this scorching fire only he seemed to ignite. If he stopped touching her now, she would die.

Grinning, he moved away and stripped off his shirt and shorts. She allowed him to slide her clothing down her legs. As he did, his hands stroked the inside of her thighs and she squirmed against his hand. When he came down over her, his lips melded to hers. She wanted this overwhelming, deep ache to be filled by him and no other. When he slipped his finger inside her, she moaned and raked her broken nails along his back.

Hurry, please, hurry. "Yes," she begged in surrender.

"Kelly?" Something tickled her chin.

She flung her eyes open.

"It's time we were moving." Alex's eyes held a puzzled expression as he crouched beside her. "I've been trying to wake you."

She sucked in her breath. His lips were too near hers, his body too close. It had all been too real.

"Dreaming?" he asked, brushing away a stray curl that lay on her cheek.

Warmth crept over her face as Kelly scrambled to her feet. "Yes," she said in a shaky voice.

"Did you sleep well enough?"

"No," she mumbled over her shoulder. "And when I finally did, I dreamed about bugs and snakes and those noisy parrots—and other animals," she admitted guiltily.

Unable to meet his gaze, she busied herself with collecting their supplies and packing her bag.

* * *

The sun flickered through the canopy of trees as Kelly hiked in silence behind Alex down the opposite side of the hill. She was still shaken by her dream.

Alex interrupted her thoughts. "If we don't find help, we'll have to decide what we're going to do."

She blurted, "But there has to be someone on this island who can help us."

"So far there doesn't appear to be. Didn't see any lights from camp last night either. And there's nothing I can do about that," he snapped.

He strode down the path. She hurried after him down the hill.

Did he think she blamed him for being stranded here? She couldn't tell him she feared being alone with him, so she kept her mouth shut.

At the sound of water splashing in the distance, she cried, "Alex. Do you hear that?"

He cocked his head and grinned. "Bloody hell. Water."

They cut through the thick growth and reached a stream that flowed down the hill in short waterfalls. Laughing like children, they removed their shoes and waded into a shallow part.

Kelly cupped her hands and sipped the delicious water. "I am so parched. Water has never tasted so good."

Alex filled the thermos. "We should probably filter it, but I'm willing to take the risk for now." After satisfying their thirst, they followed the stream down to the bottom of the hill. Eventually it cascaded over rocks and boulders into a large pool that looked like a jewel in a tropical setting of flowers of varying hues. Sweet scents mixed with the earthy smells of mud.

Kelly stripped down to her bikini and waded into the water, wishing she could have a real bath. She rinsed out her clothing and towel, and Alex did the same with his. She took everything and laid them out on bushes to dry. She joined him in the cool, refreshing water.

"This is heavenly," she said, savoring the soak. Then she glimpsed another surprise through the trees. "Alex, a hut. People *are* here." She splashed out of the water, with him right behind her.

They ran the short distance to where a small thatched building stood shaded beneath coconut palms. Clusters of banana trees and other fruit trees grew nearby.

"Is anyone home?" Kelly called out, but no one answered.

Alex reached for the door, which fell off in his hands. He set the door aside, and they entered the hut.

He put his hands on his hips and looked around. "This place hasn't been lived in for a long time."

Kelly's spirits plummeted. Dirt and leaves littered the crude hut's floor. One side wall had collapsed outward. All hope of finding anyone on the island vanished. Her shoulders slumped in defeat as she followed Alex out of the hut.

His brows also drew together in disappointment. "Must be some sort of outpost fishing camp?" He pulled off a couple of bananas from a tree and handed one to her. "I know these are safe."

After devouring the banana, she plucked a fruit from another tree. "This *is* a papaya, Alex." She broke the peel with her fingers and bit into the fruit. Between delicious bites, she said, "My thanks to whoever planted these, but where are they now?"

He shrugged. "If they've left the island, let's hope they're coming back."

They headed back to the lagoon. Kelly crept over the slippery, moss-covered rocks and sat on a flat rock next to a little waterfall. She dangled her feet into the transparent pool, and with a sigh, leaned against the rock to allow the water to splash over her shoulders. Despite their disappointment at not finding help, the cool water was heavenly and the fruit a godsend.

Something nibbled at her toes. She giggled and turned to Alex. "Fish. Plenty of them."

He had already waded into the lagoon. "Yes, more food. I'm considering how to catch them."

Kelly pulled out the elastic band that held her braid and raked her fingers through her snarled hair. She leaned back and the water rushed through her long hair. She closed her eyes and luxuriated in feeling cleaner.

When she looked back toward the water, Alex rose from the surface, looking like a sexy Apollo, muscular and fit. The sight of him wet and scantily dressed made her mouth go dry. An aching desire passed over her and shook her to her soul.

She brushed back a wet strand of hair from her face. Goodness, if she didn't detest him, and they weren't lost and worried for their lives, what a heavenly fantasy—the island was a tropical paradise and the man gorgeous.

Alex flicked his gaze to her. "So you're marrying Hillyard because you have some idiotic notion you're in love with him?"

Fantasy, busted.

She stiffened at what she considered a personal attack. "There's nothing idiotic about being in love," she said, evading the question.

Before the dive incident, she had thought the kind of love she had for Robert was enough. Now, with her attraction to Alex, she questioned some of that belief.

Alex's sensual gaze swept over her. "I don't believe in romantic love. Just lust and sex."

She crossed her arms over her chest. "Alex, I'm not up for a temporary fling with you."

However, the thought of being in his arms sent an unwelcomed heat spiraling through her. She jumped from the rocks and into the water to cool off. When she surfaced, she felt ready for some accusations of her own.

"On the day I overheard you talking to Vanessa, you told her you didn't love her when you married her. I feel sorry for you."

A bleak expression crossed Alex's features. "I'm not commenting on my relationship with her." He pointed toward the darkening horizon. "Another bloody storm. We need to find shelter."

CHAPTER SEVEN

As the storm swiftly approached, Alex's stomach tightened with apprehension. He helped Kelly gather their wet clothing and the bags containing their supplies.

"Let's head for the hills. We might find a cave there to weather the storm."

The rain came down in bands, sometimes pelting, sometimes drizzling, as they climbed the hill. He half-dragged her with him as they trudged upward. *Were they in for a tropical storm? Or worse?*

Rain ran in rivulets down her face. "We're going to die on this island," she said, her bottom lip quivering.

He squeezed her hand in reassurance. "No. We're in the tropics. Think of this as an adventure. One day, you'll be able to look back on this and laugh about it with your grandchildren."

"I sure hope you're right." She looked so frightened and vulnerable, he wanted to reach out and pull her to him. They had endured so much.

He let out a deep sigh and continued onward. They were soaked by the time they found a niche jutting about twenty feet into the surface of the rock.

"We'll stop here," he said.

She swiped the water from her face. "How I wish we were back on the ship."

"Consider yourself lucky. Now, you won't have to worry about getting divorced later."

"You're so cynical. Don't you want someone to love you?"

"You mean *own*? But you'll learn for yourself. Marriage is a trap. I don't have anything good to say about it, except it's one mistake I won't repeat."

She shivered and wrapped her arms around herself. "You don't have to worry about getting married again, because we're never going to get off this island."

He decided not to war with her. She looked like a wet kitten ready to collapse at his feet.

"Let's clean out this space."

With palm branches, they brushed out the dirt and leaves. The breeze changed direction and ripped through, blasting them with another band of hard rain.

After Alex spread the tarp and towels in the niche, he yelled over the howling wind, "Get in." Stepping into survival mode, he was past any proprieties now. He boosted her by her firm bottom into the recesses of the rock wall and climbed in after her. He urged her as far back into the chamber as possible.

They had some protection, but barely enough room to sit.

Her slender shoulders shook. He could tell she was trying not to break down, but she was beginning to crack. She must have recognized his concern because she dropped her face in her hands and turned away from him.

Although despair threatened to overwhelm him as well, oddly, the need to comfort her gave him courage. "I swear we're going to be all right, love." He took a towel from one of the canvas bags and briskly wiped the water from his face and dried his arms and chest. "Now you."

She didn't respond so he lifted her heavy hair and rubbed the strands with the towel.

"What?" She pulled back and stared at him.

"You need to get dry."

She didn't protest, but her eyes widened.

He gave her a faint smile. "Stunned that I'm helping you?"

She nodded.

He finished by dabbing at her face and patting her shoulders and arms dry. "Now, lie down." He guided her to face the wall.

"What does it matter if we survive a few more days?" she said, through choppy breaths. She looked back at him. "Don't you get it? They've given up looking for us, and there's no one on this island."

When he saw her tear-streaked face, something tightened in his chest. "We're not sure of that. I'll do everything in my power to get you home to Hillyard."

At the mention of her fiancé's name, she burst out in a sob. He'd only wanted to comfort her by saying the words he thought she wanted to hear.

Baffled, he lay down beside her and pulled the tarp over them. He hated to hear her cry. Ignoring his intuition not to touch her, he draped his arm over her waist and pulled her closer to his warmth.

"Please, don't cry," he said in a soothing voice. He pressed his lips against her damp hair. "I've admired your courage through this ordeal."

"You have?" she asked.

"Yes."

She shivered again. "I'm sorry. I can't help being afraid."

"It's all right. Even if we are alone on this island, we've found enough food to survive until we're rescued. I'm not ready to die, and I'll do whatever it takes for us to last until we're rescued." He pulled her closer and stroked his fingers through the loose curls at her temple. "Someone has been here. They'll return, or someone else will eventually come upon the island. Or if we can figure out how to bring enough supplies, maybe we can take the raft and go back out on the ocean."

He shuddered at that thought—but if they became desperate, he would do it.

"Alex, so you still think we'll be rescued?"

"Yes. Eventually," he said as reassuringly as he could. He wouldn't believe anything else.

Appeased, Kelly relaxed in his arms. They lay quietly and listened to the storm rage about them.

His eyes adjusted to the dim light diffusing through the niche. Her long hair fell over her bare shoulder, exposing the curve of her neck and the string of her bikini top. Her fresh scent lingered like an aphrodisiac.

Despite their predicament—or maybe fueled by it—desire, hot and strong, assailed him. It caught him off guard. He wanted to lower his lips to her neck, but fought for control. She was distraught and missed Hillyard, and that definitely didn't complement his overpowering urge to make love to *her.*

Clenching his jaw, he reminded himself that circumstances had forced them together. She'd made it abundantly clear she didn't even like him, and he'd seen her leave Hillyard's cabin.

Still, he'd vowed to protect her until they were rescued. He would return her safely to her home, untouched by him, because he now knew she was the type of woman who wanted a commitment and marriage.

He averted his gaze from sweet temptation. How long would they have to remain on this island and cling to each other to survive? And how long could he ignore the clamoring of his raging desire?

* * *

Morning air warmed the niche in the rocky hillside. Kelly sat and stretched, surprised to find she'd slept soundly on the rocky bed.

Next to her lay Alex. Funny how the rules changed when two people needed each other. She might as well get used to being alone with him. No longer could she consider him a stranger. Last night when she'd been upset, he'd held her tenderly in his arms.

She wanted to touch the curve of his provocative mouth, and run her fingers along the smooth skin of his tanned chest and taut abs. Smiling faintly, she knew she'd take that chance if she didn't think he'd wake. He would accuse her of finding him appealing. *Well, Alex, that might be true, but I'll never say it out loud.*

There seemed to be much more to Alex than his looks, and he wasn't as rough or uncaring as he would have people believe.

Realizing she should be fighting the warm glow spreading through her, she slipped on her now dry shirt and skirt. All the while, she looked over his muscular body. When she glanced back at his face, his eyes were open. He watched her with a glint in his eyes.

Blushing, she waited for him to make his usual cynical remark.

The amused look faded from his eyes. "Better after yesterday's deluge?"

She offered him a smile. "Yeah, a deluge in more ways than one. Sorry for the outburst. I'm not going to fall apart anymore. Now, I'm just hungry." She cringed at her faux pas and added quickly, "I'm hungry . . . for food." That sounded even worse. She clapped her hand to her face.

He let her remark slide. After they bundled up the towels and the tarp, he tossed them to the ground and jumped from the niche. He held out his hand and helped her down, and then turned his back on her and strode away.

She frowned. *Was something wrong?*

The trek down the hill proved how badly the tropical storm had ravaged the island. Leaves, palm fronds and coconuts littered the ground.

Creeped out a bit, she shuddered inwardly. *Were they truly alone?*

In the shade of a palm, Alex sat on the grass. From her bag, she pulled a couple of bananas she had picked at the hut yesterday, and then settled beside him. They shared the meal in silence.

Finally, he stood. "Let's go. We can't rely on being rescued. We need to make a camp and find food that is more substantial. I'm beginning to feel weak."

She strode after him down the hill toward the beach and the lagoon. "We really can't stay here. Maybe we should take our chances with the raft?"

He swung around to face her. "I want to leave as much as you do, but we can't go unless we take supplies. Do you want to be lost out in the ocean again, this time without food or water?"

Her shoulders sagged. "No." He was right, of course, but he didn't understand the full implications. She had welcomed his arms around her last night.

Alex sighed. "We don't have a choice, love. Do you have ideas for food? Do you know how to cook?"

"Sure, if you take me to the nearest microwave oven, I'll whip you up something." At the distressed look in his eyes, she added, "Actually, I'm a good cook, and I did see a demonstration of several traditional native dishes. Perhaps I could try to cook one. That's if we can catch some fish."

"Then we'll camp at the abandoned hut to start with. It's close to the lagoon."

It took only a few minutes to reach the lagoon that lay sparkling in the morning sun. Kelly once again stripped off her shirt and skirt with a sense of unease. She hadn't realized when she bought this skimpy bikini that she'd be living in it twenty-four-seven.

When Alex's gaze raked over her, her face warmed.

He smiled ruefully. "We've come a long way from gowns and tuxedos, haven't we?"

She nodded and sank back on a flat boulder, waiting to hold out the cooler to retrieve any fish he caught.

He took his diving knife and cut six sticks, shaping the end of each into a point. After he climbed on a higher edge of the bank, he peered into the water, then raised his arm to throw the spear. He looked entirely too gorgeous to be doing this with her.

She chuckled. "I feel like I'm on a set. Your pose must be from something like . . . uh let's see—*Tarzan and the Ape Girl.*"

He flashed her a grin. "There is no film by that title and I've never played King of the Jungle. However, I'll consider it, if you'll play Jane."

"Me?" Kelly leaned back on her elbows. Was he suggesting she play Jane to his Tarzan? Tarzan was always picking Jane up and swinging her around on vines, carrying her off somewhere.

At the thought of Alex carrying her to a private place, an unsettling heat lodged in the pit of Kelly's stomach. She hadn't forgotten her amazingly real dream. She moistened her lips with her tongue. Perhaps he would carry her to the soft patch of grass near the waterfall where tropical flowers grew in a tangle of colors . . .

He would kiss her. She closed her eyes and relived the pleasure of his lips on hers.

Cool water droplets sprinkled on her skin and startled her out of her reverie. Her eyelids flew open.

Alex had waded into the lagoon to retrieve the spears and now gazed at her with a puzzled expression. "Are you sleeping, Kelly?" He flicked more water on her. "We have a dinner to catch. Remember?"

Her cheeks burned with shame as she sat up. God help her, now she fantasized about him in broad daylight. She forced herself to concentrate on his attempts to spear a fish—and not on the hard ripple of muscles playing in his arms and back when he moved.

He gave her another curious gaze, climbed back onto the bank and threw the spears. With each throw, he missed the mark.

His eyebrows slanted into a frown. "Perhaps they're too light. I'll have to make heavier ones." He glanced at her. "You want to give it a go?"

She smiled at him. "No, I'm having too much fun watching you."

"Watch your tongue," he teased, amusement glinting in his eyes. "Or I'll be playing Petruchio to your Katharina. You have seen *Taming of the Shrew*?"

She cleared her throat and glanced sideways under veiled lashes. "Do I really come across to you as a shrew, Alex?"

Grinning, he left her hanging on that question and waded in up to his thighs to retrieve the spears.

He waved one spear in the air like a make-believe foil. "When all else fails, I say try another tactic. On guard."

"Are you going to slay them with your sword or make them laugh themselves to death?"

"I'll do that next." He swished the stick in the air, then lunged his makeshift spear into the water without success. He tried a few more thrusts, but still no hits. "Damn," he said, folding his arms across his chest. "This is harder than I expected."

She giggled. "I'm partial to restaurants myself."

He narrowed his eyes. "Why don't you try, madam? You were so successful at opening those coconuts."

She tossed her long hair over her shoulders. "All right, Tarzan, but I think I need a lesson." She waded into the water.

Alex came up behind her and placed a spear in her hand. He raised her arm to throw the stick, but when his chest pressed against her back, her mind went blank. Strong desire raged through her. She gasped. He must have felt something, because he paused, his heart racing at a mad tempo against her back.

Abruptly, he released her and stepped away. "That part of the lesson is over," he said in a low husky voice. "Now, try it, Kelly. Give it a go." He was all seriousness.

Still quivering from his touch, she closed her eyes and jabbed the spear into the water. "I probably couldn't hit Moby Dick," she muttered, but she hit something and it moved, aggressively. She winced, hoping it wasn't Alex—but she hadn't heard a scream.

"Bloody hell, Kelly. Bulls eye."

Her eyes flew open.

He took the spear from her hand. She gaped at the large, wriggling fish Alex pulled out of the lagoon. "Remind me never to make you angry when you have one of these things in your hand."

She grimaced at the poor, unlucky creature. "It was pure luck."

"Nevertheless, it appears we have dinner for tonight." He placed the fish in the cooler. "For the sake of my pride, I'll try to catch one and make a contribution."

She tramped out of the water. "Next time, I'm making a net. If I have to spear fish, I'll quickly become a vegetarian." She plopped down on the bank to watch him.

It didn't take long before he'd lanced another one.

He chuckled with amusement. "Thanks to my excellent instructor, I think I've learned the method. Now, we have to clean them."

Kelly wrinkled her nose.

He laughed, his dimples evident. "By the look on your face, I'd better do the cleaning." He gave her a sideways glance. "If you think that's the man's job . . . well since you're the woman, you can cook then. Unless, of course, you'd prefer to eat sushi tonight?"

"No. Let's try to cook the fish."

Within a few minutes, she found the tarot plant she remembered from the tour.

Choosing a site not too far from the hut to construct the pit, she instructed him to build an oven like she'd seen on the Suva tour. With empty split coconut shells, they scooped out the sand. Then they lined the pit with coconut husks and layered stones on top.

Alex took one of their precious matches and carefully lit the husks. They blew and fanned furiously to get the embers going, and cheered when the fire took hold.

"We did it," she cried.

She wrapped the fresh fish in leaves and layered it with roots of the tarot plant, like potatoes, to roast on the fire.

She covered the food with more leaves to hold in heat. "It will take hours to cook. Let's hope this turns out to be edible."

They turned their attention to the hut, which had suffered even more damage in the storm. All the while, the delicious aroma of baked fish wafted through the camp. Her stomach growled.

As she worked with him on cleaning out the hut, her thoughts drifted to their sleeping arrangements. How could her heart survive, night after night alone with him on this island, when her loyalty belonged to Robert? Alex would probably laugh at her foolishness if he knew she had grown attached to him.

* * *

A gentle breeze stirred the picture-perfect evening as Kelly served dinner. She sat next to Alex on the grass beneath a tree, happy to be alive.

He peeled back the leaves and a trickle of steam rose from the fish. He blew on it, then took a bite. "Superb. I've never tasted anything so delicious."

She laughed. "Liar. Anything tastes good when you're this hungry." She nibbled on the food. "The tarot leaf tastes a little like spinach." He agreed.

After they had eaten the main course, Kelly made an announcement, "And now I have a surprise for you."

She walked to the pit and returned with a dessert similar to what she'd seen the natives make—papaya sprinkled with coconut milk and wrapped in tarot leaves.

Alex bit into the concoction, his eyes lighting with contentment.

"Delicious," he said between bites. While he ate, she watched his sexy mouth. Once again, he sent her senses spinning.

Exhaling a deep breath, she jumped to her feet and headed to the lagoon to clean the plastic plates. By the time she returned, dusk had spread over the island, and squawking parrots heralded the approaching night.

Alex dozed against a palm tree. He must have thrown more sticks into the pit for the fire burned brightly. She didn't think she'd ever get used to the idea of complete darkness. Glad to have Alex near, she sat cross-legged beside him on the soft grass.

He opened his eyes. "Dinner was fabulous. I feel better already."

She gazed at the palms silhouetted against the sunset. "It's such a beautiful place, Alex."

"A lonely paradise."

"If only we had the comforts of home."

"Or of the cruise ship—excluding Vanessa, of course."

"You weren't too happy to see her."

His mouth took on an unpleasant twist. "Hardly. She manipulates everything. Hillyard only asked me to be in the film so he could sign Vanessa. I should have known the part was too good to be true. I'm unknown in the States, except for being notorious in the tabloids as Vanessa Caine's errant husband."

"How did you meet her?"

He raked back a lock of hair from his forehead. "While I was a drama student in London, she visited the school. You can imagine, I was flattered when she asked me out that night." He exhaled a deep breath. "I soon discovered Vanessa to be the most cunning person I had ever met." He pressed his fingertips to his temples. "I don't know why I'm telling you all of this."

Not wanting to lose this moment of sincerity and his trust, she whispered, "I'll keep your secret. I'll never forget you saved my life."

A wave of guilt tormented her. She had her own secrets. Those horrible men had been after her. She yanked out a long blade of grass and twined it through her fingers. Alex had spoken honestly. Maybe, she needed to open up, too, and he had every right to know who had caused the dive boat explosion.

She was about to confess everything, when he said, "I want you to know that I've been separated from Vanessa from almost the beginning, but she wouldn't consent to a divorce, so I've had to wait five years."

"Five years," she blurted. Then she stiffened, remembering Robert had said Alex had married the actress for her money and to further his career.

"Vanessa wouldn't agree to the divorce. In England one must be separated for five years without consent."

"That's a long time."

His lips twisted in a cynical expression. "I suppose all women are not like Vanessa."

Did Alex deserve his fate for using Vanessa? "No," she retorted. "Many people have happy marriages."

His brow rose. "My parents did until my father died."

Not hers. Someone had deliberately taken her parents' lives. How many of her father's disgruntled clients wanted her dead? A lump stuck in her throat.

"Are you all right, Kelly?"

She wasn't, but she nodded anyway. "My parents seemed happy, until my father cheated with an actress. I suppose that's one of the reasons why I've never had a high opinion of actors. Mom and Dad had just reconciled and were killed in a plane crash."

"Both your parents? Do you have siblings?"

She shook her head. "I have only my great-aunt Kaye. I went to live with her after they died. My life changed drastically." She went from a pampered rich girl to being financially devastated.

"Sorry to hear that." He looked away, and then went on in a flat voice, "I knew I wasn't in love with Vanessa when I married her."

She couldn't believe he admitted it. "How did you ever expect to be happy, if you only married her to help your career?"

His expression held a note of mockery. "So you damn me along with everyone else?"

"But you just said you didn't love her."

"People get married for other reasons, Kelly."

She folded her arms across her chest. "So it would seem."

He sighed. "I don't expect you to believe me, but the truth is I hadn't known Vanessa very long, when we . . ." He seemed embarrassed, but he shrugged it off. "My ego swelled. Bloody hell, I was twenty-two years old and this famous actress wanted *me*. She took me places around the world I'd never even dreamed of seeing. It was brief and exciting. She turned up a month later, after I'd ended it, saying she was pregnant."

A grim expression crossed his handsome features. "Within three months of knowing her, I made the worst mistake of my life. I married her." He sagged against the tree. "I've been living a nightmare ever since."

Kelly frowned. "You married her because she was *pregnant?*"

"At the time, I thought it was the right thing to do."

Disappointment assailed her. Alex had a child with Vanessa? Why should she be surprised? Married people usually had children. Even after the divorce, he'd be forever tied to Vanessa.

She yanked another blade of grass. "That was a noble thing to do."

"Yes, that was back when I was noble, young, and stupid." He picked up a pebble from the ground and tossed it in his hands. "Not anymore."

"But, no matter how you feel about her, it was probably the best thing for your child."

"There never was a child," he said sharply. "On our supposed *honeymoon*, I found out my bride was a habitual liar." He sailed the pebble into the fire. "She told me she lost the baby, but had wanted to marry me anyway. *What a lie.* She'd never been pregnant."

He paused for a moment, exhaling a deep breath. "Because of my family's reputation and the scandal of divorce, I was obligated to make it work, but it was impossible. Vanessa is insanely jealous." His brooding gaze caught Kelly's. "I've never told *anyone* the truth about my marriage . . . until you."

She put her hand on his arm. "I'll keep your secret." Now, Alex and Vanessa's story made sense. Robert had been right, but so wrong. "If Vanessa is so awful, what I don't understand is how Robert can adore her."

"Hillyard should. He helped create her and put her in his films. In turn, her stardom helped make him rich."

Kelly gaped. "I know they're friends, but Robert never told me he had such a long history with her."

Alex exhaled deeply. "I've said more than I should. I don't need any more stories in the press."

They had that in common. She took a deep breath. "I have something to tell you, too."

He crossed his arms over his chest. "I'm listening."

"Remember the day I ran into your cabin?"

His mouth quirked at the corner. "How could I forget, love? You were wearing all lace and sheer silk and nothing more."

Her heart beat faster at his words. She wore about the same skimpy amount tonight in this tiny bikini. "Please, don't tease me. This isn't easy for me."

He watched her thoughtfully. "All right, go on."

She cleared her throat. "The day I ran into your cabin, I had received a death threat. You found the letter on the floor." His expression stilled, but he let her speak. "I thought someone was in my cabin to kill me because in L.A., a man had attacked me. He tried to strangle me, to be exact."

Alex's eyebrows drew together in shock. "The bruises on your throat . . ."

She nodded. "Yes, and there's more to it. On the day of the explosion, those men were looking for *me*. I'm the one they wanted to kill."

Alex gripped her arms and hauled her to her feet. "Why the bloody hell didn't you tell me?"

She winced at the pressure of his hands on her arms. "I was afraid of the attack getting into the news and hurting Cochran Investments even further. I had planned to tell the police when we were rescued." She drew in a shaky breath. "You have every right to be mad at me. I should have told you the danger you were in just by being with me."

"I'm not angry with you," he snapped, loosening his hold.

"You certainly sound like it." She tried to twist out of his grasp, but he didn't release her.

He sighed and said in a softer voice, "Kelly, I'm concerned, that's all." He stroked her arms lightly where he had held her. "I didn't mean to hurt you."

"You didn't hurt me," she said, barely able to whisper. She had merely gone soft all over when he touched her.

"It's just they could have come back to make sure you were dead. I wouldn't have known there was any danger."

"I'm sure they *think* I'm dead or they would have come back."

"But why would anyone want to kill you?"

"The police think my father was embezzling from his clients and sending the money out of the country. A seven-million-dollar bank withdrawal had been made by my father a few days before the crash." She choked back a sob. "The plane had been rigged to go down. I was supposed to be on the plane, too, but I was sick and stayed with Aunt Kaye. At the time, I'd wished I had been with them. I wanted to die, too."

Alex pulled her into his arms and stroked her back.

"They're all lying about my father." She pressed her face against his shoulder. "He wouldn't steal money, and he wasn't skipping the country because he wouldn't have left without me. He was nothing like they say he was."

Finally, she became conscious of his warm, naked chest touching her breasts. He must have realized it, too, for he abruptly released her and stepped back.

She dried the tears in her eyes with her fingers and choked out, "I have to get back. If I can save the company and repay all the clients, I can clear my father's name, at least somewhat, and appease whoever wants to kill me."

He ran his fingers through his hair, a gesture becoming familiar to her. "You've taken all this responsibility on yourself?"

"Not by myself. Robert oversees the business as Trustee. I inherit partial control on my twenty-fifth birthday, coming up in August."

"Is this why you're marrying him?"

"Of course not." She whirled around, giving him her back. "I've known Robert for years. Do you know how many women would love to be in my place?"

"Hillyard likes controlling the company, doesn't he?" Alex asked, over her shoulder. "And I've heard he's ruthless in business."

She turned toward him. "You don't know him. He's the kindest man."

Alex raised a skeptical eyebrow.

She hugged herself. "You don't understand. I don't have any money. He's aware of that more than anyone. If anything it's a burden to him, but he watches over the company as a friend. He and my father were raised practically like brothers as his mother worked for my grandparents for years."

She refrained from telling Alex she owed the largest sum of money to Robert. On top of the seven million dollar loan, before they left, Robert had further propped up the company with another two million dollars.

Alex stepped toward her, and she didn't like the accusation in his eyes.

"So, Alex, you're implying Robert doesn't love me and only wants the company?"

"He wants you, which I can understand." Alex cupped her chin. "Don't get upset. It's your business if you want to marry him. I'm just trying to figure you two out." When he dropped his hand from her face, she sighed, because she had liked it there too much. "Why not let the company dissolve and start over?"

"It's complicated. Too many people have lost their money and need to be repaid. The employees would lose their livelihood, and I have to salvage my father's ruined reputation. Not to mention, Mister X has sworn to kill me if I don't pay."

"Mister X?"

"I call him that because I don't know who is sending the letters, but he might be one of the men who attacked the boat. Will I always be looking over my shoulder wondering if I, or worse, someone I love . . . ?" She gasped and cried out, "Oh, my God, what if he goes after Aunt Kaye now? She could pay the ultimate price."

"Bloody hell, Kelly. A lot of people have already paid the price."

Tears trickled down her cheeks. She nodded. "And you could have been one of them." She put a hand up to her wet face. "If I had gone with those men, then they wouldn't have shot at the boat. I don't deserve to be the one alive."

She whirled and hurried from the camp.

* * *

Alex ran after Kelly, caught her arm and gently shook her.

"Don't blame yourself. You had nothing to do with those killers." With his thumbs, he dabbed away the hot moisture from beneath her eyes. "You've been through hell, while I've done nothing but goad you from the moment I met you. Truce?"

She considered him for a moment. "Truce."

He lowered his gaze to her full, red lips. He wanted to take her mouth with his in an almost violent action. An image flitted through his mind of her lying beneath him on the grass, his hips between her thighs. He nearly groaned. As pretty and alluring as she was, she wasn't worth the complication.

He dropped his hand from her arm and backed away as if she were one of those hot rocks in the pit. "Don't distress yourself about it. It's late. Let's talk about this tomorrow. You stay here and sleep. I'm going for a walk on the beach."

She nodded. "Goodnight."

His gaze lingered on the soft sway of her hips as she walked toward the hut. He'd love to go with her. It would be heavenly to sleep with her in his arms again, but bloody hell, he couldn't think of one excuse to do so tonight—except to comfort her. No, he couldn't do it.

Exhaling a deep breath, he turned in the direction of the beach.

His thoughts turned to his obsession to sleep with Kelly—especially now. But knowing all she'd gone through, he vowed he wouldn't add to her pain. He had thought his life had been a nightmare, but it was nothing compared to what she had experienced, and what the two of them were going through now. Tomorrow, he'd begin building a privacy partition in the hut. Until then, he'd sleep on the tarp outside.

He headed back to the hut, trying to think of something negative or very cold to squash his desire for her—something other than his career being ruined by Hillyard. *Pregnancy.* There was no birth control out here. The thought cooled him considerably. His hormones had gotten him into trouble before. He wouldn't be a fool again.

CHAPTER EIGHT

Two days later, Kelly dusted sand from her palms after the exhausting morning's work of lugging rocks with Alex. Every muscle in her back throbbed, but the words *Help* and *SOS* now lay spelled out on the beach. Swiping the sweat from her brow, she studied the blue sky. Maybe one day soon a plane would fly over and see their plea for help.

Leaving Alex finishing up the last letter, she hurried to sneak a private bath at the lagoon.

After stripping off her bikini, she waded in and let the cool water refresh her hot skin. Under the waterfall, she scrubbed her hair with the last piece of soap she'd had in her bag. A flicker of apprehension coursed through her that while she'd always been irregular, she couldn't ignore the cramps she'd had all morning. Her period would begin soon, and she didn't have any idea how she was going to handle that.

She'd just splashed out of the water and slipped on the bottom half of her bathing suit when Alex strolled through the trees. Fumbling with the ties of her top, she whirled, giving him her back.

He chuckled. "Need my assistance?"

"No. Done," she said in a shaky voice. She turned to face him. They had made an unspoken agreement to keep their distance, but the huskiness in his voice caused warm sensations in the pit of her stomach.

"A bath with soap sounds great. Do you have any?" His gaze dropped to her bag lying on the bank.

Deciding to be fair, she pulled the soap from the bag. "Here you go."

"You seem to have quite a few things in your bag?"

"Yeah, I have some things, but this is getting way too personal. We barely know each other, and it's as if we've been

thrown together in this instant marriage. In all ways except for . . . "
She winced.

He raised an eyebrow. "*Sex?*"

Not wanting to go there, she shrugged. "I've shared my toothpaste and now my soap. You're lucky we found an extra toothbrush in another bag, or you'd be out of luck."

He frowned. "What's wrong with you?"

"Nothing." She whirled and rubbed the towel through the strands of her hair. Her stomach cramped again, making her bitterly aware how easy men had it. What did Alex have to worry about? Nothing. "Well, if you must know, I have issues I'm worried about. Being a woman out here in the wilderness has its problems. I need, uh, certain things . . . "

"What problems? What things? *Tell me.*"

Her face warmed. "You know, women things. Things I have to figure out on my own."

"Ah, I think I get it. If there's anything I can do for you, you'll tell me?"

"Yeah."

"Kelly, do you have a razor by any chance?"

She retrieved the bag and pulled out the razor. When he took it, he caught her gaze. "Thanks. I won't use it every day."

After all he'd done for her, she'd be a bitch to refuse to share everything she had with him. "Here take the bag. Feel free to use whatever you'd like."

A short time later, he returned to camp with his face clean-shaven, his perfect features more evident. Kelly's heart did a flip-flop. He looked like a handsome model from *GQ* or some other magazine, yet he seemed unaware of how beautiful he was.

Kelly blew out a deep breath. For her own self-preservation, she should fling the razor into the ocean.

* * *

Perhaps stress caused her to skip her monthly flow, but Kelly was greatly relieved. She hoped to be rescued before she had to deal with that issue again.

With every day that passed, they became more accustomed to their wild environment. Alex repaired the hut and built a partition to provide a space for him and a space for her. She'd woven pallets for them to sleep on.

Today, on a makeshift table left by the natives, Kelly placed chopped papaya into split coconut shells they used for bowls. She had not given up hope someone would find them and had shoved her worries about Cochran Investments to the back of her mind— the need to find food outweighed everything.

During the next two weeks, when darkness descended, her link with Alex became closer and more desperate. If they could keep an ember burning in the pit from dinner, they'd have a campfire. Otherwise, they couldn't waste their precious matches or lighter. They spent some nights in total darkness, beneath the stars, talking about their hopes and dreams, and of a future for each of them off the island.

She learned he had several older sisters, who had spoiled him, and a younger brother. His mother was somewhat of a socialite. She'd been shocked when he decided to become an actor as it wasn't something done in their family. His responsibility as the oldest son was to pick a more 'worthy' profession.

Kelly told him about her family's ranch in California, how much she loved horses, her 4-H honors, and her life with her mom and dad.

Although the search for food was a priority, they had some leisure time. With an excellent singing voice, Alex performed a few parts from his days in the theater, revealing his tremendous talent. When he sang love songs, and her heartbeat increased, she reminded herself not to take the words personally. Sometimes she sang along with him. He coached her with voice lessons, and she was amazed by her improvement. At other times, he instructed her in dramatic techniques. When they recited the balcony scene from Romeo and Juliet, her heart beat at a rapid tempo.

Although he said she had a pretty voice, he teased her about her acting talent. "Good thing you have a business degree, love. But we'll keep working on it."

Now, Kelly looked out over the waves again as she prepared their food. *Would they be here forever? Did she really mind spending the rest of her life with him?* She was afraid of her answer. Although it was urgent that she return home for the company, she enjoyed Alex's company more than she ever thought possible and found herself far too content in the island home they shared.

Watching his attempts to make a chair, she smiled. Dear Alex was an inventor at heart. He sang while he worked, twining a vine around some pieces of bamboo.

When finished, he sat. The chair swayed and collapsed. He sprawled on the ground, but gave her a cocky grin. Brushing off the dirt, he went back to work, retying the vines. She smiled proudly when he made a slight modification, and the chair held his weight.

At the evening meal, he waved her toward the chair. "You may have the honor first."

Warmth flowed through her as she laughed. "I see I'm the guinea pig . . . but thank you. There was a time when I thought you were frivolous because you're an actor. I've changed my mind."

"Oh?"

She didn't elaborate and glanced away from the unsettling glimmer in his eyes. It was hard to remain coherent when he held a warm look like that for her, but being affected by that gaze would only lead her into trouble. She was merely a second away from stepping into his arms. *What would he think or say if he knew she cared for him more than she should?*

So instead, she sat on the chair and ate her food in silence, pondering how their relationship had slowly changed. She'd like to think that they'd become friends, but there was something more. It was surprising, that in this place, he soothed her aching loneliness as no one had before.

* * *

The next morning, Kelly slipped the second wriggling fish from the net into the cooler. "Hey, the net I wove worked, I think we have enough for dinner in half the time." She closed the lid, trying to think of a new recipe to try.

"Are you making fun of my spearing techniques again?" Alex said with a wry smile. "You know, I haven't caught anything today."

"Yeah, but I need to be better than you at something. I won't even try for those lobsters you're so good at getting from the rocks on the beach."

When she stepped back, her foot faltered on the bank. Her arms flailed and she landed with a soft whoosh in the squishy, deep mud.

As he waited to spear a fish a short distance away, Alex's laughter rang out.

She struggled to stand, flinging the mud from her hands. "I'm glad you find this funny." When she tried to walk, her feet made sucking sounds. She swiped the black muck from the back of her hair.

"You're not hurt, are you?" He came to her rescue and stood above her on the bank. He crouched down and extended his hand.

"The only thing bruised is my pride."

"Good." Still, he had that smirk on his face as if he tried hard not to laugh.

She narrowed her eyes. "I'm so glad you think this is amusing." She grasped his hand, a little too firmly perhaps, for they both lost their balance and tumbled back into the soft mud. When he fell on top of her, the force almost knocked the wind out of her, though the mud cushioned their fall.

He rose on his forearms and scrutinized her. "Are you all right?"

At the concern on his face, she giggled. "Yes. But it was worth it to see the surprise on your face."

His eyes narrowed. "You did that intentionally?"

"No, I . . . Well maybe." They both laughed.

He shifted his weight on top of her. "You could've been hurt."

"I'm fine." She drew in her breath, suddenly aware how intimately he pressed against her.

A smile played at the corner of his lips. "You do seem to find ways to get yourself into trouble."

She silently agreed, because she tingled everywhere his body met hers. Her palm resting on his bare chest, she detected his racing heart. It took a moment for her to find her voice. "You must think I'm so clumsy."

His grin was irresistibly devastating. "No, but this time you'll pay a price for getting us into this predicament." The blue in his eyes suddenly darkened.

Breathlessly, she watched his mouth descend on hers. Their lips touched. His kiss, warm and gentle, sent spirals of ecstasy swirling through her.

He resettled his hard body between her parting thighs. She almost protested, but when he deepened the kiss, all she could concentrate on were the sensations he evoked.

His breathing heavy, he brushed feathery kisses down her throat. "I've wanted to kiss you again since the first time, but that's as far as I can go unless . . . you're ready to take a bath with me."

Did he say 'bath?' All she could think was 'kiss me again.'

Not waiting for an answer, he scooped her up in his arms and waded into the clear water. He swished them around and washed away most of the mud. Then, still holding her, he brought his mouth down on her lips with a toe-curling kiss that sent waves of longing flooding through her. With a moan, she looped her arms around his neck, pressing her breasts to his chest, unable to get close enough.

He raised his lips from hers. With an intense gaze, he set her on her feet. He cupped her face between his hands and lowered his lips to hers—this kiss was more demanding. The sensual feel of his tongue exploring her mouth sent passion exploding through her. Not until his palm slid under her bathing suit top and kneaded her bare breast, and his other hand on her backside pulled her tightly against his hard erection, did she jolt to awareness as to where this would all lead.

She pushed out of his embrace. "I'm sorry. It's my fault. We can't do this. You're still married."

With a pained expression on his face, he groaned. "Kelly—"

"Alex, I have to respect your marriage vows, even if you don't. And I can't be your temporary lover. I just can't." She hurried from the lagoon.

* * *

Using a walking stick, Alex plodded down the hill, away from their camp and on toward the side of the island where they'd first landed. Scowling, he admitted he was like a moth flying closer to a flame.

After kissing Kelly at the lagoon, things between them had become strained, so he had come to a decision. He'd get the raft ready so they could leave because he'd go mad if he stayed here with her any longer.

This past week, he'd found he had to tear himself away from their camp at every opportunity he could—while all he wanted was the barest glimpse of her—but he *had* to stay away. At night, he returned to sleep outside the hut because he couldn't leave her unprotected. However, sometimes he wondered if he wasn't the biggest threat she faced.

If they didn't leave soon, he *would* make love to her. Despite her holding out, it was only a matter of time. She had been far too receptive to his advances, and he'd lost any willpower he possessed.

And if they should become lovers?

At the thought of a serious involvement, a shudder rippled through him. Emotionally empty, he could never give Kelly more than a casual love affair. He would hurt her. And as much as he disliked the idea, she had everything to gain by marrying Hillyard, who was rich enough to keep her safe from her father's enemies. Maybe she did deserve someone like Hillyard.

When Alex neared the beach, he saw the raft where they'd left it, but it looked like a huge, deflated mushroom. He groaned and ran across the sand. He found a gaping hole in the side, and the raft looked irreparably damaged. It had been their one and only form of transportation if they were ever desperate to leave.

He hurled a coconut into the ocean, and then trudged back over the hill toward camp. He didn't relish the idea of telling Kelly about this latest disaster. They *really* could be here for the rest of their lives.

Just how long had they been on the island? He calculated four weeks. That made today April 30th. *His divorce was final.*

He had to tell Kelly. Even the damaged raft couldn't dampen his relief to be free of Vanessa. Tonight, they'd put aside their differences and celebrate his freedom.

Kelly wasn't at the hut so he headed toward the lagoon where he spotted her undressing. He stopped dead in his tracks. As he watched, she tossed her bathing suit over a bush. Her shapely backside was bared until she stepped into the water up to her waist. His groin tightened.

Sucking in his breath, he realized these past few days had been merely a temporary distraction. He approached her. "Hello."

When she whirled around, her full, beautiful breasts, in all their glory, took his breath away.

She gasped and ducked into the water, crimson spreading on her face and up to the roots of her auburn hair. "I thought you went to the other side of the island to check on the raft."

"I did, but I have bad news. The raft has been damaged. There's a large hole in one side."

"Oh, no."

He shrugged. "I'll try to repair it." He wouldn't worry her by telling her it might be hopeless without the necessary supplies.

He threw down his walking stick and dove into the deepest part of the lagoon, surfacing near her.

"Alex, I'm not dressed."

"Doesn't bother me." He flicked his gaze to the bush on which she'd hung her bathing suit. "I saw you undress."

Her mouth dropped open. She splashed water on him. "Get out."

"You should be more careful," he said in a clipped voice. "But then you never were careful about showing me your body, were you?"

"You don't think I meant to? It's just as hard for me to see you wearing practically nothing every day." She clamped her mouth shut.

"Damn." They might as well get this mutual suffering over and become lovers. He found that idea pleased him immensely.

"I thought you'd be gone for hours."

"All right, perhaps we're both to blame, but I'm here now, and I need to cool off." He sighed. The temperature had risen about twenty degrees, in his estimation. "I do have some good news to tell you. My divorce is final. I want us to celebrate."

Her face paled. "Oh, uh, that's good news."

At her dismay, he smiled to himself. The last time when he'd kissed her, her one excuse had been he was married, even though he'd been separated from the witch for years.

"Alex, I can't believe I'm having a conversation with you without anything on." She made a circular motion with her finger. "Do you mind turning around? If you want to stay, I'll put on my suit."

"Why bother? I can see just about everything you're trying to hide through the clear water, love."

She followed the direction of his gaze. With a groan, she flipped her hair over her shoulders to cover her breasts. The sexy move did nothing to quench his desire.

Irritation gnawed his gut. "Bloody hell, Kelly, go ahead and get dressed." He turned to give her the privacy she so desired. She splashed to the shore, however, he wasn't strong enough to stop himself from stealing a glimpse of her backside as she grabbed her bathing suit and ran behind a bush to dress.

He dove under the water, hoping to cool his simmering ardor. He wearied of this childish game. When he resurfaced, he called out, "I may have to move to the farthest end of the island."

Through the rustling bushes, she said, "Don't be ridiculous. We need each other."

"Exactly. And I find I need you more every day."

Dressed in her suit, she stepped from behind the bush.

His constant arousal around her caused him great discomfort. "Don't you understand what you do to me?" He sighed. "Forget it."

From the kisses they had shared, and the way she looked at him, he had always believed she found him appealing. Sure, there were issues between them, but now, he couldn't think of one damned reason why they shouldn't become lovers.

"Why don't you let me wash your hair?" he asked.

When she picked up the split coconut with a mixture he had made from a variety of plants and fruits and waded toward him, he sucked in his breath. He took the bowl and massaged the concoction onto her scalp and through her hair.

She tensed beneath his hands. "This is by far the stupidest idea I've allowed you to talk me into."

"I'm only washing your hair," he said as innocently as he could. He scooped more of the creamy mixture onto her tresses. "Let it stay on for a moment." Then he dropped his hands to her neck and shoulders for a massage.

"And now what are you doing?" she asked, with a tremble in her voice. She obviously wanted him as well. *Why did she resist then?*

"Kelly, why shouldn't we take some comfort from our situation? Anyone else would, even your bloody St. Hillyard." *Did she really love her fiancé so much?* He scowled. He brushed his fingers over her bare shoulders. "Turn around and look at me."

She obliged. At the panic in her eyes, concern shot through him. He'd been with many women, but he couldn't figure Kelly out. One moment, she enticed with those full, red lips. The next, she evaded, ready to run like a frightened deer. He frowned. *Had something bad happened to her? Could he help her work through it?*

She frowned. "Alex, do you think we could play another game of chess later?" She'd improvised a set by using different shaped stones on a mat she'd woven and stained. She won nearly as many times as he did.

"After you soundly beat me the last time? You think I'm crazy?"

"Well, my dad did teach me well, and you beat me the time before that—"

He cupped her cheek. "I'll take the challenge, Kelly, but that's not really what I want to do with you at the moment."

And the truth was, he didn't care to fight his attraction to her anymore. The desire had burned too long. They weren't going anywhere, and no amount of reasoning could change how much he wanted her.

"Kiss me, Kelly. I know you want to."

"I do, but I'm not sure about all the rest that goes with it."

He sighed with relief when her arms encircled his neck. He captured her lips with his, softly at first. She tasted like papaya. While her fingers played with the hair at his nape, he deepened the kiss. She had to feel how hard he pressed against her.

Unable to take any more, he tore his lips from hers. "Kelly, I can't just kiss you and not do anything more. Let's not deny ourselves any longer."

"Why do you want me? Is it because I'm the only woman on the island?"

"That's not true. I'd choose you if there were a thousand ladies here."

"I don't believe you."

"You know I was attracted to you from the first time we met." He touched her hair and pulled a wavy strand to his lips. "'O, she doth teach the torches to burn bright,'" he said, quoting Shakespeare. "Kelly, your hair is like a flame. Your eyes are the bluest of sapphires. . ." He placed his finger on her lips. "You're so beautiful, you don't even need makeup. But that's your outward beauty. Inwardly, you're strong, resourceful and—"

"What about Robert? I can't hurt him. He's done everything for me."

Her engagement to Hillyard grated like stones in Alex's stomach.

He pressed his lips to her temple. "Don't think of him. Right now, we're all we have."

She flattened her palm on his chest. "So this is to be a moment-by-moment thing between us? And as soon as we're rescued, it will be 'good-bye, Kelly?'"

He tightened his hands on her waist and pulled her close. "I won't lie to you. I won't get married again. But at this moment, you want me as much as I want you."

"I do," she said, in a shaky voice. "But I can't give in to it."

"Sweetheart, you can't say you want me and then expect me not to try." He cradled her face in his palms, his thumbs caressing her jaw. "You'll have to tell me to stop because I've tried to keep my hands off you. I can't do it on my own anymore."

Trailing his fingers over her shoulders, he lowered his mouth to hers in a long, possessive kiss.

She tore her lips from his. "This isn't right."

"Why not?" He could hear the anguish in his own voice. With the last shred of self-control he possessed, he loosened his hold.

She slipped out of his embrace and hurried from the water. "Because you don't love me. That's what it will take. Can you give me that?"

His heart pounded as if it would burst, but he wouldn't lie to her. He shook his head.

She left him and ran through the trees, her auburn hair flying behind her as if she fled for her life.

For one fleeting second, he had a primitive urge to go after her, to drag her down into the grass and prove she wanted him as much as he wanted her, and to do what was driving them both crazy—and to hell with calling it *love*. At that insane thought, he rubbed his forehead wearily.

Bloody hell, you are losing it.

* * *

The next day, at the hut, Alex sat at the table and reached for a chunk of coconut. His fingers accidentally brushed Kelly's hand as she reached out at the same time. They both sprang back.

Her eyes widened in accusation. "You care so little for me that you would use me?"

He flicked his gaze over her. "You know, I hate this damnable and unwanted attraction between us."

She gasped. "Now, you've said it."

Gone was the easy companionship they had developed. In frustration, he stalked out of camp only to return later to sleep outside the hut. When rain pelted him, he grabbed his bedding and stepped inside. He shook off the water that had fallen on him.

Kelly sat up on her bed. "What do you want, Alex?" The air sizzled between them.

"Don't think I've come to ravish you, love. It's raining. I have to sleep in here tonight."

On his side of the thin partition, he punched his makeshift pillow before he lay his head down. Their relationship had come to this—nerves stretched to the breaking point.

Trying to get comfortable, he rolled around on the pallet, but he couldn't forget Kelly lounged soft and warm on the other side. He throbbed with the need to pull her into his arms, which swept away his common sense to avoid her.

"Do you think I like this any more than you do?" he whispered. "Do you think I want to complicate our lives by getting involved with you? You don't know how much I wish we could go home."

He had plenty of time over the sleepless night to decide he'd somehow repair the hole in the raft. Come hell or high water, as the old saying went, he'd find a way off this damned island—and soon. He just didn't know which would happen first.

* * *

Kelly followed Alex's long strides toward the crest of the hill, the shortest route to where they'd landed. This past week, she had not needed to avoid him because he had stayed away from camp. He claimed he worked on various projects, but refused any offers of help. However, he always returned to sleep outside the hut at night.

He wouldn't even sit with her to eat anymore, but opted to take his food on the run, to wherever it was he would go.

With heaviness in her heart, she realized how much she missed his company, how much he meant to her, and now, how much he wanted to avoid her. But she also knew she was too attracted to him.

When he had approached her that morning, he seemed perturbed to have to ask for her assistance to drag the raft back to their camp. "I would do this alone, but I can't. I need your help."

"Okay."

His gaze swept over her. "I'm going to find a plant to make glue and use the tarp to make a patch. If that doesn't work, I'll build a raft out of fallen trees and fashion a sail out of the canvas. I'll get us off this island somehow."

As she followed him under the canopy of thick trees, his pace was too fast for her to keep up. It was slippery underfoot from the recent rains and her feet skidded in a few places on the wet ground. Once she nearly wrenched her ankle, so she took careful steps as they climbed up the steep hill. Occasionally, he would stop and turn, give her a cool assessing look, and wait for her to catch up to him. Then he was off again. Clearly, he didn't want to be in her presence for too long.

When they reached the crest of the hill, Kelly sucked in her breath at the view below. Banks of clouds drifted over an ocean of endless blue. She stared at the ends of the earth, reminding herself of just how alone they were, and how much they depended on each other for everything.

Hating this distance between them, she wanted to make amends. She hurried to catch up, wanted to take his hand and walk the rest of the way—*with him.*

Without warning, the earth shook like a dynamite blast and then it crumbled before her feet. She fell backwards into the dirt. Dust spewed. Rocks tumbled into a mudslide. Alex slipped over the edge of the newly made cliff.

"Alex," she screamed, her heart pounding. She waited for the ground to collapse beneath her, but the earth remained solid.

With tears streaming down her cheeks and rocks cutting into her hands and knees, she crawled near the edge. Her head swam with horror. He couldn't have survived the fall. Her tears flowed as her body and mind were racked with the pain of losing him.

CHAPTER NINE

How would she survive without Alex? She lay in the dirt, with her head hanging over the edge and scanned the base of the cliff. Tears slid down her cheeks as she cried out, "Alex, Alex! Please answer me." She hadn't been immobilized with such searing pain since her parents had died.

"Kelly," Alex shouted.

Choking back a sob, she lifted her head. "Alex?"

She leaned farther. Twenty feet below, he dangled from a tree barely rooted there. His foot had wedged in a tenuous ledge on the cliff face.

"Get something I can climb," he yelled. "Hurry. This tree won't last long."

Her thoughts spun. Their rope was at the camp, at least an hour away. She scanned the forest where thick vines hung from the trees.

"Hang on." She took her knife and hacked through a few, then trailed them back to the ledge. After wrapping and tying them around a sturdy looking tree, she yanked to test their strength.

"Here I come." Carefully, she crawled to the edge and tossed the ends to Alex. Though the vines chafed her hands, she clung tightly. When her engagement ring slipped from her finger, she didn't care. The diamond flashed in the sunlight before bouncing over the cliff.

"Dear God, please, don't let him fall."

Alex tugged on the vines and shouted, "I've got them."

The seconds dragged and her heart pounded as he slowly climbed. When he neared the top of the cliff, she grasped his t-shirt and helped him scramble to safety.

His breathing came in heavy gasps as he sank to his knees. He ran his hand down his dirt-streaked face. His shirt and shorts were ripped. A layer of dust coated his body.

He exhaled a deep breath and collapsed next to her. "My thanks, Kelly."

The enormity of how close he'd come to death shook her. While tears blinded her, she threw her arms around him and sobbed into his chest.

"I thought you were dead," she sobbed.

Trembling as badly as she did, he held her close. "Let's get out of here. It could still be dangerous," he said, his breath heating the curve of her shoulder.

Clinging to each other, they descended the hill heading toward camp, with him limping and her arm draped around his waist. Something warm and sticky dripped on her hand. Frowning, she glanced at his side. Blood seeped through his torn clothing.

"You're hurt," she said in a choked voice. *Would he be okay?*

When they reached the lagoon, she helped him peel off his clothes that stuck to his injuries.

Naked, he limped toward the water.

After this brush with death, she wasn't embarrassed. Nothing mattered anymore. On this island, he had become her entire world.

After washing off her own dust, she settled on the grassy bank to watch him. He winced as he washed off the dirt and blood on his ribs. She glanced at the abrasion on his left hip and then stared, mesmerized by how beautiful he was.

"Are you all right?" she called out to him in a shaky voice. "Your ribs?"

"Nothing's broken, only bruised and scraped, I think." When he glanced toward her, his eyes flared with awareness that she watched him.

Her cheeks warmed as she stood. "I think I'll just run to the hut for the first aid kit."

He nodded and turned to splash more water on his wounds.

When she returned with the kit and a towel in hand, he stepped out of the lagoon. His gaze enveloped her with an intensity that nearly buckled her knees.

Gratitude shone in his eyes. He took the towel she offered and dried his tanned body. "You saved my life."

"Then we're even," she quipped. Her attempt at humor failed because this moment between them was fraught with too much emotion.

"Let me see how badly you've been hurt." She smeared the antibiotic ointment on his ribs and he sucked in his breath. "Sorry. You have some cuts and that must hurt."

"It stings a little."

However, now that the danger and fear had abated, his nakedness impacted every one of her senses. Her hand shook as she applied medicine to the abrasion on his bare hip. Beneath her fingertips, a shudder rippled through him, and she didn't think it had anything to do with pain.

She bit her lip and continued her work even though he became fully aroused before her eyes.

"You're not afraid of a naked man, are you?" he asked.

"No comment."

When she finished covering his scrapes with the ointment, she glanced up at his face. Their gazes locked and awareness pulsed between them.

Bursting into more tears, she threw her arms around him, careful of his wounds. "I was so scared that I'd lost you." She pulled a little out of his embrace and swiped at her eyes. "Don't ever do that to me again."

His eyebrows drew together in a frown and he lifted her chin with his knuckle. "Don't cry, love."

She lay her hand against his cheek. "You could've been killed."

"But I'm all right." He bent and brushed her lips with his. Her fingers crept up his arms.

His tongue flicked over her lips—teasing at first. When her lips parted, he thrust his tongue into her mouth with fierce urgency. Sensations rocked her.

He groaned and threaded his fingers through her hair and pressed closer for a deeper kiss . . . as if he couldn't get enough. Passion ignited in her soul.

When he slid his hand under the edge of her shirt, and beneath her bathing suit top, she caught her breath. His palm lingered upon her breast and caressed. Her nipples hardened and her breathing became labored. Her knees sagged and she leaned toward him.

"Kelly?" he murmured in a savage groan against her lips. His erection pressed into her belly. "If you don't want this—"

"Don't stop." She entwined her arms around his neck.

* * *

After expelling a ragged breath along her cheek, Alex untied the top of her bikini. His heart pounded in a racing rhythm. He'd never wanted a woman more than Kelly. Looking him directly in the eyes, she pushed her bathing suit bottom down her legs. He bent and slipped the bikini off her feet. His breathing quickened at the sight of her bared to his view.

He led her to a grassy spot by the waterfall and spread out the towel on the grass. He pulled her down beside him on the ground, then cupped and molded her rose-tipped breasts in his hands. He lowered his head to her breasts and took a nipple into his mouth. She gasped, then relaxed, and allowed him access to her body.

Her breathing came in little rasps, causing waves of excitement to course through him. Groaning, he returned his lips to hers and kissed her with all the pent-up passion he'd suppressed since their first meeting. He ran his hands over her silky body, down to her most sensitive spot. Slipping his hand between her satin-smooth thighs, he parted her with his fingers and found her wet and ready.

She moved against his hand. "Alex." His name drifted across her lips in a plea. "I want you. Please—"

He stopped her words with a searing kiss. The urge to be inside her engulfed him like a flame, and he fitted himself to her entrance. He joined her body, but she was so tight. He pushed and drove into her. A barrier broke.

She stifled a cry against his lips.

Tearing his mouth from hers, he gazed into her flushed face, now understanding her earlier skittishness. "Bloody hell, Kelly. I thought something bad had happened to you, to make you fearful, but . . . you're a virgin."

She clamped her eyes shut. "*Was.* I hoped you wouldn't notice."

"*Notice?*" Her tight body clenched him and erased all rational discussion after that. An extraordinary chemistry existed between them, but he'd been unprepared for how good it would feel to be inside her.

While he'd thrust into her, driven by need, but trying to seek pleasure for both of them, she'd lain motionless beneath him. In the back of his mind, he feared he'd hurt her and vowed to make this up to her.

"Kelly, I'm. . .oh damn. . ." He shot off like a rocket and exploded into a thousand pieces, and shattered into a million more. Grasping her hips, he convulsed deeply inside her.

Spent, he collapsed and slumped, panting in her arms. The parrots squawked in the trees above but everything else was silent. Finally, he drifted back to reality. They lay partially on the towel with grass beneath her back and his hand. He closed his eyes, drained of energy. They were the perfect match. He'd reacted like a bloody schoolboy, not a man of considerable experience. He groaned—*and she'd been a virgin.*

And though now wasn't the time to mention it, he should have withdrawn at the last minute for birth control purposes. How reckless he'd been, but with her, his feelings had never been under control.

Still joined to her, and trembling with the aftermath of lovemaking, he raised up on his forearms. "Kelly, you should've told me."

"What difference does it make?" Her gaze dared him to make a big deal about her virginity.

Narrowing his eyes, he studied her as she lay beneath him, her glorious red hair fanned around her as he'd fantasized for weeks. Never had he dreamed that as beautiful as she was, and engaged to a man like Robert Hillyard, she would be untouched. Now, things were considerably more complicated and everything had changed.

With a sigh, he traced his finger along her cheek. She shivered, her eyes widening. How badly had he hurt her?

Smiling faintly, he flicked her chin. "If you'd told me, somehow I would have gone slower and avoided hurting you so much." He brushed his thumb over her swollen lips. She looked well kissed, the way he wanted her to look from now on.

He withdrew from her, shuddering at those intense sensations. He rolled over onto his back on the grass. With a relaxed sigh, he flung his arm over his head. "You're full of surprises, aren't you, love?"

She crossed her arms, shielding her breasts. "I'm going to bathe."

Frowning, he sat up beside her. "No, not yet." He tugged her arms away from her breasts. Her wide-eyed gaze met his. "Please don't hide from me. I realize things went too fast. I was out of control after wanting you for so long." He raised her hand to his lips.

"I'm sorry if I hurt you. I'm not so selfish. I'll make it good for you. I swear it."

* * *

As Kelly sat with Alex on the towel in this beautiful tropical setting, with the waterfall splashing near them, she found his smile disarming. She wanted to believe him and more than anything she wanted to be his lover. "I always thought I'd hate sex, and I'd been right."

"No, Kelly, no." He ran his hands over her shoulders and breasts.

She closed her eyes. "I do love it when you touch me."

"It was your first time. You know you're beautiful, Kelly." When he lowered his mouth to her breasts, warm sensations spread through her. Although the stubble of his face scratched her skin, made tender by their previous lovemaking, desire leaped again like a flame.

"Do you like this?" he asked, his lips against her skin.

"Yes." Despite the pain she had experienced, she wanted him to love her.

"Put your hands on me, Kelly."

She placed her palms on his chest, and did what she'd secretly longed to do. She ran her hands along the ripple of his muscles and his smooth skin, mindful of the cuts and bruises. With a mind of their own, her fingertips traced his nipples. Small and flat, they stiffened like hers.

She trailed her fingers lightly around the cut on his ribs and lifted a shy gaze to his face. "Does your wound hurt too much?"

"What wound?" he asked with heavy-lidded eyes.

"All right, Mr. Tough Guy." She returned her hand to his chest and explored the feel of him. "*Hmmmm,* I must say, I like this part. Did you know your eyes change to a darker blue?"

He shook his head. "Now, let me touch you."

He smoothed his hand over her breasts, caressed her flat stomach, and down to the juncture of her thighs. She swallowed to relieve her dry throat, engulfed with exquisite feelings as he parted her.

He inserted one finger and then another within her. "I'm hard again. I promise you that this time I'll go slower, love."

He settled on top of her. Kelly glanced down to see him positioned between her bare thighs. She tensed, waiting for the pain.

He eased inside. The initial stretching and burning disappeared when he thrust within her. She clasped her arms around him tightly, caught his rhythm, and let the pleasure carry her away.

His breath warmed her cheek. "It feels incredibly good to be inside you."

"Kiss me." She grasped his head and brought his mouth to hers, his lips intoxicating.

With a moan, she climbed toward something out of reach. When intense pleasure engulfed her, she gasped in surprise as strong sensations overtook her, and she contracted beneath him.

"Kelly." His eyes flared as he gave himself up to his own simultaneous release. When he collapsed on top of her, seeming all tired and happy, she smiled and raked her nails along his back. Now, she understood the satisfaction their bodies could give each other.

When he finally moved, he pressed a kiss on her lips, rolled to his back and nestled her into the crook of his arm. They slept.

A parrot squawked overhead. She lifted her gaze to the sunlit canopy of trees swaying in the breeze above them. She was tired and strangely happy. Alex's arm was beneath her and his fingers possessively curved over her breast.

She twisted her head to see his face. His eyes closed, he looked relaxed and contented, his chest rising and falling with each breath. The sun's dancing light made golden highlights in his dark blond hair.

Smiling, she reached to pull a blade of grass from his hair when reality struck. Her body turned cold. She had been carried away by desire. Now, the enormity and the consequences of what they'd done sank in.

* * *

He opened his eyes, woken by her attempts to untangle her hair from beneath his arm. "Where are you going, Kelly?"

She scrambled to her feet. "Into the water." Her shapely body glistened in the sunlight as she headed for the lagoon.

"Wait." He rose on his elbow. "We need to talk."

Ankle-deep in the water, she turned to him, a cool expression in her eyes. "About what?"

"About what just happened here," he said in exasperation.

"Do you mean what *shouldn't* have happened here?"

He rose to his feet. "Kelly, it was inevitable. We've been attracted to each other since the day we met. Why didn't you tell me you were a virgin?"

She threw her arms out. "When should I have told you? You know, I never planned for this to happen."

"You could've told me when we began."

Her shoulders sagged. "I wasn't about to. At twenty-four, we virgins don't like to broadcast the news. Actually, I thought you'd laugh at me."

"I wouldn't laugh, but I am surprised."

"Is there something wrong with my being a virgin?"

"Having been," he corrected. "No." The type of women he dated were at the other end of the spectrum—experienced women who knew that with him the act was for the pure enjoyment of sex. "I thought that because you were engaged . . ." As he thought for the right words he realized he was extremely satisfied she'd never been with Hillyard.

"It's a long story."

"Doesn't look like we're going anywhere at the moment." He stepped toward her. When she turned away, he placed his hand on her back. "Please, talk to me."

With a sigh, she returned and sat on the towel. He sat beside her and put his arm around her shoulders.

Though she still looked proud, sadness tinged her voice. "A few years ago, I was engaged to someone else. I knew I had a problem because I would freeze and feel sick when he tried to touch me, even when I thought I loved him. Then I went to see a psychologist who said my father's affairs had influenced me. My fiancé and I broke up soon afterwards. I cancelled my appointments and never finished therapy."

He squeezed her hand. "Go on. Tell me why you think you felt like that."

She shrugged. "I suppose the nights I spent hearing my mother cry, wondering who her cheating husband was with, affected me." A melancholy frown drifted across her features. "Call me old-fashioned, but I wanted to be married when I had sex for the first time."

She'd been saving herself for Hillyard.

That truth hit Alex like a crippling blow to his stomach. He had taken something special from her, something he could never give back.

He brushed his fingers along her collarbone. "I don't want you to be sorry."

She frowned creased her forehead. "I don't know why this happened. I guess I was so frightened when you almost died."

"You regret it already?" he asked, afraid to hear her answer. When she didn't respond, he put an arm around her and nestled her head against his shoulder. "Well, I don't regret anything. Who knows how long we'll be here?"

"Are you justifying our actions?"

He stroked her hair, warring again with his own desire for her. "Don't blame yourself. We've been lost for weeks. They probably think we're dead."

"I know. I'm going into the water." She slipped from his embrace and waded into the lagoon. He made a move to join her, but she backed away. "Please, I need some time alone. And some space."

* * *

Kelly strode away from the lagoon. She had to have time to think. To do so clearly, she needed to be away from Alex's presence. With his charismatic influence over her, he could convince her the sky was purple.

Fifteen minutes later, she reached the bottom of the steep cliff, where he had nearly fallen to his death. A shiver ran through her as she gazed up at the crest jutting against the blue sky. If not for the one tree still dangling by its roots, he would be dead.

"Thank you, God, for sparing his life," she whispered.

With a half-hearted effort, she scrambled over the heap of rocks and dirt at the foot of the hill. After searching unsuccessfully for her engagement ring, she dusted off her hands. The expensive ring was trivial, except to return it to Robert. What was important to her was that Alex lived, and she wasn't alone.

She left the site to stroll the sandy beach. Her body attested to their lovemaking. She was sore in places she never knew she could be. Ever since they'd met, Alex had wanted to have sex with her. And even if her mind had never condoned it, her body certainly had triumphed and won the battle.

He gave her an emotional jolt she'd never dreamed of feeling. However, unless they were stuck here forever, nothing would be permanent with him. That truth hurt.

Inhaling the fresh salt air, she plopped on the sand. The ocean spread in gentle waves across the beach. The loud cries of the seagulls filled the air. Tiny birds on stilted legs foraged for food in the surf.

Despite the warmth of the day, she shivered when she considered the isolation of the island. Alex was right. They didn't know when they would be rescued.

When the sky turned into pink and red hues, she made her way back to camp. A fire crackled in the pit and dinner lay on the makeshift table.

Alex sat staring into the fire. He jumped to his feet when he saw her and limped toward her, a muscle flexing in his jaw and his hands clenched at his side. "It's dark. Where have you been? I've been worried about you."

She shrank back from the simmering angst in his eyes. He looked so much like a concerned husband she wanted to laugh. "Where could I go?" she asked softly.

"You could've been hurt."

"I went for a walk. Did I tell you earlier I lost my ring over the cliff when I was throwing the vines to you?"

"No," he said through clenched teeth.

"I had to search for it."

He crossed his arms over his chest. "Did you find it?"

"No."

"You can't manage to hang onto that ring," he muttered. "Maybe there's a meaning behind the fact."

"I guess it's just as well. How can I go back to Robert after this?"

He stepped closer. "Still chastising yourself for being bloody human? What happened between us was not your fault."

"I despised my dad's meaningless affairs and the way he cheated on my mother."

Alex's eyebrows rose in an affronted frown. "You think what happened between us was meaningless? I care for you, and I think you feel the same way about me." He clasped her shoulders. "Besides, I don't think civilization's rules mean a bloody lot out here.

We need each other." He tenderly moved a strand of her hair from her face.

"But I know how you feel about a relationship. Don't you understand this goes against all my morals?" Even knowing this, her knees grew weak at his touch.

He sighed. "We might not want to talk about it, but we've been here for over a month. We could be here another five years or fifty."

"But *if* we're rescued?" she asked, already knowing the answer. She lifted her chin. "You want an affair with me while on the island with no later obligations?"

He expelled an exasperated breath. "I care about you, but don't fall in love with me. I can't give you that in return."

She bit her lip. Falling in love with him would be a sure way to a broken heart. She wrenched away from him. "Then don't expect anything more from me. You'll have to hold out until we're rescued." He clasped her elbow, but she jerked her arm away. "Don't touch me."

"Kelly, I don't want to hurt you. Can't you see that's the last thing I want to do? That's why I'm being completely honest with you."

Ignoring him, she paced back and forth across the camp, the crackling fire casting her long shadow. Finally, she halted and crossed her arms over her chest. "Perhaps *you should* move to the other side of the island."

His expression revealed that he knew she couldn't live here alone and that irked her. "We need each other to survive."

"And I'm the only girl available."

"That's not true, Kelly," he said, shaking his head emphatically. "I asked you to have dinner with me on the cruise. I wanted you then, and I do care about you now."

But he didn't say love. *Love.* She whirled away from him. Robert truly loved her, and she had betrayed him in the most horrible way. Robert would do anything for her, but she'd given her virginity to a man who would never have any deep feelings for her.

She choked back a half-crazed laugh. Could she have done any worse in screwing up her life? Oh, hell, what was she thinking? They were never going to get off this island. Alex would be hers for life, as much as if he were chained to her.

He placed his hands on her shoulders and turned her to face him. "Would you rather I lie to you?" he asked in a clipped voice. "Pretend that when we're rescued I'd want to get married, love?"

She bristled at those stabbing words. "I'm not your 'love,' remember?"

However, she wasn't surprised at her own secret longing he'd want her for more. She'd bet he had women declaring their love for him all the time. Besides, he'd make a terrible husband.

Her shoulders stiffened. "I wouldn't want to marry you either. We would be incompatible. Our lifestyles would clash." Inside, she knew she lied to both of them.

"Exactly. My life is not conducive to a normal marriage. I'm gone for months at a time."

She didn't really care. If they truly loved each other, they could make their relationship work, but she could tell he needed an out, a way to avoid any commitment to her.

He strode to the fire, and threw a piece of wood onto the embers. He gave her a brief look, then knelt, took a stick, and stoked the blaze. A shower of sparks flew in the night air.

He stared into the burning flames. "If my film, *The Spy,* isn't a success, my career will probably be over. Vanessa will make sure of that. She's a master at manipulating the paparazzi, which is one of the reasons for her fame. I expect losing what I want to do most in the world might be the price for my freedom. After the hell I've been through, can you understand why I won't get married again?"

"You want to remain single forever? Never have children?"

He limped to her and reached out and stroked her arm. "Kelly, I made a mistake once. I'm not about to repeat it. But I was attracted to you from the beginning."

"I know what effect I had on you," she replied tartly.

"With the unusual way we met, I've been unable to take my eyes off you. Honestly, I can say I've never felt this way before, but if we're rescued, I couldn't offer you any commitment."

"Then let's forget this ever happened."

"That's impossible. How can we? I *would* have to move to the other side of the island." He pulled her into his arms and gazed down at her. "Do you really want me to? I could not live this close and not touch you. But if you tell me to leave, I will."

They had already made love twice. She was being ridiculous and couldn't turn back the clock on what had happened today. "I want you to stay," she whispered.

He lowered his forehead against hers. No humor reflected in his husky voice when he said, "Good."

He cupped her chin and tilted her face up to his. Lacing her arms around his neck, she pressed her lips to his and relaxed in his arms. She would surrender herself to him—and on his terms. No turning back. For now, this primitive world was their home.

She broke away from his kiss.

"What are you thinking?" he asked.

"If we're going to do this, then I think we need an *agreement*."

He chuckled and put his arms around her. "Now you sound like a business woman."

"I do," she said wistfully. What she really wanted was a love agreement, but a business one might help protect her heart from expecting more than he could give. "I want everything up front so there won't be any misunderstandings later."

Smiling, he flicked her nose. "What do you suggest?"

She gazed into his eyes. "Stop grinning. I'm serious." At his sobered look, she continued, "Until we go home, we may remain . . ." She almost said 'lovers,' but that wasn't the correct term for their relationship. "I know you don't want anything permanent, so when we're rescued, our relationship ends as if it never existed."

"Is that all, love?"

"No. If at any time, either of us wants to end this affair, for whatever reason, the other person will not judge or condemn the other. We'll have a clean break."

He leaned toward her. "I guess I can live with your agreement. Let's seal our pact with a kiss."

She placed her fingers on his lips. "No."

"What? There's to be no kissing in this arrangement?"

"No. Yes." She offered him a crooked smile. "I mean there is one more thing I must ask of you. As far as anyone else is concerned, this never happened. Do you promise never to speak of it?" The real possibility crossed her mind that she could get pregnant, and then what?

"What happens on the island stays on the island. Where do I sign?" he asked, trying unsuccessfully to keep a straight face.

She poked her finger into his chest. "I'm serious. You can't tell anybody. There is to be complete and utter silence on this matter." This way, if and when they ever returned, she'd break up with Robert quietly, but the whole world wouldn't have to know she'd been Alex Drake's temporary lover. That news would humiliate Robert—or for that matter, her.

"Yes, I'll agree to whatever you say, but I think I'm under—what's that legal term—duress." He pulled her closer. She melted into his embrace and his slow, drugging kiss. Placing his hands on her buttocks, he lifted her and pressed his hard, aroused body against hers, enticing her. She wrapped her legs around him.

After an urgent kiss, he set her down on her feet, his breathing heavy as he gazed down at her. "This is not good, Kelly," he said in a husky voice. "I want to carry you inside the hut—*now*. But we haven't even discussed birth control."

Besides ending up with a broken heart, she'd already thought of the consequences to what they did. "What do you suggest?"

Still embracing her, he shrugged. "I do know we're past abstaining. I'm shaking just holding you now," he admitted with a sigh. "There are ways to avoid pregnancy. I admit, not always reliable, but better than doing nothing."

She nodded. "Okay."

When he leaned forward to kiss her, her eyes blurred with tears as all the emotions of the day came rushing back.

He cupped her chin. "Now what's wrong, baby? Have my kisses made you cry?"

She gave him a watery smile. "That's not it. Just thinking about today—you could have been killed. I am so relived you're here with me."

He rested his cheek against her hair. "I'll do my best to make you not regret this." He brazenly flattened his palm on her breast. She drew in a sharp breath. "Do you know how long I've ached to touch you this way?"

She nodded, still a little shaky, uncertain if their agreement would set her free to be his temporary lover and still protect her from hurt later.

Returning his lips to her mouth, he gave her a thorough kiss. Desire pooled in her. Beyond words and speech, she'd known what she wanted since the first day she'd met him.

He rubbed his thumb where her engagement ring used to be. "I'm sorry you lost your ring, but not sorry to see it off your finger." He kissed her palm. "On this island, you're mine."

She glanced at his left hand, now ringless, too. When had he removed his wedding band?

With that thought, she tilted her head, prompting him to bend to kiss her. She ran her fingers through his hair.

She was going to let this gorgeous actor, who didn't profess dying devotion to her, and didn't want a permanent relationship with her, make love to her.

This was a dangerous game she played, one in which she would probably get hurt, but she wanted nothing more than to savor every moment with him, come what may.

She was probably out of her mind.

He swung her up in his arms, and nuzzled his face to her ear. "Let's go to bed." As he carried her into the hut, Kelly's blood thudded through her veins in expectation.

* * *

The next morning, Alex hummed as he ripped out the partition in the hut that had separated them. Perhaps, because their relationship wasn't permanent, he found himself content to play the lover in every way. He'd even collected a bouquet of wild flowers for her this morning. If he could, he would have sent her dozens of red roses.

He wouldn't dwell on the fact he'd taken her virginity, or why he was ecstatic she'd never slept with Hillyard. He swore to take the utmost care not to get her pregnant, not only because he didn't want the entanglement of children, but because childbirth without medical care on this remote island could be life-threatening. Hadn't one of his aunts died when something went terribly wrong?

Over the next two weeks, he couldn't get enough of Kelly. Having sex became their main recreation. He stopped working on the raft and spent his days and nights teaching her about her body and his. He loved being creative in their lovemaking. Sometimes, to avoid pregnancy, they only did a lot of touching and exploring. He reveled in using his hands and mouth to make her shiver with delight. She learned, all too quickly, how to equally drive him wild. He was always careful to pull out, and not to make her sorry they'd made love.

Every night, they slept exhausted in each other's arms from the best sex he'd ever had.

Did she know how involved one's emotions could become in their psychological state of being lost from the world, in a life and death situation? Because of that, he feared she might become attached to him and think she was in love. The days wore on.

* * *

A little, old stone church stood in a gray, swirling mist.

Confusion on where she was swept Kelly. Disoriented, she stepped through the doors and approached the minister at the altar.

"Kelly Cochran, do you take this man to be your lawfully wedded husband?"

Her beautiful white wedding gown swished around her as she turned to face her groom. On seeing it was Robert, she gasped.

He grinned. "Make this the happiest day of my life, Kelly."

Bolting upright, she clasped her hands to her pounding heart. Her frantic gaze swept around and she searched to orientate herself in the blackness of the night. Her eyes adjusted to the moonlight that shimmered through the window, illuminating Alex's tousled hair and his back as he slept unclothed beside her on their bed in the hut.

Alex—Not Robert. She exhaled a deep breath.

Swiping her hand across her perspiring forehead, she reclined and stared into the darkness. She couldn't picture herself with Robert in this intimate way, but only seven weeks ago, she'd been about to marry him.

Alex rolled and faced her. He stretched lazily. With a possessive groan, he hauled her against his naked body. "You're awake, love?" he asked sleepily. "Why?" He pressed a warm kiss to her temple.

"Bad dream. It's nothing," she lied.

He ran his hand along her stomach and then stroked her inner thigh. "Would you rather go back to sleep?" he asked in a puzzled tone.

Unable to resist him, she sighed. "No."

Shutting her eyes, she cuddled closer to him, determined to savor every moment of their time together. Her unease over the dream subsided. She pressed her mouth to his lips, but couldn't lie to herself. Even in the face of being on a deserted island forever, she was ecstatic to be with him.

Alex entered her and began that deep thrusting she had come to crave. *Was she addicted to his love?* She wrapped her legs around him and trembled at the tingles his hands and body created within her. When she could take no more, she gasped and writhed beneath him, while he kept on with his rhythmic movement. Yearning to give him as much pleasure as he gave her, she slipped her hand between them and caressed him intimately. He thrust a few more times and groaned as he collapsed on top of her.

The warmth pooling inside her shot a wave of panic through her. She struggled to get out from under him, but his weight pinned her down. He was still inside her.

Panic swept her. Except for the first day they'd made love, he'd always been careful to withdraw. "Alex, get off me."

Panting, he rolled onto his back. "Oh, sweetheart. The way you touched me. I'm not made of stone."

"What are we doing, Alex? We don't want to have a baby on this island." Though she would love to carry Alex's baby if circumstances were different, she jerked from his embrace and dragged her pallet to the other side of the hut. Lying down, she pillowed her face in her arms and clamped her eyes shut.

In the next moment, he lay down beside her, stroking her hair. "I promise I'll be more careful the next time, love. We can't be that unlucky."

"We're marooned on a deserted island, Alex," she said dryly. "We *are* unlucky." She pillowed her face in her arms. "Please, go away. I can't believe we're doing this. We're crazy to take these risks."

"Kelly, if we were so unlucky we would be like everyone else on the dive boat—dead."

After a moment of silence, she heard the soft swing of the door as he left the hut.

Pressing her fist to her mouth, she trembled. She was the one who risked everything by sleeping with him, all for a roll in the hay, and in her case, that was pretty literal.

Finally, after worrying about where he'd gone for the next hour, she slept.

She dreamed she lay on her pallet. Alex knelt between her spread thighs, having delivered their baby. He leaned over and placed the child in her arms.

"This time we have a little red-haired girl as beautiful as you," he said, with a satisfied grin.

She frowned. "This time?"

Then he called over four, adorable, blond boys, all in his image, from ages two to ten. She gasped in horror as he introduced each one by name.

He took a drag from a cigar and flicked the ashes. "Kelly, enjoy the children, I'm off to London." He winked. "And if you're ever in England, do give me a ring."

He headed out the hut's door. The boys ran in a circle around her yelling, "Mummy, mummy, mummy."

The baby wailed. Kelly gaped in horror. She knew nothing about babies.

* * *

When he heard muffled sounds outside, Alex raised his head from the pallet. *Must be an animal.*

Already sunlight poured through the cracks and warmed the thatched hut. Perspiration coated his arms and chest. The heat too stifling to go back to sleep. He stretched and glanced to where Kelly slept on the other side of the hut. Her auburn hair spilled around her in a burst of color. Although she had begun sleeping in her clothing again, one bare shoulder peeped out of her ripped black t-shirt, enticing him.

His groin tightened and he stifled a groan. How out of control he had become in his desire for her. Even now, knowing the risks, he ached to hold her in his arms, but how could they—putting aside their token attempts at birth control—expect her *not* to get pregnant with all the time they spent making love?

With a pang of regret, he realized he missed the intimacy of sleeping with her. He'd agonized about the worry he had caused her. Whenever he tried to apologize, she reminded him of the bloody 'cancellation clause' in their damned agreement.

Would they be having a child together?

Primitive male satisfaction surged through him. Then he was appalled. They'd been out here far too long, living like Adam and Eve, if his thoughts took that course.

He rolled to his back. The entire idea of making love to Kelly proved he'd taken leave of his senses. He'd hoped their lovemaking would quench his desire . . . instead, he found he wanted her even more.

At the sound of voices, he sat up.

Kelly yawned and stretched. "Did you hear something?"

He threw on his shorts. "Someone's here."

CHAPTER TEN

A few minutes later, Alex stepped outside the hut to find six dark-skinned natives gawking at him. One man was of sumo-wrestler proportions and towered over his companions. The other three men were of average build.

Of the two women in the group, a small, rotund woman grinned up at Alex, showing more gaps in her smile than teeth. The other female of the group would be beautiful anywhere with her lovely cocoa complexion. She wore western-style clothing and colored beads in her short, dark hair. When she smiled at him, the gigantic man grunted unhappily.

Kelly emerged from the hut to stand behind Alex.

"I assume they're the ones who built the camp," Alex said to her over his shoulder.

Holding out his hand in welcome, he stepped forward. "Do you speak English?" Their lack of response gave him the answer. He tried French. Kelly spoke in Spanish. At both their attempts, the natives shook their heads.

How could they communicate their need for help to return home?

Standing on her toes, the small woman giggled. She placed her palms on Alex's chest and raked chubby fingers through his hair, which now brushed his shoulders. Not wanting to offend their only hope of rescue, he gently eased her hands away from her bold exploration of his body.

"I think she likes you," Kelly quipped, flicking him a cool gaze to him. "There you go, Alex. My replacement."

"Not my type, love," he said dryly. "However, they might be able to help us and they seem friendly enough."

The gigantic native stomped up to Kelly. His black eyes ogled her as if she were some kind of treat.

Alex clenched his jaw. "Perhaps I spoke too soon."

Kelly's hand rose to cover the swell of her breasts over her bikini top. "This one might be dangerous."

"Probably not, but I'm sure he's never seen anything like you before."

The huge man uttered a few words at his group. As abruptly as they had arrived, they turned and strode toward the beach.

"Wait a minute," Alex called out, but his English was useless. "Kelly, we have to make them understand we need their help."

"Do you think we can trust them?" she asked, staring after them.

"You want to go home, don't you?"

"Of course. I'll grab our things."

At the shore, the large native gripped an old fiberglass motorboat beached in the sand.

Alex strode up and grasped the other side to prevent him from shoving the boat out to sea. The huge man dropped his end in the sand. Hands on hips, he pierced Alex with unfriendly, dark eyes. Alex ignored his ire and motioned with his hands that he wanted to go with them, but the natives shrugged. Alex exhaled in frustration.

"I'm ready," Kelly called from behind. He turned to see her tromping through the sand, carrying two bags stuffed with their belongings.

His mouth twitched with amusement as he took one bag from her arms. "You brought everything, love?" he drawled.

She shrugged. "You never know what we'll need."

"I haven't been able to convince them to take us yet."

Her eyes narrowed. "You haven't? Perhaps I should try." She bestowed a brilliant smile on each person, the last of which came to rest on the burly native. The giant's mouth lifted in a bedazzled grin. Kelly pointed at the boat and made a stepping motion as if getting inside.

Alex stifled his urge to interfere with what seemed like flirting.

When the huge native nodded, and his mouth lifted in a bedazzled grin, Alex liked the man even less.

With a glint of humor in her eyes. Kelly smiled sweetly up at Alex. "I think he wants *me* to get in."

Alex unclenched his teeth. "Not without *me* you don't." They dragged the vessel past the breaking waves. He climbed in after her, along with the rest of the group.

The natives fired up the rickety outboard engine, and the motor sputtered to life. Alex watched the island they had survived on for two months grow smaller until it disappeared from his sight. Despite his relief to get away, a sense of loss enveloped him.

Wearing a baseball cap, and with her thick auburn hair twisted into a long braid, Kelly sat in front of him. She turned and gave him a serene smile. "We're leaving, Alex. Your wish has come true."

His expression stilled. *Did she look forward to the moment when they would part?*

* * *

After a couple of hours on the ocean, they arrived at a large island. Kelly got her first glimpse of a village lining the shore. The natives escorted them into a clearing where there was a gathering of long tables surrounded by thatched huts.

The islanders paused, then greeted them with friendly smiles. Kelly exhaled in relief. She'd been half-worried these people might want to turn them into slaves.

A group of children ran up to them. One wide-eyed boy reached out and touched their hair and skin, causing two girls to feel comfortable enough to do the same. Once their curiosity was satisfied, they ran off, kicking up swirls of dust in their departure.

The pretty native who had traveled with them hovered close to Alex and offered him a cup of water. He handed the cup to Kelly first. She sipped and quenched her parched throat. After Alex drank, he returned the cup, smiling at the woman. A twinge of jealousy hit Kelly. He probably smiled at all women the same—just like he had at her.

She smacked him on the back of his shoulder.

He frowned at her. "What was that for?"

She shrugged and lied, "Poisonous fly. I believe I heard about it on the tour."

Cringing at her jealous feelings, she crossed her arms over her chest and decided to find someone to help them return to the mainland. She glanced around and found the huge native watching her. When he grinned, he did nothing to hide his lustful gaze.

Her stomach knotted and she edged closer to Alex. "Didn't that giant's mother tell him it isn't polite to stare?"

Alex's eyes crinkled with mischief. "That one could eat you for dinner."

"Alex!"

"Sorry." But he looked anything but contrite.

She shuddered. "But you don't really think they could be cannibals?"

He shook his head and laughed. "Heavens no, love. Not in this day and age. I'd be more concerned they'll want money from us. Or, maybe they'll take pity on us when they see our condition—and give *us* money. However, I think he likes you." He winked. "I knew your beauty would get me into trouble in more ways than one."

"Very funny. Don't tease me." She hooked her arm through his. "But I wish he'd stop staring. He gives me the creeps."

Alex's expression held a note of mockery. "What did you expect after the way you flirted with him on *our* island?"

"I got us here," she said, satisfied that she noted a hint of jealousy in his voice. "There must be some way to explain to him that I'm with you."

He leaned and whispered in her ear. *"Are you?* You haven't been for a week. I've missed you."

His warm breath sent a shiver of excitement through her. If only he knew how much she wanted to be with him, every minute. Staying away from him had been sheer torture. At night, her treacherous body throbbed for his touch. But with the risk of pregnancy, and because he didn't want to get involved with her for the long term, it seemed better this way for both of them.

"And you know why I haven't," she said coolly. "What would happen to our plans, Alex, if I returned home *pregnant* . . . or with *your* child?"

An odd expression flitted across his face before his skin paled.

She gritted her teeth. Just as she'd expected. Heaven forbid if he might somehow be tied to her.

"You're not, are you?" he asked, catching her gaze.

Even though it was her turn to let him squirm, she couldn't stand the stricken look. "No. I'm sure I'm not pregnant," she stated flatly. This past week, she'd had to handle that challenge.

His color returned. "Good. I'm glad we don't have to worry about that problem." Giving her a faint smile, he placed his warm hand over hers, still in the crook of his arm.

He certainly took the news well. Didn't he know she'd never trap him in a relationship like his ex-wife?

She would've removed her hand, if the huge native wasn't standing nearby, constantly leering. His buddies surrounded him like he was the big Kahuna among them. At her glance, he flexed his biceps.

An elderly man strode into the clearing, obviously important because he wore a decorated robe flowing over his otherwise western clothes. The man threw his arms out wide.

"Welcome to Yangono. I'm Wamba and leader of these people."

Dizzy with relief that he spoke English, Kelly grinned at Alex. While Alex always seemed to take things in stride, she'd been half-afraid of these natives and what they might want from Alex and her.

Stepping forward, Alex shook Wamba's hand. "I'm Alex Drake."

"Unfortunately for you, I'm the only one who speaks your Queen's English." Wamba turned in Kelly's direction. "And who is your beautiful companion?"

"This is Kelly Cochran, my . . . my . . . *friend*." Alex's hesitancy on what to call her, stung. He could have at least called her his girlfriend—even if it were only temporary.

Wamba nodded. "I understand. She's your woman, but not your wife."

As if that explained their relationship. "I don't belong to anyone," Kelly snapped. "I'm here on my own. Besides, we barely know each other."

Alex frowned at her. "What?"

Raising her chin, she crossed her arms over her chest and refused to speak.

Alex glanced back at the chief. "We were stranded after a boating accident and need your help. We need to contact the mainland. Do you have a telephone?"

The leader shook his head, but at their obvious dejection, he added, "We have an old radio you might be able to repair."

Alex's face lit up and he squeezed her hand. "It's worth a try, love. Maybe we can fix it."

They followed Wamba to a storage hut. He threw open the door. Several squawking chickens ran past them. When she entered behind Wamba and Alex, she batted at the cobwebs overhead. Nestled in a corner, among boxes of miscellaneous junk, an ancient radio lay with the cover off. A quarter-inch of dirt blanketed its broken, glass tubes.

Alex picked up the radio and blew off the dust. "It's more than a few years beyond repair—more like seventy."

"Carrier pigeon, anyone?" she muttered dryly.

Missing her sarcasm, Wamba shook his head at that. "Parrots only."

Clasping her hand, Alex led her out of the hut and whispered in her ear, "I'm sorry, sweetheart. I know how eager you were to escape my presence. Now, it appears you'll have to endure my company for a little while longer."

Flustered by his comment, she gaped. If anything, she stayed away from him all week—partly because she'd had her period—but she was worried about her strong feelings for him, and if they continued to sleep together, the possibility of trapping him with a child. To hear him act as if she were the one who wanted them to be separated . . .

After Wamba spoke a few words to an older woman, she scurried toward the clearing. "I told her to cook you for food." He grinned at them.

Kelly's heart skipped a beat. "Did he say, c*ook you for food?*" She dug her nails into Alex's arm. He smiled, too. "What's wrong with you? We should never have trusted them."

Chuckling, Alex put his arm around her shoulders and squeezed. "Kelly, he's joking."

Wamba cackled with laughter. "Gets you tourists every time. I meant to say, *cook food for you*. We haven't had visitors in a while. Tonight, we welcome you with a party."

Kelly narrowed her eyes, then disregarded the fact their leader was a practical joker. She glanced at the friendly faces of the villagers and expelled a deep breath. The tension slid from her body. She did think the giant man might be a threat, but there didn't seem to be any danger as long as she stayed clear of his path. Why not enjoy this exotic experience for what it was? Alex didn't seem to be concerned.

"Well, I don't mind being dessert," she quipped, giving Alex and the chief a challenging gaze, "as long as Alex is the main course." They both laughed at her remark, while Alex squeezed her hand.

When they returned to the clearing, many of the locals had gathered around the tables. In a harsh voice, the huge native said something to the leader. In return, Wamba spoke in muted tones. Kelly watched with interest. The large native hunched his massive shoulders and gave her one last leering look before he skulked away.

Frowning, Alex crossed his arms over his chest. "What's going on with him, Chief?"

Wamba stared after the retreating giant. "Moto wants to wed Kelly, but I told him she's with you." His weathered face turned grim.

Kelly frowned. Her fears about the man returned.

For the first time since meeting the natives, concern reflected in Alex's blue eyes. "I have the distinct feeling I should have introduced you as my wife."

Wamba shook his head in disgust. "Our lives would be peaceful if not for Moto. Like a vulture, he awaits my death." He pointed to the pretty native girl who had traveled with them. "Besides my daughter, Aleah, I have only one other child. A son, Calb." He gestured to a skinny boy playing a game with rocks in the dirt. "If Calb was any competition to Moto, I don't think he'd reach manhood."

"Why is Moto so much larger than everyone else?" Alex asked. "I'm six-foot-one and he dwarfs me."

"His mother left our island and lived on Viti Levu. She returned alone and with him. She said he's large like his father. I say his body grew to compensate for his lack of brains." Wamba thumped a fist to his chest. "My people do not need a moron for a leader."

"Chief, we need your help. Will you take us to the mainland?" Alex asked.

"We just returned. It'll be six months before we travel so far again."

Alex frowned. "But we can't wait that long. We need to go home. How far away are we?"

"About one hundred miles."

Alex exhaled a deep breath. "During the storm, Kelly, we must have been picked up by a strong current to have come so far."

With a sweeping motion of his hand, the leader said, "We invite you to stay as our guests."

Kelly bit her lip, unable to reconcile a strange relief she felt. Ever since they'd left their island to travel with these natives, she'd been half-afraid her adventure with Alex was over. She stole a glance at him from under her lashes. His handsome face had become so familiar and dear to her. Perhaps more time together would give him the chance to fall in love with her.

Was it selfish to think this way? He lived an exciting life and probably hated the idea of six more months out here. Plus, she really needed to get back to the company and L.A., despite someone wanting her dead. She exhaled a deep breath. She'd not given a lot of thought to Cochran Investments lately, not when she spent night after night in Alex's arms.

Wamba clapped his hand on Alex's back. "I can see your disappointment. But for tonight, we will show you our hospitality. As you say in English, it's party time." He cackled at his joke, and then said something in his language to his people. The crowd cheered.

Wamba winked. "They love any excuse to celebrate. Kelly, you go with the women. Alex, I'll show you the village and a hut where you can stay while you're with us."

With the way Moto had stared, Kelly folded her arms over her chest, rooted to the spot. "No, thanks. I'd rather stay with Alex."

Alex nudged her shoulder. "Go on, Kelly. It's all right."

Didn't he realize that giant brute could be dangerous?

A friendly woman smiled warmly and touched a loose strand of Kelly's hair. Despite her worries about Moto, Kelly felt it would be churlish to refuse these kind people. Wamba seemed to think it was okay if she went with them. Alex didn't seem bothered either. Perhaps she worried needlessly.

She shook a finger at Alex. "All right, I'll go with them, but if I end up on the menu, it's your fault."

Both he and Wamba chuckled.

* * *

While Alex walked through the village with the chief, Wamba pointed to a small hut. "I'll have this one prepared for you and your woman."

Alex crossed his arms over his chest. "Is there anyone nearby who can help us return to the mainland sooner?"

"I'll think about the options. Once in a while we have visitors who may be able to help you."

They entered one of the larger huts decorated with a tattered flag. Some of the village men sat cross-legged on mats around a wide bowl.

Wamba motioned to the ground.

Alex sat on a mat and took an offered cup. He sipped and nearly gagged. "What is this?"

Wamba raised his drink. "Ceremonial drink—kava. Not known for its great taste, but you'll like how it makes you feel."

The other men smiled and lifted their cups.

Thinking it was better to participate in their ceremony than to insult them, Alex sipped the bitter brew. They urged him to drink more. Gradually, he became aware of the drink's euphoric effect. The air around him began to swim. A few men laughed, which echoed in his brain.

Alex swayed. "I think I'd better find Kelly." His words sounded slurred to his own ears and he struggled to find his feet. When his vision righted itself, he stood. Waving away the laughter the men directed at him, he staggered away.

He found the hut, which Wamba had provided for them, and fell face down on the cot and slept.

When fingers stroked his shoulders and down his back to his buttocks, he sighed. "Does this mean you've forgiven me for my carelessness, love?"

He twisted toward Kelly, but it was the squat woman with missing teeth who returned a smile.

Bloody hell. He scrambled to his feet and pointed toward the door. "Go. Out." With her head sinking low, she skulked out of the hut.

How long had he been asleep? He'd been foolish to leave Kelly for so long. He dashed outside to find the afternoon sun lowering in the sky. Whirling in a circle, he tried to remember the direction to the village center.

When he found his way to the clearing, the party was already in progress. A table was laden with exotic flowers and various dishes. A whole roasted pig lay on a platter at the center.

Where was Kelly? A glimmer of uneasiness ran through him. Finally, he spotted her. His breath rushed out in relief. She looked beautiful and happy. He stared at her as if seeing her for the first time. She wore a red and white-flowered halter top and wraparound skirt, which showed her bare midriff. Flowers and beads were entwined in braids, which encircled her head. The rest of her hair fell in loose curls down her back. She stood beside a table of women who were also admiring her new look.

He strode toward her. "I've been looking for you."

"I wondered where you were."

"You look beautiful."

Her lips curved. "Since we've been stranded, this is the first time I've felt remotely pretty." She twirled and showed him her outfit. "You like it?"

"Yes. I'd like to demonstrate the profound effect you have on me. Unfortunately, now isn't the time, in this very public place."

He tore his gaze from hers and glanced around at the villagers who were eating, drinking, and socializing. He spotted Moto. "Bloody hell, he's still staring at you. I hope he's not going to be a problem. You'd better stay close to me."

While he wasn't truly worried the man would cause problems as long as she was with him, Alex used the excuse to pull her against the length of him. She always felt so right in his arms. He inhaled the scent of the exotic flowers in her hair.

He brushed away a loose curl at her temple. "No more going off alone, Kelly. I shouldn't have pushed you into it. What would you say if I give you a kiss to show your entranced swain Moto that you're with me?"

Her eyes widened. "But . . . I'm not really with you. Circumstances only stranded us together."

"To hell you're not with me." Not giving her a chance to protest, he crushed his mouth down on hers.

Her warm lips trembled beneath his, causing liquid heat to pulse through his veins. He clasped her tighter until her full breasts and hips pressed against him.

"Enjoying the party, Alex Drake?" Wamba called from a nearby table.

Alex groaned. Reluctantly, he lifted his mouth from Kelly's.

When their lips parted, she cried, "Oh."

He cupped her cheek. "We're not used to having an audience." Then he brushed his thumb across her lower lip. Bloody hell, he wanted to kiss her again, but he would have to be satisfied that her flushed face revealed she'd been just as affected as he. However, he'd only meant to give her a quick kiss, not get swept up in the moment. Now, he was afraid her effect on him would be obvious to everyone around.

Sighing, he took her hand and led her to a table where Wamba sat with his young son, Calb, and his daughter, Aleah. "Good evening, Chief."

Wamba pointed to the end of his table. "Join us."

Alex settled on a bench with Kelly. He raked his gaze over her, still disturbed by their kiss. Had she been as electrified by it as he? He found her to be the most beautiful and exciting woman he'd ever met. Then he scoffed. Surely, it was because he'd been forced to spend two months alone with her that such an attachment and regard had grown.

Bowls of food were passed around the table. He watched her cautiously eye each item before she spooned food onto her plate.

Kelly handed him a bowl of fruit. "While you were gone, did you find anyone to help us?"

A guilty heat rose on his face. "No."

She gave him a sideways glance. "Neither did I." She passed him another dish. "Who knows what weird foods these people eat," she said with an impish grin. "Could that concoction be iguana? Or is that a roasted parrot in that bowl? I just might lose my appetite."

"Hush. You don't want to insult our hosts. We need their help. Now smile, eat it, and act like you enjoy it."

"Well, this fish with its entire body and head intact seems safe enough." She lifted a portion onto her plate, then selected rice and fruit. She eyed the next dish, then quickly passed the bowl to him. "You be the polite, brave one with this dish, Alex," she said with a smirk.

"Imp."

The food, however, tasted delicious.

Wamba told them a few stories about the village. The day cooled as dusk settled over the island. Some islanders lit torches around a raised platform, then with painted faces, a group of male dancers, wearing traditional garb, brandished spears. The beat of island music filled the air. Many of the villagers rushed up to dance before the stage.

Kelly caught Alex's arm. "You never told me what you did all afternoon. You were gone for hours."

"I tried their local brew and realized it was their version of alcohol. I ended up sleeping in the hut they've provided for us."

Kelly laughed. "Do you mean you got drunk?"

He shrugged. "Wamba called the drink 'kava.'"

"I've heard of it."

"I went to sleep it off, but then I had a surprise visitor in the hut."

She glanced at him sharply. "A visitor? I bet it was Wamba's daughter." He shrugged, knowing he was misleading her. Her face paled. "Did you sleep with her?" she blurted.

He dropped all teasing and slanted her a look. "And if I had?"

Her brow furrowed as she flicked her gaze away from him. "You're free to do whatever you like."

Grasping her chin, he tilted her face toward him. "Do you care what I do?"

She pulled away from his touch. "I never had any real claim on you, and I terminated our agreement."

When she stalked off, the words 'to hell with our agreement' died on his lips. And he didn't care one bit for the stabbing jealousy and possessiveness clenching his gut when she joined the group of dancers, and the men on the stage smiled down at her.

Bloody hell. His teasing had backfired this time.

* * *

Kelly couldn't get away from Alex fast enough. Grass skirts rustled against her dress as she strode through the crowd. Her chest was tight and her eyes burned. She knew Alex didn't equate sex with love. For him, it was a necessary biological function. She meant nothing to him beyond being a female body to use to satisfy his male lusts.

Let him have hundreds of women—he wouldn't have her again. She swiped at the tears spilling on her cheeks. Damn him. She wouldn't cry. Although she had always known how this would play out, this closing scene still hurt too much.

I want to go home. I want to get as far away from him as I can.

Resolving to never let Alex know how much she cared, she pasted a fake smile on her face. She threw herself into dancing, hoping the beating drums would take her away from her heartache.

When a pathway opened through the dancers, and Moto appeared, she gasped. He wore decorated clothing and a brightly colored loincloth. Grinning, he gyrated his massive hips at her. She flinched and sashayed through the crowd. When she found he wasn't following her, she blew out a deep sigh. Surely, nothing could happen to her in a crowd of this size?

She stopped at a table where a woman handed her a cup of something a few of the women were sipping. Gulping the awful tasting liquid, she winced. *Kava.*

Across the crowd, she spotted Alex. With his arms folded over his chest, he looked as if he was irked with her. However, beside him, Aleah gazed at him with an enraptured face.

Jealousy ripped through her. Kelly returned a defiant look to Alex, then downed more of the drink. Tonight, she wanted to forget she'd ever let herself care for him, forget all those times she'd let him make love to her when she'd known she shouldn't—and this pain in her heart and soul was why. He was nothing but a playboy.

Determined to have a good time, if it killed her, she marched back to the dancers.

When euphoria swept her, she giggled. At least, she wouldn't be crying over Alex, not tonight anyway. Swirling and swaying her hips to the beat, she tried to copy some of the other dancers. A few of those moves and a few villagers encircled her to watch, and—

Someone clasped her elbow. She whirled, exhaling in relief when she saw Alex and not Moto. "You scared me. I was just getting into this dance." She shooed him away with her hand and added bitterly, "So why don't *you* just go away."

When he picked her up and half-carried, half-dragged her away, she gaped at his heavy-handedness. "What are you doing, Alex?"

"You have all of these men watching you," he grumbled. "Not to mention your friend Moto." When they reached their table, he ordered, "Sit."

She crossed her arms over her chest. "Don't tell me what to do, Alex."

His eyes flashed with annoyance. "With the way your huge friend has been drooling over you, I don't think it's wise to flaunt your body in front of him, or drink kava."

"Flaunt my body?" she repeated, incredulously. She thrust her face toward his and felt dizzy. When she swayed, he caught her arm. "Okay. Perhaps you're right. I'll sit."

Glaring at her, he sat beside her.

"Why, I think you're jealous," she blurted. "Good. You deserve it."

"No, I'm not jealous. The word is not in my vocabulary, sweetheart." He folded his arms over his chest. "But *you* are *intoxicated*," he said, grinding out the words.

She poked her finger into his chest. "Okay, so it's all right for you to do whatever you please, but not for me?"

"I never said that."

"So tell me, did you enjoy your time with Aleah?" Giving him a withering stare, she couldn't keep her anger and hurt to herself anymore—so much for pretending she didn't care.

He clasped her shoulder and gently shook her. Her head fell back, and she realized how lightheaded she was. "Kelly, I didn't have sex with her."

She focused her eyes on his for the truth. "You didn't?"

"No. While I slept, someone did come into the hut. It was the woman with the missing teeth. I ran her out as fast as I could."

"Then why did you let me think you'd been with Aleah?"

His gaze locked on her, he shrugged. "I don't know. Perhaps I wanted to experience *your* jealousy. I took it too far."

"And if it had been Aleah?"

"No, Kelly. I wouldn't have."

Happiness blossomed recklessly inside her. Maybe he did care after all.

Clasping her wrists, he pulled her to him. "However, if you'd come into the hut and rubbed my back, love," he said, his voice dropping to a husky tone, "we'd still be in there. And what I'd like to do . . . You know certain spots on you are so tender—"

She sucked in her breath. "Alex . . ."

Five tables away, an argument broke out between Wamba and Moto. Kelly tore her gaze from Alex to see what was happening. He noticed, too, for he released her wrists and turned to watch.

However, they could fight all they wanted for tonight, because her heart sang with joy. Alex did care. He *had* been jealous.

Wanting to enjoy the evening, she stood and tugged his arm. "Why don't we dance?"

"Not now, love."

"You never let me have any fun," she said with a feigned pout.

His face grew serious. "Something is going on, and we need to keep our wits about us. Your dancing attracts attention. Maybe the wrong kind."

"Years of ballet and tap." Her slurred words surprised her. She frowned. "Perhaps, I've had a little too much to drink."

He settled her onto his lap. "Be a good girl and sit with me until we find out why they are arguing. I don't like this Moto character in the least. No more kava for either of us. All right?"

Comfortably snuggled against his chest, she smiled into his face. "If you're truly worried, I won't dance anymore—not as long as I get to sit on your lap."

He winked. "All right, but don't wiggle so much, love."

She grinned. "Okay, but it does feel good to be at a party, even with people who don't speak English." She walked her fingers over his chest and teased, "Gee, Alex, you never take me to any parties." At the strong impulse to trail her tongue down his neck, she sucked in her breath and tempered her passion.

He tightened his arms around her, smiling indulgently. "And you know why?" he said lightly. "At every invitation we've received on our island, I've said to myself, 'I can't take my Kelly to a party. She'll drink too much and dance like a wild woman.'"

She liked the sound of being *his*.

"I don't usually drink more than an occasional glass of wine, but this kava surprised me." She placed her palms on his chest, loving the feel of his muscles beneath her hands. "It makes me want to get you *alone*," she said, lowering her voice on the last word. At that thought, heat flooded through her. She no longer felt like laughing.

"Any more talk like that," he whispered in her ear, while he stroked his hand along her bare midriff, "and I'll throw you over my shoulder and carry you into the hut. And you can show *me* that dance in private. And damn the consequences."

"Promises, promises," she murmured, nestling closer, happier than she ever thought possible. Her gaze searched his. "Alex, I lov—"

Wamba and Moto's voices rose to an angry pitch, capturing Alex's attention.

Shock ran through her and Kelly pressed her fingers to her lips, shaken at what she'd nearly blurted out to him.

Wamba strode up to their table. "Moto says it's time he married and insists he take Kelly for his bride."

"What?" Alex and Kelly said in unison. Her stomach clenched as she glanced at Alex in panic.

He stood, sliding Kelly off his lap. "Tell Moto he can't have her. She's with me."

"But you said you weren't married," Wamba complained.

Kelly whirled toward the giant. "We're not. And I'm going to tell Moto the last thing I want is to be his bride."

When she took an unsteady step, Alex grabbed her arm and spun her around. He set her down on the bench with a thud.

Then he pressed his hands on her shoulders to keep her there. "Hey, Little Hot Head. Can't you see your gigantic swain is dressed in some kind of bridal loincloth? He means business. This could be a dangerous situation for you. We're not back in the States. A more primitive law exists here. You're a single woman and this giant wants to make you his bride. *Tonight.* Do you get my meaning?"

She cringed. "Yes, I get it."

"Good." He turned to the chief. "Tell him she's with me."

After Wamba called out the translation, Moto stomped up to their table. Any lingering thoughts Kelly had about this festive getup only being his fancy party outfit, were shot to hell. She surveyed the clearing. Not one of the other males had taken such care to decorate their bodies.

Wamba frowned. "Moto says her beauty has ripped his heart from his chest, and he'll fight for her."

She winced. "But I don't want his heart—or anything else."

Alex stepped forward and said in a calm voice, "Chief, explain to him about our Western culture of allowing women to choose their partners. You can't make a woman go with you, when she doesn't want to."

As if he understood Alex's words, Moto threw back his head and roared with laughter, his great belly shaking. Speaking a few words to his buddies, he picked up a nearby branch and broke it into two pieces as if it were Alex's body.

Wamba translated. "He says 'who's going to stop him from taking her for his wife?'"

CHAPTER ELEVEN

Alex exhaled a deep breath as he surveyed the massive native. "I'm glad he thinks this is hilarious," he said dryly. "What am I supposed to do, Chief? Fight him?"

Wamba's expression grew pensive. "Rule of the village . . . Every man handles Moto any way he can. Let him have her peacefully. You'll lose in the end. No man has been able to stand up to Moto."

Alex glanced at Kelly. "Did I tell you I'm an *actor*, not a fighter?"

Her eyes widened. "I know that. You can't mean to do this."

"Blast it, Kelly. You would attract the biggest bully on the island." He turned to Wamba. "Tell him he can't have her."

She clasped his arm. "This isn't one of your movies. He'll kill you."

Believing this bastard would do Kelly harm, a surge of protectiveness swept over him. He gazed down at her. "Do we have a choice, love? I don't like the alternative, do you?"

Moto stepped toward Kelly and flexed his chest muscles and biceps.

She frowned. "Is that supposed to impress me?"

Alex's anger rose at Moto's audacity. "He looks ridiculous."

Kelly turned to the chief. "I'm not going anywhere with that monster. On your island, doesn't a woman have any rights?"

Wamba threw out his hands. "Most the time, but sometimes Moto tries to make his own laws."

Waving his gigantic fist in the air, the huge native shouted something in his native tongue. The music and dancing halted.

The islanders gathered around, whispering amongst themselves.

Even in the torchlight, their faces reflected fear. How many men had Moto thrashed?

Wamba translated. "He says anyone who interferes is tomorrow's fishing bait."

Not wanting to fight, Alex said, "Do something, Chief."

"There's nothing I can do," Wamba grumbled. "Everyone is afraid of him." His shoulders drooped under his regal finery. Alex realized the aging leader's power was tenuous at best. "The only compensation I have for you is my beautiful daughter who expresses an interest in wedding you." Aleah blew a kiss toward Alex.

"That's a great honor, Chief, but I feel a certain responsibility to this woman." Alex narrowed his gaze on Kelly. "Even if she is a magnet for trouble. God knows, I've been up to my neck in it, since the day we met."

She winced. "Alex, please don't fight. I don't want you to get hurt."

Wamba patted Alex on the back. "Consider it an honor for her to marry Moto. If he becomes the next leader, she'll be his queen."

Alex lifted his chin. "I'm not impressed."

"Consider you'll be able to walk away with your life," Wamba countered blandly, straightening his robes around himself.

Alex squared his shoulders. "I intend to live." With a troubled expression, Kelly glanced toward him, and then back at his competition. He lifted his chin. "Kelly, have a little faith in me."

Moto taunted Alex with a wide grin. Alex rubbed his palms on his shorts. Damn it. The bloody bastard really meant to fight for her. He flicked his gaze to Aleah who beamed a smile at him. Did Moto have another reason to hate him? How many women had refused the giant?

Moto grabbed Kelly's wrist and yanked her to him.

"Let me go," she cried, her voice muffled against his big body. She stomped his foot, but he only wrenched her arm and proceeded to drag her away.

Alex stared, unable to move.

Kelly dug her heels into the dusty ground. *"A-l-l-e-e-e-x-x!"*

Her cry snapped him to his senses. For a moment, he'd been waiting for a director to end the scene. This was something out of a film . . . having to fight a native over a beautiful girl.

Alex swore, "Bloody hell!"

Clamping his hands on his hips, he strode toward them to block Moto's exit.

Moto glared as if Alex were crazy to even attempt to mess with him. Was this how he got away with whatever he wanted, frightening everyone until they backed down?

Alex clenched his fist. He wasn't backing down. He turned toward the chief. "Tell Moto I demand he release her—"

"Watch out, Alex!" Kelly yelled from behind him.

Moto lunged into Alex, sending him crashing into a table leg. Food landed on him as he sprawled face-first on the ground. Alex swiped the gritty dirt from his mouth. So much for this only being a scare tactic on Moto's part.

Freeing herself, Kelly ran and crouched beside Alex. "Are you all right?"

He lifted his head and shook off some fruit that had fallen on him. "Yes, but I've been better, damn it." He rolled onto his back and cringed to find Moto standing over them.

Kelly grasped a nearby wooden spoon from the ground and shook her tiny weapon at Moto. "I mean it. Stop this, this instant."

Moto laughed and glanced around at his buddies. He yanked the utensil from Kelly's hand. A startled expression swept her face. Then Moto turned toward Alex and pounced.

Alex gasped for air, crushed beneath the mammoth's great weight.

* * *

When Moto smashed his beefy fist into Alex's eye, Kelly winced. Unable to stand by and do nothing to help Alex, she glanced around for a more substantial weapon.

Nearby, stood the woman with the toothless grin and the chief's daughter Aleah. Both appeared to be waiting to console whatever was left of Alex. She grasped a nearby chair and swung as hard as she could at Moto's head . . . but missed. The bamboo chair landed with a thud on the ground, inches from Alex's face.

He gazed up at her from where he lay flat on his back. "Are you trying to help me?" he asked sardonically.

She cringed. "Sorry."

She lifted the chair again. Moto swiped out with his huge hand and shoved her aside. She stumbled, but with the distraction, Alex managed to roll away from Moto's bulk.

His breathing coming in gasps, Alex hastened to his feet. "My thanks, love. I can't let him get me down again." He stripped off his t-shirt and flung it aside and circled the giant. When an opportunity appeared, Alex landed an upper cut against the giant's jaw. "He's like a bloody brick wall."

Moto's eyes rolled in astonishment. He shook off his dazed expression and lunged, but Alex moved out of the way as Moto charged past, then struck him from behind with a kick. The huge native landed in the dirt.

Then the giant lumbered to his feet and became an angry bull ready to charge.

Kelly shrieked, "Run, Alex. Run."

A sheen coated Alex's lean, muscular frame as he circled Moto near her. "Not *today*, love."

When Moto moved toward him, Alex kicked him in the stomach. Finally, with another punch, Moto's mouth dropped open. Alex followed with an uppercut that made the giant's teeth snap, a chop to his throat, and finished with a kick in the groin. The large man let out a painful yelp, then doubled over and sank to the ground.

Kelly exhaled a ragged sigh of relief.

Breathing hard, Alex staggered to a nearby bench.

Running to him, she threw her trembling arms around his neck and kissed his perspiring cheek. "You've won. When did you learn martial arts?"

Alex grinned, his lip cut and bleeding. "When I was a boy, after several brawls, my mother insisted I take lessons. Kelly, did you think I got the leading role in the movie about a spy who kicked butt, for nothing? Bloody hell, I wasn't going to let that gigantic moron force himself on you."

"You're amazing," she said, squeezing him. "Thank you so much."

Moto lay in a moaning heap on the ground. Dogs gathered around and licked his face. His friends helped him to his feet.

Kelly didn't miss the threatening glance he shot at Alex before departing with his buddies.

A feeling passed over her that Moto wasn't through with them.

Wamba pounded Alex on the back. "Moto won't be bullying anyone for a while. He's in disgrace." He held Alex's arm up in a victory salute. The villagers cheered.

When Wamba took their hands, everyone grew silent. He spoke a few words in his native language, then gave Alex and Kelly a broad grin. "Congratulations. I've blessed your union and told my people that according to laws of our Yangono, you are husband and wife."

Kelly shot a glance toward Alex, surprised to find him smiling, busted lip and all. *But then, why not?* He knew this marriage wasn't binding in their world and that it was only a device to save her from Moto.

On the stage, musicians beat drums in a celebration song. The only ones who appeared not to be jubilant were the two women interested in Alex.

No matter what Alex wanted from their relationship, he deserved her tender care for all he had done for her. She picked up his discarded shirt and reached for his hand.

"My hero, come with me," she said.

They walked the short distance to the stream. After he dove in and splashed off the dust, they sat on a bench near a torch.

"Let me see the damage." In the torchlight, and using Alex's wet shirt, she dabbed at the blood on his face. "I'm so sorry you were hurt because of me. You saved me again."

"I don't know. Even if he'd thrashed me to a bloodied pulp, I think you would have figured some way out, love. The way you swung that chair—"

"And the way I almost slammed you with it." She lightly touched his mouth. "Too bad we don't have any ice. You're going to have a black eye, and your lip is cut, but your beautiful face is still intact."

He snorted, as if to say he wasn't beautiful, but he was, and he was way too good looking for her own good. And tonight, he was the man she loved with all of her heart.

Kelly gently pressed the wet shirt to his cheek. "I think we should go to *bed . . . early*."

At her suggestion, his eyes flared with heat.

They walked hand-in-hand back to their hut. Inside, with only the light of the moon shining through a window, she stood before him. "You didn't have to risk yourself and fight Moto, or do all the things you've done for me since we've been lost. Thank you." Rising on her toes, she gave him a quick kiss on the cheek. "If you don't want to, I understand."

With a chuckle, Alex drew her close, pressing his face against her hair. "Oh, I want to and you know it, but I won't have you sleeping with me to thank me."

Thanking him wasn't it at all. She wanted to tell him she'd fallen hopelessly in love with him.

Aware he wouldn't want to hear those words though, she shrugged. "I've missed being with you."

He grinned in the moonlight. "Then stop talking and kiss me."

She wound her arms around his neck and pressed her lips to his. He placed his hands on her waist. If temporary was the best she would have with him, she'd take what she could get.

Before things progressed too far, she gently touched her finger to his bottom lip. "Does it hurt much?"

"No," he said, his voice light with warmth. "And you heard what Wamba announced. On this island, we're married." He drifted his fingers down her back and fumbled for the ties on her top and skirt. With little effort, the outfit fluttered to the floor. "How convenient," he quipped.

With only flowers and beads in her hair, she stood before him. The breeze cooled her hot, naked skin.

He stripped off his wet shorts and pulled her down beside him on the cot. "You were angry with me the last time."

"No, not at all. I was afraid of the risks we were taking." Now, even those risks couldn't affect how much she wanted him.

His demanding lips caressed hers in a long kiss. She relished the feel of his naked skin against hers. Being in his arms, with her mouth pressed to his, all seemed so right. She swirled again into a pool of desire.

"You're not under the influence of too much kava?" he asked, his breath warm and fanning her ear.

"No," she said with a sweet shiver. "It's worn off." At this point, she didn't think either of them could have stopped, for he already nibbled a trail of kisses down the column of her throat.

His stubbled cheeks bristled against her bare shoulder. "Good. I want your full consent. Just promise me you won't be sorry later."

"I won't be."

His mouth sought hers and he kissed her tenderly, while his hands stroked her breasts. She ached inside, not only to satisfy their desire, but for something magical to happen between them. Although he might not want her love, she wanted to surrender her entire being to him.

While she moved her hands over him, his hands and lips touched her everywhere, stoking a fire. "I need you, Kelly."

She responded by wrapping her hand around his erection and guiding him into her slick wetness.

Her surrender was more than the physical act of love, and she knew she'd never be the same without him. While he stroked inside her, their heartbeats beat in time together, a union of two souls.

Afterwards, she rested in the security of his arms, thinking uneasily about how much she loved him. What was she going to do?

* * *

The sun's first rays crept through the window. Somewhere a rooster crowed. Alex traced his finger down Kelly's bare spine, delighted when she wiggled her hips. His smile dimmed at the memory of yesterday. If he hadn't brushed up on his martial arts fighting skills, enough to look good for his role in the *The Spy* . . . He hated to think of yesterday's outcome if he'd lost the fight.

He leaned over and nibbled on the delectable curve between her neck and shoulder, while his fingers trailed up the silky skin of her warm stomach. She heaved a sigh and rolled over to face him.

She pulled the towel over her breasts. "After last night, I guess we're shameless."

He caressed an auburn curl and gazed into her sapphire eyes. "Having regrets already?"

She shook her head. "I'll never regret being with you."

Realizing his desire for her never remained extinguished for long, he sighed. "I'm glad as I had the most amazing night with you. What do you say we have a repeat performance, love?"

Her gaze traveled down to his bulge against the towel. She pulled it back for a peep. "Oh, I *see*," she said, with an impish grin. "But it looks like a huge, personal problem to me."

"Brat." He tugged the towel out of her grasp. "But it's you I don't see enough of." She laughed and let him look his fill. His blood stirred hotly as he cupped and molded her breasts with his hands. "I like to look at you. You have such a lovely body. I also want to touch and taste." He leaned over and drew lazy circles with his tongue on her nipple, causing it to pucker. She gasped in pleasure. He smiled and ran his fingers over her bare stomach, working his way lower.

When he reached what he sought and sunk his fingers into her warmth, she sighed and relaxed on the pallet. "Oh my."

He chuckled. "You heard what Wamba said. We might be here for a while, and I intend to enjoy every moment we work on this mutual sensual pleasure." He leaned forward and kissed her sweet lips, taken aback by the depth of the emotions she stirred in him.

From outside the door of the hut, Wamba said, "Alex Drake, we need to talk."

Kelly whispered, *"Now?"*

"Chief, we'll be out in a moment." He gave her a light kiss and then tapped her chin. "Later, love. All right?"

After dressing, they stepped out of the hut to find Wamba wrenching his hands. "Moto is running wild. The fool has set fire to one hut. We've tied him down, but we won't be able to hold him forever. He says he'll kill you for making him lose the respect of the people, and then he'll claim Kelly as his wife. You won't be safe here."

Alex clasped Kelly's hand in a reassuring grip. "But where can we go?"

"There is one place," Wamba said in a rushed voice. "A small island close by. It belongs to an American. From there you should be able to make your way home. We have observed their boats occasionally, but mostly their island is uninhabited."

Alex removed his diamond wedding band from his pocket. "We can pay you with this ring to take us there."

Wamba pushed away his extended hand and the offering. "Keep it. You might need it to barter with these other people. If they don't help you, we'll take you with us to the mainland in six months." He patted Alex's back. "Moto's angry, but you've done much for us, proving that Moto can be beaten. When I die, they will stand up to Motto and pick a more worthy leader until my son is grown to lead them."

* * *

The trip took over an hour in the rundown motorboat. When they reached an island with a high peak, the natives motored into a cove where an unoccupied dock came into view. Alex didn't see any other evidence of habitation until the men pointed up the hill to where a roof peeked out through heavy foliage.

He hauled their bags out, and the islanders waved and left the cove.

"Seems rustic, but it's a real house," Kelly said in awe.

"I feel it. We're closer to going home."

They trudged up the steep hill. From the beach, the two-story house had been barely detectable, blending in with the natural surroundings. From further up, they saw the building took advantage of its perch overlooking the ocean. An antenna, satellite dish, and a large array of solar panels were mounted on the roof.

"Alex, do you think they'll take us to the mainland?"

"We'll give them my ring, with the promise to pay more, but it doesn't look as if they're in need of money."

Her brow wrinkled with worry. "My thoughts, too. I wonder what business they're in."

He shrugged. "It's probably some rich man's holiday home." He didn't feel as confident as his words and chalked his uneasiness up to the fact that it was hard to believe their luck could be changing. He reassured Kelly with a grin. "Let's find out if anyone's home."

Before he knocked on the door, he glanced at Kelly. His smile faded. Her provocative beauty had gotten him into trouble with the natives. His sore ribs and face attested to that fact.

He didn't want to chance her generating more problems on this island. "Come here." He smoothed her hair with his hands, but her thick auburn curls would not behave. Frowning, he straightened the worn and ripped t-shirt that exposed her left shoulder. She raised her gaze to his, silently questioning his actions.

He gave her a weak smile. "You look entirely too enticing and adorable for our own good." Heaven help them if these people weren't honorable. "Let me do the talking."

He knocked on the door. When no one answered, they walked around to the side of the house and peered into the windows—still no sign of anyone. "Let's check the lower level."

When they found everything locked, Alex picked up a rock.

Kelly grabbed his arm. "You're not going to break a window?"

"If I have to, love. These aren't normal circumstances. We can't wait out here for their return. But if it makes you feel better, I'll try something else first." He retrieved the rope from one of the bags and knotted it tightly to the rock. "Jack Stone, my character in *The Spy,* had to do this."

Her lips pursed and she crossed her arms over her chest.

"Now don't frown at me like I'm crazy . . . Let's give it a go." He threw the rock a few times until the rope wrapped around the railing. He yanked and lodged the stone securely, then scaled the wall to the second floor. "The door is unlocked," he yelled over the balcony.

A minute later, he opened the door on the lower level. With a bow, he gestured for her to enter the room. "I've had enough rusticating, haven't you? Welcome to our temporary home."

* * *

While she explored the house, Kelly tried to push aside her guilt about invading someone's home.

"Don't worry so much," Alex said, "We'll explain our situation and pay them handsomely for the use of everything, once we get home."

A living area with a television, bar, table, sofa and a galley kitchen, with a well-stocked pantry, took up most of the lower floor. Game machines and a pool table were located on one end. She frowned, perplexed by the nearby utility room with a row of bunk beds.

Upstairs, they found three, nicely furnished bedrooms, each with a private bathroom, and another living area with an entertainment center and a more elaborate kitchen. Kelly stepped through sliding glass doors onto a large balcony. Over the treetops, one could see the ocean and anyone who approached the house.

Her stomach growled so she headed to the kitchen and rummaged through the cabinets.

Alex walked in. "The two-way radio doesn't work because the power supply has been removed, and the computer requires a password."

Kelly sighed. "We had such hope. What do we do now?"

"It's only a setback, love."

She pulled out a box of spaghetti from the pantry. "Are you hungry?"

"Famished."

She took a saucepan from a cabinet. "At least we'll live in comparative luxury while we wait for the owners. There's plenty of food."

Alex walked to the bar. "Let's celebrate some good fortune then." He opened a bottle of red wine and handed her a glass. "We *are* going to make ourselves at home."

The nagging in the back of her mind refused to be stilled. "I can't help it, but I feel weird taking over their house. And there is something about this place I don't like."

"We'll explain our situation when the owners arrive." She knew he always thought everything would work out, but her stomach tensed into a tight ball of nerves.

She blew out a deep breath, deciding to shove away her doubts. "You're right. These aren't ordinary circumstances. As long as you think they'll understand," she added with a rueful smile. "I like the comforts of a house as much as you do. I've found coffee and books. It's like we've died and gone to Heaven." She held her wine glass out to him for a toast. "To getting home."

He clinked his glass to hers. "To going home." They sipped the dry, fruity wine.

"This tastes great, but before I drink it, I'm taking a shower. I found scissors. When I'm finished, will you trim my hair?"

"Sure. Can I trust you with mine as well?" he asked.

Kelly entered a bathroom, stripped off her clothes and stepped into the large shower. She basked in the welcome luxury of warm water, shampoo, and scented soap.

Alex opened the frosted glass door. His gaze traveled down her naked body. "Since our hosts aren't here, do you mind if I join you?" he asked, his voice turning husky.

She smiled. "There's room for two."

He joined her in the shower and lathered himself with soap, but then he couldn't seem to keep his hands off her. He bent and drank the water running off one of her breasts and then latched onto her nipple. Heat exploded through her. She threaded her fingers through his hair. He lifted his head and kissed her lips while running his soapy hands over her body, caressing her. Kelly arched her back and moaned. When his fingers stroked her intimately, her knees grew weak and she clung to him for support.

"Alex," she cried.

He groaned and clasped her shoulders, drawing her closer. He pulled her hand down to wrap around his swollen member.

She shuddered at the hot desire quickly rising inside her. "I need you now."

As he entered her, she sucked in her breath. She clasped the towel bar and as he proceeded to satisfy them both, she moaned and cried his name and took every inch of him, over and over again, until she climaxed.

He groaned and swiftly pulled out, muttering, "Almost didn't make it."

* * *

Wrapped in large, white towels, Alex sat before Kelly on the stool he'd brought up from the lower level. Holding a pair of scissors, she picked up a lock of his hair and breathed in his clean scent. She clipped a strand. "You *do* like to live dangerously, Mr. Drake, when you have me cut your hair. I think 'Danger' must be your middle name."

His gaze met hers in the mirror and he chuckled. "I didn't know the meaning of the word until I met you. By the way, my full name is Alexander Maxim Langford Drake. Quite a mouthful, isn't it?"

She edged around him, snipping his thick, dark blond hair, which curled at his shoulders. "I like it." Her next thoughts strayed to her being *Mrs.* Alexander Maxim Langford Drake. She thrust that thought aside. "Are you worried about how your hair's going to turn out?"

"Should I be?"

Kelly forced herself to concentrate on following his previous style. "Actually, you're lucky. I have a friend who cuts hair for a living. I've watched her many times. I think I can pull it off."

When Kelly moved in front of him, she noticed his gaze lowered to the swell of her breasts above the towel. Despite that distracting her, she managed to finish, and then blew his hair dry with the blow dryer she found under the sink.

When it was her turn, she sat on the stool. Alex stood behind her and gazed at her in the mirror. He tugged on the ends of the curls cascading more than halfway down her back. "I don't want to cut much. I love your hair."

"On the cruise ship you said it was wild, so I thought you hated it."

He tugged a strand. "Hush. Did you really believe that? I was baiting you on the ship, trying to torment you . . . like the torment I felt after meeting you and discovering you were engaged to someone else." That information left her stunned into silence.

After he finished, Kelly enjoyed the luxury of blow-drying her own hair while he shaved. She hadn't seen her reflection in over two months, except for in her little compact. Glancing in the mirror, she thought she looked a little more mature. She *had* changed. They'd been through so much, and she was no longer a virgin or fearful of sex. She carried herself with a heightened level of confidence and awareness now.

He wiped away the shaving cream and turned to face her. When he smiled, his slight dimples and high cheekbones were more evident. "What do you think? Better?"

Her heart did a flip-flop and then nose-dived to her toes.

As gorgeous as he had been with the stubble and the occasional shave, now with shorter hair and freshly shaved, he was devastatingly handsome, even with the black eye, swollen lip, and smattering of bruises on his arms and chest. His beautiful face and golden good looks reminded her that he was an up-and-coming movie star—and she just an ordinary girl.

Now he looked like he had when they'd first met on the ship, when he'd worn only a white towel and that look was daunting. Her throat ached with despair. She had gotten used to him in her life, despite his warning that she shouldn't fall in love with him.

To regroup, she stroked her thumb along his jaw line and noticed more bruises. "Thanks again for saving me from Moto. Does your face hurt much?"

He shrugged. "I'm all right." She knew him well enough to know he wouldn't make a big deal about any pain.

Kelly gazed into his glorious aqua-blue eyes and bit her lip. She would be the biggest fool to imagine there was any chance of them staying together once they went home.

A frown creased his forehead. "Is something the matter, Kelly?"

"No. Everything is fine." She ducked her head and straightened things on the counter. "I wanted to say that after we're rescued, I'll always remember you and our adventure." She dashed out of the bathroom, calling over her shoulder, "Our clothing has had it. Let's see if we can find something else to wear."

* * *

Kelly returned to the kitchen wearing a simple white cotton nightgown despite numerous articles of sexy lingerie she'd found. Alex didn't need any enticing.

For her own self-preservation, she had to accept that if things went well—Alex might be able to figure out the two-way radio or hack into the computer— she could be in California in a matter of days. He would be happy to get back to his life, and she might never see him again.

After dinner, he found an acoustic guitar. He tuned the instrument and played, and sang her a song, which only reminded her that he was more talented than anyone she'd ever met. Tired, and with guilt tugging at her conscience, she decided to slip off and go to bed—by herself. With just the trappings of modern civilization and their potential return, he had to be aware they needed to end this affair if they were going to live up to their agreement. Besides, what would happen if the owners returned? Maybe he wouldn't be, but she would feel uncomfortable being caught sleeping with him, without being married.

She didn't want to offend the people who owned this house any more than they probably would be when they found their home invaded in the first place, so she picked the smallest, sparsely furnished bedroom with an empty closet. Sighing, she drifted to sleep in the comfortable queen-sized bed, a blissful luxury compared to what they had grown used to these past two months.

She was half-asleep when Alex clicked on the lamp. "Kelly?" he whispered. "Are you hiding from me?"

Her eyes flew open. She winced, because there was no doubt in her mind her heart was going to be broken. "I thought with a houseful of beds you might want to sleep somewhere else."

"No, Kelly," he scoffed, frowning. "I want to sleep with you."

She winced and clasped the sheet to her throat. "But we could be going home soon."

He lifted an eyebrow in amusement. "Does it matter at this point?"

She shrugged. "Some."

What was between them might just be sex and having a good time to him. But the way pain seeped into her heart at the thought of him leaving her, she didn't find the situation funny at all.

He sat on the edge of the bed and ruffled the hair at her temple. "After all we've been through, don't you want to actually sleep with me in a real bed? Or would it be too traditional for us?"

She blurted out the other reason that bothered her. "What will our hosts think if they arrive and find us in bed together . . . and *unmarried?*"

He chuckled and tugged her hand from the sheet. "Unless the house belongs to a bunch of nuns or priests, then I think we're all right. But for your safety, I had planned to tell them we're married anyway. They won't know if it's true or not. Let's enjoy what time we have together."

"I shouldn't." Her voice sounded weak, even to herself.

"But you want to." His eyes gleamed with that smoldering look she couldn't resist.

Yes. He was going to hurt her, but it wasn't his fault. She had tried not to fall hopelessly in love with him, but she was.

"But we'll be going home soon."

"You want to break our agreement now?"

"We should." However, he looked so handsome, and she loved him so much. Her heart wrenched.

He sighed. "All right, Kelly. I'll talk to you in the morning." He turned off the lamp and rose from the bed, then paused, becoming a silhouette in the doorway. "Good night, love. Sleep well."

Anguish searing her heart, she extended her arms. "Don't leave me," she said in barely a whisper. "Not yet."

He strode to the bed, sat, and again turned on the lamp. She threw her arms around him, desperate for some assurance he cared.

He returned her tight embrace, giving her a light kiss on the ear. "Then don't talk like this." He held her close, his cheek against her forehead. Her heart soared, until he said, "We're not back yet. We're together, at least until then."

At least until then. Kelly blinked back the tears burning at the back of her eyes. She nodded. "Sure." He intended to go his own way. Still, she'd hold onto him until the last minute.

He cupped her chin in his hand. "Shall our lessons in love go on, Kelly? Or do you prefer to sleep tonight?"

"Sleep? I can sleep later." She'd take one day at a time.

His face took on a serious quality as he fondled her breasts. His thumb flicked her nipple through the thin fabric. "I can't get enough of you. You're like a drug that's gotten into my blood."

Those words pleased her and gave her hope. She took his face between her hands and kissed him.

* * *

Morning light streaked through the slats in the shutters. The fan above circulated the air.

In the comfortable bed, Alex leaned over Kelly and frowned at the dark circles under her eyes. She had been restless last night so he decided he wouldn't wake her.

He'd be an idiot if he didn't realize she might think she was in love with him. He shoved his hand through his hair. He did care for her—deeply. That he would admit. Moreover, the last thing he wanted was to hurt her, but it was only because of their desperate situation that they had needed each other like they had. It was nothing more than that—or was it?

While he dressed in shorts and a shirt he'd found in the house, he watched her sleep. He blew out a deep breath. He'd never intended for them to become emotionally involved.

Perhaps she'd been right last night about severing this bond between them, which had grown like an entangling vine. Maybe, since chance of rescue loomed closer, he should have left her alone last night, tried to put distance between them.

Didn't she realize she was better off without him? He had been suffocated far too long, had lived in virtual hell, and needed his freedom. He wouldn't be good for her, and she didn't fit in with his plans.

After brewing coffee, he took a cup into the office. He disliked invading someone's privacy as much as she did, but damn it, what else could they do? He tugged on the center drawer and found the desk locked. His gaze turned to a pegboard on a wall, holding keys. He retrieved them, but none fit the door or the desk.

Sighing, he knew he couldn't go so far as to break the lock on the desk—at least not yet. He'd give the owners one week to return—a week he'd spend with Kelly. During that time, he'd work his way up to saying good-bye.

He spent the next hour exploring outside, until he found padlocked doors into the side of the hill. Camouflaged with paint, the doors blended into the surroundings.

What was inside?

They might find a dingy with a motor or even a radio. Anything.

He hurried to the house for the key ring. Bloody hell, these were *not* normal circumstances.

Dressed in a yellow sundress, Kelly sat at the table sipping a cup of coffee. She was beginning to know him well, for she abruptly stood. "What's wrong?"

He ran his fingers through his hair. "I've discovered something. Come with me."

He led her outside to the hill. Removing the deadbolt, he swung open the bulky doors. Cool air hit his face, perhaps from being built into the hillside or was the space climate-controlled by the solar panels?

When he flicked a switch, lights flooded the area and revealed a huge warehouse. Inside, they discovered most of the shelves were empty. However, some of the shelves held what he thought were museum-quality paintings and antiques.

He glanced at Kelly's pale face. "Judging by the island's remote location and concealment of the building, I'm speculating we've landed ourselves in a den of modern day pirates. My guess is this is a clearing station for expensive, stolen goods—some may be priceless. I recognize a famous oil painting reported stolen over a year ago."

"Smugglers? You're scaring me."

He clasped her hand. "I'm sorry, love. They're not the most desirable group to run into. If they suspect we've found out their secret, I don't think they'll let us go."

At the horror creeping over her face, he said, "Let's pack up. We'll have to take what we need from the house . . . food, tools, and all the guns we can lay our hands on."

Outside, he replaced the padlock. When they turned around, a man stalked out of the shadows. He leveled an assault weapon in their direction.

Alex's heart slammed in his chest.

"Too late," Kelly whispered.

CHAPTER TWELVE

Kelly's heart pounded at a ferocious tempo as she gaped at the gun in the man's hands.

"You can put that down," Alex said. "We weren't stealing."

Wearing a camouflage hunter's cap, the stubble-cheeked man, dressed in a t-shirt and shorts, waved the weapon in Alex's face.

"Shut the hell up. Put your hands on top of your head, or I'll splatter it in the bushes. Now, come with me." He marched them through the trees and toward the house. "You, lover boy, up the stairs first. I'm aimed at your girl's back, so don't try anything, or she gets it first—then you."

When they stepped inside the living area, he motioned toward the sofa. "Plant your fucking asses on the couch." They did as he instructed. Keeping his eyes on them, the guy yelled, "Ralph, I found someone poking around in the warehouse."

Kelly threw Alex a desperate look. While his façade was one of calm indifference, she thought she might faint. In addition, he didn't know what else she knew. She recognized him as one of the men who had attacked the dive boat. She inhaled a deep breath to keep from hyperventilating.

Alex put his arm around her. "It's alright, love. We'll explain everything."

A stocky, middle-aged man with salt-and-pepper gray hair sauntered into the room. His most distinguishing feature was his flattened nose. Smoke rose in wisps from the cigar he clenched between his teeth. She remembered him, too, from the dive boat that fateful day.

Kelly's heart slammed in her chest. She gripped Alex's thigh. He turned narrowed eyes on her, but she had no way to communicate that she recognized these men.

The man called Ralph rubbed his chin, while sizing them up. "Well, well, Mick, what do we have here?"

"Boss, they were coming out of the warehouse with these." Mick dangled the set of keys.

"Caught ourselves some thieves, huh?" Ralph puffed on his cigar and then blew a stream of smoke into their faces. Kelly coughed. "You've been living in the house, too." He jammed his face toward Alex. "Do you have any idea what we do to people who steal from us?" he bellowed. "It's not pretty."

"Do we look like thieves?" Alex asked. "We planned to explain everything once you arrived."

An attractive Asian woman, with straight, black, shoulder-length hair strode into the room.

Ralph folded his arms across his chest. "Ming, we have visitors." He turned to Alex. "Now, start explaining."

"This is my wife, Kelly, and I'm Alex—"

"Alex Douglas," Kelly said, interrupting. She couldn't chance these men realizing who they were. Alex's curious gaze rested on her, but he let her speak. "Our sailboat sank nearby. Some of the locals brought us here, believing you would help us." She smiled sweetly up at Alex, hoping he liked her performance. "We're newlyweds, on our honeymoon." She bit down on her lip for a shy effect. "We thought it would be fun to travel the world, just the two of us."

With his inquisitive gaze searching her eyes, Alex kissed the back of her hand, then he addressed Ralph. "Yes, we do apologize for imposing on you. All along, we planned to pay you for your trouble, your hospitality, and the use of your house."

A smile lighting her face, Ming gave Alex a thorough going-over. "Oh my, he's gorgeous, and I love the accent."

Kelly caught Alex's eyes narrowing defensively. She had already witnessed him putting up with unwanted attention from women because of his looks.

Ming scrutinized Kelly next. "Why, she's adorable, too. So you're the one who's been borrowing my clothes."

Kelly cringed. "We didn't have a chance to save anything from the sailboat. Sorry to have barged in on you, but we had nowhere else to go."

"You poor things." Ming bestowed a smile on Ralph. "Can't we help them, Ralph? You know, true love and all . . ."

Ralph grunted. "I may not want them to leave in such a hurry." He took a slow drag on his cigar and studied Alex. "You've been snooping around. What were you doing in the warehouse?"

"I had hoped to find something to help us leave," Alex answered. "All we want is to go home."

"It's a damned inconvenience for us to have to worry about you two." Ralph turned to the man who had discovered them. "Mick, find a way to secure them. I need to think on what we'll do about our uninvited guests."

* * *

After spending the afternoon handcuffed to each other in the living room, they were escorted to the bedroom they had shared. Kelly trembled as she nervously eyed the gun pointed in their direction.

Ralph cocked his head toward the bed. "Lie down."

Alex lay down next to her on the bed, while Mick secured their hands to the headboard with the cuffs.

Ralph paused in the doorway. "No hanky-panky." He chuckled at his joke, then turned out the light, and shut the door.

The only light was from the moonlight through the slats of the shuttered window.

She tugged, trying to free herself, but the metal cut painfully into her wrist. "Ouch."

"Don't. If you struggle, the handcuffs will only tighten." Alex slammed his palm against the bed frame's spindles. "Damn, these won't give without some leverage or making a lot of noise."

Exhaling a deep breath, Kelly dropped her head on the pillow. "We're in more trouble than you know. These are the men who tried to kidnap me from the dive boat, but neither seemed to recognize me."

Alex groaned. "Bloody hell, Kelly. You must never let them know who you are."

"I'll do my best."

"Another fine predicament we've gotten ourselves into, Kelly lass," he said in an Irish brogue.

Despite her fears, she laughed. He did, too.

"If they can hear us they must think we're crazy, but our situation is going from bad to worse."

"If I didn't laugh . . ." His voice trailed off.

"I think I'd cry," she finished solemnly. "Here we are handcuffed to a bed by murderers and smugglers. Can this get any worse? How are we going to get out of this?"

"I don't know. They've made it bloody inconvenient for us to leave."

"I wish we were back on *our* island. Do you think they'll let us go?"

He sighed. "We'll have to persuade them. Just don't let them know who you are. Now, try to get some sleep. We need our strength to find our way out of here tomorrow."

She snuggled close to him, but sleep didn't come easily for her.

* * *

The next morning, Mick, the stubble-faced, younger one, with the camouflage cap, stood over Alex and Kelly. With a sneer, Mick released the cuffs. Alex's hands tingled as blood returned.

Rubbing their wrists, they were escorted by gunpoint to the living area.

Haggard looking from what Alex guessed was an evening of heavy drinking, Ralph sat at the breakfast table eating a bowl of cereal. Dressed in a pink satin robe, Ming sipped a cup of tea.

How could they convince these people they weren't a threat to their operation? He glanced at Kelly. Her hair was disheveled and her yellow dress wrinkled from sleeping in their clothes. She returned a brave smile, but her trembling bottom lip gave her away.

Despite the cool demeanor he tried to present, Alex struggled to keep his anger in check. He'd like to further flatten Ralph's nose for what they were doing to them, and for everyone who had died on the dive boat. But with Mick's magnum aimed at his heart, Alex didn't think he would live long enough.

Ralph pointed toward the table. "Take a seat." Their chairs scraped the wooden floor as they sat. He drummed his fingers on the tabletop. "I've made my decision. I'm not willing to let you go until our work is done here. So I'll make a deal with you, Alex. We could use your help to bring our shipments from the boats to the warehouse. When we leave, we'll take you and your lovely wife with us."

Although his insides knotted, Alex had no choice but to agree. "All right."

Ralph leaned toward Alex. "*But*, I won't put up with any bullshit. If you try to escape, I'll have you shot. Then afterwards, your beautiful, grieving widow can entertain the lonely men around here."

Kelly's face paled.

Mick grinned as if he liked the idea and wouldn't have any problem using the gun resting on his thigh. Mick might even enjoy killing him, especially knowing Kelly would be the prize. How easy was it for these bastards to take a life?

"I have men working for me who haven't seen the outside of a prison in a decade," Ralph said, his cool voice unsettling Alex. "Probably haven't been with a woman in all those years. I'm sure they could make good use of Kelly after your death."

Alex's jaw tightened. If he did something now, he'd only get himself killed. He squeezed Kelly's hand, trying to reassure her that somehow he'd protect her and get them out of this mess.

Ralph leaned back in his chair. "*But*, if you do exactly as you're told, I'll drop you and your sweet wife off at one of the local villages. Once there, you should eventually make your way back to the mainland. However, if you ever even whisper one word of what you've seen here, we'll hunt you down and kill you. Our acquaintances are far and wide. We'll find you."

Alex didn't doubt that. There had to be numerous international contacts in an illegal smuggling operation such as this one.

"Even if you chanced going to the authorities," Ralph said smugly, "they'd never find this tiny remote island."

"You can take us blindfolded for all we care," Alex stated flatly. Still, he didn't buy that Ralph would help them. These men were ruthless and couldn't be trusted. They'd use them for their purposes and kill them if they suspected they'd be reported to the police. However, he had no choice, but to go along, for now.

Ralph read his mind. "In case you have other ideas, Alex, while you work, your wife will be our collateral in the deal. You do your part, and she remains unharmed here in the house. But then there's always that chance that you might willingly leave her behind to save your own hide . . ."

At the man's insinuation that he'd leave Kelly, Alex curled his fists.

Ralph chuckled. "Well, do you agree to these conditions?"

It was a bargain made with the devil, but he had no alternative.

"Yes," Alex ground the word out between his clenched teeth.

On the way out, he glanced at Kelly. A surge of protectiveness swept through him. He had to find a way for them to escape.

* * *

Alex squinted when he stepped into the bright sunlight. With Mick standing behind him carrying an assault weapon, they headed down the hill to the cove. Tied to a dock was a massive yacht, a luxury speedboat, and a sailboat. Hope rose inside him that he could steal one.

When they boarded the ship, Ralph met them on the back deck. "Alex, you'll be helping, Sam, Juan, and Joe transport the cargo to the warehouse."

Alex gave him a terse nod. He assumed the stolen articles needed a cooling-off period, or perhaps would remain here until buyers were found on the black market.

For the next several hours, he sweated and hauled antique furniture and artwork worth a fortune.

He searched for anything he could use as a weapon, but Mick guarded him closely. In the warehouse, Ralph photographed and cataloged the items.

The three men he worked with were a nefarious crew—an unkempt but organized gang of thieves. Alex doubted he could make any deal with them to help them escape. Belligerent and rude, they often snickered at him, as if he were on the outside of some crude joke.

That evening, he found out the extent of their humor. Mick escorted him, not to the bedroom he'd shared with Kelly, but to the bunkroom on the first floor. His hands were cuffed securely to a wood slat on a lower bunk bed. Exhausted from the long day's work, he fell asleep as soon as his head hit the pillow.

A light flicked on. Still groggy from sleep, Alex twisted with the handcuffs and rolled to his back. Sam and Juan stood over him, while Joe leaned casually against the wall. Alex froze at the predatory gleam in their eyes.

The scruffy man, Sam, nudged Alex's knee with his foot. "Yep, boys, a guy like him probably gets any woman he wants. While *we* was doing *time*, he's been having himself a helluva good time. I'd enjoy taking him down a peg or two. Wipe off that 'better than thou' attitude. Let's show him what prison would be like for someone like him."

Adrenaline pumped through Alex. "Get the bloody hell away from me."

"You know, boys, he wouldn't last a week in the slammer. Let's give him a lesson that'll keep him on the straight and narrow path." Sam moved closer. "Ready?"

"I think not." Alex lashed out with a kick to Sam's groin, sending the man flying back against the wall with a crash.

Sam gasped and doubled over, sinking to the floor. "*Sonafabitch.* Sonafabitch."

Juan's laughter echoed in the room. "Hey, Sam, he knows how to fight, no? Beats you with his hands tied. Now, let's see how much defense you have against this, gringo." He slapped a billy club against his palm.

Alex's heart pounded as if it would burst from his chest. "Stay the bloody hell away from me," he warned through rasps of breath. He yanked at the handcuffs that imprisoned him. Pain shot through his wrists.

The door thrust open. Ralph strode into the room. "What's going on here?" he asked calmly. "I do hope you're all getting along."

Alex said through heavy breaths, "You didn't say in this deal I might be attacked."

Ralph leveled his gaze on him. "As I said before, these three have been in prison for over ten years. Now imagine what they'd do if they get their hands on your pretty little wife."

Sam croaked from the floor. "He's got a woman here?"

"Yeah," Ralph drawled, "and she's a real looker."

Joe cracked his knuckles. "Can we have her?"

Alex's stomach tightened in knots. He swiped the perspiration from his brow on his arm. How could he protect Kelly, when he might not be able to defend himself?

Ralph chuckled. "No, you *cannot.* Alex and his wife are my guests. Both she and *he* are off-limits to you." Raising an eyebrow, he shot a glance at Alex. "As long as they do as they're told, *you are to keep your hands off them.*"

Alex gritted his teeth. Ralph had known what these men might attempt. The man's earlier words were reinforced, loud and clear and had been for effect—to terrorize, and to make Alex afraid to attempt an escape.

Joe pushed away from the wall. "We weren't doing nothin'. Sam just wanted to scare him."

Ralph whirled on Joe. "Sure." He turned to the other two convicts. "I can't afford to lose any of you. If you want to earn your money, don't make trouble."

Getting up from the floor, Sam leveled heavy-lidded eyes on Alex before turning his gaze to Ralph. "Yeah, boss. Whatever you say. But if he crosses that line, I want to be the first one at him. I owe the punk."

* * *

During the next week, except for the occasional crude remarks, the ex-cons left Alex alone.

Meanwhile, he watched for a means of escape and found something to help when he opened the drawer to get leverage to move an eighteenth-century dresser. He'd barely slipped the tiny switchblade inside his pocket when Juan approached to assist in the move.

That night, Alex discreetly palmed the knife before being handcuffed to the bed. Afterwards, he kept the knife hidden on the narrow ledge of the headboard where he could reach it.

Every night, as long as footsteps trampled on the wooden floors upstairs, and sounds from the game machines and the pool table reverberated outside the closed bunkroom door, he worked. He scraped and cut away at the wood from behind the slat they had handcuffed him to, so he could soon break through.

He prayed his attempt wouldn't be noticed.

* * *

Except for one glimpse of him, Kelly hadn't seen Alex during the next week. In the main living area, Kelly sat at the table with Ming, listlessly stirring a bowl of cereal, unable to eat. The last two days, Ming had convinced Ralph to allow her out of the bedroom. Having heard murderers had difficulty killing their victims if they knew them, Kelly tried to befriend Ming, asking her if she could assist in cooking or help with the housework.

Despite the thieves she associated with, Ming had a generous nature and treated Kelly kindly. She didn't consider herself a criminal because she never personally participated in any of the heists. She invited Kelly to watch movies from the satellite dish or from her collection of DVDs.

Sighing, Kelly rubbed her forehead with the palm of her hand. She'd been trying to work up a plan of escape. All she had to do was steal the keys to a boat, and to the handcuffs Alex wore.

She'd have to climb out through her third-storey window by tying the sheets together, then sneak into the downstairs bunkroom and release Alex. She exhaled an exasperated breath. Her task seemed insurmountable.

Yesterday, she'd seen the men trudging up the hill, returning to the house. Desperately wanting a glimpse of Alex, she ran to the window and leaned out. At the site of her, the men made loud whooping sounds. Alex threw her a warning look. One of the men elbowed him, and another shoved him, saying words she couldn't hear. He reared back to throw a punch, but Mick intervened by waving a gun in Alex's face. He backed down. Embarrassed and worried that she could've gotten him killed, she'd withdrawn into the shadows of the room.

"You're not eating?" Ming asked with concern, breaking into Kelly's thoughts.

Biting her lip, Kelly shook her head. "I'm worried that Alex and I don't have a future."

"It won't be much longer, maybe a few more weeks, and they'll be finished with the shipments. Ralph will drop you off where you can find your way home." Ming added softly, "You love Alex very much, don't you?"

Seeing no reason to lie to her, Kelly choked back a sob. "Yes. I only wish I could talk to him to make sure he's all right."

"Alex is fine, but I'll talk to Ralph. You'll see. He's a decent man."

Ming might have faith in Ralph, but Kelly knew he was a no-good murderer and smuggler, however, she couldn't say this. Instead, she asked, "Are you Ralph's wife?"

"Oh, no, I'm David's girlfriend. He'll be here shortly. I love him as much as you do your Alex." She held out her hand with a large emerald ring. "It's from David. He likes to give me nice things. I met him when I was a dancer at a club in Los Angeles."

Los Angeles? Was it a coincidence? Kelly swallowed hard? Was David, *the* David Lewis? The man wanted for killing her father? Was he 'Mister X' and the reason why she had been attacked on the dive boat?

Kelly choked out, "Your ring is beautiful."

"I know what you're thinking. How could he be in this business? But at one time, he had legitimate work in the U.S., until some man ripped him off," Ming said, finishing in a flat tone. "David got into some kind of trouble after that and had to leave the country. He's always said he wanted to pay back those responsible in the U.S."

Kelly flushed miserably at more proof that her father had cheated his clients and that many people wished her dead for it.

Ming frowned. "Are you all right?"

Forcing a smile, Kelly nodded. To prove it, she forced down a few bites of her cereal.

Ming patted Kelly's hand. "Everything will be all right. You'll see. Come on. Let's get our work done so we can watch a movie. Not much else to do around here while we wait to for the job to be finished."

Kelly's stomach rolled into knots. She had to get those keys before David arrived.

When Ralph returned to the house, she saw him lock a set of keys in the cabinet. He turned and his gaze slid over Kelly as she sat there with Ming. "She's to be in her room, unless I'm here or Mick is. Do you understand, Ming? Lock her up. I have to go down to the warehouse."

* * *

The next afternoon, Kelly answered a knock on the bedroom door. She had expected Ming, but at the welcome sight of Alex, she wanted to weep. She would have thrown herself at him, but Mick stood behind him with the gun. Alex stepped into the room.

While Mick remained in the hall, Ming smiled and carried in a tray of food. "I told Ralph you've lived up to your end of the bargain and to let you honeymooners have some time alone. He'll give you until eight. Now don't make me sorry that I've asked for this favor. If Ralph thinks he can trust you, he might let you spend more time together."

The door closed and the outside lock clicked into place. Although they had been apart for only a week, it had seemed an eternity. She threw herself into his arms.

He hugged her tightly and then held her away by her shoulders. "You look pale. Has anyone hurt you?" he demanded.

She shook her head. "No. Actually, Ming has been nice to me."

"Good." Once again, he held her close. "I must smell like a sewer. Let's continue this in the shower."

Really, she didn't care that he smelled of sweat. It was pure heaven just to cling to him.

He gazed into her eyes and brushed stray tendrils of hair away from her temple. "Everything will be all right, sweetheart. Before you know it, you'll be back in the States and this will all seem like a bad dream." He smiled down at her and her heart sang with love for him.

He released her and went to the window. Tilting the slats of the shutters, he peered out. "Bloody hell. Mick's below. I didn't think they'd give us the chance to escape today. Come," he said, pulling her into the bathroom. "Take a shower with me. Let's put some color back into those cheeks."

She managed a smile. "I've missed you."

He shaved at the sink, amazed that a simple action returned a level of normalcy despite their daunting ordeal. They spoke little . . . being together was enough.

After stripping off their clothes, he reached for her. She sighed as he pulled her with him into the steamy shower. He washed his hair and scrubbed his body, then coaxed more smiles to her lips. She became lost in their foreplay.

With his fingers, Alex teased her until she writhed in ecstasy. "Alex, now, please . . . I can't take any more."

He led her out of the shower, and after wrapping a towel around him, he took another one and slowly dried her naked body. "I've dreamed of doing this."

"I have, too," she said breathlessly.

He swung her up in his arms and laid her on the bed. He kissed her lips and ran his hands all over her body. She threw her head back, completely lost to everything but what he did. He took his time nibbling down to her breasts. He trailed a blaze of kisses to her navel—and lower. She moaned with pleasure when he explored her intimately with his tongue and mouth, but whenever she came close to climaxing, he stopped and denied her release.

When he positioned himself on top of her, ready to thrust inside of her, she said, "No."

"No?" His expression and ramrod hard erection told her he'd have trouble stopping at this point.

"Not yet. I want to please you just as much."

"I can tell you I'm very well pleased at the moment."

"No, lie down." Letting her long hair glide teasingly across his bare, toned chest, she lowered her mouth to take little nibbles of his smooth skin, fresh from the shower. Kelly continued with her tongue, leaving a dampening trail downward. She lingered at his navel before she headed to her next destination. She returned his tantalizing foreplay and smiled to herself when he trembled and breathed just as heavily as she had.

He groaned. "Kelly, stop. Unless you want to end this now."

Only then did she allow him to enter her. She wrapped her legs around his hips, matching his rhythm.

When she climaxed, he murmured, "Oh, Kelly, love." Alex pulled her hips closer, thrusting deeper. He collapsed on top of her, that part of him still inside her.

After a deep sigh, he raised his head, his eyes drowsy with after-passion. "Sorry, Kelly. That's all we need. To worry about a pregnancy."

She smoothed the damp lock of hair that had fallen on his forehead. "It's okay. We might die on this island, and I want to experience all this closeness with you."

Alex held her close. "We'll find a way out of here." He propped up on his elbow. "I don't think we have much time left." He kissed her once more, and then rolled off the bed.

Kelly admired his naked body as he headed for the shower. After a languid stretch, she joined him in the refreshing water. If only he could stay here with her, she wouldn't be so afraid, or so unhappy.

When dressed, they sat on the bed and ate the food Ming had left.

Looking out the window, Kelly's gaze fell on a dark-haired man who strode up the hill toward the house. She gasped. "Who is that man?"

Frowning, Alex raised an eyebrow. "Ralph's brother and the head of the operation. He arrived this morning. Why?"

Her heart skipped a beat. "I'm pretty sure his name is David Lewis. He was the one who tried to take me from the dive boat. I think he killed my parents, too."

"Do you think he'll recognize you?"

Her stomach churned. "I don't know. I wore a wetsuit and diving gear, but my hair . . . He must have had some description of me when he looked for me on the dive boat."

"Try to stay out of his sight. If you have to confront him, act like you've never met him before." He gathered her in his arms, cupped her chin, and tilted her face toward his. "I know you can pull it off. You did a fine job with Ralph."

She sighed. "I've never been good at pretense. I hope he doesn't recognize me because Ming thinks Ralph will let us leave."

Alex shrugged. "So Ralph's said, but I don't trust them, Kelly. Not one bit. They're more despicable than you know."

"What do you mean?"

"Nothing." She frowned and asked again, but he shook his head and refused to say more except, "They have too much at stake to let us go. If there's a chance for escape, I'll come for you. Be prepared."

A shiver of panic ran through her. "If you can leave, save yourself. My father brought this all down on me. If he really did embezzle his client's money, I don't want you killed because of that."

Alex leaned his face against her hair. "Bloody hell, Kelly. Put that thought—I would leave you behind—out of your head."

"That scares me even more." Wincing, she put her hand to his cheek. "Please, I couldn't bear it if anything happened to you."

After a sharp rap on the door, Mick called out, "Time's up."

Alex squeezed her tightly. "Take care until I come for you."

She murmured into his chest, "I mean it, Alex, if it's too risky . . . I won't think any less of you if you go. You can send help for me—"

Mick thrust open the door. "I said honeymoon's over."

Alex's gaze seared hers as Mick escorted him by gunpoint from the room.

* * *

His muscles aching, Alex deposited the last valuable on a shelf. As he was led from the warehouse, he squinted and caught the sun's setting rays glinting on the cove. In the distance, a powerfully built man of huge proportions motored a small, rickety boat toward the dock.

Alex's stomach knotted. Ralph stepped down the sandy beach to greet their visitor.

Adjusting his camouflage cap, Mick grinned at Alex. "Moto's here to help on the next shipment. Can't speak two words of English, but we'll get the job done faster. He makes you guys look like a bunch of pansies."

If Mick meant to goad him, Alex didn't take the bait.

Ralph and the big islander headed up the hill. Moto halted when he neared Alex. His wide features registered surprise. He clenched his fists, then stalked with Ralph toward the house. Alex had the distinct feeling he'd not seen the last of Moto.

With a chuckle, Mick escorted Alex back to the bunkroom. "If looks could kill, you'd be six feet under and pushing up daisies. What did you ever do to him? Or it must be that face of yours that pisses everybody off."

Alex's jaw tightened, but he didn't comment. At the moment, he had more problems than Mick. He knew he didn't have the energy to confront Moto, not tonight, not handcuffed to a bed.

* * *

When Kelly entered the living area, she found David sitting with Ralph at the table, cards spread before them. A shiver of panic ran through her. She had thought David had left this morning when the yacht had sailed away with the workers to retrieve what Ming had told her would be the last shipment.

He seemed absorbed in the card game. Biting her lip, she settled on the sofa, keeping her back toward the men. If only she had a scarf to cover her incriminating hair color.

"So this is the woman who's staying here?" Her stomach clenched at David's deep voice. "We've not met."

Her throat went dry. She turned to see him watching her from the table and remembered those cruel, dark eyes and the zigzagged scar across his cheek from the dive boat. His piratical presence fit his smuggling operation.

Ralph put down his beer mug. "I told you about the young couple who wrecked their sailboat nearby."

Although she felt more like shrinking down into the couch, she brazened out David's intimidating stare. *Was he really responsible for her parents' deaths?*

David crossed the room and stood over her. "How long have you been stranded?"

"About a month," she lied.

"You must be anxious to return."

"We are." He couldn't know how desperately she wanted to be away from this place. She lied some more. "I'm sure someone will be looking for us, so if you could just help us get away, we will be less of a problem for you."

David glanced toward the table. "Ralph, you've searched them to make sure they're not cops?"

Ralph nodded. "Yeah, they're not."

"We can't be too careful." David's gaze settled on her face, appreciation gleaming in his dark eyes. "However, you are one beautiful woman."

"Thank you," she said not knowing what else to say. "My husband thinks so, too."

Glancing at her ring-less left hand, he lifted an eyebrow.

She cleared her throat. "I lost my ring when our sailboat sank."

He tipped his head in puzzlement. "There is something familiar about you. Have we met before?"

She practically choked. "N-no."

From the table, Ralph grunted. "Are we going to play cards or are you going to ogle her all night?"

David shrugged. "Oh, yeah, the game." He returned to the table.

Ming frowned at David when he walked away, then she placed a stack of movies before Kelly on the coffee table. "David always brings me the latest."

Kelly's heart hammered when she read one title, *The Spy*.

"Anything in particular you'd like to see?" Ming asked.

Kelly couldn't risk them recognizing Alex. She feared they might put two and two together and realize they were both from the exploded dive boat. Kelly pulled a comedy from the stack. "How about this one?"

Ming popped the DVD into the machine. Kelly exhaled a deep breath, trying to calm her racing heart. She had passed the first hurdle and sank back on the sofa. David hadn't recognized her.

As the evening wore on, the voices of the men grew louder. Kelly's stomach rolled from cigarette smoke that permeated the air.

"Damn you," Ralph growled. "Are you cheating again, David?"

David chuckled and slammed down a card. "You always were a sore loser, brother."

When the movie ended, Kelly whispered to Ming, "I'd like to go back to my room."

In the hall, Kelly whirled around at the sound of footsteps behind her. She gasped to find it was David.

His lip curled into a smile. "Did I frighten you? You know someone has to lock the door. I relieved Ming of that duty, but the jealous woman wasn't too happy about it."

The dim light highlighted the swirls of smoke in the air and gave him a threatening appearance. If he was trying to intimidate her, it worked. Her heart pounded as she retreated from him and bumped into the wall. Coming up closer, with one hand around her, he effectively trapped her and leaned toward her. She caught a strong whiff of whiskey.

He ran his finger down her cheek to her lips. "Why don't we scratch that itch together?"

Kelly shuddered and jerked her face away. "No. Let me go."

He ignored her request. "With your husband working hard for us, I thought you might enjoy a little company tonight."

"Not yours."

He grinned. "I like spunk in a woman, especially one in my safekeeping." His finger traced down to where Kelly's dress dipped into a 'V' and paused where her chest heaved in fear. He let his fingers linger. "You're sure now? Your husband never needs to know."

After squeezing out from behind him, Kelly fled into her room. She slammed the door shut and leaned against it, gasping for air. The handle turned. She shoved with all of her weight to keep him out.

David chuckled and said through the door, "Don't think I couldn't come in if I wanted to. Lucky for you I have Ming to satisfy my needs or your ass would be flat on that mattress."

The lock clicked into place, securing her in the room. She sagged against the door, trembling from head to toe. His hearty laughter grew fainter as he went down the hall.

* * *

The next evening Kelly stared out the window and wrung her hands together. Now, she couldn't even leave the room for fear she'd run into David.

When the door opened, her heart leaped in her chest. She exhaled in relief at seeing Ming, but that didn't last long. "Kelly, David says you're to come out."

"Tell him I don't feel well."

Not wanting to hurt Ming, Kelly refrained from saying David was a two-timing slug, but from Ming's somber attitude as she turned to go, she probably already knew.

"Please, wait," Kelly cried. "Can you arrange for me to see Alex again?"

"David won't allow it." After Ming left, Kelly sat on the bed and dropped her face into her hands. They had to find a way out of here and fast.

A minute later, David flung open the door and stalked toward her. "Come out, princess, unless you want me to join you on that bed."

Fear gripping her, Kelly jumped to her feet. "I-I'll come out."

He grabbed her elbow in a tight grip and jerked her to his chest. "Don't forget this is *my* island. I make the rules. And if I want you, I'll take you. If you prove to be good, you might even persuade me to help you and your husband leave sooner."

Kelly yanked her arm from his grasp. He was worse than Ralph. He may have been forced into this line of work, but this man obviously enjoyed the power he wielded over others.

She headed to the living area and dropped onto the sofa next to Ming as if Ming could protect her. Ming turned on the DVD. When the movie began, Kelly's heart slammed in her chest. Oh, no. Not *The Spy*. The blood rushed to her head.

"Popcorn?" Ming asked, passing a bowl to Kelly.

Kelly shook her head. Somehow, she had to stop Ming. "Oh, but I've seen this one. Why don't we watch something else?"

"Couldn't have. It's newly released and received excellent reviews. There's an interesting story. Only several months ago, the lead actor died in a terrible boating accident, not far from here."

"Oh?" was all Kelly could think to comment. Apparently, Ming didn't know about the attempted kidnapping and explosion, or David's involvement. Kelly glimpsed him out of the corner of her eye. David stared at them, then returned his attention to the game. Kelly swallowed her fear.

Obviously a fan of tabloid news, Ming shuffled through her stash of magazines lying on the coffee table. "Alex Drake was married to Vanessa Caine. They say she took his death badly." Ming handed Kelly a magazine. "But she's all recovered and will be shooting the film that stalled before the accident. I just love her, don't you?"

"Not really," Kelly answered truthfully. Frowning, she returned the magazine. She didn't want to read about Vanessa, or see her in a designer gown, smiling as if she hadn't a care in the world, while their lives hung at the mercy of killers. "Ming, can we please watch something else?" She reached for the stack of movies.

"I insist. Give it a chance."

To stop Ming, she'd have to wrestle the movie from her, which would only draw more attention. She only hoped Alex wouldn't be recognized. She glanced over her shoulder, glad to find the men absorbed in their card game. Perhaps her fears were groundless. How could anyone connect a movie star with the down and out people they had become?

After the camera angled across London, Kelly found herself engrossed. *The Spy* was humorous, and action-packed with karate fights and car-chase scenes. Funny as Jack Stone, Alex was a secret agent who always managed to get himself in over his head. Somehow, he always managed to get himself out of the predicament, too. He kissed three women within twenty minutes of the movie's opening and had one sensual bedroom scene where he was completely naked from the back. She covered her eyes, unable to watch him make love to another woman, even if it was only pretend.

David's chair crashed backwards, startling Kelly. He jumped to his feet, his gaze riveted on the TV. "Alex Douglas, my ass. Mick, bring him up here."

CHAPTER THIRTEEN

When the lights clicked on, Alex squinted and rolled to his back.

Ralph leaned over him and roughly unlocked the handcuffs. "Get up."

Stone-faced, Mick stood a few feet away with his magnum trained on Alex.

The look on their faces made him uneasy as Alex rose from the bed. "What's the problem?"

Ralph re-cuffed Alex's hands behind his back with a jerk. "You'll find out soon enough."

A wave of trepidation spread through Alex as he was escorted upstairs to where David sat with a semi-automatic lying near him on the table. Taking one glance at Kelly's pale face as she sat on the couch, Alex swore under his breath. *They knew.*

Ralph shoved Alex into one of the wooden chairs at the table. David clicked on the DVD player and let the film run for a minute.

"Enough?" David lifted a sardonic eyebrow. He turned off the TV and slammed his fist on the table, sending cards and money scattering. "You're the damned actor in the movie and you didn't sink some sailboat."

Pulse racing, Alex tried to think of a reasonable explanation for keeping their identities a secret. "We thought if you knew, you might hold us for ransom."

From the sofa, Ming clapped her hands in delight. "A movie star. Of course, you're so handsome. And Vanessa is the most wonderful actress. . ." She gaped at Kelly. "But all of this time you told us you were his *wife.*"

"She's not his *wife,*" David ground out.

Alex gritted his teeth at the lewd look David gave Kelly. "Vanessa Caine is my *ex*-wife. Kelly's with me."

"Your *lover?*" David sneered. He strode to Alex and glared down at him. "Ralph, he is correct about the ransom. Instead of working for us, he'll be more valuable in other ways."

"I'm willing to pay whatever you want if you'll let us leave," Alex said in agreement. They were in such trouble at this point, maybe offering large sums of money would help.

"Oh, yeah," David scoffed. "I'm to let you go and trust you'll send the money back to me. Hardly." He paced the floor. "Ralph, get in touch with this Vanessa Caine."

"She won't pay. We're divorced," Alex pointed out. "She may sooner see me dead."

David whirled on him. "She just might get her wish." He tapped Ming on the shoulder. "You said the movie was a hit."

Ming blinked. "Yes."

"Good." David gloated at Alex. "When it's discovered you're alive, there will be money for your return." He waved the gun under Alex's nose. "Give Ralph the details on how we can contact this actress."

Alex frowned. "There's no deal unless Kelly goes with me."

"You're in no fucking position to bargain, Hollywood."

Elbowing David, Mick guffawed, "What kind of movies is he in, boss? How about him and the girl giving us a little show? Maybe we'll make our own *movies*, if you know what I mean." Alex gritted his teeth at what Mick was alluding to.

Ming said, "He can sing—"

"Yeah, I can sing and dance, and play guitar," Alex said sarcastically, "but not with my hands tied behind my back." He needed to get free of the handcuffs. If he had the guitar as a weapon, maybe he could go for one of the guns.

"Come on, David," Ming cried. "I'd like to hear him sing. We have so little entertainment around here. I'll get the guitar."

"Not quite the *skin show* I had in mind," Mick muttered.

"*No,*" David roared. "*No show.*"

Then he thrust his face at Alex and exclaimed in a mocking voice, "Because it doesn't matter what kind of entertainment you two provide for us, or if I get ransom money for you, because I know you were *both* on the diving boat, and she's *Kelly Cochran.* Her father cheated me out of millions, so she isn't going anywhere until I get my hands on my money." He crossed the floor to Kelly. "Damned bitch, you've caused me a lot of trouble."

Kelly shrank back, but he grasped her wrist and yanked her off the couch and up against him as if she weighed nothing. Her hair tumbled wildly around her.

Alex's jaw tightened. He attempted to rise, but Ralph and Mick jammed him into the chair, clamping their hands down on his shoulders.

"How did you manage to survive?" David asked, circling his arms around Kelly.

She shoved her palms again his chest. "Alex saved my life. We made it to an island."

David gripped her chin, forcing her head up. "You must have been a charming companion these last three months."

She slapped at his hands. "How did you know I'd be on that dive boat?"

His smile showed he enjoyed her outrage as David grabbed her wrists. "I was tipped off. I intended to take you alive, but the explosion happened. I thought you were dead. Now, as I originally planned, you're going to take me to my money, plus everyone else's."

Kelly shoved against him. "My father wouldn't steal."

He laughed bitterly. "Oh, no? Richard Cochran deluded many people before he skipped town with millions. He ruined my life."

"You ran from the police. You caused the plane to crash."

"What if I did?" David asked. "He deserved to die."

She pounded her fists into his chest. "My mother was on that plane, too. You killed my mother, you bastard."

He slapped Kelly. She sagged into his arms. "If anything happened to Cochran and his wife, he was entirely to blame for it. He screwed everyone, so don't push me, bitch."

Alex's hands tightened into fists behind his back. "Only a *coward* would make a daughter pay for her father's sins."

David snorted and dragged Kelly toward Alex. "Coward? When I'm finished with her, I'll give *you* a damned lesson in cowardice."

"Let her go," Alex demanded. David raised his fist in Alex's face and he flinched, preparing to be struck.

"I'm sorry to have gotten you into this trouble, Alex," Kelly cried.

David burst out in laughter and didn't strike him. "She's mine now, Hollywood. All of her." He wrapped his arm around Kelly and pinched her cheek. "Your lover's not too happy he'll be leaving you behind as soon as we get the ransom, but I'm glad you didn't die."

Kelly struggled against David's chest. "I'm not staying with you, you bastard."

"You little hellcat." David twisted her arm behind her. She yelped as he hauled her to a chair and brought her down upon his lap. His hands on her back tangled into her long hair and forced her against his chest. "I'll convince you to take me to the money, but damn I didn't think I would enjoy it so much. Lucky for me you are a beauty. Fancy me having Richard Cochran's daughter to do with as I please. Kill her if I want. Have her if I want. What sweet revenge."

Unbridled anger rose in Alex. "She told you she doesn't know about any stashed money."

"I believe them." Ming wrung her hands together. "Haven't you been bitter over this long enough? She can't undo what her father did to you."

David grabbed Kelly's chin. "Then you'll pay with your skin for every dollar your father stole from me, if I have to sell you into prostitution on the white-slave market. I think the Orient would be a good place to start. They'll love the novelty of your blue eyes and red hair."

When he laid his palm over her breast, she slapped his hand away.

Although his hands were cuffed behind his back, Alex couldn't stop his rage. He broke free of Mick and Ralph's hold. When he shouldered Mick in the ribs, the magnum flew from Mick's hand.

Alex headed toward David, but he was shoved him from behind. Unable to catch his fall, Alex slammed into the wall. Pain shot through his head and shoulder, and he crumpled to the floor. Darkness threatened to engulf him.

"Alex," Kelly cried.

With his cheek pressed against the rough wooden boards, he opened his eyes and met her worried gaze. He had failed her. "I'm sorry, Kelly."

Mick jammed a booted foot into Alex's back. "Damn it. If you do anything like that again, you'll make it back to L.A. in a body bag."

Mick bound Alex's ankles with painful jerks of a rope.

"I know how you feel, Hollywood. *Impotent*," David said, standing over him, with his arms around Kelly. "Just like her father made me feel. Now, she's landed in my hands, literally. We're going to her room, where she'll talk and do much, much more."

She twisted against David's hold. "No."

"Why not? You're just a whore for that actor, and you're mine until you come up with my money." David wagged his fist in Kelly's face. "I don't want to mess up the merchandise, baby, so don't make me bruise you too much, but damn it, how can I convince you?"

He shot a glance toward Alex. Abruptly, he thrust Kelly toward Ralph. "Don't let her run." With a sneer on his face, David kicked Alex in the side. In excruciating pain, Alex doubled over on his stomach. "Enough, *Miss* Cochran?" David asked. "Or do you want me to hurt him—badly?"

"Please, don't," Kelly pleaded. "I'll go with you."

"Don't, Kelly," Alex said with a groan.

David picked up a gun and crouched beside Alex, pressing the barrel to his temple. "I don't have to return you at all to collect the ransom. What was that you called me, Alex? A *coward*? Not wise when I'm holding a gun." Alex glared back at him.

"David, stop," Ming cried.

"I'll do anything you say," Kelly begged. "Just please don't kill him."

"Ah, the lady pulls through for her lover." David's eyes glittered as he withdrew the gun from Alex's temple. "You're a lucky man. I wasn't prepared to make a mess in the house. However, I can't let you off the hook for that 'coward' comment."

He raised the magnum in the air and crashed the butt down on Alex's head.

Pain exploded through him.

* * *

Kelly tried to run to Alex, but David grasped her and pulled her away.

Turning on him, she slammed her fists into his chest. "Why did you have to hit him? I told you I would do what you wanted."

He clasped his arm around her waist, hurting her. "I didn't kill him, just like you asked." He jerked his thumb at Alex. "Mick, take our *movie star* downstairs to the bunks. Make sure he's doubly secured at all times."

Tears flowed down her cheeks as Kelly watched Mick and Ralph drag Alex from the room.

"Ming, come." David propelled Kelly down the hall and into her bedroom.

Inside, he released her wrist. "You lover's not dead yet, and won't be, as long as you do as I say. Ming, find something pretty for her to wear. You know what I like."

"Yes, David." With a dark, angry expression hardening her face, Ming turned and left.

David's gaze smoldered with heat and swept over Kelly. "Change into whatever she brings. I'll be right back. Remember, I expect your full cooperation. Later, after you've satisfied me, we'll talk about my money."

After David left the bedroom, Ming returned with a black negligee, thong panties, and a pair of high-heeled shoes. She held out the articles to Kelly. "These are mine. David likes them."

Kelly stood frozen by the door. "I'm not wearing those things."

"I wouldn't cross him."

"Oh, how can I do this?" Kelly cried, her shoulders sagging. "But if I don't, he'll hurt Alex."

She swiped at her tears with the back of her hand and went into the bathroom to change. Through the partially opened door, she pleaded, "Ming, please, help us escape. You can come with us."

"Me? Where would I go? What would I do?"

One glance in the mirror told Kelly she might as well have worn nothing in the single layer of sheer silk. She crossed her arms over her chest and stepped out of the bathroom. "We'll get the money for you to start over."

"I love David. Life with him is all I want."

Kelly expelled a breath. "Then how can you let him do this to me?"

At the loud rap on the door, and in spite of the balmy breeze through the window a shiver ran up her Kelly's spine. "Please, Ming . . . you . . . you have to stop him."

"I can't—"

David thrust open the door and stepped into the room. Ming sulked past him and closed the bedroom door behind her, leaving Kelly with him . . . alone.

David stared at her. "Hey, sexy. Come here. You might like it. Ming tells me I'm a great lover."

"Please don't do this?" Trembling, she twisted the fabric of the negligee in her hands.

He traced the white line slashing his cheek. "Am I not handsome enough? I got this scar escaping from the police when they tried to arrest me for murdering your father. Do you want me to tell you all he's done to me? I'm warning you. I might really get pissed off and not go easy on you. Now, why not relax and enjoy it?"

She crossed her arms. "Drop dead. I'm only doing this for Alex."

"Have it your way." He shoved her onto the bed. Her stomach heaved as he threw himself on top of her. He tried to kiss her, but she turned her head. Every impulse in her wanted to fight him—and she would have, except for Alex. She tasted her salty tears and let the sobs overtake her. She didn't fight him, but she'd never enjoy anything with this man.

His wet lips nuzzled her earlobe. "That's better."

She shuddered with disgust. "I hate you."

He squeezed her shoulders. "Good. Maybe night after night of my loving will convince you to take me to the money. Did your old man stash it in some foreign bank account?"

"I don't know what happened to the money," she said through her quivering lips.

When he fondled her breasts through the sheer negligee, revulsion rose in her throat. "I'm going to be sick."

"No, you're not."

She lay stiffly, trying to think of other things to take her mind away from what David did to her.

"Good, that's better." He ran his hands over her back and hips, and she endured it for Alex. However, when he slipped his hand between her thighs, bile rose in her throat. On reflex, she kneed him in the groin.

Doubling over, he shot out a fist, striking her cheek. "You bitch."

She slumped across the bed, hoping she'd lose consciousness. Unfortunately, the darkness receded.

"Damn you, you bitch." The mattress moved as he rolled from the bed. "Pull another stunt like that and the next beating for your boyfriend will make the last look like child's play."

Squeezing her eyes shut, she pressed her hands together and bowed her head. "I'm sorry. I'm sorry. Don't hurt him. I'll do whatever you say."

"You bet you will." He yanked open the door. "Maybe a little starvation will make you more cooperative. Ming," he yelled into the hallway. "No food for her, and no food or water for Hollywood until I say so."

He glanced back at Kelly. "You'll come to me willingly and you'll give me the answers I want about the money." He slammed the door behind him and the lock clicked into place.

* * *

Ming sighed in relief when David emerged so quickly from the bedroom. Had he realized how much she'd be hurt by his actions? She stood in the kitchen, while he sat hunched over his cards in the living area, but he didn't even glance her way.

Grinning, Ralph slapped a card down on the table. "You weren't gone long."

"You want the truth? The damn bitch kneed me in the balls."

Ming steadied her hand on the counter. His feelings for her had nothing to do with why he left Kelly so soon.

"Maybe I'm more her type," Ralph said with a chuckle.

Mick hooted with laughter. "Neither of you could pass for a movie star, so I'm definitely the next best looking man here. I'll have her squealing—"

"Kelly is mine." David smacked a card down on the table. "After some convincing, I'll have the Cochran bitch begging for me before the week is out, *and* I'll get my money. That amount of cash is not just misplaced."

Ralph said, "And how do you propose to manage this feat?"

He steepled his hands on the table. "Her boyfriend's the ace-in-the-hole to make her do whatever I want. Tomorrow, Mick, I want you to chain Hollywood in one of the smaller closets in the warehouse. He needs to be secured. He's not to be ransomed until I get my money from the Cochran bitch." He rubbed his chin. "Before we put him away, I'll rough him up again real good in front of the girl. Then he can go rot away in darkness until she does exactly what I want. She'll come around."

Too absorbed in their game, the men didn't see Ming's back grow rigid.

* * *

Alex's throbbing head tugged him from oblivion . . . and to awareness that his ribs hurt like hell, and he had the metallic taste of blood in his mouth. Memories of what had happened flooded his mind. *Kelly.* When he raised his head, pain shot through his entire body. Groaning, he closed his eyes. Slowly testing his arms, he discovered not only was he secured to the bed frame with the handcuffs, but his feet were bound and tied to the footboard.

How long had he been unconscious? No light filtered through the shutters and only dim light filtered under the door.

With great effort, and enough slack of the rope at his ankles, he twisted onto his stomach. The throbbing pain in his lower back a reminder of how vital it was for them to leave immediately. Stretching sent agony screaming through his back, but that was the only way he could reach the switchblade. He grasped the knife and worked, shaving away more of the wood slat.

Finally, he yanked the chain, hoping to break through, but the wood didn't snap. His heart raced. If he couldn't break free, there would be no way to hide the damage to the bed for another night. Using all of his strength, he yanked again. The weakened wood splintered.

Fairly certain he'd not made too much noise, he expelled a deep breath. He loosened the knots of the rope binding his ankles to the end of the bed.

As soon as he rose from the bed, the door opened and quickly closed again. He had the advantage for his eyes were accustomed to the absence of light. He jumped the figure from behind and put the handcuffs against the small person's throat. Not any man on this island. Not Kelly either—he'd know her body anywhere.

Alex loosened his hold. "Ming?"

"Yes. I want to help you and Kelly escape."

After he released her, she flicked on the light switch. She rubbed her throat with her hand.

"Why would you help us?" he said in a hoarse voice. "Bloody hell, is this another sadistic game you people are playing? I leave this room and someone jumps me?"

"No, but you two are nothing but trouble. David told me the dive boat explosion was an accident." She held up a small key. "I don't think he killed her father either."

Alex thrust out his hands, and she unlocked the handcuffs. Now, he had a fighting chance. He rubbed his sore wrists.

"I love David, and this revenge is eating him alive. Kelly is right too. I won't share him."

They slipped outside into the night where a sliver of moon cast a dim light as they strode around to the side of the house.

Ming handed Alex a basket. "David's hatred for what Richard Cochran did to him has been brewing for too many years. You both need to get away from here. They're playing cards upstairs in the living room. You wait here. I'll get a rope and Kelly can climb out the window." She held out another key. "This is to the smaller speedboat. A guard won't be posted on the dock tonight since the captain has taken the yacht."

"Ming, you're taking a chance to help us. Thank you."

"Good luck and go quickly. Don't make me sorry I helped you. I don't want to see what he'll do to you if he catches you." She entered the house while Alex waited in the shadows.

* * *

When the door squeaked open, Kelly scrambled from the bed with a strangled gasp.

The light flipped on. "Ming," she cried in relief. "Thank goodness it's you." Then fear assailed her. "Alex is he . . . Is he all right?"

"Yes, and he's waiting below. You have to go out the window." Ming handed Kelly the rope. "Quickly."

Hope bubbled inside her at the sight of Alex standing below. She paused and turned to Ming. "Are you coming with us? David will be so angry with you."

Ming shook her head. "I'll hide the evidence I helped."

Kelly contemplated the three-story drop, realizing she wasn't afraid of going down as much as staying.

Seconds later her hands burned as she slipped down the rope, inch by inch.

When she reached the ground, Alex wrapped her in his arms. "Are you all right, love?"

Nodding, she sighed into his chest. "And you?"

He released her. "My head's killing me, but we've got to get out of here."

They crept around the side of the house. Ahead of them a cigarette glowed. *Mick.* Alex clenched Kelly's arm and pulled her back into the shadows. "For once I don't think the bastard has a gun in his hand. Stay here."

Alex rushed the man from behind and slammed Mick's head several times against the wall, then took the rope and bound Mick's legs and arms and tied him to a tree. "Works as well for him as it did for me. Let's go."

Through darkness, Alex and Kelly raced hand-in-hand down the hill toward the glistening water. Her heart pounded madly. They were almost to the bottom, when shouts rang out. Footsteps echoed as people chased them down the hill.

David shouted, "Stop, or I'll shoot."

Alex clasped Kelly's elbow. "We don't have time to untie the boat and start the engine before they'll be on us. Come."

He dragged her away from the direction of the dock and toward the beach. Every inch of her body trembled with fear. She ran with him, knowing they fled for their lives.

* * *

"Damn it to hell. We've lost them." David stamped his foot on the wooden dock. He turned to Ralph and paused. "But where *are* they going to go? I'll have Moto track them tonight. If he doesn't find them, in the morning, you, Mick and I'll take the rifles."

"Where the hell *is* Mick?"

David handed Ralph the flashlight. "I don't know. You take the first watch. I have Ming to deal with. If I hadn't seen her coming out of Kelly's room, I wouldn't have thought to check on her. I know Ming will deny it, but if she's helped them, I'll wring the jealous bitch's neck."

David stalked off the dock. He paused and glanced over his shoulder. "Ralph, I want the girl alive."

"And Alex?"

"I want them both alive, but if he gets in the way—*kill him.*"

* * *

Kelly sank to her knees in the wet sand. "I can't run any farther."

Alex kneeled beside her. "That's all right because I don't think they're following us any longer."

"No?" she said, her breathing coming in rasps. "Maybe they'll let us go?"

"They're not coming after us because they know we have nowhere to go."

"Then they'll guard the boats and know we're stuck here."

He nodded. "Yes." He held out his hand and helped her to her feet. "Let's find a place to rest."

"But what will we do?" she asked as she trudged with him to a stand of coconut palms.

He paused, and after a moment of silence, he said, "I think I have an idea. From a film."

Kelly gaped and then blurted, "We're going to risk our lives on some make-believe plan?"

"You have any other ideas, love?"

Her shoulders drooped. "No."

"Then I'll swim down the shore and take the speedboat from the water. I don't think they'll expect it. I'll come back here for you."

"You're not going without me," she blurted.

"Bloody hell, Kelly. It's too risky."

"It's too risky for you, too. You might need my help. You're already hurt. The beating he gave you—"

Alex exhaled in exasperation. "All right, we go together, but if we're caught, Kelly, I don't know what's going to happen."

She nodded, knowing what they faced—some form of torture and maybe death.

"Let's rest here, love."

They sat under the group of palms, the fronds rustling in the breeze. He leaned back against the trunk of a tree and gathered her in his arms.

She touched his cheek. "I was so afraid for you. Are you going to be able to do this tonight?"

"We can't wait for me to recover. They'll look for us tomorrow. It'll be much harder to hide in the daylight. After things settle down, we go." He stroked the fabric of her black negligee. "Did he hurt you?" he asked softly.

"He tried to force himself on me. I tried to give in for you, but I couldn't help myself. When he touched me, I kneed him and stopped his amorous ideas pretty quickly. He hit me for it, but I'm afraid I could've gotten you *killed.*"

"The bastard. I'm glad you did it."

She opened the basket Ming had given them and picked up a stack of bills. "Ming must have anticipated we'd need money."

Alex stuffed the cash into his pockets, while she pulled out bottles of water and several cold-cut sandwiches. Despite all that had happened, they both ate quickly. From their days of hunger, they'd both learned to eat when food was available.

After about an hour, he said, "Let's give it a go, love."

They strode down the beach to about two hundred yards away from the long pier. Dim solar dock lights illuminated three boats—a sailboat, and two other craft built for speed.

Alex stripped off his shirt and tucked it into the waistband of his shorts. He gave her a quick kiss on the lips. "Say a prayer. Even the swim might be treacherous with sharks."

Slowly, they swam toward the boats. At the final forty feet, she followed Alex's lead and dove underwater and resurfaced under the dock. Peering out, Kelly spotted Ralph seated at the entrance to the dock, facing the house. Abruptly, he stood. A tight knot formed in Kelly's stomach.

Alex clasped her elbow and pulled her under the dock. They waited while Ralph trampled the planks over their heads. His footsteps retreated, indicating he had walked back to his chair. Kelly exhaled the breath she'd been holding.

"I'll climb the ladder," Alex whispered. "Once I'm certain he hasn't seen me, I'll wave for you to come aboard."

Shivering, she caught his arm. "He'll catch us."

"Not if I can help it." He shrugged. "At least it worked in the film."

She frowned. His words did not reassure her.

The boat rocked on gentle waves. She cringed at every slight squeak the ladder made as he climbed. Once he was on the dive platform, he leaned over and motioned for her to follow.

When she stepped up the ladder, the cool water plastered the sheer negligee to her like a second skin. Alex grasped her hand and helped her onboard. She crouched beside him on the deck of the boat.

"I can't untie the lines without him seeing me," he whispered. "I don't recall that part in the film. I'll have to improvise to get Ralph over here."

Improvise? Here? What did he plan to do? She bit her lip and her stomach churned as he crossed to the helm and picked up a shiny gold lighter from the dashboard. "Stay down." He tossed the lighter on the dock.

She kept her head low while Ralph's footsteps pounded across the wooden boards toward them and the sound of the object that Alex had thrown. Alex vaulted off the boat. Her heart slammed in her chest as she peered over the edge to see him landing on Ralph's back. They both crashed to the dock.

"Help," Ralph shouted.

They rolled around.

Kelly jumped to the dock and untied the back rope.

She glanced to see Alex punch Ralph in the mouth, silencing him.

Ralph went for his gun and they wrestled for the weapon. A blast pierced the night air.

Fear paralyzed Kelly. Both Alex and Ralph lay in a heap on the dock. After what seemed an eternity, Alex rolled off Ralph. Dark stains covered both of them.

As if shocked by the moment, Alex scooped up Ralph's semi-automatic and backed away, gaping at the still man. "I think he's dead."

She grasped Alex's arm and pulled him away from Ralph's lifeless body. "It was either you or him, and I'm glad about the outcome. Let's go. It'll be a matter of minutes before they're all down here."

While she untied the front rope, Alex leaped onto the boat and tried the engine. "Come on . . . Bloody hell, start."

She climbed back in and shoved away from the dock, pushing the boat out into the cove. It slowly floated away.

He turned the key again. "The engine won't turn over."

Massive footsteps pounded like beating drums across the wooden dock. Moto dove into the water with a huge splash.

In a few powerful strokes, the giant reached the boat. With a wide grin, he took the first rung of the ladder.

Kelly grabbed an oar and whacked him on the head. "Grin at this, you son of a bitch."

He plunged into the dark water and came up sputtering.

She stepped to the console. "Hurry, Alex. Please hurry."

He turned the key again. The twin engines rumbled to life. They exhaled in mutual relief.

Kelly swiped her perspiring forehead. "Thank, God."

He pushed the throttle forward and the boat glided out of the cove.

She turned to see David hitting the dock, running.

He knelt over Ralph's lifeless form. "*No!*" he bellowed.

His rage confirmed their suspicion that Ralph was dead. David lifted his gun. A shot crackled in the night air and struck the control panel.

"Get the gun, Kelly. Shoot back."

She did as he requested, but as she held the gun and aimed, she trembled so much, she couldn't keep her hands from sweeping back and forth in an unsteady arc.

Alex glanced back at her as another shot plugged the dashboard.

"Kelly. Drive. They're going to follow us in the other boat." He grabbed the gun from her and fired as she took over the wheel. "Mick's gotten free, and he's running down the hill. Pick up your speed."

Alex crouched down at the back of the boat and fired several shots. A sudden explosion pounded Kelly's ears.

She whipped her head to look over her shoulder. What had been the other speedboat was now a tower of flames. "*Whohoo*, Alex. Great shot. You took out the other speedboat. You're incredible."

Alex stood watching. "Not intended, Kelly."

She frowned. "What?"

"Lucky shot. I aimed at Mick, but I was a bit off, don't you think, since he's about thirty feet away from the boat that I hit?" He shot her a cocky grin, his teeth gleaming white in the dark night. "But I'll take it. We need some luck. Now they can only follow us in the sailboat."

"Oh, no, Alex," Kelly cried. "Mick's picking up a rifle. We've got to get out of here." She turned back to the console, periodically peering over her shoulder at what was happening on the island. Alex was crouched at the back of the boat. Aiming the gun with both hands, he fired. This time he must have hit Mick in the leg because Mick dropped to his knees.

David grabbed the rifle from Mick's hands and aimed toward them.

With a hand on her shoulder, Alex pushed her to the floor. "Get down, Kelly, and stay down. Don't get up until I tell you it's safe."

He took control of the boat and rammed the throttle into full speed, and the boat lurched forward. She clung to the base of the captain's chair and her hip pounded against the floor with each wave as they roared out into the open ocean.

More gunshots rang in the night and several slammed into the console. Alex let out a loud groan. "Ouch. Bloody, damn hell. Damn it."

"What is it?" she cried.

"Just stay down, Kelly," he ordered.

After they drove for several more minutes, the boat slowed.

A little shaken, but relieved, Kelly asked, "Are we at a safe distance now so that I can get up?"

"Yeah, should be. You'll have to drive." When she stood, he staggered toward her. Her arms went around him. His was breathing jerky and labored. He leaned on her. She brushed his back and brought her hand away covered with blood.

"Oh, my God. You've been shot."

CHAPTER FOURTEEN

While the boat rocked on the waves, Kelly supported Alex to the bench seating along the stern of the boat. His trembling alarmed her. After all they'd been through, he couldn't die on her now.

Putting his hand over his shoulder to cover the wound, he sat with a groan. "Hurts badly, Kelly."

"Let me see if I can find bandages."

Her stomach churned with anxiety as she hurried below. In minutes, she returned with the first aid kit and a towel. After flipping on a deck light, she leaned over him and inspected the wound. Blood oozed. "Thankfully, it's only your shoulder, but I need to get this bleeding stopped."

She pressed the towel to his wound. "Now aren't you glad I came along with you?" she asked, trying to sound calm and light for his sake. Inside her nerves quaked. "I don't suppose the hero was shot in the movie version?"

"In the film, they got off without a hitch. But it worked for us, love. We did get away."

"Yes, *we* did." Her hands shook as she tied the bandage. He grimaced. She bit her lip. "Sorry. Now, you're going below while I drive this thing. Just point me in the direction you want to go."

"Help me to the console." He staggered to the captain's chair and set the waypoints on the Global Positioning System. "Kelly, all you have to do is follow the arrows. I've set the GPS for Nadi, Fiji. There's an airport."

After she led him down to one of the staterooms and helped him strip off his wet clothing, he eased onto the bed. Something tightened in her chest at the sight of the many bruises covering his naked body.

"Kelly," he said through chattering teeth. "I'll rest for a while. Wake me soon?"

"Sure." Tears slipped down her cheeks as she spread a sheet and blanket over him. She put her hand to his face. "Are you going to be okay?"

"I'll be as good as new . . . soon," he said with a groan that didn't reassure her. "And I'm not too concerned they'll catch us with their sailboat, but we still need to get to Fiji and the police quickly. David may have notified his friends. He also knows what Ming probably didn't. With the GPS, the authorities will be able to backtrack to the island because I saved the coordinates. He'll be hell-bent to stop us, love. It's up to you . . ." He closed his eyes.

"*Alex*," she cried. She lifted his limp wrist. She'd never dealt with a seriously injured person before. She felt for a pulse and was relieved it was steady. She lay his hand down and tucked the blankets in around him.

Then she ran her fingers through her hair and blew out a deep breath as she returned to the cockpit. Alex had to be okay.

She sat down in the captain's chair that smelled of new leather. Obviously, David's smuggling business was lucrative, judging by the ultra-luxurious features of the vessel.

Her father had taken her with friends on excursions, but she'd never done much more than steer. Now, their lives depended on her getting them back to civilization.

"I can do this." She brushed the stray curls from her perspiring forehead. With one last glance toward David's cutthroat island blanketed in darkness beneath the stars, she pushed the dual throttles forward and the boat moved through the water.

As steered the boat, she was sure she would bless this GPS for the rest of her life. It made guiding the boat easy. It pointed to the Fiji mainland on a small screen and chirped when she strayed off course. Although she was exhausted, she had to get Alex to a hospital. She drove the boat straight through the remainder of the night, only taking short breaks to check on him.

Not long after the sun rose over the horizon, she spotted land. With a deep sigh, she glanced down at the sheer black negligee she still wore. It blew like fine gauze in the breeze. She needed to find something decent for them both to wear before heading into port.

She pulled back on the throttle and stepped down to the stateroom. After a quick, cold, reviving shower, she leaned over the bed where Alex lay twisted in the sheets. She touched his hot forehead, then patted his cheeks. "Wake up, baby. Wake up."

He opened his eyes and blinked.

"We're almost there. I've got to get you to a doctor. I'll be right back with something for you to wear."

With a quick search of the stateroom's closet, she found a blue sundress for herself and jeans and a shirt for him. "Here, put these on." After she pulled on the sundress, she helped him dress. "Now, go back to sleep. I'll wake you when we get to the dock."

She drove into the inlet. When she reached the docks, she scraped the edge of the boat, but she didn't care. Waving her arms, she caught the attention of one kind tourist who took a glance at Alex and stopped a taxi. She told the driver they didn't have a lot of money. He sped them to a free clinic.

Once inside, Kelly frowned at the filth, but they could hardly walk out now as they had barely enough money to cover plane fare.

The staff there allowed her to stay with Alex. As he lay on his side on an examination table, she held his hand and his gaze, while an elderly, American doctor injected a local anesthetic into his shoulder.

"Got yourselves into some kind of trouble?" the doctor asked with a sweeping gaze over them. Then he returned to work on removing the bullet . . .

"Yes. I'm going to report it to the police." Kelly explained what had happened and how David Lewis's accomplices might be in hot pursuit.

The doctor finished with thick bandages. "You have a slight concussion, son, and you're going to be sore for while." He handed Alex a bottle. "Take these antibiotics and pain pills." Then he held up a huge needle, and lifted Alex's hospital gown, prepared to inject him in the backside.

Making a face, Alex squeezed his eyes shut. "Bloody hell, Kelly, I hate pills and shots."

Giving him an encouraging smile, she gripped his fingers. "Come on. This is going to make you feel better."

After enduring the shot, he hauled himself up to sitting position on the table. "If you say so." He swayed and the doctor caught his arm. "Not so fast." After placing Alex's arm in a sling, he said, "The shot and a night at the clinic will have you on the mend."

"But he can't stay," Kelly blurted. "I'm afraid they're looking for us. But can he rest here while I file a report with the Fiji Police?"

* * *

Kelly made arrangements with the American and British consulates for passports so they could leave the country immediately. Several hours had passed by the time she rushed back to the hospital.

She smiled that a little color had returned to Alex's face. "I hope you're feeling up to traveling. I've spent most of Ming's money on flights to Hawaii. We are *so* out of here."

They took the first cab. When a car followed closely, she glanced out the rear window to see two men, looking like they could fit the profile of David's accomplices, trailing behind them.

She clutched Alex's arm as they walked through the airport. When she looked over her shoulder and saw the same two men behind them, her knees nearly buckled. "Alex, I think we're being followed."

He clenched her hand. When they passed an elevator almost full of people, he said, "Get on." They quickly stepped inside. They went up another floor and took another elevator down, and continued toward their gate.

It wasn't until they were boarding the plane, that the tension faded from Kelly's shoulders. She sighed. "Thank, God, we lost them and we're on our way home."

An attractive brunette flight attendant stopped Alex as soon as they stepped on. "Mr. Drake, we've heard the news that you're alive. Since the flight's not full, we have room in first class. Let me show you to your seats."

Once they were seated, the other female attendants swarmed around Alex, and he was the celebrity of the moment. One pretty blonde fawned all over him. "I'll personally wait on you for the duration of the trip." She winked at him before she walked off to assist another passenger.

Alex's eyebrows shot up. "I didn't expect this."

"No?" Kelly asked, amused. "Are you sure you didn't plan our disappearance to gain publicity?"

He chuckled and patted her hand. "No amount of fame would be worth what we've gone through, love."

Glad to be alive, she settled into the comfortable seat, unable to believe they were on their way home. "I think I'll just pinch myself to make sure it's real." The plane taxied down the runway and soared into the air, leaving Fiji far behind.

"Let's get some sleep," she said, turning to Alex, but his eyes were already closed.

Thoughts of their future whirled through her head. She suppressed an urge to smooth back the lock of dark blond hair falling onto his forehead. She shouldn't, since so many attendants had recognized him.

Sleep eluded her. Perhaps she should have taken one of his pain pills.

She stared out the window, her thoughts churning inside. *Did he love her?* Even during their most intimate times together, he'd never once said so.

* * *

As soon as the plane touched down at the Honolulu Airport, an officer escorted them to the police station. Now dead tired, Kelly sipped a cup of strong coffee and filled out yet another detailed report for the U.S. authorities. After midnight, they were finished. The detective closed his file.

"You'll be free to go to a hotel once this paperwork has cleared." He left them alone at his desk and allowed them the use of his telephone.

Alex handed Kelly the receiver. "News will travel fast. Would you like to ring first?"

"Okay, but won't they all be surprised? After three months, how do you tell people you're alive?" She dialed her aunt's number, while Alex leaned back in the chair, eyes closed.

"Hello," answered Kaye in her gravelly voice.

Kelly exhaled in relief that nothing had happened to her aunt during her absence. "Aunt Kaye. It's me—Kelly. I'm alive. I'm so sorry—it's the middle of the night—but we just made it back where I could finally call you."

"Oh, my Dear Lord in Heaven. We were told you'd either drowned or were killed in the explosion." Her aunt started crying, sending tears down Kelly's cheeks.

After Kelly reassured her aunt she was very much alive, she said, "Aunt Kaye, I have to go, but I'll talk to you soon. I need you to send money for a hotel and expenses."

She gave her aunt the address of the Crystal Polynesian, a nearby hotel they'd seen on the way to the police station.

"Shall I call Robert for you, sweetie?"

Kelly's stomach clenched into a knot. Guilt coursed through her at what her being alive and with Alex would mean to Robert. She frowned and stole a sideways glance at Alex. He leaned back in the chair with his eyes closed, as if asleep. "No, I guess I'd better do that myself."

She punched in Robert's telephone number.

"Hello," he answered groggily.

"I know this is unexpected, but this is Kelly. I didn't die in the dive boat explosion as everyone assumed. I'm very much alive."

There was a moment of silence where she wasn't sure if he believed her or not. Then he said, "Can't be . . . Oh, honey, this is amazing. I searched for you, but they insisted you were dead. I shouldn't have believed them. I would never have given up. Do you believe me?"

"Of course."

"Tell me what happened."

Kelly couldn't concentrate. "I'm so dead tired, I'll tell you everything when we . . . when *I* get back." She told him where she intended to stay. "I'll be home in a day or two. I'm sure we have a lot to talk about."

"No. Don't move from the hotel. I'll bring my private plane down tomorrow." *Click.*

Gasping, she sagged back in the chair. "Alex, Robert is coming here tomorrow."

"Hillyard?" Alex's eyebrows slanted into a frown. "Why did you call him?"

"I had to. I couldn't have him hear it in the news. You probably can't understand this, but he's always been a big part of my life. He's like family. Besides he runs my company, and we have so much to talk about."

While Alex used the telephone, she went into the hall and collapsed on the wooden bench outside the detective's office.

Worry and guilt grasped her heart like a fisted hand. After all Robert had done for her, by keeping her company afloat, by extending loans and being her staunchest supporter of her dad's innocence.

Now, she was going to have to hurt him.

* * *

"Hello." Vanessa's voice hit Alex like a sucker punch.

Why the hell was she answering? She'd never lived at his house. The estate should have gone to his mother on the 'presumption' of his death.

"Is anyone there?" Vanessa demanded.

"This is Alex," he said bluntly. He heard glass breaking and the receiver bouncing on the stone floor, and then the rattle of Vanessa retrieving the phone.

"Damn it," she hissed. "What kind of prank is this?"

"It's not a prank," he forced himself to stay calm. "It's a long story, but I didn't die after all." He could hear people talking in the background. What was going on at *his* house? "I survived the dive boat explosion, and I'm in a hotel in Hawaii. Is my mother there?"

"No. Whatever you need I can help you with." He couldn't even tell if Vanessa was telling the truth about his mother's whereabouts. He was suspicious when Vanessa said, "I'll be there."

"*No.* Don't even think of it." He tried to keep the hostility out of his voice. He didn't have the strength to fight with her now, and they were divorced. "Sounds like you have guests. I'll ring her again."

"Alex, she'll be here soon. If you give me the hotel's address, I'll have her send anything you'd like."

"I need money." If Vanessa had any ideas, he repeated, "Don't come." He had hoped she had accepted their divorce, but her voice held an edge of excitement. "Please, tell her I'm all right as well, and it's late here. I'll speak to her tomorrow."

He hung up the phone and exhaled a deep breath.

His memories of his miserable marriage tumbled through his mind. Vanessa had been a clever seducer. Once he'd signed his life away, she had considered him no more than a hot stud to show off and use for her pleasure. Within the first month, he despised her. He'd soon realized how crude and kinky she was in her sexual appetite.

One of the last times he'd endured an evening with Vanessa had been dinner at her friend's home. After the entree, Vanessa made an excuse to go with him into the kitchen. After closing the door, she flung herself on him.

Although he'd firmly said 'no,' she'd deftly unzipped his trousers. "You'll learn, Alex, when I want something, I take it. Besides, Nell is occupied with her dinner date." She lowered her mouth to him.

Nell hadn't been too occupied because she walked in on them. In humiliation, he'd turned to fasten his trousers and realized Vanessa had achieved the results she intended.

Not caring to be publicly fondled for her friends' enjoyment, he avoided her after that. She accused him of affairs, became insanely jealous, and imagined situations that never existed. It wasn't long before he refused to have sex with her, which brought out the very devil in her. So after nine months of marriage, he filed for separation and moved into a London flat.

She harassed his friends and ruined what had been a budding career as producers and directors learned that with him came the excess baggage of a demanding and often hysterical wife. When Vanessa wouldn't consent to the divorce, he moved on with his life anyway, refusing to feel guilty.

Now, he was finally free of the witch.

He walked out of the detective's office. Kelly had fallen asleep on a bench in the hallway. Dark circles under her eyes revealed how little she'd slept in the last forty-eight hours. A burst of tenderness swelled in his heart. He dropped beside her and gathered her close, nestling her in the crook of his good arm. It was his turn to take care of her.

Her eyes flickered open. "Alex? What's going on?"

"Vanessa was at my house. Strange, since she never lived there." He leaned his head against the hard wooden bench. "Go back to sleep, love, looks like clearing us might drag on through the night."

"I couldn't wake up if I tried," she murmured, snuggling close.

With her head resting against his chest, they both slept soundly, oblivious to a few clicks and flashes of a camera.

* * *

After hanging up the phone, Vanessa laughed and twirled around the room in her wedding dress, trying not to step on the millions of fragments of an expensive, crystal vase smashed on the slate floor.

Needing to call off the wedding, she strode out on the lawn where the rental people were busy setting up tables and chairs for the garden wedding at noon.

She waved her arms at the caterer. "Get all of this out of here and send me the bill."

She grabbed her mother-in-law's hands, not regretting for one moment that she'd lied to Alex. His mother was already at the house. Poor Mrs. Drake. She had been too mousy to even put up a fight to keep the family ancestral home. "Explain to Reginald that Alex is alive. I can't get married."

"My son? He's alive?" Alex's mother fainted on the grass.

Vanessa stepped over her and ordered to a passing maid, "Help Mrs. Drake. Then have my bags packed immediately. I'm flying to Hawaii."

* * *

At his Beverly Hill's mansion, Robert sat immobilized on the edge of his bed, stunned by the news—his Kelly had not died after all. When his racing heart quieted, he turned on the lamp and nudged his assistant who had been his constant companion these past three months.

"Robert? You look like you've seen a ghost." Tammy ran a hand through her short blond hair and squinted at the light.

"Close. Kelly's alive."

She pulled the sheet up over her breasts. "How? No . . . You can't be serious?"

"I am. And I can't have her coming back to find you living here." He placed his hands on Tammy's shoulders. Years ago, there had only been one other woman he'd ever wanted as desperately as Kelly and she had died. "I never lied to you about my feelings for her. You always knew."

"You're obsessed with that girl. I gave up my marriage for you, you jerk." Tammy slipped off the bed and fled from the room.

Robert decided to let her go and vent her anger. He only hoped she wasn't angry enough to tell Kelly about their affair, especially the part before their engagement.

If Tammy valued her job, she'd keep her damned mouth shut.

* * *

The four-story hotel lobby of the Crystal Polynesian surrounded a manmade waterfall and tropical palm trees under a huge, domed skylight. Alex agreed with Kelly it was prudent they get separate rooms in each of their names. However, when he made the reservation, he asked for those rooms to be adjoining. She raised an eyebrow at him as if to say he wasn't being prudent enough. Perhaps he wasn't. He shrugged.

After she showered and crawled into bed to sleep, he decided to buy a newspaper.

As soon as he entered the lobby, a local news reporter with a crew wielding cameras and microphones cornered him. "Did you anticipate the enormous success of your movie, *The Spy*, Mr. Drake, after the publicity of your supposed 'death'?"

"I had no idea?" With his arm aching like hell and himself feeling weaker than a newborn kitten, he wasn't exactly up for an impromptu interview, so he kept it brief.

When he turned to enter the elevator lobby, he found a second reporter. "Hey, Mr. Drake, what's with the arm sling and bruises?"

He didn't get the chance to answer when a third reporter with a beefy face stuck a microphone in his face. "Three months on a deserted island with a hot number. Not bad, eh? A little pleasure in paradise?"

Alex glowered at the man. These last two men were the lowest of the low, only out to discover dirt. He'd had enough exposure to their kind while married to Vanessa. "Aren't you in the least concerned for those who died in the boat explosion?"

"Yeah, sure, yeah, but all of our readers are more interested in hearing about how you and Robert Hillyard's lovely fiancée survived for three months stranded alone on a deserted island. Does Vanessa Caine know yet?"

"Why the bloody hell would I care what she thinks?" Alex snapped. "We have gone through hell, people have died, and you want to make an issue of my time with Ms. Cochran?" He turned on his heel and sought refuge back in the bedroom that Kelly had claimed as hers.

Her eyelids fluttered open. "Alex, is something wrong?"

"You won't believe it, but it's a nightmare down there with the press. They're more interested in a story about *us* than how this happened."

"Oh, no."

He sank into the chair in the sitting area of the hotel room. "There is nothing we can do about it. Let's stay up here. You need more sleep. My mother wired money. I'll have clothing delivered and order room service. We'll slip out when you're ready to go."

After she told him what she needed, he called an expensive department store.

* * *

Kelly yawned and hugged the soft pillow, refreshed after a few hours of sleep. She cocked her ear and realized Alex was talking to a woman in the other bedroom.

"Yes, these are all the packages that were delivered to the front desk, Mr. Drake," the woman said. "I realize you've been hurt. I wanted to let you know, if you need *anything* . . ." The woman's voice lowered seductively. "You can call me."

Alex cleared his throat. "I'm all set for now."

Kelly frowned. Was he always propositioned like this? Probably. She remembered the women on the cruise ship. There were the girls on Wamba's island, the flight attendants, the way women's heads swiveled just this morning when they'd entered the hotel. Alex would create a stir of feminine interest no matter where he went.

After lunch, she helped him undress in the bathroom and ran the water in the bathtub so he wouldn't get his bandages wet. He stepped into the bath.

She sat on the edge of the wide marble platform, the luxury of it feeling odd after the island.

"How are you?" she asked him.

"Better."

"I think you're worse than you're letting on."

His gaze searched hers. "Do you care?" He clasped her wrist with his left hand.

She almost fell into the bathtub with him and warm water splashed onto her leg. She laughed. "Of course, I care, and I'm trying to help you."

He grinned and steadied her. "I know. I like it." He released her. A pained expression flitted across his handsome features. "Kelly, we need to talk. So much has happened between us."

She sighed. "That's putting it mildly. Here, let me wash your back. Talk." She lathered the thick washcloth with scented soap and ran it over his smooth skin, avoiding the bandages. His back was a perfection of muscles and lean strength.

"Come back with me to England," he said in a low voice.

Her heart beat faster. Had he grown to love her as much as she loved him? Giddy and blissfully happy, she would definitely say 'yes.' This time, unlike with Robert, there was no doubt in her mind she loved this man with all of her heart and soul.

She was about to tell Alex she'd go with him anywhere, when he said, "You don't have to go back with Hillyard. And it's probably not safe for you in L.A. You could stay with me for a while, at least until you decide what you want to do."

The words that she returned his love died on her lips.

"You understand, don't you?" he said over his shoulder again. "I've always been upfront with you about what I wanted in my life."

Her throat aching, she couldn't say anything. For her, she didn't want to contemplate a day without him. Obviously, she was the only one in love here.

"I wouldn't be any good at a commitment. I'd only hurt and disappoint you in the long run." He stated calmly.

If he didn't know by now what they had, he would never realize it.

Crushed on the inside, with tears burning at the back of her eyes, she tried hard to keep her voice from shaking. "You know, that's fine. I-I have to get back to California . . . I have things to do with the business . . . I, uh, I have to check on my aunt." She bit down on her lip to keep from sobbing out loud.

He glanced back at her, his eyes narrowing. If he expected her to make a scene like Vanessa did, he wouldn't get one. She had endured more pain in her young life than most people did in a lifetime, and she could survive losing one man who didn't love her.

"I'd better go." She placed the washcloth on the ledge and tried to sound light. "You know, on my part, I don't think I would be any good at fighting through the hoards of women anyway. I think it's time we honored our agreement and said good-bye. That's why we made it. We knew this day would come. I'll see you later."

He narrowed his eyes. "Is this what you want?"

She nodded, blinked back tears, and hurried from the bathroom. She could never be his short-term lover or his built-in playmate while he had other women on the side.

* * *

Alex dragged himself out of the bathtub and managed to dry himself with a towel and shave. Although his fever was down, his shoulder throbbed painfully so he took a pain pill. He'd not meant to hurt Kelly, and he could have used more finesse when asking her to live with him. He should've let her know she was special to him, but he just couldn't give her his heart.

He curled his good hand into a fist as he considered the reality. He was going to lose her. She had her pride. She wasn't going to be like Vanessa or like the other women who had begged him to stay with them.

He should be relieved. She'd make it easy for him to walk away. Damn.

Isn't that what you wanted, not to have her hanging on, expecting something you can't give? From the beginning, you made it clear you could never offer her love and marriage.

Bloody, bloody hell. If this was what he wanted, why did he feel like hell—and like the biggest cad of all time?

He stepped into the bedroom and paced the floor. Besides his arm, his head and body ached wickedly from David Lewis's beating, and he was starting to feel worse.

When would those damned pills kick in? He rubbed his palm against his forehead. With this searing pain, he was unable to think clearly about anything, especially something as important as his relationship with Kelly.

Perhaps a quick breakup was better for both of them. He'd been with her far too long, and they had become attached—that was all. And his injury and this throbbing pain in his shoulder, made him feel as if he needed her and couldn't let her go. He'd be damned if he would ask for help in getting dressed.

He managed to get partially dressed, but he was exhausted from just that amount of exertion. His hand shook when he tried to fasten his trousers. After a few minutes, he gave up trying.

He straightened his shoulders, knowing he had no choice but to seek her assistance. Besides, with his swelling shoulder and all of the bandages, he might need her to cut the shirt and jacket.

With a shudder, he thought of scissors, zippers, and an angry woman. He shook his head in disgust. He really did live dangerously.

* * *

At a brief, seemingly impatient knock, Kelly unlocked the adjoining-room door to find Alex standing in unfastened black slacks. His underwear peeked out through the fly, and his arm was in the sling over his naked chest. It was somewhat irrational of her, but how unfair of him to display himself in front of her when he looked so good—and she couldn't have him.

"I need your assistance to dress," he said it as if he regretted having to ask her—and he should, since he'd rejected her love.

Knowing all he had gone through in the past two days, she didn't have the heart to slam the door in his face. She waved him into the room. "Come on in." She'd help him and get through this ordeal without breaking down. She could cry in L.A. where she'd never see him again. That thought caused her throat to constrict.

He handed her a pair of scissors. "I had the desk clerk bring these in case you require them."

She flicked him an ironic gaze. After cutting the sleeve to fit his bandages, she buttoned his shirt. She helped him into the jacket, slipped on the sling again, then bent down and put her fingers on the zipper of his slacks. He sucked in his breath.

She lifted her gaze to find him regarding her with heavy-lidded eyes.

"Are you going to marry Hillyard?" he asked coolly.

Frowning, she didn't want to think of Robert now. With a quick jerk, she zipped up Alex's pants, nearly catching him in the zipper.

"Watch it," he growled.

Her face warming, she fumbled and finished fastening his pants and belt. "I'd rather not talk about that, okay?" She stepped away from him and to the window. Below was a sparkling pool, only steps from the beach—the kind of hotel she had wanted to find when they'd first landed on their beautiful, desolate island. Her heart ached at the sight of a couple strolling by the pool, obviously in love.

"Kelly, I hope you don't regret anything that has happened between us. I'm sorry if I hurt you."

She didn't look back at him. "I'll be fine."

He came up behind her, and with his good arm, he turned her to face him. Her body throbbed for his touch.

Her face heated with shame that even with his rejection, she still desired him. Not wanting him to see this weakness in her, she leveled her gaze on the buttons of his shirt and blinked back her tears.

He tipped her chin and forced her to look into his eyes. "I don't think you're being honest about your feelings."

Speechless, she gaped at him. *Why wouldn't he let it go? Let her hold on to some dignity. Did he want to make her cry?* "There is nothing to say."

"I have nothing but the utmost respect for you. Not only have we been lovers, I also consider you the best of my friends. I admire your courage and humor during these trying days. I enjoyed having you as my 'wife.'"

Kelly touched her finger to his lips. "Please, you don't have to try to make me feel better. I'm okay. Really I am."

He wrapped his arm around her and pulled her close, his face against her hair. "Above all things, I don't want you to feel badly."

That was hardly the case. Desire pooled in the pit of her stomach, and her legs threatened to give out. His heart also pounded rapidly beneath the palm of her hand.

She couldn't be in his bed again, not now that she knew for sure he didn't return her love. She pushed at his chest. "I'd better go. I need to shower and dress."

Hurrying into the bathroom, she locked the door behind her as a sob tore loose from her throat. She sagged against the door. All the tears she had tried to arrest escaped down her cheeks.

She slowly slid to the floor.

* * *

Kelly took a long, warm shower and finally calmed herself enough to apply makeup and to dress. She was determined to get through this, although a headache pounded her skull. She went to the lobby for aspirin.

At a magazine rack, a reporter clasped her elbow. "Could you answer some questions about yourself and Alex Drake, Miss Cochran?"

Surprised to be recognized, she gaped at the man and jerked her arm away. "No. How did you know who I am?"

He thrust his florid face toward her. "Miss Cochran, we all know who you are so how about a picture, babe?"

She held up her hand. "No to that, too." But he snapped pictures anyway. The flashes burned her eyes, sensitive from crying.

"Miss Cochran, did Alex Drake find you a good substitute for Vanessa Caine?" As she hurried for the elevators, he bellowed to her back what she dreaded the most, "Aren't you the daughter of Richard Cochran, the embezzler? Living it up on his clients' money, aren't you? Taking South Pacific cruises and having secret rendezvous with actors? All I want to do is talk to you about it. Get your side of the story. Clear the air."

She rushed to her hotel room. After stepping inside, she slammed the door and paced the floor. Downstairs was a bitter reminder of her earlier distaste for public life. She couldn't go through this again. With Alex's skyrocketing fame, she'd been caught in another publicity scandal. Everything about her father would be dredged up again.

Unable to even share her pain with Alex, she dropped wearily onto the loveseat. Only when Robert called and said he was on his way from the airport, did she knock on Alex's door.

His appreciative gaze swept over her from head to toe as he entered her bedroom. "You look beautiful," he said huskily. Then he added in a mocking voice, "I'm sure Hillyard will be pleased."

Her chin shot up. *Now he was glad she would be attractive for Robert.* "Thank you," she said flatly.

Alex sat down in the chair and stretched his legs out on the ottoman, closing his eyes. Just look at him, she thought bitterly. Even though he was battered and bruised, he still looked as handsome as ever. He'd have no trouble finding women and would soon forget what they had shared. Perhaps, he even wanted her looking good for Robert to ease his guilt over dumping her.

Trying not to get upset again, she paced the floor. Their relationship really was over, with nothing left to discuss. They'd been like that old saying about two ships passing in the night, and in Alex's case, now his ship was ready to sail on again.

At a rap, she opened the door. "Robert," she cried. He'd always been the one who stood with her in her time of need. She hugged him and then stepped back. Although he was still as attractive as ever, in a rugged way, a few more stands of silver streaked his dark hair and deeper lines etched his tanned face—or was she unfairly comparing him to Alex's youth?

"Kelly, I. . . ." He stopped mid-sentence when Alex came to stand beside her.

Robert's happy expression faded to anger. "*You . . . Drake?*"

Alex returned Robert's savage stare. "Yes, this is the right room. Come on in," he said with a sweeping hand. Kelly gaped at Alex's hostile tone. What was he up to? How would they keep their affair a secret if he acted like this?

A frown furrowed Robert's brow. "Kelly, I heard he was alive too, but why the hell is he in your room?"

CHAPTER FIFTEEN

As Robert stalked past Kelly and entered the hotel room, Alex's arrogant stance and the challenging glint in his eyes made them appear as guilty as sin. The rumpled, king-sized bed in the room didn't help matters either. Kelly closed the door.

Why was Alex doing this? Obviously, he didn't want her, but she didn't want Robert hurt either. After closing the door, she caught Alex's gaze and silently pleaded with him to stop.

Under Robert's unwavering gaze, she swallowed the lump in her throat. "We can explain everything. It's not like we planned to be lost together."

Someone knocked on the front door in the adjoining room, which sounded through the door connecting the two hotel suites. "See," she said brightly. "Alex has the suite next door."

"Excuse me." Alex strode into the other suite. "Vanessa," he ground out in a disgusted voice. "Why are you here?" Kelly's shoulders drooped.

Vanessa's voice carried through the opening between the two suites. "I was afraid your phone call was a cruel joke so I had to come and see for myself." After a moment of silence, in a harsher voice, the actress exclaimed, "You look like hell."

"Thank you very much," Alex snapped. "Now, why don't you hop back on whatever broomstick you rode in on and get the hell out of here."

"How can you speak to me like that? I've come all this way out of my deepest concern for you."

"Damn," he said. "Come with me."

Alex strode into Kelly's suite with Vanessa in tow. Uneasiness gripped Kelly's stomach.

Vanessa's winged eyebrows rose sharply over her green eyes. "Robert, what a surprise? What's this all about?"

Robert walked to Vanessa and kissed her cheek. "I'd say it's the most unbelievable news."

"Is it?" The actress asked, crossing her arms over her chest. "I suppose, Robert, you're also wondering as I am, was their disappearance all these months a publicity stunt, or an opportunity to get *laid?*"

Kelly's face heated. "Of all . . ." Appalled at the accusation, she shook her finger at the famous movie star. "I don't care, Vanessa, if you are Robert's friend, or a famous movie star. *You* are the rudest person I've ever met."

"Vanessa, retract the claws. Let them explain before you skewer them." Robert nodded toward the sitting area of the room. "Can we sit?"

Kelly sat on the love seat. Robert dropped beside her, while Vanessa remained standing, tapping her foot.

Alex returned to the upholstered chair. "There has been no hoax." He explained briefly the attempted kidnapping, the boat explosion, and being marooned.

Kelly crossed her arms over her chest. "It took us this long to find our way back. We nearly died—many times."

Robert scowled. "Is there anything between you two I should know about?"

From beneath her lashes, she stole a glance at Alex. He didn't seem to mind handing her over to Robert. She recalled how adamant he had always been about her expecting too much from their relationship. No, she thought bitterly, there was nothing Robert needed to know. What had happened was private and over.

"Please, don't insult us by reading anything more into this. In the beginning," she said truthfully, "we could barely keep ourselves from tearing each other apart. Now, we've managed to become friends." Certainly, that was how Alex wanted her to feel. Although he'd warned her not to fall in love with him, it had been impossible to protect her heart.

"*Friends?*" Robert asked, piercing her with his dark gaze.

Kelly frowned. "We had more problems to worry about than what you're thinking. It was a struggle to survive, and we went through hell to get here. We're lucky to be alive."

Robert lightly touched his fingers to the bruise on her cheek. "How did you get this?"

"Someone hit me."

"Hell," Robert said, pulling her close. "I had no idea, you poor sweetheart. None of this has been your fault." When he kissed the top of her head, guilt seared her. Did he still plan to marry her, as if these three months hadn't gone by, and she hadn't been changed at all from the ordeal?

"Have the police even tried to find who attacked us?" Alex's sarcastic tone matched his stony expression.

Robert's brow wrinkled. "We were told the explosion was an accident."

"*Accident?*" Alex echoed. He sagged back in the chair, his face pale and bruised, his discomfort from injury even more evident. Kelly stifled the urge to go to him. He didn't love her.

She turned to Robert. "Did you go to the police with the letter?"

He squeezed her hand. "I didn't know there was a connection, honey."

"There must have been," Alex muttered, "and we nearly died because of it. And David Lewis might still come after Kelly."

She shuddered. "Robert, why did you choose the South Pacific for our cruise—the very place where David set up an illegal business?" The question was followed by a silence.

Robert shook his head in shock. "David Lewis was involved? I'll check with Tammy and find out if she knows who left those brochures at the office about the cruise, but anyone could have found out what trip we were taking." He gripped her fingers. "Damn, Kelly, the police told us the explosion was an accident. I searched for you for days. Believe me?"

Sighing, Kelly nodded. "I knew you would have. Have there been any other threats against the company?"

Robert lifted her hand to his lips. "No." She noticed the barely perceptible tightening of Alex's jaw. "Honey, you need to know your apartment has been re-rented. All of your possessions have been sold or given away, although Kaye has some of your things."

Kelly sucked in her breath, having had about all she could bear for one day. "I never considered my 'death' might have erased my life. We were so preoccupied with . . . with surviving."

"Kelly?" Alex asked, concern in his voice.

She tried to glance at him, but Robert crushed her against his chest. "Everything will be all right."

Bracing her hands against his chest, she eased away. She couldn't let him try to take over her life again.

Vanessa knelt beside Alex's chair. "The same is true for you, except for your house. Since you've been hurt, why don't you come back with me?"

Anger twisted Alex's features. "I'm not going anywhere with you. My mother told me you were planning to marry yesterday. Why did you cancel? I'm happy for you."

She plucked his sleeve. "Darling, after the accident, I went to court. The date we thought you died . . . was before the divorce was finalized. I legally became your widow, which now means I'm still *your* wife."

Kelly's stomach clenched. If Alex had been pale before, he looked deathly ill now.

"What the hell?" His good hand gripped the arm of the chair. "I don't know what tricks you pulled, Vanessa, but I'll see my solicitor about this."

Vanessa ran a long nail along his arm. "You might want to wait a while, darling. *The Spy* became a surprise hit. Take my advice, if you want to hang onto your success, the public won't think kindly of your dumping your wife as soon as you're famous."

The same bitter look he'd had when Kelly first met him returned as Vanessa wormed her way back into his life.

Robert stood and held out his hand. "I'm starving, Kelly. Why don't we give these two a chance to talk and have a quick dinner before we leave? We have our own private matters to discuss."

* * *

While he chewed a bite of his steak at the hotel's restaurant, Robert surveyed Kelly over the table. What was she trying to conceal? She'd never been good at hiding her feelings.

"Of course," he said, "we'll straighten out everything with Cochran Investments when we get back to L.A. Hillyard Pictures has its own problems with the movie delayed because of this fiasco. Vanessa has agreed to do the picture with Timothy Michaels, but with Drake's newfound fame—and that contract he signed—I'll insist he play the lead." Robert sipped his wine, waiting for her response.

"That should be good for Alex."

His sweet Kelly pushed around more pasta with her fork than she ate as if she only half-listened to what he said. Hell, he didn't like it. She'd been distracted all during the meal. Aside from her initial, friendly greeting, she didn't seem overjoyed to see him.

"Kelly?" Robert waited until she glanced at him, then his gaze locked on hers. "The filming of the movie will keep Drake near Vanessa, and married to her, which is what she wants."

Sadness tinged her eyes and that angered him. He should just ask her point-blank if she'd slept with Drake, but he'd find out soon enough. He intended to take control of this situation before he lost her for good.

Gripping his hand on the glass, he drained his Chivas Regal. What might have happened over the three months taunted him. She'd blossomed into an even more beautiful woman, and all this time she's been alone with Drake. Robert was positive she'd been a virgin because her fiancé told him, and she'd been a frigid block of ice with him on the cruise. Damn it. If Drake used her, he would pay dearly. However, he couldn't let his temper spiral out of control and scare her off. She meant everything to him. Nothing had changed for him. He still desired her for his wife.

He set his glass on the table. "I'll arrange for our marriage as soon as possible."

"We need to talk about our engagement." Color seeped into her cheeks. "I can't marry you."

"What? Why the hell not?"

"I need to rest—I'm exhausted. And I need to work on the business. I don't think marriage right now would be a good idea when I've gone through such an ordeal. I just can't think of anything that important. So I'm breaking—"

"Does Drake have anything to do with this?" he snapped. "I can promise you, I'll crush him. He won't work in Hollywood again."

She gasped. "No. Oh, no. This has nothing to do with him."

Although anger simmered in him, Robert kept a lid on it. He didn't need to come on too strong, but he needed the time to change her mind back to wanting to marry him.

He hoped understanding filled his eyes. "All right. We'll put the marriage on hold—for now. I realize you need time to recover. Let's go home." He clasped her hand over the table. "I was devastated when I lost you." He stroked her finger. "Your ring?"

"I'm sorry, Robert. As you know, it was loose. Unfortunately, I lost it."

"That's all right. What really counts is that you're back safely."

Actually, he was more worried about something else she might have lost, but he couldn't say it. "Let's go home. I need you, the company needs you, but more importantly, you need to recover."

"But I. . . . I can't leave just yet."

"Why not?"

Her face reddened. "I'd like to say good-bye to Alex."

Him again. Keeping his spiraling anger and jealousy in check, he gave her a peck on the cheek. He could be a piece of furniture for all she seemed to care.

"Let's make it quick, Kelly. I have the plane standing by."

* * *

After Kelly and Hillyard re-entered the hotel rooms, Alex's jaw tightened at the older man's smug expression . . . as if Kelly was already his for the taking. *Had they discussed wedding plans over dinner?*

Kelly stepped forward. "Good-bye, Alex," she said stiffly. "Take care of yourself."

Ignoring Hillyard, who would be able to hear every word that was said, Alex clasped her cold fingers and tried to read her thoughts. "We've had some adventure, haven't we? Do you look forward to going home?"

"Yes," she whispered, but she didn't seem happy. Why was she going to L.A. with Hillyard, instead of to England with him?

Sighing, he knew he could never give her the commitment she needed, and she deserved the best in life. Maybe a clean, swift break was what they both needed, to make leaving each other easier, but those tears shining in her eyes almost undid him.

He touched her cheek. "I owe you everything. You saved my life."

"You saved mine—too many times to count—so I think we're even."

He nodded. "We were a good team, love."

"We were. I'll never forget you." He hated the tears brimming in her eyes, and the ones he felt pricking his own.

Not caring what Hillyard thought, Alex pulled her close. He didn't like the guilt that burned his gut. "Please, be happy. We've made it back." He breathed in the sweetness of her hair and wanted to recapture her the way she'd been on their island, soft, sensual, loving, and giving. God help him, but he wanted to kiss her one last time. He cupped her chin, his gaze dropping to her full lips.

Hillyard cleared his throat. "Let's go, Kelly. The plane's waiting."

Alex mustered all of his restraint and released her. She turned away from him. He wanted to reach out, force her to look at him, and make her realize this scene was tearing them both up.

This had not turned out at all as he'd planned . . . with her leaving without him. Perhaps he should have stressed to her they could take their relationship one day at a time. They could go on as they had been and see what happened. All she had to do was tell Hillyard she wasn't going with him. *Why didn't she tell him?*

Then the knowledge came back to him like a roar. If Vanessa wasn't lying . . . If for once in her bloody life she was telling truth— *he was still legally married.* His offer to Kelly to live with him would never work for her now.

Speaking of the witch, Vanessa sauntered into the room, waving a magazine in her hand. "Well, you *both* are an overnight scandal. This won't do at all."

Kelly reached her hand for the magazine, but Vanessa arrogantly retracted the paper from her grasp and thrust it toward Hillyard. "Why, Robert, I thought you might like to read this one first."

Alex read the caption: Adultery in Paradise: Vanessa Caine's Husband and Embezzler's Daughter Marooned on a Tropical Island.

The color drained from Kelly's face.

Vanessa handed another magazine to Alex. "And this one's even worse. My name is only mentioned in small print." Alex didn't comment and handed the magazine to Kelly.

Biting her lip, Kelly flipped to the article. "It's just like when my father died." Her hand shook as she thrust the magazine back at Alex and whirled away. "Robert, I'm ready to go now."

Alex frowned. He couldn't let her go this way, being devastated. "Kelly, they'll be on to something else next week."

"Or perhaps she'll be the next slut of the century for the tabloids," Vanessa quipped.

"Shut up, Vanessa." Alex stepped toward Kelly and addressed her back. "The press really will be on to something else soon. However, I'm worried about your safety. If you ever need anything, you can count on me. I'm only a plane ride away."

When Kelly began to turn, Hillyard caught her around the shoulders. "That won't be necessary, Drake. After her parents were brutally murdered, I stepped in. And I'll take care of her now, just as I did then. Come on, Kelly."

She didn't look at Alex again. He met the older man's gaze, in mutual dislike, before Hillyard escorted Kelly out into the hall.

Alex followed and watched them leave. He reached out his hand to stop her, but he couldn't move.

She was walking out of his life forever. That realization shook him and squeezed his heart.

He hastily brushed the moisture from his eyes.

CHAPTER SIXTEEN

After returning to Los Angeles, Kelly moved into her aunt's townhouse and resumed her job at Cochran Investments. Over the past month, she welcomed the numbness that dulled her heartbreak over losing Alex. She hadn't heard one word from him, which was probably for the best. She couldn't be just his friend. He had moved on, and she needed to do the same—even though pain twisted like a knife in her heart every time she thought about him.

Kelly tapped the tip of her pen against her lips and stared at the computer as she went over the accounts again. The company was in even worse shape than she had previously thought. They weren't even close to the nine million dollars needed to repay Robert's loan.

In a month, unless she asked him for another extension, the company would be forced to file bankruptcy. Now, with their engagement called off—although she wasn't sure Robert had actually accepted that—she wasn't sure if he'd give her more time.

With a brief knock, Tammy strode into the office. "You left a message to see me?"

Kelly gazed up from her desk. "Yes, I couldn't find the general ledger from just before my father died, or any other records he might have left."

Her face defiant, Tammy clamped her hands on her hips. "You don't need to be concerned with old history."

Anger simmered at these constant attempts to thwart her. This time Kelly stood and glared at Tammy. "Why, yes, I do."

Tammy clamped her arms over her chest. "I'll have to speak to Robert first."

"At the moment, Tammy, this is still *my* company."

Robert sauntered into the room. "Problems?"

"I'd like to see the old books. But your assistant thinks it's unnecessary. I have so little time left to clear my dad's name."

A frown furrowed his forehead. "Kelly, why don't you let me take care of everything? You should be home resting."

Kelly clenched her hands. "Don't patronize me, Robert. Dad wouldn't steal, so I need to find out what happened. At the time of his death, I'd been too young to even think the evidence could be at the company, right under my nose." She whirled on Tammy. "You were his secretary. Did he leave any personal records, letters . . . a journal? *Anything?*"

Tammy pursed her lips. "No. And I went over every record with the police."

"See, Kelly, it's all been analyzed."

"I want to see for myself."

Robert sat in the chair across from Kelly's desk. "Tammy, bring her whatever books and documentation she wants."

His assistant's lips compressed, then she strode out of the office.

Kelly dropped into her chair. "She's hiding something from me."

He snorted. "She's not a conspirator, if that's what you're thinking. More likely, she's concerned you're pointing a finger at her."

"But I'm not—"

"She thinks you are. And dwelling on the past is not going to get us anywhere. Tammy's concerned about the company. She lost money, too."

Kelly drew in a sharp breath. "Even she's owed money?" she asked, her shoulders drooping.

He nodded. "As soon as we get the books, we'll go over them together."

"No, Robert. I want to take them to Aunt Kaye's house. I want to do this . . . alone."

A wave of discomfort crossed his features. She winced, but he had to know they weren't right for each other. Now, with the hurt he must feel, she couldn't even bring up the topic about a loan extension.

Robert dipped his head. "All right." He gave her a wan smile, while waving a tabloid magazine at her. "I wanted to give you this. Someone left it on my desk and is deliberately trying to irritate me."

Kelly's stomach tightened into a ball. *Tammy.*

"You can't imagine, how I hate to see your picture with Drake's. And now, they're spewing how romantic and heroic your time was with him, as if you were on some grand adventure."

"*What?*" Although reluctant to read how well Alex was doing without her, she took the magazine from Robert's hand. The earliest tabloids had ripped them to shreds. Calling their disappearance a publicity stunt for Alex. Some even accused her of trying to escape her financial obligations. Others charged they were on a vacation having a steamy love affair at the expense of Alex's wonderful wife.

"You haven't seen them?"

"No." After a painful glance at Alex's picture, she returned the tabloid to Robert.

He leaned toward her. "Let's put an end to these senseless rumors you had an affair with Vanessa's husband. Marry me."

Kelly cringed at this reminder that Alex had not really been divorced when they'd made love. "Listen to me, Robert. I'm sorry if this hurts you, but I can't marry you."

His face darkened. "I promised myself I'd give you time to get back to normal. Let's not even discuss this . . . but you've got to know, you're not safe in L.A. I want to take you to the ranch."

"Of course I'd love to see my old home. But at the moment, I need to be *here*."

"You'll have computer access."

"I've done nothing wrong. I won't hide out like I'm a criminal."

"People think you've benefited—"

Tammy strode through the door. Her face held a calm expression and betrayed nothing more than the dutiful assistant when she placed two leather-bound ledgers on Kelly's desk.

"Come on, Tammy. Let's leave Kelly to her work." Robert quickly escorted his assistant into the hallway.

For an hour, Kelly poured through the files and discovered the incriminating evidence that implicated her father. Before the plane crash, over a six-month period, her father had made ten, large, withdrawal transactions.

Releasing a ragged breath, she gathered her laptop and the heavy books and headed for the elevator. As soon as she stepped into the nearly empty parking garage, a tingle ran up her spine. How foolish she'd been to stay so late and not leave with the usual five o'clock crowd.

She hurried toward her car, then halted in her steps. Twenty feet away, the man who had attacked her months ago in her apartment sat on the curb. With greasy hair and wearing a dirty t-shirt, he sneered up at her.

Fear pumped in her heart and she backed away. He jumped to his feet and lunged for her. She tossed the books at him and fumbled for the pepper spray on her key chain. A steady stream hit his shirt. He jumped backwards.

"Kelly," Robert shouted. His voice and footsteps echoed as he ran across the parking garage.

Her attacker shook his fist at her. "Next time, bitch." Then he turned to run in the opposite direction and disappeared down the ramp.

Shaking uncontrollably, she didn't have the strength to refuse Robert when he pulled her into his arms.

Her cheek rested against his jacket as she mumbled, "I was stupid to think these attacks were over. It's never going to be over." How utterly alone she was in this mess. The thought overwhelmed her and she choked back a sob to keep from breaking down.

He squeezed her tightly and pressed his lips to her temple. "That's why you need me. I'll protect you."

Alex had moved on with his life. She'd never be able to repay everyone without Robert's help. And he loved her . . .

* * *

A week later, across the globe in an English, country house, Alex sat in his study thumbing distractedly through a stack of scripts. Surprisingly, two of them were great roles.

With a heavy sigh, he tossed down the last of the brandy in his glass.

He should make a decision on what work to accept, but instead, all he could think about was Kelly. He missed her in his life, missed waking beside her in the morning and sharing their days.

He blew out a deep breath. All he had to remind him of her were pictures in the stack of tabloids and magazines that lay on his desk.

Although he was finally recovering, this past month had sped by in a blur of sheer hell. He'd endured fever, infection, and pain. When his shoulder hadn't healed properly, he had surgery.

He flexed his still-aching arm, but at least he was out of the sling and off the pain pills.

The worst of it, his agent had pleaded with him not to go to the courts to straighten out the mess of his divorce, not while his popularity was rising.

"Wait," Paul had insisted.

And Vanessa? He exhaled an exasperated breath. He couldn't manage to get a divorce from her. Ironically, people thought he'd married her for money. He wouldn't get anything from her in the divorce settlement. And he'd discovered he hadn't been the only thing she wanted when she'd tricked him into marriage. She wanted his home, and he wouldn't let her have it.

This ancient pile of stone and bricks had been in his family for over two hundred years. Until recently, it took more money than he made to pay the taxes and maintain the manor house he loved from further decay. If he lost the house, it would be a blow to his family and his heritage. Now, with his income from *The Spy*, and new work on the horizon, he could begin the much needed restoration projects.

His thoughts returned to Kelly, and he blew out a deep breath. Was she happy and living with Hillyard? At an image of Hillyard laying his hands on her, jealousy ripped through Alex. He drained the rest of the brandy and lobbed the snifter into the fireplace. The glass shattered and the fire flared.

His vision blurry, he realized his life was out of control. Perhaps drinking this past week to forget Kelly hadn't been such a good idea. He stumbled to the couch and stretched out on his back to sleep off his over indulgence. Tomorrow he'd get his life together and think of what he should do.

When the door was flung open with a bang, he lifted one eyelid.

"Hello, darling." Vanessa flounced into the study, wearing a barely-buttoned red silk blouse, a short, black leather skirt, and boots. The tray in her hand held a bottle of champagne and fluted glasses.

"Why are you here?" He struggled to sit, but didn't have the strength to get up. Had he consumed so much brandy?

She sat on the edge of the couch and brushed the hair away from his eyes. "Did you forget we're still married?"

He rasped, "Get the hell out of my house."

"Yours?" she asked with a shake of her head. "No, darling, while you were gone, I paid for expensive repairs to the roof, or this place would be falling down around our ears. You owe me, bucko."

"I'll get your bloody money. Now get out." His eyes drifted closed. He didn't even have the strength to lift his hand to force the witch out.

"Don't you dare fall asleep on me. It's not money I want."

"Vanessa, forget it . . . *No.*"

"I know what your problem is—Kelly Cochran. You might as well get over her. She and Robert married several days ago."

The news hit Alex like a sledgehammer. "*Married?*"

"You insisted you two were only friends," she said, her voice laced with heavy sarcasm. "Or else I would have told you sooner. Right now, Robert is probably giving her exactly what *I* want."

His sluggish brain wouldn't accept that Kelly was married. "You're lying. And whatever you did to stop our divorce, I'll find out."

She laughed and gripped his cheek. "I still remember our time together. Alex, I'm telling you now, I won't let you publicly humiliate me with this divorce." The last words he heard her saying, "I didn't go from a filthy tenement house to becoming a major star by playing fair."

* * *

Hours later, a beam of light fell through a crack in the heavy, velvet curtains, illuminating the darkened room. Shivering, Alex pressed his fingertips to his throbbing temples. His stomach heaving, he raised his head. He lay on the floor, with only a blanket for warmth—naked.

Bloody hell. How did he end up this way? And what a horrible nightmare? He'd actually dreamed Vanessa had attacked him in his study. He squinted at the clock. Eleven a.m. He recoiled. He never slept this late.

He staggered into the bathroom. Maybe he'd learned his lesson about drinking to forget Kelly.

Swaying, he put his hand on the sink and peered at his bloodshot eyes in the mirror. He gaped at the red-lipstick on his cheeks. Further evidence that Vanessa had been here trailed down over his chest, his stomach and lower in bright red smudges . . . Bile rose in his throat.

Trembling, he stepped into the shower and scrubbed his body, allowing warm water to beat down and remove all traces of her.

He returned to his desk, sank into the chair, and dropped his face into his hands.

* * *

A few hours later, and with his suitcase packed, Alex headed down to the front hall just as Vanessa breezed through the door, as if she already owned the place. At the brilliant smile on her face, he cringed.

She rushed up to him. "Good morning, darling. I'm late because—"

He held up a stopping hand to keep her from getting too close. He wanted to shove her, but kept his restraint in check as he just might send her crashing through the window. No matter how much he felt like it, he'd never strike a woman. "I don't give a damn where you've been. Was I having a nightmare last night or were you really here?"

"Yes and you were so eager, Alex. You called me 'your love.'"

He lifted his hand to his pounding head. "You're a damned liar and always have been."

She smiled. "You've denied your love for me, but proved yourself last night. I know you were disappointed after we lost the baby."

"There never was a baby," he roared.

With a glance at the suitcase by the door, she grasped his sore shoulder, sending pain rippling through him. "Where are you going? I'll pack and go with you."

"No, damn it." He wanted to throttle her. He pried her fingers from his sore arm.

"You fucking bastard? Nobody leaves me until I'm ready. If you do, I'll make sure I get this house. Your mother and family will think you're a failure." She raked sharp fingernails across his cheek. "Oh, that's right. You are."

His face stinging, he slapped her hand away. "My biggest failure, and regret, was marrying you."

Her winged eyebrows drew together. "Or is it Kelly Cochran you're moping about? You can't deny you found your way into her pants. That slut broke up our marriage. I'll have you both slaughtered in the press for this."

"Leave Kelly out of this," he said in an icy tone. He stalked toward the exit, and then took one last glaring look at her. "You forced yourself on me with your tricks from the first day I met you." He shook his head in disgust. "You're sick. Get help. When I return, I want you out of *my* house."

He slammed the door, just as something crashed against the wood on the inside.

* * *

Less than twenty-four hours later, Alex drove his rented Jaguar through the sunny, palm-lined streets of Los Angeles with one destination in mind—to see Kelly.

His cell phone rang.

When he answered, his agent said, "Your housekeeper told me you're in L.A."

He wasn't confiding in Paul the real reason he'd flown to California. "There's a detective that might need my input on the South Pacific case."

"I've got bad news for you. I have to pull two of the scripts you were interested in. They've found another actor. I don't know what happened."

"Vanessa's what's happened. Which ones?" As he listened, he clenched his hands on the steering wheel.

"What would you like me to do now?"

Anger struck Alex to his core. "She's pushed me too far this time. Everything's in motion. I have to get out, no matter the cost to my career."

And the cost to Kelly? More reason to see her. He had to warn her things might get ugly in the media.

Paul sighed on the other end of the line. "At least you have the Hillyard Pictures' film lined up."

Alex took the next corner too fast, his tires squealing on the pavement. "Probably not for long,"

"What did you say?"

"Nothing."

"You have another request for an interview."

"Yeah, and as usual, it will only be twisted into a story of what I've done to their precious Vanessa, just to make a headline."

"But this is with the American interviewer, Sandra Weaver. She wants to discuss the attack in Fiji."

Alex frowned. She was one of the biggest names in celebrity interviews and known for her integrity. "I'll think about it, but I have something important to do first."

He had important things to do all right, like visit an auburn-haired woman, who had firmly entrenched herself in his soul. He had to see her, make sure she was safe and happy, and then get over her, once and for all.

CHAPTER SEVENTEEN

Friday morning, Kelly sat alone in Detective Spagnola's office, awaiting his update on the case in Fiji. Robert and Tammy had just dropped her off and were parking the car, while the detective had stepped out to clarify an issue with his staff.

Sipping strong coffee, Kelly frowned, her stomach queasy as she glanced over the latest financial report for Cochran Investments.

"Hello, Kelly," Alex said in his English accent. Her head jerked up to find him standing in the doorway.

Her breath rushed out. His charismatic good looks were as startling as ever. He lit up the office. Dressed in a navy-blue suit, which contrasted with his dark, blond hair, he looked the epitome of the handsome movie star. They were a matching set, because she wore the same color in her jacket and skirt. Without the sling and bruises, he appeared recovered.

The report slipped from her hands and scattered on the floor. She curled her hand into a fist, digging her nails into her palm as it took all of her self-control not to fling herself into his arms and tell him how much she'd missed him.

She had rehearsed her cool reaction if she were to see him again, but was failing. She cringed and bent to retrieve the papers. "Uh. . . hi there."

"Let me help you."

He crouched beside her. After neatly stacking the papers, he handed them to her.

When his hand brushed hers, her skin tingled in response. Biting her lip in dismay, she slipped the report into her briefcase and inhaled a deep breath to compose her.

After they stood, she held out her trembling hand for him to shake. Finally, she allowed herself to meet his eyes. Her love for him burst out.

Wincing at the racing of her pulse, she dropped her gaze to his cheek. "How did you get those scratches on your face?"

Ignoring her question, he flashed her that devastating smile she'd never been able to erase from her heart. "What? No hug for your old friend?"

He pulled her close. She inhaled his sandalwood cologne and fisted her hands on his back to keep from clutching his jacket and never letting him go. Why did it feel so right in his arms? She tilted her head to see if he experienced any similar feelings.

His intense gaze held sizzling warmth and surprise, too. He abruptly released her.

Frowning, she stepped back. "Why are you here?"

"A few days ago, I rang up Detective Spagnola. He told me you were meeting today."

"He'll be right back. Would you like coffee?"

"No, thank you." He sat in a chair, his long legs stretched out in front of him.

She took a seat in one of the other chairs. Her nerves were rattled that he still could totally undo her.

He gave her a pointed look. "Are you married yet to Hillyard? Should I wish you congratulations?" He asked it as casually as if he were asking her about the weather.

Pain twisted in her heart. Had he so little feelings for her he would be happy if she were already married to Robert?

Smarter than she'd been on the island, she was determined to never let him know how deeply he'd hurt her. "No. We're not married." Her were eyes burning and she had to get away from him. She leapt to her feet. Darkness threatened her as the dizziness she'd felt off and on all week returned.

Alex caught her arm. "What's wrong with you? Are you ill?"

"Maybe. And I'm so glad you're concerned about what happens to me," she snapped, unable to keep the bitterness out of her voice.

"Of course I care. Have you seen a doctor since you've been home?"

"No. Please, just help me to the sofa."

When she swayed toward him, he swept her up in his arms and strode to the leather couch, and gently placed her down. "Kelly, speak to me."

At his concern, she croaked, "What do you want me to say?"

Sitting beside her on the edge of the couch, he loosened her jacket and unbuttoned the top of her white blouse. "I want you to tell me you're all right."

"What the hell is going on here?" Robert demanded. Kelly's stomach clenched. She twisted to see Robert standing in the doorway. He looked as if he could tear Alex apart as he stared at Alex's fingers hovering over her neckline.

"She's ill," Alex said, taking her hand in his. "What's wrong with you, sweetheart?"

She shook her head. "I don't know. With so many people hating me, I wouldn't be surprised if I've been poisoned."

Alex brushed back the hair from her temple. "Is that possible?"

She gazed into his blue eyes. "No, really, I think it's just a virus . . . or stress."

"It's so charming the way you help her, Drake," Robert drawled.

Continuing to hold her gaze, Alex didn't move from his position beside her. "I'm sure you'll read whatever you want into it."

With a strained expression, Tammy stepped beside Robert, but Kelly was too ill to care what either of them thought. Alex was here, and she never wanted him to leave.

"Kelly, is he helping you like he did on the island?" Robert grumbled.

"Old habits die hard," Alex said. A soft gasp escaped from Kelly's lips. Alex released her hand. "I'll take you to your doctor, Kelly."

"I'll see that she gets medical care," Robert ground out.

Kelly lifted her hand to her forehead. *Why was Robert acting as if they were still engaged?* "Really, I feel better already."

When she tried to sit, the room spun.

Dropping her head, she raised a pensive gaze. Both men watched over her protectively.

"All right," she said with a sigh. "I'll go to the doctor as soon as I can get an appointment."

Tammy dropped into one of the chairs. "What do you think is wrong with her, Alex?"

Alex raised an eyebrow, but didn't answer.

"She's picked up some tropical bug," Robert snapped. Then he glared at Alex. "So here you are, Drake, at the LAPD, acting all concerned about Kelly, and I hear from Vanessa you're practically on a second honeymoon. What are you up to?"

Alex expression tightened, and he rose from the couch. Kelly frowned. *Why didn't he deny the allegation?*

Or, was it as Robert had said previously—that all along, Alex had never really planned to divorce Vanessa? Had it only been a ploy to bed other women?

Although it tore at her insides, she'd let Alex know he meant nothing to her.

She struggled and sat up. "Robert, how long do we have to stay here? Why don't we take the detective's advice and go to the ranch together?"

When she glanced at Alex, his gaze was shuttered, and his mouth was drawn into a taut line, satisfying her.

With a warm glint in his eyes that promised much more, Robert said, "As soon as Detective Spagnola gets here, and we finish our business, we'll leave."

As quickly as anger had hit her over Alex's lies, guilt now assailed her. She'd not meant to use Robert, but Alex's rejection hurt so much she had wanted to strike back.

Papers in hand, Detective Spagnola strode into the room and sat at his desk. "Excuse me for being late, but I've been waiting for this fax from the Fiji Police. They're closing in on the suspects. Miss Cochran, can we count on your testimony at trial?"

Although apprehension tensed her shoulders, Kelly nodded. "Of course."

Robert put his hands on the desk and shoved his face toward the detective. "It's *too* dangerous. I won't have it."

Kelly frowned. "But, Robert, I can't forget all those people who died on the diving boat."

The detective peered over his steepled hands. "Mr. Hillyard is correct. I can't discount the danger to you, Miss Cochran. Because of his brother Ralph's death, David Lewis has more reason to want revenge against you. In addition, he'll do his best to avoid being prosecuted for the boat explosion."

Alex crossed his arms over his chest. "I'll identify Lewis, which will leave Kelly out of this."

With a sigh, Robert walked to the couch and sat beside Kelly, putting his arm around her shoulders. "Good. Then she won't be involved. I'll watch over her and keep her safe."

Through her half-lowered lashes, she glanced at Alex. He seemed genuinely concerned for her. *No.* She dug her nails into her palms. For a month, he'd forgotten all about her and perhaps had lied all along about divorcing Vanessa. Tears burned the back of her eyes. *I just want to get out of here.*

The detective shook his head. "Mr. Drake, there is a problem with only your testimony. In your statement you said you were underwater when the explosion occurred."

Alex nodded. "That's true."

The detective jotted something on a pad of paper. "Then Miss Cochran's eyewitness testimony will be needed to support any murder charges."

"What about kidnapping charges?" Alex interjected. "I can testify to attempted murder and keep her out of this."

"Yes, your testimony is vital in the matter." Detective Spagnola flipped through the file. "Now, according to your statement, you and Miss Cochran were handcuffed and locked together in a bedroom at the house?"

Alex hesitated and glanced at Kelly.

Robert frowned. "What are you saying, Detective Spagnola?"

Not wanting Robert hurt, Kelly rushed to explain, "For my safety, Alex told them we were married, so naturally they put us together in the same bedroom."

"*Naturally,*" Robert grumbled in a sarcastic tone. "I'll *bet* he said you were married."

Alex countered. "Seven men—all criminals—were on the island. She was at risk. What would you have had us do?"

Robert's brow furrowed. "Did any of these men hurt you, Kelly?"

She shook her head. "Not in the way you mean."

Besides being fondled and struck by David, Alex was the only man who'd hurt her, but she had slept with him willingly.

Robert dipped his head toward Alex. "I suppose you did the right thing, Drake. Although I can't help but think you had an ulterior motive."

Detective Spagnola interrupted, "Miss Cochran is the only one who can identify the men who caused the explosion."

"No way," Robert ground out. "She's not going to risk her life for an international crime problem."

The detective shook his head. "She's already in danger. Safest solution for her would be to put these men in prison for life. Someone tipped them off that she'd be in the South Pacific and on that particular diving boat. It was all too convenient."

"Anyone could have gotten that information easily," Robert muttered. He squeezed Kelly's shoulders. "Lewis obviously kept close tabs on her."

The detective leaned back in his chair. "The perpetrator probably figured if Ms. Cochran disappeared outside the country, there wouldn't be much of an investigation."

Kelly held up her hand. "When David Lewis is arrested, I'll testify for all of the people who died. Even though his girlfriend, Ming, denied he killed my parents, I'm sure of it. He's so ruthless."

The detective jotted more notes on a pad. "Now this latest attack on Miss Cochran is worrisome—"

"What attack?" Alex asked, frowning.

Robert launched into what had happened in the parking garage. He described how he'd charged in and saved her, but he neglected to mention she'd stopped the hitman with pepper spray first.

"Miss Cochran, can you go somewhere safe and keep a low profile?" Detective Spagnola asked.

Robert patted her thigh. "She's just agreed to go to my ranch. I'll hire a bodyguard to protect her, several if it's required." She stiffened at his touch and knew she had been an idiot to lead him on. Later, she'd beg his forgiveness and explain why.

"That would be wise." Detective Spagnola escorted them to the hallway. "Mr. Drake, before you leave town, I'd like to ask you a few more questions about the case."

"Give me a few minutes." Alex turned to Kelly. "I'd like to speak to you . . . *alone*."

Her hands clenched. She refused to be weakened by his false concern. "No point to it, Alex, as I *am* going to testify. And I'm sure you're anxious to get back to your *wife*. I don't want to hold you up."

With simmering anger in his eyes, he dipped his head.

She whirled. As she strode toward the door, Robert caught her arm.

"One moment, Kelly." He swung around to Alex. "Drake, in three weeks, I'm hosting a party to celebrate the upcoming production of the movie. Be there. Your job depends on it."

With an acute sense of loss, and the certainty that truly hearts did break, Kelly stepped into the warm Los Angeles sunshine and down the police department steps with Robert and Tammy. Foolishly, she'd let Alex upset her once again, despite knowing, that to him, she'd only been a convenient woman to satisfy his needs while on the island.

Once they were in Robert's car, they pulled out into traffic. Tammy, in the back seat, leaned forward and waved a tabloid at Kelly and Robert as they sat in the front. "I'm sorry about this, Kelly, but Robert needs to know the truth. There was more between you and Alex than you're telling him."

Kelly grasped the magazine and stared at pictures from the night she'd slept in Alex's arms at the police station in Hawaii. No words could explain away this evidence of an intimate embrace with his arm draped around her shoulders and her face pressed against his chest as she half-lay on top of him as they slept on the bench in the hallway.

"Yes," Kelly whispered. "There was more."

When Robert stopped at a light, he took the tabloid from Kelly's trembling hands. "Stay out of this, Tammy." Then he looked at Kelly. "It's all right, honey. You were vulnerable on that island. I suspected that gigolo used you, but I never once blamed you." He tossed the magazine into the back seat.

"Tammy, I don't want to hear another word about this. It's a closed matter."

* * *

Later in the day, Kelly and Robert drove the several hours north to the ranch—her childhood home. She stared out the window, guilt enveloping her. She'd given Robert false hope. She sighed. If only she could bring herself to marry him. No mess. No fuss. No pain. She'd have her beloved childhood home and a family. He'd be happy.

She inhaled a deep, shaky breath. But marriage for the wrong reason hurt everyone. A few months ago, she'd been ready to marry him, but she had to admit, perhaps the overwhelming financial mess had frightened her—not to mention that a man had tried to strangle her—and to endure it all alone had seemed overwhelming.

Perhaps, also, she'd been 'settling' with Robert and afraid to feel too deeply. She couldn't bear the pain of again losing someone she loved beyond her own life. An image of Alex came to mind, and she had to thrust him from her thoughts.

Robert steered the car. "Can you handle another surprise, Kelly? Do you remember the Westwood Grande Hotel, near the ranch?"

"Yes," she said numbly, finding it hard to get excited about anything.

"That's where I'm holding the celebration for the beginning of production on the movie. I also want to celebrate your birthday at the same time."

"You don't have to."

"But I want to. It's a big day for you. You're inheriting partial control of Cochran Investments."

"It won't matter. I've seen the reports, Robert. The company will have to file bankruptcy." *Unless, I ask you for an extension on the loan.*

He turned the car onto the road leading to the ranch. Gravel crunched beneath the tires and dirt puffed up as they drove down the long driveway. "I had a large section of the ranch walled in. I want to keep you safe."

The new wrought-iron gates swung open and he steered the vehicle down the tree-lined drive. She'd spent so much of her youth on horseback, galloping over these hills.

"Kelly, I can't wait for you to see the house."

"I can't either, but I don't like the idea I need walls and bodyguards to keep me safe here."

"For now you do," he said firmly.

She sighed. Here, alone with her memories, maybe she could figure out what to do with her life once Cochran Investments was dissolved. Perhaps she'd find answers about her father here in her family home? Her heartbeat quickened. *Perhaps the truth has been here all along.*

"Kelly, I've made a few changes to the place."

At first sight, Kelly felt as if she'd been punched in the stomach. Instead of the traditional, Spanish-style home she'd loved as a child, the 1920's mansion, she'd thought he was buying partly to please her, had been converted into a mammoth, contemporary of glass and straight lines. The house gleamed white in the hot, afternoon sunlight.

"But we must be at the wrong house, Robert."

"No. This is it."

She gaped and took in the facade. *How could she have ever thought he was sensitive to her feelings?* She slid out of the car and wanted to rant at him.

He took her elbow. "I hope you don't mind the changes."

Speechless, she stepped up to the house with him. The back of her throat tasted bitter. When they entered the etched glass doors and encountered the soaring, but stark, cold entry, her stomach heaved.

She ran in the direction of what she hoped was still a bathroom. She locked the door and lost her lunch in the ultra-modern toilet. Trembling all over, she sank to the cold marble floor and hugged her knees. She hadn't expected Robert to keep the house as a shrine to her parents, but why had he bought her home when he had planned to obliterate everything? Tears spilled down her cheeks. She'd lost even this last part of her parents.

CHAPTER EIGHTEEN

Two days later, Alex drove up to gates near a sign that displayed the bold words: *Hillyard Rancho*. At the sight of Hillyard's name on Kelly's old, childhood home, Alex clenched his hands on the steering wheel. Purchasing her home had been another way for Hillyard to manipulate her into marriage, and Alex planned to tell her so. Besides, Hillyard was too old for her. If he could think of any other reasons why she shouldn't marry a man who could give her everything she wanted—and was rich enough to protect her from a killer—he'd tell her that as well.

Reaching through the car window, Alex jabbed the button on the intercom.

A deep, gravelly voice sounded on the speaker. "How can I help you?"

Was he the bodyguard hired to protect her? "This is Alex Drake. I'm here to see Kelly."

"Miss Cochran's not home."

Impatience grinded Alex's nerves. "When will she return?"

"Can't give out that information, mister." *Click.*

"Bloody, bloody hell." He'd never speak to her at this rate.

Alex was about to back up his car and leave when a motion caught his attention. Kelly galloped on horseback across the rolling hills, dust swirling beneath her horse's hooves.

He slid out of his car and stepped to the closed gate. Of course, Hillyard would instruct his employees to lie at the mention of Alex's name. He waved his arms to get her attention. She galloped the horse in his direction.

In the distance, a burly man, looking like an ex-lineman, stepped out of the house. Two Rottweilers shot out the door and passed him as they all ran toward him. The growling dogs made the gate first and jammed their heads through the bars, snapping at Alex.

Kelly trotted the horse up to him, then, tightening the reins, held the horse in place. Her auburn hair was pulled back into a thick ponytail of waves and curls. She wore a riding helmet, boots, and tight riding pants. Seeing her, gave his senses a jolt.

"Why are you here, Alex?" she asked, glaring down at him.

"We need to have a chat."

The bodyguard bounded up, which caused the dogs to go even crazier with their barking.

"Max," Kelly said, "call off the dogs."

The man gave a command and the animals fell silent. He jerked his thumb toward Alex. "Mr. Hillyard said if Drake was to come here, I was to turn him away. I don't want to lose my job over this."

Kelly sighed. "It's all right, Max. I take full responsibility. Now open the gate."

Max punched in the security code. "The boss will machete my head off for this."

When the gate swung open, Kelly turned to Alex and said coolly, "Get in your car. I'll meet you at the house, but first I have to take care of the horse and shower."

Alex drove his car down the lane. At the house, the bodyguard opened the door and allowed Alex inside, then shook a beefy fist in Alex's face. "You hurt, Miss Cochran—"

"I'm not here to hurt her."

"That's not what I've heard from Mr. Hillyard. He said you're a *dangerous* man." After one last sneering glance, Max left Alex alone in the three-storey foyer.

Alex gazed at the marble sculpture placed in the center, barely recognizable as a naked woman. While cooling his heels for a good forty minutes, he studied the contemporary artwork that decorated the foyer and living room walls. To his taste, the pieces felt cold and empty.

What the hell was keeping Kelly?

At last, she descended the stairs, looking fetching in a white blouse and blue jean skirt. Her hair hung in damp spirals down her back. Her full red lips, and her cheeks rosy from her ride, reminded him of her face flushed with passion and all the times they'd made love.

She crossed her arms over her chest. "What do you want?"

You. Seeing her again took his breath away. He lifted his gaze from her mouth to her deep blue eyes that sizzled with anger.

He forced himself to focus on why he'd come. Even he wasn't sure. Except to see her again. *To get over her?* He didn't know. He was a wreck, confused at what she did to him. She sparked weakness and longing, plus jealousy—because she was staying at Hillyard's house—all at the same time.

"I suppose you're safe here, but can't you see what Hillyard's doing, buying your childhood home? He's manipulating you into marrying him."

"Not a chance. If he had, he wouldn't have made all these changes. It's not the same house that I lived in and loved."

Alex blurted, "I've missed you horribly, Kelly." In those words, he acknowledged the feelings he'd been fighting and that had twisted his gut since their return from the island. His intense feelings for her frightened him, and he didn't know what to do with them.

"And what about your *wife*, Alex? I was nothing to you." She turned and hurried up the stairs. "Excuse me, but I have something to do while Robert is away. I found my father's old desk."

"I'm coming with you." Alex grasped the handrail and followed her. "Why haven't you returned my calls these last two days?"

She turned mid-stair and gazed down at him from her higher elevation. "I misplaced my cell phone." Her face paled and she gasped. "I can't believe it. Robert must have hidden it from me." Then her eyes narrowed as she snapped, "But if he didn't want me to speak to you, it's only because he's trying to protect me."

Alex mounted the steps behind her. "You don't need to be protected from me. Bloody hell, Kelly, I never lied to you. Everything I've ever told you was the truth." He followed her through a door to a second set of stairs.

* * *

A minute later, Kelly strode into the large attic, with Alex following. The space, with a high peaked ceiling, was filled with stacks of boxes and discarded furniture. Everything was all old junk to Robert, but to her it was remnants of her life. In one corner was her old dollhouse and rocking horse. In another were crates of their old books and the family's CD collection. Robert had told her she could have anything she wanted up here.

She struggled to control her mixed emotions of anger, hurt, and love—just being near Alex caused her heart to pound rapidly.

When she'd first seen him, he looked so good dressed in a black shirt and black jeans, she wanted to throw herself at him and cry again every tear she'd shed on his behalf.

With a shaky breath to control her emotions, she whirled and picked up a hammer and screwdriver from the huge, antique desk. "This was my father's. I can't wait any longer for Robert to find the key. I'm breaking the lock."

She wedged the screwdriver into the keyhole and swung the hammer. The lock didn't break, but dust motes swirled in the sunlight pouring through the attic window. She backed away from the desk. While waiting for the dust to settled, she flicked a bitter gaze to Alex. "I'm surprised you could tear yourself away from Vanessa and your second honeymoon."

He took the hammer and screwdriver from her trembling hands. Taking four sharp hits, he broke the lock. "Vanessa's lying."

Was she? "Then why didn't you say so in the detective's office?"

Gritting her teeth, Kelly opened the drawers and found only a few desk supplies.

She flipped through miscellaneous loose papers, her shoulders sagging. "Nothing. I'd hope to find my dad's journal, or something to clear him." She swallowed the despair. When she regained control of her emotions, she raised her gaze to Alex. "I'm going to lose the company, too."

"Kelly, I'm sorry to hear that."

"I can't even ask Robert for an extension. He would . . . if I marry him."

Alex gripped her arms above her elbows. "I was told you'd married him. I'm so relieved. You're not still thinking of doing that are you? Have you been with him?"

She pulled away. "What do you think? I'm living here."

His face grew grim. He whirled and stalked to the door. He paused with his hand on the frame, but he didn't turn to look at her. "Bloody hell, Kelly. I'm such a fool. I shouldn't have come. I should've stayed on the other side of the world."

"I haven't been with Robert," she blurted out, "but I'm not sure what business it is of yours." She swiped away the tears in her eyes and turned her back to the desk. "And am I supposed to believe you gave me one thought when you didn't call for the entire month that we'd been back? So now you try to call me?"

Alex strode across the room. "I thought about you every day. Kelly, the night Vanessa's talking about, I was drinking too much—trying to forget about *you*. She turned up at my house, and I passed out. She's trying to say something happened to prevent our divorce, but I know I wouldn't, Kelly. Even drunk . . . she disgusts me." He ran his hand down his face in anguish. "I left England the next day to come here to see you."

"You did?"

"Yes." He gathered her in his arms. "Come back to England with me. There was magic between us." He brushed his finger against her cheek. The simplest touch from him sent heat crashing through her. "There still is." His blue eyes deepened in color. "Life will be unbearable if I should lose you to Hillyard. I'll have the courts straighten out the paperwork for my divorce." His gaze dropped to her lips. "Kelly, I'm going to prove to you that you can't marry him."

Cupping her jaw, he crushed his lips down on hers and sank the other hand in her hair. He tasted of mint. Twining her hands around his neck, she crushed her breasts against his chest. He belonged to her. His arm was around her, pulling her closer and she felt the hardness of him against her as if he couldn't get close enough to her either.

He exhaled a ragged breath along her cheek and tugged at her shirt, freeing it from her skirt. Wanting him bare as much as he wanted her, she yanked at his shirttail, slid her hand underneath and trailed her fingers over his taut abs. His heart raced against her palm. He slipped one hand beneath her bra and cupped her breast. His thumb caressed her nipple, causing heat to flood to her lower body.

She sucked in her breath and dropped her shaking hands to his belt. He was rock hard against her palm and groaned at her touch. Still kissing her, he lifted her on the desk and slid his hands up her legs, bunching up her skirt. His fingers sunk inside her underwear and sensations shot through her.

"Oh, Alex. Please, now."

He groaned and kissed her again. Then, he lifted his lips from hers as if it took every effort to stop. Both their breathing came in heavy rasps. "No, Kelly, we can't do it this way. Not in Hillyard's attic. You have to leave this house." He held her securely in his arms and rested his forehead on her head.

Wincing, she raised her face to him. "I can't believe we just did that . . . " She checked her watch and gasped. "I have to go. I have an appointment with Dr. Hubbard in an hour."

Disregarding her shock, Alex stroked his thumb across her cheek. "Pack up. You're coming back to England with me. I'll get my divorce finalized, like it should've been months ago if Vanessa hadn't found a way to change it, and you'll stop this nonsense. We're going to *live* together."

"I need more."

He released her. "Blast it, Kelly. I'm not going to be trapped into another marriage. We don't need some man-made laws to legally bind us. I want you. You want me. Let's don't make it any more complicated than that."

She shoved her shirttail into her skirt. "Is that what you think a commitment to me would be? You're going to be an unhappy and lonely old man someday."

"Yes, but I'll have had my freedom."

"But do you *love* me or is this only about sex? If you love me, I'll go with you anywhere and live with you."

"I care for you . . . but I can't give you marriage," he said flatly. "It's unrealistic to expect that such an institution or feelings can last a lifetime."

She choked out a harsh laugh. "I can't seem to reach you inside, can I? You obviously don't love me and probably never will. You know, Robert *does*. I'm a fool not to marry him."

Alex clamped his arms over his chest. "Maybe you should . . . So I should just leave?" But he didn't go, and then he narrowed his eyes. "Well, he's doing a good job of trying to manipulate you into it. Exactly what hold does he have over you?"

The blood drained from her face. "What?" she asked in a shaky breath.

"It looks like I hit the bloody nail on the head. Just how much blasted money do you owe him that he can hold guilt over you to convince you to marry him?"

Kelly floundered under Alex's intense gaze. "He's done everything for me . . . He helped me through college." She winced, and then sighed. "Okay, I owe him nine million dollars, but that won't convince me to marry him."

"*Nine million dollars!*"

The dogs barked loudly outside the dormer windows.

"Someone's here," she blurted.

Alex strode to the window. "A black Mercedes just drove through the gate. Hillyard?"

She nodded and straightened her clothing. "I didn't expect him until this evening. Max must've called him. Alex, he's done so much for me. I don't want him hurt, finding us up here."

Frowning, he pinned her with his gaze, while he tucked his shirt into his jeans.

Kelly hurried down the steps with Alex following her. Tears burned her eyes. He might desire her as a lover, but he didn't love her. Had he any idea how much that hurt? And she had to protect Robert.

They reached the foyer just as Robert jerked open the door. "Max called me. Drake, what the hell are you doing here?" he demanded.

"I stopped to speak to Kelly before returning to England. Good-bye."

Kelly exhaled the breath she'd been holding. Alex was civil enough. She was glad, for his sake, too. Didn't he realize the power Robert wielded in Hollywood?

"And I have a doctor's appointment." Kelly reached for her purse on the table in the foyer and headed out the front doors.

The two men stepped out of the house and onto the drive with her.

"Wait, Drake. Before you go," Robert said in an irritated voice. "I need to speak to you."

Alex nodded and leaned against his dark blue Jaguar. Although his expression was grim, he was still the handsomest man she'd ever seen.

Robert clasped Kelly's hand and led her to his car. "Take mine." He opened the door for her to slide inside. "I'd like to go with you, honey, but there's some business I have to handle. I'll tell Max you're ready."

Evidently, Robert didn't want to leave her alone with Alex for even a moment because he shouted through the doors for Max to go with her to town.

A minute later, the glass doors from the house opened. Tammy stepped out, purse in hand. "Max is on the phone. I'll go with Kelly."

"No, Kelly," Robert ground out. "Wait for Max."

"I can't." Kelly moved to the driver's seat and tapped her watch. "I don't want to be late for my appointment."

Tammy slipped into the passenger seat and shut the door.

* * *

A few minutes later, Alex watched the gates shut behind the Mercedes as Kelly drove away from the ranch with Hillyard's assistant—without even a backward glance. Inner turmoil stabbed at his heart.

Hillyard rounded on him. "Drake, why are you here? Trying to seduce her again? I know all about you two."

Alex didn't answer. Hillyard had every right to be angry, but that didn't explain the overwhelming jealousy surging through him that she'd decided to stay here with this man.

Hillyard clenched his hands at his side. "Stay out of my way. She's going to marry me. I love her."

"Really?" Alex mocked. "I know how much you grieved for her after we were lost. The day you returned from the cruise, your assistant moved into your house."

Hillyard's face darkened. "I thought Kelly was dead."

"I haven't told her, but I'd suspected you and Tammy were having an affair before the cruise. I had only to ask around L.A. to get that information. While we struggled to survive, you were living with her. Not to mention, you had no one scouring the islands to see if Kelly had survived. Your love for her is deep, isn't it?" Alex took a long, hard look at the arrogant man. "I don't want Kelly hurt."

Fury blazed in Hillyard's eyes. "Me, hurt her? I want to make her my wife. You used her, you bastard. I bet you laughed behind my back the entire time you took what should've been mine."

Alex's loathing for Hillyard increased. "She's not your plaything."

"She's not yours either. You knew she was my fiancée, yet you couldn't keep your hands off her." Hillyard slammed his fist into Alex's face.

Alex lifted his hand to his throbbing jaw. "I suppose from your perspective, I deserved that, but don't try it again."

Hillyard snorted. "I know what you're thinking, Drake, that Kelly's rich. Don't waste your time. She's in deep debt, and Cochran Investments is in shambles."

"I'm aware of Kelly's situation."

"Damn it. I won't have you interfering. And when I think about you two . . . and what you did with her . . . " Hillyard swung again, but this time, Alex blocked the punch. With one quick movement, he flipped Hillyard flat on his back onto the concrete driveway.

Hillyard groaned and then snarled up at Alex, "Damn you to hell, Drake."

Max strode out of the house, portable phone in hand. "Boss, you have a call." Shock rose on his face. "What happened?"

Hillyard shoved away Max's extended hand and rose to his feet, clutching his back. "Drake, I don't give a damn that I promised Kelly I wouldn't take it out on you. I'll make sure you never work in Hollywood again. You're fired. *Finished.*"

Alex's jaw tightened. So, Kelly had protected him as well— another one of Hillyard's manipulations used to control her?

Max held out his hand with the phone. "It's Detective Spagnola. The Fiji Police found David Lewis's island house deserted. He wanted to warn you and Miss Cochran as they have reason to believe he's come to the U.S."

"Damn it," Hillyard said, swearing. "I shouldn't have let her go alone. We've got to go after her." He took the phone. Before he spoke into it, he put his hand over the receiver. "Drake, if you're ever on my property again, I give Max permission to show you what we do to trespassers."

* * *

Driving the winding road through the hills, toward town, Kelly kept her trembling hands clenched on the steering wheel, blinking back tears. *How can you do this to me, Alex? I don't have much more heart to break.*

She drove toward the main street of the small town and lifted her gaze to the rearview mirror. A black Cadillac followed closely behind. She pulled into the doctor's parking lot. As the car behind her drove on, she exhaled in relief and shut off the engine.

She glanced at Tammy who had not spoken one word in the past twenty minutes. "Why did you volunteer to go into town with me? You don't like me and went to great lengths to produce that incriminating picture from Fiji to hurt Robert. You could've driven your own car if you wanted to go shopping."

Tammy shifted in her seat. "It's not that I don't like you, but if you marry Robert, you're going to ruin all our lives. Did you know he and I lived together while you were missing?"

Shock ripped through Kelly. *What a liar he's been.*

Then a huge blast of relief ricocheted back. She didn't *owe him* anything. Well, anything except nine million dollars, but he'd been fine with her gone, so she didn't owe him any loyalty as his fiancée.

Stunned by Tammy's confession, Kelly strode into her physician's office. She stepped out later in even more shock, the elderly doctor's words still ringing in her ears, "Young lady, I hope you're prepared for this. You're three month's along."

She had hoped he was joking, but by the look on his face he was deadly serious. "You mean I'm *pregnant?* I've always been irregular—I can't be."

* * *

Her worst fears confirmed, moments later she walked down the sidewalk on wobbly legs and in a trance, her surroundings a blur. The only man she'd ever been with was Alex. He'd turned her life upside down, stolen her heart, showed her what passion could be, and then deserted her.

She couldn't handle a baby right now. *And Alex's baby?* She put her hand to her mouth. That thought was scary and thrilling at the same time. She blew out a shallow breath. He wouldn't be happy about this at all. How could she tell him? He'd think she was trying to trap him as Vanessa had done.

The only good thing about a pregnancy was Robert would have to give up insisting she marry him. He'd lied by omission about his affair with Tammy—so he wasn't spotless, and if he married Tammy, Kelly would be free of the guilt he continually heaped on her.

Still jittery about the baby news, she strode to the boutique where Tammy shopped. When she reached for the door handle, a hard, metal object poked into her back.

"I've been waiting for you to step outside your fortress," said a familiar, deep male voice. "Get in the car."

Fear edged Kelly's spine as she turned. David Lewis lifted the jacket draping his arm and flashed a semi-automatic with a silencer on the tip. A shudder ran through her. She glanced around, but the sidewalk was empty.

"I'm not going anywhere with you," she whispered.

"If that's your answer, here's mine." He raised the butt of the pistol and swung.

CHAPTER NINETEEN

Wanting to warn Kelly, Alex raced the car toward town, wishing the damned car could fly. Even if Hillyard was on his way, he was going to make damn sure she was safe—for himself. Remembering the name of her doctor, Alex found the location on his phone, then drove down the main street of the quaint town. A few people strolled along the sidewalks, past boutiques and shops. At the curb ahead, David Lewis shoved an auburn-haired woman into a black Cadillac. *Kelly!*

Fear tightened in his chest as Alex followed David's car. With three cars between them, he was afraid he'd lose them. The light turned red, two cars in front of him. He slammed his fist on the steering wheel. Finally, the light changed and he moved through the intersection. Traffic cleared, and he continued to drive. He reached the parking lot of a warehouse where he spotted the parked car. Lewis carried Kelly's limp body in his arms and entered the second of the huge metal buildings.

Alex called 911. With adrenalin pumping, he popped the trunk, opened his suitcase, and pulled out the gun he'd recently begun to carry. Clutching the weapon in his palm, he blew out a deep breath. *This was real.*

With no time to wait for the police, he pounded his fist on the warehouse door. "Mister, someone's impounding your car," he lied, in his best Californian accent.

David Lewis yanked open the metal door with a squeak. "What the hell? I paid cash—"

Alex aimed the gun at Lewis. "I'm here for Kelly."

With a smirk of satisfaction, Lewis said, "Oh, what a sweet reunion this is, Hollywood. Come on in. I was going to track you next. You've saved me a lot of trouble."

Alex advanced forward. "I'm the one with the gun this time, so shut up. Put your hands over your head."

Lewis raised his arms and backed into the cavernous warehouse. "Despite your killing Ralph, I don't believe you got the guts to pull the trigger."

"Try me." Alex thrust the weapon toward Lewis's ribs. "Now take me to her."

With a sneer, Lewis shrugged and led Alex to Kelly. "I didn't get my money, but I got my revenge. You can have her rotting corpse."

Limp, with her eyes closed, she lay on a pile of rags on the concrete floor, a coiled rope lay nearby.

"Kelly?" Alex asked numbly. When she didn't respond, his throat ached in despair. "You bastard, what've you done to her?"

Lewis took advantage of Alex's distraction and lunged. They crashed into a wall, knocking the gun from Alex's hand. Pain shot through his head and his recovering shoulder. He connected his knuckles with Lewis's jaw. Lewis swung and hit Alex in the eye. Alex landed a round of punches until the bastard staggered backwards.

Rage shot through Alex and took over as he wrestled the man to the floor. "You've hurt her—you die." He slammed his fist over and over in Lewis's face, satisfied with each bone-crunching sound and the blood spurting from his nose.

Sirens blaring, the sound screeched closer. Alex heard the police cars tearing into the parking lot. He took a deep breath and reigned in his anger.

Through bloodied lips, Lewis mumbled, "I'm not the only one who wants her dead."

Though disgust and fear edged him, Alex took a deep breath and moved away as the police stormed in and leveled their guns on them.

Rubbing his jaw, Alex rose from the floor. "He's your man," he said, in heavy gasps. "He grabbed this woman and I came after him." He handed the officer his driver's license. "Call Detective Spagnola at the LAPD You'll find out that David Lewis is wanted on multiple murder charges and his accomplice is a guy named Mick. I'm sure you'll find him nearby."

He dropped beside Kelly and pulled her into his arms. She was warm. He pressed his wet face against her hair and felt for a pulse.

"Kelly, you're alive," he whispered, tenderly rocking her in his arms. "You're going to be all right, love."

When the officer got off the phone, he said, "An ambulance is on the way. And you've been cleared."

The police led Lewis away.

Lewis last words to Alex were, "Mick will get her."

Alex clenched his jaw, satisfied he'd beaten the man, for what he'd done to Kelly—to both of them—on the island. Although Lewis would go to jail, Kelly still wouldn't be safe. Not when Mick was out there along with anyone else who'd hated her father.

The medical emergency team rushed through the door. Alex moved back while the paramedics lifted her onto a stretcher.

Then one of the paramedic's lifted her eyelids and checked her pulse. "She has a lump on her head and might have a concussion, but based on this quick check, she should be okay," the man said.

Another paramedic dabbed something that stung onto Alex's eyebrow and then his chin. "You okay?"

Alex nodded. "Yeah."

The team wheeled Kelly to the ambulance.

Hillyard, along with his bodyguard, strode toward the truck and shoved past Alex. "What happened?"

One of the officers said, "David Lewis tried to kidnap her. He's been taken into custody."

When a news crew arrived and wielded cameras, Alex grew tense.

When Hillyard leaned over Kelly, her eyelids fluttered open. "Robert. You're here? I thought Alex was. . . I guess I was wrong . . . David Lewis hit me."

Hillyard ran a long finger down her cheek. "I'm always here for you, honey. It's always me."

Clenching his aching hands, Alex stifled the impulse to swoop Kelly up in his arms and make his way out of here, but he'd have to fight both Hillyard and Max, and she needed to go to hospital.

"I'll be right back, Kelly." Hillyard stepped up to Alex. "Drake, *I* can protect her. I'm hiring six more men to guard her at the ranch, and wherever she wants to go. I have the money to help her stabilize the company, so we can pay back all of her debts so one day her life can be normal. What can you do for her?"

Simmering with anger, Alex kept his temper under control, but everything Hillyard said was true.

"Besides, hell," Hillyard said under his breath, "you're a married man. How seedy, Drake? She deserves better than to be dragged through the mud as your mistress. With you out of the picture, she might rethink her life with me again. Don't you want what's best for her?"

Alex clenched his jaw, and despite the nasty look from Hillyard, Alex moved into her field of vision on the other side of the stretcher and leaned close. "Kelly? I'm here as well."

"You didn't leave me after all?" she said groggily. She reached out and her hand fluttered down his cheek. "You're hurt again. Did you fight with David? Please . . . ride with me in the ambulance," she begged.

Alex shook his head. With him out of the picture, he thought Kelly might decide to marry Hillyard. Could she be happy?

He leaned over her and kissed her on the brow. "Hillyard and Max will accompany you. I've some things I need to take care of." He gave her a bland smile and hated the look of disappointment on her face. "You're safer with him."

* * *

The next day, released from the hospital and back at Hillyard Rancho, Kelly hung up the phone. Her head ached miserably, but she was relieved that Doctor Arnold had assured her the baby would be okay.

And Alex? She sighed. Detective Spagnola had called this morning and said the police had a Mick Shepherd in custody. "Alex Drake helped us track down the man last night." She had such hope welling up inside her that that was the reason Alex had left her, but then when she'd ask the detective if he would be meeting Mr. Drake soon and that perhaps they could all get together, he'd said, "No. Mr. Drake said he was on his way back to England and he'd only been happy to help capture the man."

So that was that. Tears gushed in Kelly's eyes. After having rescued her yet once more, he'd left her again to go back to his home in England. Perhaps, after yesterday's ordeal, he thought she was just too much trouble, even to live with. And last night, his sending her off with Robert spoke volumes.

You're safer with him.

Her mouth turned down unhappily. Perhaps for Alex it *was* better. Look at how many times he'd been hurt on her behalf, and she didn't want anything to happen to him. She'd be the most selfish woman in the world if she wanted him to endure any more of all they'd been through. She had to let him go.

* * *

Acutely aware she needed to confide in someone, Kelly had called Aunt Kaye from the hospital and asked her to come stay with her. Kelly was grateful when she arrived later that day. She gave her dear aunt a tight squeeze.

"Oh, my poor niece, I can't believe that horrible man hit you."

"I'm fine, but I have to take it easy for a couple of days."

"After all he's done to you and our family, I'm glad the police have that nasty man in custody."

"Me, too. There will be a trial to deal with, Aunt Kaye, but Detective Spagnola assured me David Lewis should go to prison for life for what he's done."

Kelly escorted her aunt into the once-inviting library. Its mahogany shelves and overstuffed leather furniture had been replaced with chilling art and lean, white chenille sofas and glass tables. Even the magnificent stone fireplace had been changed to black ceramic tile.

Aunt Kaye slapped her hands to her face. "Oh, my! Robert hasn't left one inch of this house alone."

"Unbelievable, huh? The attic is the only place that's the same," Kelly said with a sigh. "This used to be one of my favorite rooms."

"He can't expect you to be happy about this?"

"I don't even think he really notices what I like or don't like. But it doesn't matter anymore. This is his home now. I only came here because he convinced me it was for my safety, and I'm getting tired of him telling me that. No way will I allow Robert to talk me into marrying him." She squeezed her hands together. How could she tell her aunt the rest?

"What else is bothering you, sweetie?"

Kelly let out a deep breath. "I'm pregnant. Alex Drake is the father."

Aunt Kaye's hand rose to her throat. "Oh, my."

"I've shocked you. You'll be embarrassed that I'm going to be an unwed mother?"

"Sweetie, nothing you could ever do would embarrass me. I'm so proud of you." Aunt Kaye embraced Kelly. "I never wanted to say it, but I didn't think Robert was right for you. He's too controlling. Have you told him you can't marry him?"

"Over and over again," Kelly said rolling her eyes. "But he still thinks he can change my mind. I hate to hurt him, but news about the baby should do it. I'm telling him tonight, then I'm moving out."

* * *

After dinner, Kelly asked Robert to meet her in the library. "I need to talk to you."

He strode to the bar and poured a drink. "Sounds serious. What's this about?"

"This is tearing me up, but I can't let you go on thinking you'll convince me to marry you."

He strode to her. His hands were clenched and he seemed barely in control of his anger. "Haven't I done enough for you?" he snapped. "You don't like the house? What is it now, Kelly? What doesn't make you happy?"

"I'm pregnant," she said flatly.

The skin around his mouth whitened. "*Drake*? I'll kill him."

She stepped away from the hatred for Alex that blazed in his eyes. "It happened when we were lost. He doesn't know."

Robert's expression soured when his gaze dropped to her stomach. He snorted. "You'll have an abortion. Tomorrow. I'll be with you all the way, holding your hand."

Shocked, she blurted, "*No*. I'm keeping my child."

"But you. . ." His face reddened and he took a deep breath. "Hell, Kelly. I love you, and if this will make you happy, I'll raise the baby as my own . . . That is, as long as no one knows the truth about it, especially Drake."

She frowned. "I can't ask you to do that for me, Robert. What if the baby looks like him? You wouldn't be able to handle that. Besides, we're like family. I love you, but not in the way you deserve." Her gaze met his truthfully. "And I know while I was away, you were living with Tammy. I think she's a better choice for you."

"I thought you were dead," he choked out. Then his expression quickly changed to disgust. He clenched his fist. "Damn it to hell. I know what this is about. You think you're in love with *Drake*. He used you for booty calls, and then dropped you like a two-bit whore. And you're still panting after him."

She cringed. "It doesn't matter. I still can't marry you."

"Two days after your birthday, the loan is due. Cochran Investments will file bankruptcy. If that happens, I won't get a damned dime of my money and neither will anyone else."

"Give me an extension. We can still save the company. I have some ideas to generate money. I'll pay you back, every penny."

He stepped closer and glared down at her. "Are you kidding? I was willing to risk and extend myself for a wife—not for some other man's whore."

She flinched as if she'd been slapped. Her face burned with shame, yet anger sizzled inside her. "Is that so? I think I understand."

He gripped her wrist in a painful vice. "No, you don't."

She tried to jerk away. "You're hurting me."

"Am I? I've been too soft on you. Time you faced the truth. Your father was guilty as charged. He ripped us all off, and *you* are responsible to make sure the money is repaid."

The floor wavered beneath her feet. "But you told me all this time you believed in his innocence and that he must have been planning to replace the money."

"Damn it, Kelly. I didn't want you hurt. I knew how much you loved your dad. I was protecting you."

Her face burned as shame consumed her again. "You've stood up for him all these years, although he cheated you and everyone else?"

"He was my friend. But he had a dark, ugly side to him that even your mother knew nothing about." He released her. "I didn't mean to be so rough on you, but you've dragged me through pure hell with your deceit."

Her shoulders sagged and Kelly massaged her aching wrist. "I'll be out of your house as soon as possible."

"I'll be in L.A. over the next two weeks. You can stay until then. I want you to think about what's going to happen when you file bankruptcy. To do so will mean all of Cochran's employees and the investors will never recover their money." From his jacket, he retrieved a black box. He opened it to display a huge diamond ring and laid it on the bar. "A second offer and there won't be a third. Wear it. You'll come to your senses and marry me. Then I'll help you."

* * *

The constant ringing badgered Alex from a deep sleep. He opened one eye and tried to focus. He recognized the carpet of his study, rough against his cheek. He licked his dry lips. Last night, after he'd returned to England, he'd settled into his house to decide what to do and had poured himself a glass of brandy . . .

The telephone rang again, excruciatingly loud. He struggled to his feet. "All right, all right. I'll answer." He scooped up the receiver. "Hello."

"I've been trying to get in touch with you for hours," his agent said.

Alex put a hand to his throbbing temple. "Paul, don't talk so loudly. My head aches miserably."

"Do you ever think to answer the phone?"

"I was asleep."

"It's noon. Where's your staff?"

"*Noon?*" Alex raked his fingers through his hair. "I had to let them go as I can't afford to pay them. Do you have any good news for me? I'm going to lose my house."

"No. All offers have been pulled."

"Bloody hell, that's just great. Now, even though he's won, Hillyard's still had me blacklisted. He's making sure I stay away from Kelly. And no one's going to hire me here with Vanessa threatening them if they do."

"Have you considered doing the interview—" *Click.* "Hold on. Got another call."

"Sure, Paul," Alex muttered to himself while he waited. "I've got all the time in the world. My career is in ruins. I had to let my woman go for her own good."

Every time he thought of Hillyard's words, it stabbed like a knife. "Drake, I can protect her . . . What can you do for her?"

Running a hand down his face, Alex stepped to his desk and sat down. How long had he blacked out? Last night, he had returned home and had one small glass of brandy. He picked up the bottle, opened the cap and breathed in a peculiar, bitter smell.

"Bloody hell."

This was the same decanter he drank from the night Vanessa had been here. He couldn't believe it. *She must have put something in his bottle of brandy.*

He smiled for the first time in days. It was a murderous smile, but a smile nonetheless. He'd take the bottle to a lab. If Vanessa wanted to play dirty, now was the time to beat her at her own game. He had to free himself and put her in her place, once and for all. *And for the rest?* He'd bloody hell lost everything and had nothing else to lose.

When Paul clicked back on the line, Alex said, "About that interview with Sandra Weaver . . . Make the arrangements. I'll do it."

* * *

For the past week, after Robert had left the ranch, Kelly took the opportunity to scrutinize the company records and over that time had found nothing to clear her father from blame. The year before his death, there had been every indication the business was doing well. *Why steal from it then?* She even searched the entire attic to see if she had overlooked anything that could clear her father.

Kelly rose from the desk in the library and paced the floor. Ready to give up, and tired because of the growing baby, she flicked on the television, clicking through the channels. When she saw Alex being interviewed, she gaped. Her first response was to shut it off . . . Instead, she dropped to the loveseat and watched, mesmerized.

Sandra Weaver leaned toward Alex. "It's been a big year for you, with the attack on the dive boat, lost at sea, and then being marooned on a deserted island. "Kelly Cochran was with you. Many rumors have swirled about you two being involved in a romance."

"What these rumors don't take into account is Miss Cochran and I had to struggle daily just to survive." Kelly heaved a sigh of relief. Alex successfully avoided admitting on TV that they'd had an affair.

"May I call you, Alex?" Ms. Weaver proceeded to detail the deaths from the explosion, and then Alex's other heroic actions, including the latest attack by David Lewis. "You recently rescued Kelly Cochran at a warehouse, then you helped capture Mick Shepherd, wrapping up what must be a huge case for the police."

"Yes, two of the men involved are in custody, but I must also add that Ms. Cochran saved my life a couple of times as well."

"Your divorce from Vanessa Caine is final. Is there any truth to the rumors that you're dating actress Megan Daniels?"

"None at all. At this moment, my interests lie with my work."

"Vanessa Caine has made your career difficult. Would you like to elaborate?"

Alex didn't comment, so Ms. Weaver recited past incriminating details about Vanessa and her role to blacklist Alex.

A dismayed frown flitted across his face. "I hold no ill will toward Ms. Caine, and wish her the best . . . if we can move on and put these issues in the past."

"That is very gracious of you, Alex."

In the end, Kelly thought the interview was favorable to him. He didn't reveal anything negative about Vanessa, but his ex-wife was hung by her own vengeful deeds and attempts to hurt his career.

The next morning, Kelly held the newspaper in her lap, her hands shaking. In the Entertainment Section a paragraph announced Alex's divorce from Vanessa. He smiled beside actress Megan Daniels, who beamed up at him—the same actress he denied dating in the television interview. Beautiful with long dark hair, Megan probably accommodated the playboy lifestyle Alex wanted to lead.

He'd found someone else. Kelly's tears splattered on the newspaper. Now, there was no way she could tell him about the baby.

CHAPTER TWENTY

August 30th

Built in the twenties, the Westwood Grande Hotel wasn't far from the ranch and symbolized sumptuous elegance. Although tonight was Kelly's twenty-fifth birthday, she didn't feel like celebrating. However, she was determined to endure tonight's festivities with pride and dignity. No one would guess that on Monday morning, her happiness to take over partial control of the company would end—if Robert wouldn't give her an extension, the company would go into bankruptcy.

The amount she owed Robert weighed heavily on her mind and shoulders. She sighed. He'd even paid for the dress she wore.

With new disclosures by Robert that her father was guilty of the embezzlement charges, saving the company to restore her dad's reputation didn't matter anymore. However, her heart ached that she wouldn't be able to repay Robert, or the clients and employees who had lost their investments. Now, there was nothing she could do to make right the wrong her father had done to them.

However, this past week, while she stayed at the ranch, she'd come to a decision. She'd move to the east coast to make a new life for herself and the baby. She had proved she wasn't helpless. She'd survived on a deserted island, battled ruthless criminals, and made an escape to freedom. For a new name? She thought wryly, how about the aliases Kelly Smith or Kelly Jones?

However, tonight, she was still Kelly Cochran and that gave her a measure of comfort. She had her hair arranged in a partially upswept hairdo, letting the rest flow in curls down her back and over one shoulder.

Resigned to the inevitable, she stepped down the hotel's marble staircase, in a pale-yellow silk gown. The high waist, with a band of rhinestones below her breasts, and a sheer overlay of silk, effectively concealed her slightly rounded stomach—something she wouldn't be able to hide much longer.

She entered the ballroom with its high ceilings and glittering chandeliers. She might as well get this evening over with by pretending everything was wonderful at Cochran Investments.

A band played upon a stage. Tables held elaborate towering arrangements of colorful and aromatic flowers, while a wall of French doors led to lush gardens with fountains.

She pasted a smile on her lips—one she didn't feel—and joined Robert and Vanessa at the entrance.

Dressed in a black tuxedo, and looking debonair, Robert gave her a curt nod. "Hello, Kelly. I'm glad to be back from New York, especially to see you. You look like a goddess."

The way his gaze slid over her she could tell he hadn't accepted her refusal to marry him. She frowned. Surely, he hadn't expected her to change her mind?

In exasperation, Kelly glanced away. Tammy hovered nearby, overseeing anything that might go wrong. They shared a mutual, unspoken desire that Robert would realize Tammy was the right woman for him.

Appearing statuesque in a golden gown and dangling, diamond earrings, Vanessa dropped her gaze to Kelly's waistline. The movie star's mouth twisted in disgust, but she didn't say anything.

Heat stole across Kelly's face. She couldn't believe Robert would betray her secret to Vanessa—of all people.

When Robert took Kelly's elbow, she tensed at his touch. He murmured in her ear, "I'd like to introduce you to Timothy Michaels. He's the new actor in my movie—Drake's replacement—since I *fired* Drake."

Sporting a prominent chin with a deep cleft, Timothy grinned at her. She realized Alex had paid dearly for their romance on the island.

The four of them formed a line to greet guests. Standing beside Timothy, Kelly watched him flirt with every woman who passed by. He reminded her of her original stereotype of good-looking actors. With his cocky smile, he seemed in love with himself. He didn't let her down either. "Hey, my lovely sidekick, as soon as these intros are over, how about you and I *getting it on*," he said, winking, "on the dance floor."

"Let's don't," she returned in her iciest tone. She almost laughed when he appeared affronted by her rejection. Robert must have overheard because he sent Timothy a deadly look.

The guests were friends, celebrities, or Robert's clients, since most of her dad's ex-clients hated her father. Aunt Kaye was also present and had checked into one of the hotel rooms.

After the formal dinner was over, Mrs. Martin, one of her father's oldest and richest clients who had not been hurt in the financial debacle, greeted Kelly with a hug.

Mrs. Martin peered over her glasses and glared at Vanessa, ten feet away. "I can't believe Robert would bring that dreadful Caine woman around you after what she did."

Kelly flinched. "What do you mean? What did she do?"

Mr. Martin grabbed his wife's elbow. "Come on, dear. There is someone I want you to meet." He escorted her away.

Robert joined Kelly, murmuring in her ear, "I can't stand that blabbering woman. Now, what's your answer?"

"It's still *no*, Robert," she whispered in exasperation.

"Hell, is it your plan to embarrass me? And why aren't you wearing your ring? You know everyone expects me to announce our wedding plans tonight."

"Robert, please, *stop*," she hissed. "It's not going to happen. Now, don't completely ruin my feelings for you."

She whirled to leave and bumped into a little man with a red, bulbous nose. "I beg your pardon."

Coming up behind her, Robert clasped her elbow. "Kelly, I'd like you to meet the Reverend Ned Schulte and his wife, Doris."

Both unkempt, the man wore an outdated plaid suit, while his wife's bleached-blond hair looked like cotton candy. The couple didn't seem like anyone Robert would associate with.

The minister stuck out his hand. Reluctantly, Kelly extended hers.

He gripped her palm with a sweaty squeeze. "My pleasure."

"She'll make a beautiful bride," the wife cackled. A knowing gleam lit her beady eyes, as if Kelly's marriage to Robert was a sure thing. When she saw Aunt Kaye again, she'd have to tell her about Robert's sheer nerve.

Glaring at Robert, Kelly extracted her hand from Mr. Schulte's grip and resisted the urge to wipe her palm on her dress. "I need to go. Enjoy the party." She crossed the floor, muttering to herself, "I can't believe Robert."

When she noticed a tall, handsome man across the room, she gasped and stopped in her steps. In a tux, Alex stood out like a beacon in the crowd. He was stunningly gorgeous in his black tux with bow tie, looking like a movie star from Hollywood's golden days. His hair gleamed like antique gold in the chandelier light.

Why was he here? Hope washed over her. She wanted to thank him for not only saving her from David, but going after and helping the police apprehend Mick.

Alex's gaze moved around the ballroom as if he searched for someone. He must have found who he looked for because a pretty brunette in a blue sequined gown rushed over and attached herself to his arm—the actress from the newspaper photo.

Kelly's stomach clenched and tears burned her eyes. How could he be so cruel as to bring his new lover to the party?

A male guest bumped into Kelly, sending the soda in her champagne glass spilling over the rim and onto her hand. The man apologized, but she was only thankful he had snapped her back to reality so she no longer stared at Alex like an idiot.

Her heart breaking, she whirled and headed in the opposite direction.

* * *

Alex endured a brief conversation with Megan Daniels, a woman whose clinging grip on his arm reminded him of Vanessa. After he politely excused himself, he moved through the crowd.

A male colleague clapped Alex on the back. "Way to go. Everyone's talking about your interview with Sandra Weaver."

Alex shook his hand. "Thanks."

"Man, as if you hadn't done enough in the Islands, I can't imagine walking into a warehouse, knowing the man was a killer. And then to track down his accomplice."

"Miss Cochran's life was in danger."

"Brave, if you ask me."

Alex continued past people until he spotted Kelly. Across the crowded ballroom, their gazes locked. His heart lurched at how much he'd missed her. How could he have ever compared a life with Kelly to his with Vanessa?

The color drained from Kelly's face. He'd not come to upset her, only to speak to her. He made a quick cut through the crowd but by the time he reached her, a man was leading her onto the dance floor.

While they danced, a familiar jealousy roared to life in Alex's soul. He had to face the truth. When it came to Kelly, he had no control over his emotions, and his life was in a tailspin without her.

A woman bearing a resemblance to Kelly approached him, extending her hand. "You must be Alex Drake. I'm Kelly's Aunt Kaye."

After a few pleasantries, Alex's gaze strayed back to Kelly. "She looks beautiful."

"Too bad she can't marry the man she loves."

Alex lifted an eyebrow in surprise. *Just how much had Kelly told her aunt about him?*

Kaye gave him a tentative smile. "Robert's not right for her, and I don't like the way he's pressing my dear girl to marry him either. It was a pleasure meeting you, Alex. Enjoy the party." Her gown swished as she walked away.

When the song ended, he strode across the floor to Kelly's side. "Happy Birthday, love. Could I have a chat with you?"

At the same time, Megan approached and tugged on his jacket sleeve. "Alex, I'd like a dance." He groaned inwardly when Kelly's gaze dropped to the hold Megan had on his arm. Megan's mouth turned downward. "Who's this?"

Brushing past him, Kelly whispered with a cool hauteur, "While I want to thank you for what you've done for me, going after David and Mick, if you're trying to introduce me to your new girlfriend, I'd rather not meet her." Her voice choked up on her last words, "It's just too much to ask of me." She hurried through the crowd.

"Kelly," he called out, but she kept on going.

How could he convince Kelly he'd come here to see *her*?

After the rock band finished their song, he jumped on stage and spoke to the musicians. Then, holding the microphone close, he belted out a love song and sang how his heart ached for the one he'd loved and lost. He put a 1950's spin on the song, by speaking some of the words. As he intended, it was a little tongue-and-cheek because he wanted to make her smile so she'd warm up to him as he crooned about unrequited love.

Finally, Kelly paused and stared at him. She had to know the song was for her. Satisfaction simmered inside him, until a group of women gathered near the front of the stage. When the music ended, Megan rushed up to him.

Contempt flashed on Kelly's face before she whirled away.

He exhaled a frustrated breath. His singing had backfired. He'd seen Kelly's surprised face turn into an unhappy one. She'd never speak to him now, or trust him, and he'd lost her once again in the crowd.

When he stepped down from the stage, Megan followed.

Vanessa strode toward him with her hands on her hips. Talk about darkening one's day. One sneer from the witch and the women around him departed like rats from a sinking ship.

He hadn't seen the she-devil since his day in court. With her gold, statuesque gown, like plastic, wrapping her body, most men might believe her beautiful. To him, she looked as deadly as a cobra about to strike.

She grabbed a drink from a passing waiter and lifted her glass in salute. "Darling, did you change your mind and come to the party for me?"

He eyed the martini in her hand. "Only if I've died, and this is *Hell*."

"Then did you come here tonight for that home-wrecking *slut*?"

"Don't ever speak of her in such a way."

When he turned, she plucked at his jacket sleeve. "All right, Alex. Why *are* you here?"

Alex glanced at her with disgust. "I've nothing to say to you." He strode away, but her high heels clicked behind him.

Vanessa rasped, "Damn you, Alex. So destroying your career wasn't enough? That little strumpet is going to pay. Mark my words—"

He whirled on her. "Shut the hell up, Vanessa. Leave Kelly out of this." He turned on his heel, but she gripped his sore arm, pulling the jacket from his shoulder.

"Have a good time living in poverty, you bastard. At least you'll never work as an actor again."

Grasping Vanessa's elbow, he steered her into a nearby private room and closed the door.

Then with disgust, he dropped his hand, not wanting to touch her. "You're causing a scene. Don't you have any pride, Vanessa?"

"Not if you're leaving me. No one leaves me, not until I'm ready." She laughed, a little hysterically. "And I might be pregnant after our night together."

"Not by me. Lab reports confirm the brandy decanter in my office had been laced with sleeping pills—the same brand you're prescribed. I was out cold. Now, I'm giving you one last chance to stay out of my life or *else*."

Her expression soured as she straightened. "You can't prove I did anything of the sort?"

"Not smart that you left the empty bottle of your prescription in the waste can, but it doesn't matter. I don't think it would be good publicity in the press to think that you had to drug me to get my attention. It wouldn't be good for your career. According to my doctor, the medication you put in the decanter would have left me, let's say, unable to perform. That combined with knowing . . . " He leaned closer, hoping to make his meaning finally, and utterly clear to her. "That I have not the least desire to make love to *you*, proves nothing happened. I've turned the evidence over to the police and my solicitor, and they're waiting for my word to start legal action. So I suggest you stay out of my life." He splayed his hand in the air. "Or I can see the headlines in the tabloids now . . . "

Her mouth dropped open, and then she snarled, "So, Kelly's brought you back by telling you she's pregnant? You're a bigger fool than I thought."

"Kelly . . . pregnant?" He turned in shock. He had to find her.

"*You didn't know?*" she hissed. She stomped her foot. "Well, you can't marry her. Robert will stop you. Damn you." Her martini sailed toward him through the air. He stepped aside. The glass shattered against the door next to him. "I hate you, Alex!" she screeched.

He stared at her. "Now that's much better than your false, professed love." He added dryly, "You know you really should work on your aim."

She raised her fist and rushed at him. "You're going to pay for this, you bastard."

Alex shoved her out of his way. She fell into a nearby chair.

He leaned his hands on the arms, and thrust his face at her. "No, Vanessa," he warned through tight lips. "Any more bad press for Kelly or me and I'll hold you responsible. While I was in

England, I had a private investigator do some research on you. Don't you think the press will love it when I tell them all about your past? How you slept your way to the top, with about every producer in town. How about your numerous, but secretive, plastic surgeries? And your mother's sordid profession as a streetwalker, not to mention your little foray into that line of work for a time when you were a teen." He stood back and crossed his arms over his chest. "Don't think I don't know all about it."

"You wouldn't dare go public with anything like this. Why you'd look like a fool."

"I will, if you so much as attempt to harm Kelly. By the way, did you catch my interview with Sandra Weaver?"

Vanessa's winged eyebrows drew together. "What interview?"

Alex didn't bother answering. She could find the information on her own. He headed back to the party, his relief enormous to be free of the witch.

He glanced around the ballroom looking for Kelly. No wonder she was angry. And she had a lot to say for herself, especially with the secret she'd been keeping from him.

* * *

Tears pricking her eyes, Kelly clenched her arms over her chest and tried to keep her mind on the conversation with one of Cochran Investment's satisfied clients. She'd made a fool of herself, staring at Alex while he was on stage. For one brief moment, she had imagined he sang to her. It was probably part of the actor job description to make every woman feel special.

"I'm sorry . . . you were saying, Mr. Brown?" Kelly asked.

When Alex strode directly up to her and put his arm around her shoulders, she gasped.

He stroked his fingers on her bare shoulder in an intimate way, sending shock waves through her. "Hello, love."

He smiled at her in his most charming way with his teeth gleaming white and his dimples evident.

Frowning, she glanced at his hand.

"What are you doing, Alex?" she asked warily. *How could he do this to her in public?*

"I need to speak to you . . . *privately.*" He added in a low voice, "Unless you want everyone to know our business and cause more gossip."

She gritted her teeth. Robert must have told Vanessa, who in turn told Alex about her pregnancy. What else could drag him away from the eager Megan Daniels? "Excuse me, Mr. Brown. It seems this *client* can't wait until Monday morning to talk business."

Alex clasped her hand in a firm grip. "Yes, I'm certain this discussion can't wait. Let's go into the garden."

Sighing, she went with him through the French doors and onto the terrace. He led her down stone steps and along a lighted path, to a secluded bench surrounded by ornamental trees and sweet, fragrant flowers.

"Sit . . . please," he said.

With a sigh, she plopped down on the bench and crossed her arms over her chest. "What do you want, Alex, other than to humiliate me? Everyone could see us leave the ballroom together. I've endured more bad publicity about us than I can take, so please have a care for *my life*. I really don't want to meet your new girlfriend, or hear you sing love songs to her."

"I don't have a *new* girlfriend," he said, sitting down beside her. "By the way, I brought you a birthday present." He retrieved a wrapped box from his jacket pocket and presented it to her. "Open it."

She gave him a sideways glance and then tore off the wrapping. Inside, a necklace with a heart-shaped ruby, surrounded by tiny diamonds, lay against black velvet.

"The song I sang tonight was for you, sweetheart, and the lyrics, my true feelings. I want to make it official, love. You've stolen my heart. Or should I say as Moto did, 'you've ripped my heart from my chest.' It's only appropriate that you wear this around your neck."

She gaped at Alex, unable to speak.

He lifted her hand and twined their fingers together, while his gaze searched hers. "What *did* happen to us on that island? You don't need to answer my question because I already know. And I don't want to hear another tale of how lonely we were. It took me a while to figure it out, Kelly, but I'm *hopelessly*," he emphasized the word with his beautiful blue eyes gleaming at her. "I'm *hopelessly*, in love with you."

She shook her head to clear her thoughts. "Say that again?"

He grinned. "I love you, Kelly, and I always will." Putting his arm around her, he pulled her close. "I want to hold you, take care of you, *marry* you."

Stunned by his words, tears of happiness brimmed in her eyes. She was enthralled watching his gaze lower to her mouth. She licked her own lips in response to his being so preciously close.

"It's true," he said in a husky whisper that made her shiver. "I want to break our silly agreement. I'm never going to let you go. And if someone is spying on us, they can see this."

His mouth covered hers. Her hands pressed against his jacket, Kelly gave herself up to the sweetest pleasure. Returning his kiss with eager affection, she lost herself in his love for her.

Finally, he pulled away, his expression growing serious. He raised an eyebrow in question. "But perhaps I was mistaken about your feelings for me?"

Giving a little gasp of happiness, she cupped her hands to his cheek. "You've always known how I feel about you, Alex."

He held her hands in his, his eyes shining with warmth. "Sweetheart, after I left you the last time, I went to my solicitor. I'm officially divorced. They claim it was a clerical error, although I'm sure Vanessa had a friend in a high place. They corrected the date back to April 30th as it would have been." He pulled an envelope from his pocket.

In the dim light, she skimmed the papers before returning them to him.

He slipped the divorce papers into his jacket pocket, then clasped her hands. "I'm still worried about your protection, but with both Lewis and Mick going to prison, and if we live in England, far away from here, you should be safer. But, Kelly, we have more issues between us. I can't offer you anything like Hillyard. Right now, I have a lot of debt. I don't even know if or when I'll land my next acting job, but I want you to marry me . . . If you'll forgive me for behaving so stupidly."

"I want to . . . but being with me," she said, wincing. "How can we do it? I don't want you hurt or worse. You've gone through enough because of me."

He grabbed her shoulders. "Kelly, I can't go back to the way I used to be. I swear when I saw you lying there for dead in that warehouse, it was like walls crashing around me. I realized how much I loved you and there *is* no life without you."

Tears sprang to her eyes. "I never expected to hear those words from you."

"Then I'll say it again. I love you, Kelly. Marry me? I'll shout it in the ballroom if you'd like. You have stolen my heart."

"Well," she said with a watery chuckle. "I had to steal it, as it was obvious you wouldn't give it to me freely."

He grinned. "I'm not sorry. You hold my heart in your hands."

Her brow creased in concern. "Robert will go ballistic. He might hurt your career."

Alex framed her face in his hands. "Between Vanessa and Hillyard, my career *is* already over. He's already blacklisted me in Hollywood."

"Oh, no."

He nodded. "Oh yes. But I don't expect Vanessa to bother us again." He squeezed Kelly's hand and told her about the drug Vanessa put in his drink and what the doctor had said about the effects of the medication. "I passed out that night. Even out of my mind, I knew I hadn't slept with her."

"She's sick, Alex."

"No one knows that better than I do. I've threatened her with her own tactics—the media—so I don't think we have to worry about her anymore. However, Hillyard will try to make our lives miserable, but I don't care. If I have to, I'll do something else for a living."

She pulled a little out of his embrace. "I've seen how women chase you. My mother suffered because of a cheating husband."

"Ah, the jealous type?" He grinned and tapped her chin. "Bloody hell, that's all right because I've been insanely jealous over you, starting with Hillyard on the cruise ship, and Moto who nearly killed me to get to you. Not to mention—"

"Okay, so it works both ways." She ran her hand along his jaw and smiled through her tears.

"I won't cheat, Kelly. You make me more than satisfied."

"I watched your interview. What about Megan Daniels?"

He tipped Kelly's chin up and caught her gaze. "I said there was no truth to the rumor. Megan came here on her own tonight. She's followed me since my divorce, but I'm sure our marriage will dampen her enthusiasm."

"I should hope so."

His eyes brimming with tenderness, he held her hand in his. "I want only you."

He hadn't mentioned the baby. Her hands on his chest, she pushed a little away from him, narrowing her eyes.

"Is there any *other* reason why you're asking me to marry you?"

He chuckled. "Other than to keep me from being an unhappy and lonely old man someday—your words—I can't think of anything else."

Happiness enveloped her. He didn't know about the baby and wasn't asking her to marry him because he felt forced. She should've known Vanessa wouldn't tell him.

"Tell me you feel the same, Kelly."

She looked into his worried blue eyes and at that moment, nothing else mattered. She smiled. "I love you, Alex. There's never been any doubt in my mind about that. I was attracted to you from the first time I saw you in your cabin, wearing nothing but a towel." She grinned. "But it was how good you were to me while we were lost that really made me fall in love with you. I don't care how poor we'll be. I'd live in a hut, just to be with you."

"With our money situation, we might have to."

She teased, "I know of a little vacant hut on a certain deserted island."

He pulled her close. "Answer the question, love," he said in a husky voice. "Will you marry me? Will you risk whatever we have to go through?"

"Yes. Oh yes, Alex. I'll risk it all for you." She giggled, her eyes brimming with tears of happiness to be with the man she loved. Unlike her engagement to Robert, she knew deep in her soul that Alex was the right choice.

"Will you wear your birthday present?"

Smiling, she nodded eagerly, and he hooked the necklace around her neck.

Then he cradled her face in his hands. With his thumbs, he swiped the wetness from beneath her eyes and placed a light kiss on her lips. He deepened the kiss and held her as if he'd never let her go. Desire surged through her.

With a sigh, he lifted his mouth from hers and rested his cheek against her hair. "I've been utterly miserable without you. I don't want you going back to Hillyard's ranch, ever."

"I only have to get my things. After you left, I told Robert nothing he said would ever convince me to marry him, which means on Monday, I probably won't get the extension and the company will be dissolved." She ran her finger down Alex's face. "I planned to move across the country and change my name."

He stroked her cheek with his thumb. "I like the idea of a name change, but this time, you're leaving with *me*."

Pressing her lips to his, her love for him burned brightly. She decided to tell him about the baby later and hoped he didn't mind he would be getting more than he bargained for. He kissed her, slowly and with a shared hunger that swept them both up in the moment.

When his fingers tugged on the zipper of her dress, she broke their kiss. "Alex?"

He groaned. "You're right. Unless we want to cause another scandal, we'd better call a halt to this and return to the party."

She nodded and caught a glimpse of his face in the dim light. "We can't go back looking like this either. Come here." With her thumb, she gently wiped her lipstick from his mouth, giving herself credit for resisting the strongest desire to plant another kiss on his sensual lips and sink back into his arms. "I'd better go in first and repair my makeup. See you inside."

He waited several minutes. As soon as he stepped near the doors, Hillyard's bodyguard, Max, said to his back, "Drake, this is a private party." Alex turned. Six, tall bouncer-type men, glared as they surrounded him.

* * *

After leaving the ladies room, Kelly entered the ballroom, feeling wrapped in a cocoon of bliss. Even the loss of Cochran Investments couldn't dampen her happiness tonight. She didn't see Alex, which was just as well, since she could hardly spend the entire evening with him.

When she passed a table where the Reverend Schulte sat with his wife, he raised his drink in salute, sloshing liquid onto his jacket. "There's the beautiful bride-to-be."

Kelly rolled her eyes. Did Robert think she'd allow this drunken minister to perform their wedding ceremony?

Nearby, Robert conversed with Mr. and Mrs. Martin, even though earlier in the evening he'd called the woman blabbering. Must be a cordial conversation, Kelly thought sarcastically. She'd always known he never cared for the outspoken lady. Kelly tried to slip by, but Robert waved her over. Not wanting to appear rude, she sighed and crossed the floor to him.

When Robert linked his arm with hers, she stiffened. "Kelly's fine and the picture of health, aren't you, honey?" His words belied his unhappiness over her pregnancy.

"Nice to hear you survived your terrible ordeal in the South Pacific, dear," Mrs. Martin said. "I just wanted you to know, I for one have always believed in your father's innocence."

"Thank you," Kelly replied, but the Martins only believed in him because they were fortunate enough not to have lost money in the embezzlement scheme. However, if her father had been a cheat, she wasn't responsible for anything he'd done. Still, his guilt tormented her.

A movement above on the second floor balcony caught Kelly's attention. Max had his hand on Alex's jacket lapel and took a swing at him. Alex ducked.

After a light scuffle, Alex grasped one of the draperies and climbed the railing. Kelly's heart squeezed in her chest. The crowd gasped, and then the room fell silent. Then Alex slid down the curtains to the first floor safely. Kelly exhaled in relief as he straightened his jacket and bow tie.

Throwing a disgruntled look toward Alex, Robert folded his arms over his chest. "Drake was supposed to leave. He wasn't invited, and he'll pay for the damages to those draperies."

Robert gripped Kelly's arm. She knew she would have to cause a scuffle to get away. However, he couldn't hold her arm forever.

Mrs. Martin squinted over her bifocals at Alex. "Hmm. So that's Alex Drake with whom you were stranded? Extremely handsome. I would've found myself delighted to be lost on a deserted island with him."

Kelly smiled at the vision of Alex alone with the older woman, old enough to be his grandmother.

Mrs. Martin wagged her eyebrows. "Robert, you must have been insanely jealous to know she spent so much time with *him*— alone." The gleam in her eyes indicated she deliberately tweaked Robert's ego.

He flicked a piece of lint from his sleeve. "No. Since Kelly is the soul of *integrity* and *loyalty*, I had nothing to worry about."

Her face growing warm, Kelly barely restrained herself from wrenching her arm away from his grasp.

"Well, then the question of the hour is, when can we expect you two love birds to be joined in happy wedlock?" Mrs. Martin asked.

Kelly nearly gasped. Obviously, Robert was not getting the word out that they were no longer an engaged couple.

Mr. Martin grabbed his wife's hand. "Dear, why don't we get some fresh air?"

After the Martins departed, Robert grumbled, "Damned busybody."

Through clenched teeth, Kelly said, "Let go of my arm, Robert. Did you try to throw Alex out of the party?"

Robert's hold on her arm tightened. "He crashed it."

"He's *my* guest now."

Vanessa swished up to them. "Robert, aren't you curious as to why Alex is here?"

Robert sneered down at Kelly. "I was about to ask Kelly the same question?"

Kelly didn't get the chance to answer because Alex made his way through the crowd and joined them. His gaze dropped to Robert's hold on her arm. Animosity passed between the two men. Kelly winced, hoping they wouldn't fight again.

"You weren't invited, Drake," Robert snapped.

"I distinctly remember you telling me about this party at the police department," Alex countered. "You said, 'be there.'"

Robert's mouth twitched. "You damn well know that was before I *fired* your ass."

"Hillyard," said a bald man with glasses who approached them. "I'm late, but not too late to witness that little gimmick you had in store for your guests. Is he one of the actors in your new film? The staged fight, then coming down the curtains—a brilliant publicity stunt. For a movie coming out?"

Finally, Robert released Kelly's arm and said smoothly, "Sam Goldsmith." Kelly recognized the name of one of the biggest producers in Hollywood. Robert shook the man's hand vigorously. "Glad you could make it. And *no*, he doesn't work for me."

Mr. Goldsmith's nod toward Vanessa was cool. "Vanessa, it's been a long time."

"Sam, my agent will call," the actress said, slurring her words. "I've decided to accept the part—"

"You're no longer right for any of my projects," Mr. Goldsmith said, cutting her short. Vanessa's mouth snapped shut. "And your other guests?" he asked, his attention directed at Kelly and Alex.

"Kelly Cochran," Robert answered. Begrudgingly, he choked out, "Alex Drake."

Mr. Goldsmith extended his hand to Alex. "I liked your entrance, son. So you're the young man Sandra Weaver recently interviewed?"

Alex shook Goldsmith's hand. "Yes."

"You were a hero. I planned for my assistant to contact your agent on Monday, but since you're here, could I have a minute of your time? I see a lot of star quality in you, and since you're not working for Hillyard here, I have a few projects which might be of interest to you." He shrugged toward the rest in the group. "Excuse us for a moment?"

Kelly met the twinkle in Alex's eyes and they shared the moment. She smiled to herself as he walked away with Mr. Goldsmith.

"Damn it to hell," Robert said with a groan. "Hero, my ass. Star quality?"

Vanessa clenched her hands at her sides. "I can't believe this. I thought for sure Sam would give me the part."

Apparently, Vanessa's little star was slipping. Kelly lifted her hand to cover her grin.

Robert frowned. "Hell, Kelly, why *is* Drake here?"

"*For me*," she quipped. Wrapped in euphoria now, she smiled brightly.

His face contorted with anger. "It's time to make my announcements." He stepped onto the stage. With a curt wave of his hand, he stopped the band mid-song and practically wrenched the microphone from the singer. "As you all know, it was a blessing Kelly Cochran survived after an attack in the South Pacific. Now, let's congratulate Kelly on her 25th birthday and taking over partial control of Cochran Investments. She's worked hard for this."

He spoke about the future of the company, but it was all a lie—unless he gave her an extension next week. And he'd made it clear he wouldn't unless she married him.

Alex rejoined Kelly. "I have good news. I'll tell you later."

After a round of applause, Robert again spoke into the microphone, his gaze finding Kelly's in the crowd. Her heart skipped a beat. "As the celebration ends, I'd like to take this opportunity to make a more personal statement tonight. Many of you know how special Kelly Cochran is to me."

She gaped in disbelief.

Someone yelled from the crowd. "And when will we hear of a date?"

Many people turned her way and clapped.

Robert said into the microphone, "Perhaps tonight I'll press for a date, but then Kelly has a mind of her own, so you never know." He turned it into a joke. The blood rushed to Kelly's face. "But I know that as a husband-and-wife team leading the way, we would have Cochran Investments thriving. Thank you for coming."

The band began to play their last song, and the crowd thinned.

She shot a frown at Alex who looked as perplexed as she was.

Tammy made her way over to Kelly. "You're still thinking about marrying him?" she accused in a shaky voice.

"No, Tammy," Kelly whispered, shaking here head. "No. That wasn't a marriage announc—"

Tammy whirled and didn't wait to hear her explanation that this had been all Robert's idea.

Kelly's shoulders slumped as she watched Tammy flee from the ballroom. She shook her head in disgust. "Alex, I just don't know what he's up to."

"He's trying to save face, but he's lost, and he knows it." Alex trailed his finger down her bare arm. "I want to see you tonight," he said, lowering his voice. "You and I are free to do as we choose." The desire blazing in his eyes made her forget all about Robert and his ridiculous games to manipulate her.

"Your place or mine?" she asked.

"Unfortunately, the hotel's full. I don't have a room."

"I do. You can stay with me." At the thought of spending the night with Alex in the soft canopy bed upstairs, desire swept through her.

He lifted his hand to her cheek and brushed away a tendril at her temple. "I'll be there."

With tingles sweeping her, she withdrew her keycard from her handbag and said with a shaky voice, "Room 411. As a rep for the company, I need to say good-bye to a few of the guests. And I want to check on Aunt Kaye. I'll be up in a few minutes. Okay?" Besides, she didn't want to tell Alex, but she wanted to have a little private talk with Robert.

Alex took the card. "I'll be waiting. I love you," he whispered. She tore her gaze from his. All she wanted was to have the party over and be in his arms again.

After the last guest had left, Kelly confronted Robert in the empty ballroom. "You have to accept that we're never going to get married."

"Do I?"

"Yes! What's wrong with you? Why did you make it sound like we still might marry?"

"Because you'll come to your senses soon. You need this marriage. You'll lose the company. *For what?* To get laid by Drake?" he roared.

"He's asked me to marry him. We love each other."

Anger twisted Robert's features. "I won't help you then, and Cochran Investments will be dissolved. You'd better choose wisely which one of us you want. I won't be responsible for your enemies when the money isn't repaid."

"I'm pregnant with his baby. How can you even think you want to marry me?"

He clasped her forearm. "Because I love you."

She shook off his hand. "I'm sorry I hurt you, Robert."

His lips twisted in a cynical smile. "So am I."

"In the morning, I'll pick up my things from the ranch."

"I'm not going to be there until the afternoon—I've have guests to see off in the morning. You get your things and get out. It would be better that way." He blew out a breath and shook his head. "But it still bothers me, Kelly. Someone might be out there wanting to kill you."

As usual he was impressively rugged in his black tuxedo. It hit her hard just how much Robert had dominated and ruled her life since her parents had died. Well, she was through with that. "Robert, stop trying to manipulate me. It won't work. Tammy was hurt tonight by what you said. She loves you . . . as you deserve."

"I know she does. I should find her." His shoulders sagged as he glanced away, like a man finally beaten. "I've always wanted what was best for you, Kelly. And I've tried to give that to you. Now, you're on your own."

When he walked away, her heart wrenched. He'd been an important part of her life. Had she lost his friendship forever? She winced, only hoping that with time, wounds would heal and he'd forgive her.

Kelly headed toward the elevators when she heard Vanessa call from behind her, "Wait." The furious actress strode up to Kelly, the glare in her eyes threatening physical violence. "You stole my husband."

"I had nothing to do with your failed marriage, Vanessa. You did that on your own. You tricked him into a marriage, and then you wouldn't let him get out."

The actress's face reddening, she clamped her hands on her hips. "Why, I can't fathom what he sees in you."

"Possibly what he never found in you," Kelly retorted. She sidestepped the furious actress and stepped onto an elevator, leaving the woman fuming in the lobby.

CHAPTER TWENTY-ONE

On the way to her suite, she stopped by her aunt's room. "No matter what Robert tried to imply, Aunt Kaye, Alex and I are going to be married."

Aunt Kaye squeezed Kelly in a tight embrace. "That's wonderful. You two were positively beaming at each other."

Kelly smiled. "Yeah, we're in love. He doesn't even know about the baby, so he's not marrying me for that reason. I'll tell him tonight."

After departing her aunt's suite, Kelly tapped on her own hotel room door.

Alex greeted her with a wide grin. Shoeless, he'd removed his jacket and tie, and his white shirt hung unbuttoned. Her gaze dropped to his smooth skin and the muscles of his chest. A hunger to touch him made her suck in her breath.

He smiled, his dimples creasing in his cheeks. "I thought you'd never get here."

She walked straight into his arms. A peacefulness she'd never known washed over her.

With a chuckle, he lifted her off the ground and swung her around.

"I'm so happy tonight, Alex."

He set her on her feet. "What I didn't get the chance to tell you downstairs is that Mr. Goldsmith's offered me a leading role in a major film. He's also considering buying the rights to a sequel of *The Spy*. Tomorrow morning, I have a meeting with him here at the hotel."

"I'm so happy for *us*," she said, smiling. "I'm so glad he recognized your considerable talent." She wanted him to do the work he loved. "Now, this night is *perfect*."

"I'm expecting even more perfection." He pulled her against the length of his hard body, and captured her lips with his. Warmth sizzled through her and she ran her hands over his back.

He tugged on the zipper of her dress. "I don't think we need this." Her gown whooshed to the floor. She stepped out and kicked off her heels, her feet and toes sinking into the carpet.

She gazed up at him shyly, and ran her hands up his smooth chest, and pushed his shirt off his shoulders. "I'd like you bare, too."

"No problem, love," he shrugged off the shirt, and lay it over the back of the chair.

He reached around her and unhooked her bra. Holding her away a little, his blue eyes lit with hunger as his gaze roved over her.

She bit her lip. Perhaps she should have prepared him, but he didn't seem to notice the changes in her body, her fuller breasts or expanding tummy. She'd tell him later . . . and then forgot all about telling him when his mouth covered hers in a thorough, heart-pounding kiss. Fire ignited between them.

Almost frantically, they began to remove the rest of their clothing. He slid her underwear down her legs. She tugged at his belt and unzipped his pants. His slacks fell to the floor. He kicked out of his pants, scooped her up in his arms, and crossed to the canopied bed.

Yanking back the comforter with one hand, he settled her on the satin sheets.

He turned down the light and sat beside her, his hands caressing her rounded abdomen.

"Kelly? Eating well since you've returned from the island?" he asked with a grin.

She stiffened and said flatly, "I gained a little weight."

He tapped her nose with his finger. "You look as beautiful as ever and it's been so long, and now I have you in my arms." He lay down beside her and leaned over her. His tongue met the peaks of her breasts while his hands touching her lower, stoked a blazing fire within her. "I've been half-crazy wanting you, Kelly. I missed you, missed having you with me."

His smooth erection was warm against her hip. She took him in the palm of her hand.

He groaned and pressed kisses along her collarbone and neck, then to her ear. "I don't want to rush this, but I'm shaking just being near you."

Moaning with delight, she curved her fingers around his neck and pulled him to her. "I need you, too, Alex. It's been way too long."

His hardness sank into her softness, hot flesh met hot flesh. Her body tightened around him like a sheath. Their coming together occurred with a wild, explosive, physical need. He took. She gave, her body milking him until she quickened around him and he climaxed inside her. He buried his face into the curve of her neck.

Spent, they relaxed in each other's arms.

He raised his head, his eyes drowsy with spent passion. "I hope I didn't hurt you. That's not exactly the way I planned to make love to you."

"There will be many other times to take it slower."

"Yeah." He smiled and rolled over, bringing her on top of him. "Like very soon."

"Alex," she whispered, pulling away just a bit. "I have some news which might change your mind about wanting to marry me."

Gazing into her eyes, he clasped her shoulders. "What news could do that, love?" he asked softly.

"I'm having your baby," she said in a rush of words. "I found out at my doctor's appointment, just before David kidnapped me."

He chuckled. "Doesn't that sort of news usually speed up the process?"

Alarm spread through her. "*You knew.* Is that why you asked me to marry you?" She scrambled off him.

He caught her arm before she could leave the bed and pulled her back to his side. "No, Kelly. But bloody hell, when were you going to tell me? *Never?* I've been waiting all evening for you to confess."

She sighed. "I suppose I would have eventually told you, but I know your sense of honor. I didn't want you to be forced to marry me, too. I don't want you for a husband on those terms."

While his blue gaze pierced her, he stroked her chin with his fingers. "I've caused you considerable distress, haven't I?"

"You don't have to marry me. Really I'll be okay. I can take care of myself—and my baby."

He leaned over her and pressed her into the mattress, one hand coming round to cup her bare bottom. "Whoa now. *Our baby.* Last time I heard, it takes two . . . but, Kelly, you must believe me. I came here tonight to ask you to marry me before I knew you were pregnant."

"Really?" Tears burned her eyes. "You mean that?"

"Yeah. Vanessa cornered me with the accusation." He rolled to his back and adjusted the pillow beneath his head. "When will you start believing me, Kelly? Everything I've ever told you is the truth. I promise I didn't hear about the baby until tonight."

"You can't be too thrilled."

He let out a deep sigh. "I admit it's sudden, but I think we can make the best of the hand we're dealt. We always have. Frankly, I can get used to the idea of a sassy, little Kelly, just like her mother."

She slung her arm over his chest and squeezed him tightly, her lips quirking. "Or we might have a rambunctious, little Alex. What do you think?"

He grinned. "Either way, we're in trouble, huh?" He placed his finger on her bottom lip. "Before I met you, I didn't think this kind of love existed."

She cupped her hand to his face. "And that it was just a fairytale?"

He nodded and stroked her cheek. "You taught me what real love is and a lot about relations between a man and a woman."

"Me?"

"Yes, *you*. You taught me about making love—not just about having sex. I never experienced the connection before, but when I'm with you, I feel I belong. We're together, for better or for worse already. We might as well make it legal. I want you for my own." When he smiled a brilliant smile, her heart leapt with happiness. "And then you'll *have* to come back to England with me," he teased.

She ran her hand along his jaw. "We've certainly had some of the worst times, but also the best. You sure you're happy about the baby? You know, considering that playboy life you had planned."

"Yes. It wasn't what I'd planned, but it's what I never knew I wanted. I'm deliriously happy. About the baby." He proved it to her by trailing hot kisses across her stomach. "About marrying you."
He pressed more kissed to her abdomen.

She forgot everything, except making love to him again. His mouth sought her lips eagerly. They made love again, slower now that the urgency was gone.

* * *

Kelly blinked her eyes and checked the clock on the nightstand. Seven a.m. Careful not to wake Alex, she untangled herself from his arms, and the sheets, and stepped into the shower. "I know what I have to do," she whispered to herself as the warm water beat down. "I'll give the company to Robert in exchange for the money I owe him and hope he accepts it."

It had come to her in the middle of the night and made perfect sense. If she turned over the company to Robert, he could save Cochran Investments for himself and repay the investors. While she would no longer be a part of the business, this would also make things safer for the baby, Alex, Aunt Kaye, and herself.

By making things right with Robert, she might somehow salvage their lifelong friendship. She was sure with the love that Tammy had for him that he'd find happiness, too.

After she dressed, she lingered for a moment to gaze at Alex, sprawled on the bed, partially covered by the sheet. A wave of tenderness surged through her. His breathing was deep and easy, his hair tousled—he looked gorgeous and incredibly sexy.

She wanted to crawl back into bed and snuggle into his warm embrace and spend the next week with only him and room service. Smiling to herself at how much she loved him, she took her laptop and headed downstairs to print out papers for Robert. She'd leave the contract at the ranch for Robert to sign later when he returned. He could mail everything to the attorneys to finish the deal.

* * *

Kelly used her pass card to get through the gates of the ranch. Even though she'd had misgivings about coming alone, she had to clear out her father's desk and get the rest of her clothing. She was glad Robert wouldn't be there until later. She didn't want to have to face him so soon and she wanted to start her new life with Alex right away.

With an empty box in her hand, she entered the house. It was eerily quiet. *Where were Max and the dogs?* She climbed the stairs to the attic and sat in her father's chair, packing the items from his desk into the box.

When she heard a creak from the stairwell, Kelly tensed.

"Who's there?" she called out, but no one answered.

After another squeak of a floorboard outside the door, her heartbeat quickened. *Someone was here.* Slowly, she stood.

A moment later, Robert loomed in the doorway.

"Robert, you scared me," she cried. "You said you wouldn't be here until this afternoon."

His tuxedo pants and his white shirt were wrinkled, and his face was haggard as if he hadn't slept last night. Her heart wrenched. *What had she done to him?*

She winced and thrust out her hand. "I brought papers. I'm signing over the company to you."

"You spent the night with Drake. *Whore.*"

Her cheeks burned, but she let his remark slide. "I'm sorry for everything. I never wanted to hurt you."

He dipped his head in exaggerated mockery and took the papers. "At least something is salvaged from your betrayal. I regret ever letting you get under my skin."

"It won't cover what you're owed, but you'll salvage some repayment for your loan, and I hope, eventually pay back the investors. I think the company is really what you want, and since you're here . . ."

Anger simmered in his eyes. "Do you *really* know what I want?"

There might never be any salvaging of their relationship. She should've known with his controlling nature, and his perfectionist attitude, he wouldn't take being scorned very well. Now, all she wanted was to have the business transaction over and to get the heck out of there.

When he scratched his name in bold letters, she let out a sigh. She took the papers, her gaze dropping to the first letter of his name.

Robert wrote with a curlicue at the beginning of his 'R.' These past weeks, she'd been looking at her father's signature on the incriminating withdrawal slip copies from the bank—enough to know it well. The "R" in Richard Cochran—it was the same "R" on those last withdrawal slips. Her heart pounded in her ears. The "R" had been written with just a hint of such a flair. *Oh, God, had Robert been the one withdrawing money?* Cheating the clients—*and* setting up her dad?

CHAPTER TWENTY-TWO

Kelly was only several feet away from Robert in the attic. Her stomach knotted with the implication he'd forged her father's signature all those years ago. And stupidly she had trusted him. Now it all made sense. His wealth had grown enormously after their deaths, and he'd such a keen interest in helping her.

Apprehension swept through her. *Was he also responsible for the deaths of her parents?* Her breath caught in her throat. *Jerk. Traitor. Murderer.*

He stepped between her and the doorway, blocking the doorway. "What's wrong, Kelly?"

While her heart raced, she tried to hang onto a fragile appearance of calm. She had to get away from the ranch without him suspecting what she knew.

"Nothing," she murmured, hoping the quivering in her voice didn't give her away. "You have the company now, Robert. I'm leaving."

"You're not going anywhere." He grasped her arm above the elbow in a bruising hold. "And you're not a particularly good liar either. I can't let you go. So my error on the signature tipped you off? I didn't have it quite down, did I?"

Rage shot through her. "How could you have killed them? He was your best friend."

"The best friend who stole the woman I loved."

A sick knot formed in her stomach. "You did this because you had some kind of twisted thing for my mother?"

"Not entirely. I loved her, but also needed the money. He had it."

She slammed her fist against his chest. "You bastard. No wonder you wanted to marry me. You wanted to make sure *your* embezzling, by forging my father's signature, was never found out. Did you think you could hide it from me for a lifetime?"

He wrenched her arm behind her back and brought her against himself. "You little fool. I would have given you everything."

Struggling against his hold, she rasped, "You let me go to college, thinking your generosity had helped me, when you had stolen everything from me." She stomped his foot. "I hate you."

"I wanted you for my wife." He grasped the front of her blouse and with one jerk ripped it down to her waist. The buttons pinged on the floor and left her with only a lacy bra to cover herself.

Breathing hard, they stared at each other. She backed away from the hard look in his eyes.

Robert stepped toward her. "All I ever wanted was the company—and you, Kelly." He reached out and grabbed her shoulders. "So like your mother."

Her heart pounded with fright and she twisted in his grasp. "Don't."

"I have every right, my sweet fiancée. I remember a particular promise." His fingers dug into the flesh of her shoulders, hurting her. "You said, 'I promise to make you happy and be a good wife,' remember?" He mimicked the words she'd told him the night they'd become engaged on the ship. "You know, if anyone found out you were in the hotel with Drake last night, I'd look like a fool."

"I broke our engagement. I don't owe you anything."

He shook her until her head nearly snapped. "I should've killed you years ago and ran the company for your aunt. She'd never have nosed around in the books. But no, my only crime is I wanted you, too. We would've been happy."

"Eventually I would've seen through you."

"You believe that?" He slammed her against the wall, sending pain at the back of her head and up her spine. He put his hands on both sides of her and pinned her to the wall, his face twisting in a grotesque mask. The rage glittering in his eyes caused fear to twist like icy fingers around her heart. "I arranged for someone to tinker with the engine of your dad's plane. I never dreamed Jane was on that plane. Foolishly, she had just reconciled with your father."

He stroked her cheek. "But then you grew up even more beautiful than your mother. I wanted you. A *true* Cochran. What better way to get one up on them, than by marrying into the family? However, you were hard to convince I was anything other than an uncle. I even paid some men to be real jackasses to you, so you would turn to me."

"Ben?"

"Your fiancé was easy. He needed the cash."

"Alex?" She held her breath, fearful of Robert's answer, but unable to believe it.

Backing away a bit, he laughed. "I'd love to tell you 'yes,' but, 'no,' you found that bastard on your own."

Trembling, and knowing that he was determined to hurt her, she had to stall. "All the attacks were to frighten me and convince me to marry you?"

"But when it didn't seem like it worked, I told David Lewis you'd be on the dive boat."

"So knowing he hated me for thinking my father stole his money, you set him up to kill me?"

Robert shrugged. "If you didn't marry me, I didn't give a damn what happened to you. Lewis was supposed to kill you. When you said you'd marry me, I tried to stop you from going, but you didn't listen."

"What are you going to do now?"

"Why marry you, of course, but now not only will I have your signature giving me the company, I have a marriage license, signed by the Schultes, and witnessed by Vanessa. After all, she helped me all those years ago. She tried to seduce your father to have an affair and break up his marriage."

Through numb lips, she murmured, *"Vanessa?"*

He nodded. "When that didn't work, we planted evidence against him. It was overwhelming enough that your mother believed it."

"He didn't cheat on my mother? Why you bastard."

Robert removed a paper from his jacket pocket. "I don't give a damn what you think anymore. Now, sign the marriage contract. Then we'll go off on a little honeymoon on a yacht, after which you'll disappear."

"No." Kelly let the paper flutter to the floor.

She lunged toward the desk and grabbed for the pepper spray on her key chain. She turned it on him, but fumbled with the safety catch. He slapped her hand and sent the keys flying across the room.

"I can do without that." He shoved her toward the desk. "Now, sign."

Trembling all over, and knowing that she had to think of some way to defend herself, she signed the papers with a shaky hand, her signature barely legible. She handed him the paper, then turned, and reached into the box behind her. Her fingers touched the letter opener. She whirled and stabbed him in the neck.

With a groan, he yanked out the sharp instrument. "Damn it, Kelly."

But it gave her enough time. Her breath came in rasps as she bolted for the stairs. His footsteps pounded right behind her. At the bottom, she flung the door in his face.

Her heart was pounding. She raced down the main curved staircase.

"Damn it, Kelly," he shouted from the balcony above. His voice and her footsteps echoed in the stark foyer. Her heart raced as he took the stairs after her. "I won't really hurt you."

She glanced over her shoulder, and saw his face, an evil mask above her. She lost her footing and tumbled on the final steps. She cried out as she sprawled on the cold marble floor.

Please, God, help me. Alex—I'll never see him again. The baby.

Hot tears fell from her eyes but still she crawled toward the front door. Her hands and knees throbbed with pain.

Robert dug his fingers into her hair and scalp and with it, yanked her to her feet.

She turned on him, kicking at him, her feet connecting to his shins. "Let me go."

"If you'd married me, I wouldn't be forced to hurt you. You want to make me break your neck here and now?"

The intercom buzzed.

Robert hauled her to the window.

When she recognized Alex's car at the gate, hope momentarily welled inside her and was replaced by instant fear for his safety.

"Hell, if it isn't your hero," Robert sneered, his breath hot in her ear. He punched the buttons and the gate swung open. Alex drove through.

Robert unlocked the front door and then yanked her with him into the living room. He went to the desk and pulled out a gun, then sat with her on the couch. He pressed the hard metal of the gun into her back. "Keep quiet. We'll wait here."

The doorbell rang. Robert covered her mouth with his hand. After a moment, Kelly heard the squeak of the door opening.

She jerked her mouth free. "No, Alex, don't come—" Robert slapped his hand over her mouth, muffling any further cries with his palm.

Alex strode into the living room. His gaze swept over her in Robert's tight embrace. Anger flared in his eyes—until Robert pulled the gun from behind her back. Alex's face froze with deadly understanding.

Standing, Robert jerked Kelly to her feet, waving the weapon at Alex. "Come on in. Join your going away party."

She struggled against Robert's firm hold. "Robert forged my father's name to withdraw the money. He was the embezzler, all those years ago."

"I want you to know, Drake, how much it annoyed me that you got Kelly pregnant, so you'll be the first to die." Robert aimed the weapon at Alex.

Her heart pounded wildly. "You see, Alex," she said, her voice trembling, but she had to stall. "It's important for Robert to repay my grandparents' generosity and kindness. They treated him like a second son, but now I realize he always resented being the . . . *housekeeper's son*," she ground out the last words. "Is there any other way you can explain to me, Robert, why you would do this?"

Wrenching her arm, he snapped, "Don't you ever call me *that.*"

Alex glared at Robert. "Bloody hell, do you actually think you can get away with killing us? Put the gun down."

Robert choked out a bitter laugh. "Who will question *me*? Oh, I admit, I'll have trouble getting rid of your bodies, but the ranch has a lot of ground."

A shudder ran up Kelly's spine. She hadn't told anyone she was coming to the ranch, except for what she wrote in the note to Alex. No one would miss her as Aunt Kaye would think she'd left with him, and that would give Robert plenty of time to clear his tracks.

"There will be evidence you killed us in this house," Alex said.

Robert snorted. "I'll burn down the evidence."

Alex narrowed his eyes. "I knew he never loved you, Kelly."

Robert tightened his hold on her arm. "That's a lie. And damn you for interfering, Drake."

"Robert, put the gun down," she pleaded. "Don't."

His sarcastic laughter echoed in the room. "No way, honey?" He thrust the gun closer to Alex. "There's only one way out for me. By killing you both."

Alex stepped back. "If we're missing, you'll be suspected. Last night, I gave it out to some of your guests that Kelly and I are getting married."

"You lying son of a bitch." Robert's face contorted with anger, and he cocked the trigger.

Alex backed away, putting his hands up. "I did give it out."

Kelly threw herself against Robert.

He shoved her aside and fired, hitting Alex in the chest. Alex's eyes glazed over and he crumpled to the floor.

"*Alex!*" she screamed through a haze of tears.

When she tried to go to him, Robert wrenched her arm. She tore into him, hitting him. "I hate you." She clawed at his face as tears streamed in rivulets down her cheeks. "You killed everyone I've ever loved."

He set the gun down, then grabbed her and clamped his hands against the sides of her face. "And I'll finish with you. Something I should've done years ago. How easy to just snap your neck. Quick and painless."

Then there was a thump and Robert let out a groan, and went flying into a chair.

Kelly turned to see Alex holding up a small nude statue with blood on one end.

Rubbing his chest, he gave her a wry smile. "Bullet-proof vest borrowed from the studio."

Blood rushed to her head and heart. "Alex, oh Alex, you scared the life out of me." Tears fell from her eyes, but she still snatched the weapon from the table and aimed it at Robert.

Robert raised his hand and smeared the blood trickling on his forehead. "You're supposed to be dead, Drake."

"I guess I'm a better actor than you think. Detective Spagnola had been suspicious of you earlier, and when I called him this morning, he said he'd interrogated Lewis who said he didn't kill them but you might be behind the deaths of Kelly's parents. He told me to use caution if I went in after Kelly in your house."

Her hand shook but Kelly kept the gun pointed at Robert. "You're going to jail. You're nothing but a cheat and a murderer."

"No one will believe you two over me," he said through clenched teeth. "Drake, I'll have you thrown in jail for assaulting an American citizen."

"My cell's been recording everything since I stepped in the front door." Alex moved away from Robert and checked his watch. "Detective Spagnola said if he didn't hear from me by eleven a.m., he'd send over the local police. It's now five past."

"You two-bit actor," Robert sneered as he rose to his feet. "You ruined everything." He staggered toward Kelly.

Her hand was shaking as she kept the gun trained on him. "Robert, don't make me shoot you."

Alex retrieved the weapon from her. "After all he's done, I won't hesitate."

Kelly crossed her arms. "He's going to jail for the rest of his life. The humiliation will be worse than death for him."

"I'm not going to rot in prison while he screws you." Robert lunged at Alex.

Alex fired. By Robert's expression as he toppled to the floor, Kelly didn't think he was surprised at the outcome. He'd obviously made his choice. He wanted an easy way out and was too arrogant to face the public with his crimes.

Pain wrenched Robert's face as he spat out, "Now, Drake, you'll go to prison for murdering me to get to my fiancée. You'll never have her." He let out a final gasp.

Alex placed the gun on the table and pulled Kelly into his arms, and away from Robert's still body. "Are you all right, love."

With tears running down her face, she nodded against his shoulder. "I love you, Alex. Nothing in this world will ever be wrong, as long as you're okay and you're with me."

"I'm sorry I had to do that." He cupped her face with his hands and his thumbs, wiping the wetness from her cheeks. He lightly brushed his lips over hers. "It's over now, sweetheart."

"You think so, Alex?" asked a familiar shrewish voice from behind. They turned as Vanessa stepped into the room. Hatred glittered in her eyes. She grabbed the weapon lying on the table. "What a disgusting display of affection, Alex. I could kill her for that alone, not to mention that you killed Robert." With unsteady hands, she pointed the pistol toward Kelly.

Kelly sucked in her breath.

"He tried to kill *us*," Alex said, thrusting Kelly behind him. "Now, put the gun down," he ordered. "Your career's too important to you, and you don't want to go to jail."

Vanessa's mouth turned downward. "Alex, why didn't you love me? I'm beautiful. Men grovel at my feet."

Sirens blared outside and the sound grew closer.

"Damn it to hell." Vanessa whirled. She tossed the weapon on the sofa and fled from the room.

Simultaneously exhaling, Alex and Kelly sagged into each other's arms.

CHAPTER TWENTY-THREE

Two weeks later, along with her Aunt Kaye, Kelly flew into London for her wedding to Alex.

"To think I almost married Robert," Kelly shuddered at the thought as they taxied down the runway. "How could I not see how evil he was?"

"There're a lot of things we all regret in life. I wished I'd expressed my suspicions about him, too."

"Well, I think you tried to when I was on the cruise."

"But I had no idea the extent of all this—if only I'd put two-and-two together. You were almost killed. I'd never have forgiven myself."

Kelly squeezed her aunt's hand. "It's all over now."

When they got out of the car at Alex's house, Kelly clutched Aunt Kaye's elbow. Her gaze swept over the large country house, complete with expansive landscaped grounds that went down to a small lake. "I plan to have a long talk with my future husband. He'd never once let on he had such a magnificent home."

"I'm so happy for you, sweetie. He's a nice man and he took care of you when you were in need."

As Kelly took in the site of the house, she thought the old English manor of stone and brick would be the perfect place to raise their child, except—she thought with a smile—when they were living in California.

Last week, Alex had left for England to prepare everything for their wedding. She and Aunt Kaye had stayed in a hotel when they arrived last night, so the groom wouldn't see her until the ceremony.

Strangely, Robert had left her heir to his estate so the ranch and all his other property reverted to her—even his film production company. Once everything was through probate, and the production company could be sold, the money he stole to finance that company, would be returned to Cochran Investments. She would have enough funds to repay the missing money to the clients immediately and put Cochran Investments back on its feet.

In the long term, she planned to restore her family home to its original style with some of the rest of the money. Though, now seeing Alex's home, she wasn't so sure she'd have to do it so soon, but still it was her dream, and she hoped he'd want to live in both places.

Robert had done so much damage to her life, in so many ways. It took two weeks for the authorities to straighten out what he'd done to her father's company.

As they stepped to the front door, Kelly felt blissfully happy to be alive. She couldn't wait to be in Alex's arms again. She had daydreamed all week about what living with him would be like, but she'd not expected starting out in this charming house.

Vases of roses, with their sweet scent, decorated the inside hall.

Friends and relatives arrived and filled up the house. Alex's mother, aunts and uncles, cousins, and his sisters and brother were already there.

His cousin Susan gave Kelly a warm hug. "I've found another job. What a relief not to work for Vanessa any longer."

Tammy was ushered inside, along with a few of Kelly's friends from California.

Kelly greeted them all, then took Tammy aside. "I'm so glad you could be here. Thanks for everything. The company needs you more than ever now."

"I'm happy you're letting me stay. I never realized what Robert was capable of." Tammy shook her head in dismay. "And to think I loved him, left my marriage for him."

Kelly sighed. "We were all fooled. None of us knew the true Robert."

"What about Vanessa? Has she tried to interfere with your marriage to Alex?"

"No," Kelly said with a chuckle. "Thankfully, Vanessa is about to marry a rich, elderly man with a title."

When Vanessa had been questioned about the murders, she insisted she'd not known how far Robert had gone. She said she'd agreed all those years ago to help him make Kelly's father look like he was having an affair with her, in exchange for movie roles.

Both Kelly and Alex decided not to have Vanessa prosecuted as long as she stayed out of their lives and sought psychiatric care. The media and the tabloids had punished her enough and her career was nearly defunct.

The guests murmured as Alex entered with the minister. He shared a smile with Kelly from across the room.

He walked up to her and kissed her on the cheek, and said, "You look ravishingly beautiful."

His words filled her with contentment. "So do you," she croaked. "And you have a wonderful house, Alex. Funny, you never told me about all this."

"What?" he asked, with a lopsided grin. "You were expecting a hut?"

She groaned. "Not entirely, but maybe some little apartment or flat."

Linking his arm in hers, he gazed down at her. "Are you ready to make another agreement with me and become my wife, love of my life and my heart?"

"Yes, but I think this time I'll let you set the terms to our new agreement."

He grinned. "All right, but I warn you. I drive a *hard* bargain. Are you sure?"

"I'll agree to *anything* and *everything* you want," she teased in a husky voice.

"*Tsk, Tsk.* I like where your mind is going, but that's not what I meant. No, this time I'm only asking you to stay with me forever and to never leave my side."

Beaming up at him, she nodded. "That's an agreement I can live with for a lifetime."

Holding his hand, Kelly walked with him toward the minister with joy in her heart. All they'd been through had forged a strong bond that wouldn't be broken.

After their vows, the minister said, "You may kiss your bride."

Kelly returned Alex's kiss as eagerly as he gave it. Then they remembered they were in a room full of people. The broke away and shared a laugh. Everyone clapped.

* * *

Later in the evening, Alex and Kelly lay in his wide four-poster bed, with a fire crackling in the fireplace and warming the room. Tomorrow, they headed for a weeklong cruise in the South Pacific. And then a week, in a bungalow on a beach—*at a resort*—with room service.

He caressed her hand, his finger touching her diamond wedding band. "It's not the size Hillyard gave you, but it's a family heirloom. I'll buy you more jewelry later."

"I love this ring." She brushed her lips across his shoulder. "By the way, I found out neither one of Robert's engagement rings were real. The diamonds were as phony as his love for me. Besides, I love this one. I told you before what I wanted from life, and an enormous diamond ring wasn't on the list."

"Ah, what did you desire? A family . . . which we'll have very soon." He winked and patted her rounded stomach. "And a husband who loves and wants only you. You have that now. Come, let me show you again how much I love you." He lifted her hand to his lips. "Live with me, and be my love, and we will all the pleasures prove," he said, quoting Shakespeare.

"*Mmmmmm*," she said dreamily. "Did you mention pleasure, Alex?"

He stroked the smooth skin at her waist and leaned in for a kiss. "Yes, love, now and forever."

* * * * *

ABOUT THE AUTHOR

Debra Andrews has dabbled with writing fiction for most of her life. She likes to write stories with a lot of conflict, adventure and suspense. When she's not working, she's enjoying her family and pets.

Dear Reader:

I hope that you enjoyed the book. If you have time, could you please leave a review on the buy page of Amazon.com or BarnesandNoble.com, or wherever you purchased this book.

Thank you so much. I hope you will check out my future releases.

Debra

For future release information, and a mailing list, or if you have any comments about this story, please visit:

www.debraandrews.net

or

www.debraandrewsauthor.com

Coming soon in the "Nothing but Trouble Books":

DISGUISED

A woman lies about her credentials to land a job at a company to seek evidence that the owner is involved in corrupt business practices which caused the death of her brother. Not only does she fall in love with the man, she finds him innocent, and that he's the real target of sabotage. However, before she can confess her ruse, he discovers she lied and thinks she's behind the schemes to destroy him.